"You cannot resist me, Natalie, sweet."

And then he was kissing her, smothering any hint of denial with his lips, pressing tenderly at first, with no real trace of movement, just a touch. He didn't pull her into him, but stood there in the shadow of dusk, the faint sound of waves splashing against the ship beneath them, his palm softly caressing her cheek as his body came eagerly alive from nothing but the penetrating heat of her mouth . . .

Instinctively, after several seconds of shock at his daring, she tried to pull away. That's when he grabbed her around the waist and drew her against him, embracing her completely with an arm of solid strength. Her first rational thought was how this wasn't a kiss like the one in his town house only a few days ago—just a delicate brush of his warm lips. No, this was sweet desire, controlling and intense, the sudden taste of him so powerful she was flooded with the memory of their first intimate encounter five years earlier, of what he'd done to her then, both physically and emotionally. And passionately . . .

Jove titles by Adele Ashworth

STOLEN CHARMS
MY DARLING CAROLINE

Stolen Charms

ADELE ASHWORTH

JOVE BOOKS, NEW YORK

STOLEN CHARMS

A Jove Book / published by arrangement with
the author

PRINTING HISTORY
Jove edition / September 1999

The Penguin Putnam Inc. World Wide Web site address is
http://www.penguinputnam.com

ISBN: 0-515-12565-2

A JOVE BOOK®
Jove Books are published by The Berkley Publishing Group,
a division of Penguin Putnam Inc.,
375 Hudson Street, New York, New York 10014.
JOVE and the "J" design
are trademarks belonging to Penguin Putnam Inc.

PRINTED IN THE UNITED STATES OF AMERICA

10 9 8 7 6 5 4 3 2 1

This book is dedicated to Mary Ann Townsend, my wonderful mother-in-law, for being my biggest supporter, promoter, and self-appointed publicist, and to all the patrons and employees of Mr. Marvin's Barber Shop in Port Charlotte, Florida. Thank you, thank you, thank you!

And, of course, my loving thanks to Ron, Andrew, and Caroline.

Prologue

England, 1842

"Emeralds."

She blinked. "I beg your pardon?"

He smiled faintly. "I was just thinking, Miss Haislett, that on this ballroom floor, under the light of a thousand candles, your eyes sparkle like precious emeralds."

She swallowed nervously and held his gaze with her own. His voice was so very rich and deep, almost caressing, and suddenly she felt quite shy, a feeling Miss Natalie Haislett of Sherborne had never before experienced in the presence of anyone.

"Thank you," she whispered, lowering her eyes to stare at the ivory buttons of his shirt.

He continued to smile but said nothing more as he expertly twirled her around the dance floor in time to the waltz. She couldn't understand why she felt so anxious, for this was, after all, her father's masked ball, and he was only an invited guest who had graciously asked her to dance. She'd seen him before on several occasions, although they'd never spoken to each other. But this time he seemed to take particular notice of her, watching her closely, almost too closely, and the attention from such an attractive man made her breathless.

"I'd like to see you without your mask."

His smooth, husky words startled her into raising her eyes to his once again. He was unbearably handsome, with thick, almost black hair, a tall, hard body and the most mesmerizing gray-blue eyes.

She stared at him for several seconds, then quietly replied, "I'd like to see you without yours." After looking around cautiously she leaned up to murmur boldly, "Meet me outside in the flower garden, under the south balcony, in fifteen minutes."

He cocked his head fractionally, eyes narrowing behind black satin. "Are you serious, Natalie?"

His sudden use of her given name without permission reminded her, in the purest sense, of her delicate position. "I-I just thought it would be a private place to talk."

"I see."

He continued to stare down at her partially concealed face for a moment, and just as she began to feel a trifle embarrassed by her very brazen behavior, he leaned over to whisper, "I'm looking forward to our . . . talk."

She shivered from his warm breath on her cheek, then too quickly the waltz was over. He stood upright, his eyes piercing hers as he brushed his lips against the back of her hand. Then he turned and walked away.

Natalie watched him for a moment as he disappeared into the crowd of laughing, mingling people, trying to shake herself of the strange sensations the man evoked in her. She shouldn't have asked him to meet her in the garden unchaperoned, she knew that, but something inside of her compelled her to do so.

She would meet him. She was drawn to him.

Slowly she made her way toward the back of the ballroom, stopping every so often to chat nonchalantly with various members of the gentry. It took her almost fifteen minutes just to reach the balcony, then, slipping away unnoticed, she fairly raced down the stairs and into the garden.

The chill night air brushed her skin, but the moon's full

glow and her own anxious thoughts warmed her inside.

Glancing around cautiously, she tiptoed along the path in the hopes that nobody would see or hear her. Her mother would no doubt perish from shock if she knew where she was and what she was doing, and it saddened her to know she wouldn't be able to stay in his presence long without someone in the ballroom noticing her absence.

"I really didn't think you'd come."

She turned toward the sound of his voice, coming from the shadows several feet away.

"Especially," he continued, stepping toward her, "since no one else seems at all desirous of strolling through the garden on this perfect autumn evening. It appears we're all alone."

"Yes," she agreed weakly. Her pulse began to race from anticipation. He had removed his mask, and all she could see of his face under pale moonglow was a vague expression of contemplation.

"Take it off."

"I beg your pardon?"

"Your mask, Natalie. I want to see your face, remember?"

He had moved to stand directly in front of her, but she now faced the moonlight so a shadow once again blocked his features from her view. She could feel his warmth, could feel his penetrating gaze, but she couldn't move away. Timidly she reached behind her head and untied her mask, lowering it to hold at her side, growing increasingly shy and afraid to look at him. He forced her to do so, however, as his palm came up to lightly grasp her chin, raising her head in the process.

He was quiet for a moment, studying her intently, and second by second the pounding of her heart grew to a thunder.

"Beautiful . . . ," he whispered.

He glided his thumb across her lips, and she lost herself to his touch, closing her eyes and leaning her head back in response, her mask slipping out of her hands to fall to the ground unnoticed. For a moment she was unsure of what to do or say, and then she felt his warm mouth on hers as he pulled her into his arms.

She hadn't really expected to be kissed. Or had she? Perhaps this was what she'd longed for since she'd first seen him months ago, to drown herself in the splendor of his hard body, his emanating power. His tongue teased her lips apart to invade her warmth, moving, flicking, searching for hers. Oh, God, he felt wonderful. He was warm, inviting, so very masculine. Much more than she had ever imagined.

Natalie instinctively leaned her body into his as the kiss grew more demanding. She raised herself on her toes, wrapping her arms around his neck so her fingers could play with the hair on his nape. She whimpered from pure, raw pleasure as sensations she'd never before experienced melted her inside.

Groaning deeply, he placed his hand on her bottom and pulled her hips boldly against his, holding her snugly to him, his free hand gliding down her cheek, then to her neck to caress it with his fingers.

She was quite aware of the tension, the hardness of every point of him, the raw passion building between them, but she couldn't stop it. Not yet. She wanted nothing more than to stand in the moonlight, in a fragrant garden, and be with him like this for an eternity—kissing, touching, feeling, wanting. The rush of emotion was perfect, wonderful, and every nagging doubt about what she was doing vanished from her thoughts as his lips continued to torment her mouth with excruciating pleasure.

She heard herself gasp ever so slightly when, without warning, he lowered his hand over her gown to place his thumb against her nipple, gently stroking, caressing, teasing the waiting peak through the thin layer of Florentine silk. Guided by impulse, she began to move her hips against his, stroking him gently with her belly.

That action made him come alive with eagerness. He grasped the fullness of her breast with his warm hand as the one holding her bottom, without her total awareness, started to lift her skirt.

With a quick expertise she couldn't begin to understand, he placed his palm against her leg, and whether out of unsureness or simple instinct, she immediately stiffened.

Apparently he felt it as well, for his mouth relaxed against hers as his hand moved in and around to stroke her inner thighs.

"What are you doing?" she murmured, pulling her head back.

"What we've both been dreaming of for weeks," he answered in a gravelly rasp, his lips beginning a trail of feathery kisses down her neck.

His head moved ever lower, lower, until he brushed his mouth against the tops of her breasts, just above the edge of her gown. She started to relax again, closing her eyes to the luscious feelings he expertly created, until she felt him move his hand up to caress intimately the sensitive area between her legs.

That shocked her to reality.

"Don't." She gasped, pushing against his shoulders, enormously embarrassed and quickly overcome with guilt.

Slowly he withdrew his hands and raised himself to stare down at her, his breathing coming fast and heavy through the sudden stillness. Although she knew he was as affected as she by the force of attraction between them, she couldn't read the thoughts on his face through the shadows.

He stood there for a long moment before the hardness of his voice sliced through the chilly night air. "Why did you ask me to meet you, Miss Haislett?"

She couldn't think straight. Her breathing faltered, her body trembled. "I-I wanted to talk."

He remained silent for a second or two, then he drew a long, slow breath. "You've never done this, have you?"

Natalie grasped her elbows with her palms in a small measure of defense, but she didn't move or look away from his hidden expression. "I've been kissed before, if that's what you mean, but—"

"But what?"

She lowered her gaze to study what she could see of her

blue satin slippers. "It lasted three seconds and it was on my right cheek."

For a fraction of a moment she thought he might actually laugh. But he didn't. Instead, he moved up to stand directly in front of her once again, placing his hand under her chin to lift her face to his. She shut her eyes tightly against his gaze, instantly filled with an acute sense of shame.

"Look at me," he demanded in a dark, velvety voice.

She took a fast breath and opened her eyes. "I'm sorry," she said in a whisper. "I really didn't mean—"

"How old are you?"

She paused, wanting to sound mature and independent, but in the end deciding it best just to be honest. "Seventeen. Eighteen in a month."

"I see. . . ."

He began to rub his thumb across her jawline, back and forth, back and forth, and she closed her eyes to the feel of it, once again succumbing to his touch.

Finally he put his arm behind her, pulling her up against his chest, hugging her tightly to him, one hand on her head, the other on her back as he slowly ran his knuckles along her spine.

Natalie could hear his heart beating steadily beneath her cheek, could feel his slow, even breathing, and she knew she was losing herself in his embrace once again. It felt perfect to be held by him, to be doing exactly, as he'd said, what she'd been dreaming of doing for weeks.

"You just wanted to talk," he repeated coolly, contemplatively.

"I think I really wanted to be kissed," she sheepishly admitted, snuggling even tighter against his chest. "I like the way you kiss."

He groaned softly and shook his head. "You are undoubtedly the sweetest thing I've come across in ages, Miss Natalie Haislett."

She lifted her chin, gazing up at his face. "Did you like it?"

He looked down sharply. "Kissing you?"

She nodded.

"I liked it more than I probably should have."

That warmed her to her toes. "Do you think we could kiss like that again sometime?"

His body stiffened as he looked once more to the darkened garden. "I don't think it would be a good idea."

Awkwardly she lowered her gaze to his chest.

He glanced down at her again. "What did you want to talk about when you asked me out here?"

Natalie, never being one to keep her feelings wisely in check, could think of nothing to say but the truth. Quietly she confessed, "I think you're the most beautiful man I've ever seen in my life and I . . ." Her cheeks grew hot with color. Casually she tried to free herself from his embrace, but he wouldn't let her go.

"You what, Natalie?"

His voice was deeply smooth, her name sounding achingly intimate as it rolled off his tongue. She couldn't hold back any longer. "If I tell you, do you promise not to laugh?"

"Not unless it's funny."

She sighed with resolution, then closed her eyes and raised her face to the moonlight. "I think I love you."

He said nothing. But he didn't laugh, either, or release her, and for that she felt tremendous relief. She couldn't open her eyes, though; she simply couldn't. Not until he said something.

For a minute or so she heard nothing but the quiet night air charged with distant music and laughter from the ballroom above. Then she felt his lips gently touch hers again, brushing against them, not passionately but with sweet tenderness. She wanted more of him, but the second he felt her begin to respond, he pulled back.

"You'd better go inside before someone comes looking for you," he whispered against her mouth.

Natalie didn't know what to feel. Somehow she knew he wasn't being unreasonable, and that he probably wouldn't say he loved her in return, but a rush of sadness filled her nonetheless.

She moved back from him as he released her from his grasp. Then without even so much as a glance at his face, she picked up her mask, turned, and fled the garden.

One

London, 1847

"Emeralds."

"Emeralds?" he repeated, surprised.

"A rare and priceless blend of gold and precious green."

Jonathan William Rayburn Drake, second son of the late and most respected earl of Beckford, exhaled heavily and leaned back against the soft burgundy leather of his Louis Treize chair to regard his guest with speculation. Stealing precious emeralds was going to be a nightmare.

"How much are they worth?" he cautiously asked.

Sir Guy Phillips, a very blond man whose middle-aged looks could only be described as wholly unremarkable, scratched his thick side whiskers and shrugged. "I couldn't at this time put a number on their value."

"Hmm. Let's have it."

Phillips paused to collect his thoughts, then began at the beginning. "They originally belonged to the wealthy duke of Westridge who legitimately purchased them from one of the Hapsburgs, probably Charles VI, sometime in the early 1720s. The duke then gave them to his wife, Elizabeth, as a wedding gift, and she had them in her possession for almost sixty years until her death in the winter of 1781. Although

Westridge had one child, the boy was sickly and died in 1740 at the age of twelve, leaving the duke with no heir to claim his vast fortune. The lovely Elizabeth, who died fifteen years after her husband, supposedly left all her personal possessions to her cousin Matilda, a spinster who, coincidentally enough, was somehow very distantly related to King George.''

Phillips patted the ruffles of his white silk shirt and stood, brandy snifter in hand, and began to pace the room. ''Nobody is altogether sure where the jewels were kept, or who actually had rights to them after Matilda's death in ninety-two, but rumor has it that the king became the possessor sometime before his idiot son was appointed regent in 1811. Prinny inherited the emeralds, then to help pay his horrid debts when he became king in 1820, he sold them to the duke of Newark for an undisclosed, though some say an ungodly, amount. And there they remained, in the duke's possession, for more than twenty-five years, locked safely away in a vault on his estate, until three months ago when his wife discovered them missing—''

''Stolen by professionals, then,'' Jonathan cut in as he raised his glass to his lips.

Sir Guy stopped pacing to look at him directly. ''We have reason to believe the emeralds are now in France, stolen after months of keen planning, by those working for high-ranking officials who want very desperately to overthrow the current French government.''

Jonathan slumped in his chair and gave a slow whistle. ''How the devil did I know the French would be involved, Phillips?''

The blond man chuckled. ''They always seem to be, don't they?''

''Go on,'' he insisted.

Phillips sighed. ''Well, speculation has it that the jewels have turned up in the hands of French Legitimists who, of course, view Henri as the true king and want to see him back on the throne.'' He shook his head, his expression becoming grave as he lowered his voice. ''Louis Philippe's court is crumbling, Jonny. The entire country has yet to find stability. The Legitimists want Henri; the people, ever unhappy, are talking of another revolution. . . ."

After a lingering pause, Jonathan asked contemplatively, "So why steal these jewels, aside from the fact that they're worth so much? Whoever lifted them risked a great deal in coming here to do it."

The older man snorted and began pacing again. "Because—and this is only a guess—those involved in their disappearance believe the emeralds rightfully belong to the French people. A justifiable theft."

"Justifiable?"

Sir Guy tapped his fingers against his glass. "Apparently the Legitimists have convinced themselves that the emeralds were not purchased from the Hapsburgs, but confiscated illegally. Stolen. They believe the jewels were never to belong to the British because they were actually supposed to be passed from Charles to Maria Theresa and then to her daughter Marie-Antoinette, and at the time of her unfortunate demise, should have become the property of the French people."

"How convenient for the French."

"Yes, quite."

Jonathan drained the contents of his snifter, then placed the glass on the small table next to his chair and stretched his legs out in front of him. "I can only conclude that you've recently received information regarding the whereabouts of the necklace?"

Phillips nodded as he moved to a side bar to pour himself another bumper.

"A fortnight ago one of our contacts in Paris attended a gala affair, the sole purpose of which was to raise money for the Legitimists' cause. At that function, this same contact overheard an unusually frank discussion regarding jewels that had recently been stolen right from under 'haughty English noses.' After subtle questioning, it was learned that the emeralds are in Marseille for safekeeping until such time that it becomes necessary to overthrow Louis Philippe."

Phillips returned to his chair, placed his glass on the table, and reached into the pocket of his shirt to remove a small piece of paper. He handed it to Jonathan.

"My heart goes out to the duke of Newark and his lovely wife who lost her emerald necklace to French thieves," he somberly continued. "But the reason I'm sending you to France and putting your life in danger, Jonny, is to help Louis Philippe keep his government together, if we can. If the emeralds are pulled from their settings and sold, the Legitimists could come into an enormous sum to be used to further their cause. England doesn't need another war right now. Our boys don't need to die once again because of French arrogance."

Jonathan glanced at the paper. The writing was neat, precise.

Madeleine DuMais. 5 Rue de la Fleur. Twenty-seven June, ten A.M.

Quickly Sir Guy drained his glass for a second time, placed it on the table, then stood to retrieve his overcoat from the rack near the door. "I believe you already know of the enchanting Miss DuMais."

"Mmm . . . I met her once, actually."

"Good. She'll have an identity ready for you to assume, and maybe a lead by the time you arrive. When can you leave?"

Jonathan stood as well, rubbing his tired eyes with his fingertips. "I expect I could sail by Friday. That should give me enough time to make the appointment."

"We'll be awaiting word." Phillips opened the front door and turned back to him, smiling. "You understand that since you'll be in France you'll miss Lady Carlisle's gathering."

Lady Sibyl Carlisle's annual cotillion was the season's most dreaded event for eligible bachelors. Along with her four matronly daughters, the lady insisted on using the party for nothing but a matchmaking social. To have an excuse not to attend was a marked blessing.

Jonathan grinned. "Most unfortunate timing, I'm sure. You'll have to give her and her lovely daughters my regards."

Phillips shook his head wearily. "Indeed. I suppose I'll

have to make an appearance again this year. At least the lady spares no expense when it comes to good food and drink.''

"That, I admit, I will miss.''

"Speaking of good food,'' Phillips added, "dinner was excellent. Tell Gerty the roast was perfect this time.''

"She'll be pleased to know you ate every bite.''

With a nod and a click of his heels, Phillips turned, walked down the front steps, and disappeared into the foggy night.

Jonathan stood in the doorway for several minutes, breathing the damp night air until the cold began to seep into his skin. Slowly he closed the door, though he didn't bolt it since Marissa would be arriving in less than an hour for another night of romping between the sheets. She was the only mistress he'd ever had, the only one he'd ever known, who preferred to meet her gentleman friends in their homes, providing, of course, that her gentleman friends were unmarried. Truthfully, he didn't care. He wasn't hiding his sexual escapades from a nosy wife, or from anyone for that matter, and if Marissa wanted to enjoy their little liaisons in his home instead of hers, so be it.

Tonight, however, he was restless, and not really looking forward to her visit. Until just recently, Marissa had been able to satisfy every need he had, but now, even as he hated to admit the fact, he was tiring of her. Oh, she was uncommonly beautiful and very definitely experienced with the use of her body. But quite suddenly, to his confusion, he found himself wanting more—more from life and more from a woman. Marissa was a mistress for anyone who gave her the most, the nicest trinkets, and Jonathan had no qualms about giving her trinkets. She was good at what she did. But that, oddly enough, was the problem, because for the first time in ages, in his entire life really, he wanted to be more sexually aware than the woman he bedded.

With a sharp tug to loosen his neckcloth, Jonathan walked back into his study, picked up the half-empty bottle of brandy and glasses, and took them to the kitchen in back of his town house. Gerty, as usual, had left the place spotless before she'd left for the evening, so all that remained on the counter were their dinner dishes. He placed what he carried next to the rest of the things to be washed, unbuttoned the top three buttons of his shirt, dimmed the lamp on the kitchen table, then walked back to his study to sit in front of the small fire to think.

He had to admit he was growing tired and bored. Tired of the women he knew and bored with just about everything else. At twenty-nine years of age he'd done many things, but now he found himself envying those men he'd thought he would never envy. During the last several months he'd actually taken the time to consider where he was, what he was doing, and he suddenly realized he missed, even craved, stability. He'd never imagined that one day he would want a family. Until just recently, he'd thought the idea laughable. He'd known many men, even friends, who were undeniably unhappy with their marriages, and for a long while he assumed all marriages to be like that, to be painstakingly difficult and not at all worth the trouble. But after thoughtful consideration he realized that although marriage was indeed difficult, it proved for many to be enriching like no other union. He had seen it in his parents' marriage, his brother's marriage, and as if almost overnight, he wanted it for himself. What troubled him most was knowing he could never combine it with his work. He would have to choose between the two.

Leaning back in his chair, he folded his hands across his stomach, stretched out his legs, and stared at the flickering firelight as it danced on the dark ceiling above.

Ridding himself of Marissa would really be no problem. She would simply turn to the next wealthy member of society who could keep her comfortably housed and clothed in adornments. They both knew what they received from each other was purely physical, was desired by both, and from the beginning he'd made his intentions clear as to the nature of their relationship. Marissa was used to it, for she had taken many men before him, and the ones to follow would be exactly the same. The woman's job, technically, was to give pleasure in bed for an elegant living, and she was definitely an expert in her field of study.

The question he'd been asking himself over and over of late, however, had nothing to do with his mistress, but whether he could live without the excitement of his work if he took a wife. He'd been operating throughout Europe for six years, and those who used his services were unquestionably in his debt, desperately wanting him to continue what he was doing, and for everything he did, they paid him well. Very well. But money aside, he wasn't altogether certain he could give it all up, at least not completely, and if he didn't, he wasn't sure he would be able to marry. No lady of quality would want a husband who wasn't around to cater to her whims, to escort her to social functions, and no women he'd ever known had been able to match his sense of adventure, his desire to experience life at its best.

Jonathan closed his eyes. Maybe he'd just grow to be an old, cantankerous bachelor. Just him and his dog. What an attractive couple the two of them would make.

"Darling?"

Marissa's husky voice shook him from his thoughts. He turned in the direction of the door, smiling faintly to lighten his mood. "I didn't hear you come in."

Sliding her pale woolen shawl from her body with perfectly manicured fingers, she sauntered toward him. "Why is it so dark in here?" Slyly she purred, "Were you hoping to make love in front of the fire?"

He grinned, raking his eyes up and down her long, graceful figure. He was certainly going to miss her. "We need to talk, Marissa."

She stopped short and gave him a crooked smile. "Goodness, it sounds serious."

Jonathan regarded her for a moment. Then with a deep breath for encouragement and his own sense of acceptance, he quietly said, "This has nothing to do with you, sweet, but I think it's time—"

"Don't think I haven't considered this day was coming, Jonathan," she cut in brightly, tossing her shawl onto the hardwood settle to her left. "I've noticed changes in you lately and I've seen them before."

She walked to his side, gazing into his eyes and smiling as she perched her bottom on the arm of his chair. "Believe it or not," she continued thoughtfully, weaving her fingers through his thick hair, "I was also thinking it was probably time to move on, and you'll never believe who's pursuing me, darling, but the wealthy and generous Viscount Willmont."

He raised his brows in surprise. "Old Chester?"

She nodded.

"Can he still . . . walk?"

"Jealous, darling?"

He grinned again, placing his palm on a thigh he knew so well, inhaling the familiar scent of her perfume. "Very."

Marissa laughed softly and steadied his chin with her forefinger and thumb, her face only inches from his. "Nobody will ever compare to you, in or out of bed, and I envy the woman who finally steals your heart."

Jonathan grabbed her around the waist and pulled her onto his lap. "I'm sure we can still make use of tonight," he goaded huskily. "Chester has probably already drunk his warm milk and retired for the evening anyway."

Marissa reached down and cupped him fully, boldly, then leaned over and whispered against his mouth, "Let's go upstairs. . . ."

Two

Natalie Haislett threw caution to the wind as she pulled the hood of her cloak tightly around her head, looked subtly in both directions, then quietly made her way down the steps of her father's London town house toward the end of the street where her ride awaited her.

She knew she was being brash, perhaps even irrational, but the time had finally come for her to make her move, and she could think of no other way. She was ready to meet the man of her dreams, the man who would take her away from her starched, banal existence. And she'd never felt more anxious in her life.

Even through the thick, early-morning fog, she spied the hired coach arranged for her by her ever valuable maid and walked quickly toward it. Then before the sun began to warm the day, she was on her way to his home, thrilled to the core and scared out of her mind.

Jonathan Drake was the last man on earth she wanted to see, the last man she wanted to count on for help. But he was all she had; he was her only lead. His older brother, Lord Simon, twelfth earl of Beckford, was married to her closest friend Vivian, and Vivian had promised with no uncertainty that Jonathan personally knew the infamous Black Knight, the man Natalie had known for nearly two years now as the man she was destined to marry.

Drake, independent and wealthy in his own right, was something of a free spirit, a wanderer, though thoroughly accepted as one of England's most eligible bachelors. He was a trader of fine goods, a buyer and seller of antiques and unusual artifacts for his own personal satisfaction, which meant to Natalie that he was just another nobleman with too much money and the time to waste it. But that was his business. Her interest in him went no further than his knowledge of the whereabouts of Europe's most notorious thief.

According to Vivian, Jonathan Drake had apparently met and become acquainted with the Black Knight through either business or travels. Although the Black Knight was a living legend, this wasn't so difficult for Natalie to believe, as he was still flesh and bone, and he had to have a few friends who knew his identity. It was just an extraordinary coincidence that the man she intended to marry knew *him,* the only man on earth she'd give her life to avoid.

Settling into the squabs, Natalie closed her eyes, attempting to replace the anxiousness she felt at seeing Jonathan with the hope and excitement of finally meeting her future husband.

The Black Knight was a mystery throughout Europe. She'd been following his escapades in England and on the Continent for more than two years, keeping track of him and his whereabouts through newspaper articles, and yes, although she was ashamed to admit it, through gossip. He was called many names—the Black Knight, the Thief of Europe, the Knight of Shadows—mostly, she assumed, because he worked only in darkness, in clandestine operations. Although the majority of people thought him a dishonest scoundrel and a despoiler of women, Natalie felt quite certain most all of what she'd heard was embellished or fabricated by those who were simply jealous of his accomplishments.

She'd first heard him mentioned when he'd been given credit for stealing a fine collection of Sevres vases from a prominent family in Germany. That this collection had originally been stolen from a French aristocrat during the Revolution of 1792 was somehow waylaid by the fact that the stealer was the infamous Black Knight. Natalie wasn't certain, but it was rumored that the vases eventually found their way to their rightful owners who were settled once again near Orange, and that the thief was only working for money and doing a job which those in authority were unable to do for reasons of questionable propriety or legalities.

She'd heard his name mentioned indifferently several times after that, but only last January did all of London come alive with speculation once more when Lord Henry Alton was arrested and charged with attempting to sell the countess of Belmarle's stolen ruby earrings. When his property was searched, not only did the authorities find a snuffbox on his mantel stuffed with the matching necklace and ring, but clear evidence that the man was running a highly enterprising trade in bootlegged whiskey. Rumors flew, but the word was out that the Black Knight was the one to sell Lord Alton the original rubies that led to his arrest.

Others might scoff, but Natalie, naive though she may be, knew in her soul that the notorious Knight of Shadows was working for the government and doing questionably legal things to catch criminals and right wrongs that could not be done through conventional measures. This had to be the case, for what good thief would return stolen items to rightful owners? Everything about him was rumor, however, from these instances to those involving art forgery and pirated gold to the identity of the man himself. The only certainty was that he existed.

So for the last few months Natalie had learned everything she could of him with keen interest, and except for only a general outline of his physical appearance, she knew everything there was to know, including the obvious fact that he was the man for her. He was exciting, intelligent, had been everywhere she wanted to go, and had done all the remarkable things she admired. But most of all he wasn't stiff as starch like every English gentleman who brought her sweetmeats and flowers, and took her for unimpressive rides through St. James Park while discussing Lord so-and-so's antique flintlock top, hammer pocket pistols, or the hunt in bloodthirsty detail. If she married this type of man, the type of man her parents wanted for her, her life (and naturally her backside) would become one huge, unproductive lump of fat. She deserved more from life, and since she was now nearly twenty-three years of age and hadn't yet chosen a husband, which in itself was driving her mother and father into a near panic, she finally felt ready to look for the man destiny had chosen for her. Heaven help her when her parents found out, but she was going to marry the Thief of Europe. And Jonathan Drake was going to help her find him.

As her coach finally stopped in front of the man's city dwelling, Natalie pulled her collar tightly around her neck. She didn't enjoy the chill, or the knowledge that someone might see her enter his town house unchaperoned, remote as that possibility would be.

Quickly paying the driver to wait for her, she ascended the steps and without hesitation lightly tapped the knocker on the front door. It was unthinkable to be calling at such an unseemly hour, as it was probably not quite six o'clock, but she really had no choice. She had to see him early so she could return to her bed before her mother awakened and panicked over her disappearance.

After waiting several moments, coming to the conclusion that the man's servants were seriously neglecting their duties and he evidently slept like the dead, Natalie tried the knob. To her complete surprise and satisfaction, the unlocked door slowly creaked open with a gentle nudge.

Quietly, nerves fired with anticipation, she stepped inside the darkened entryway, allowing her eyes only a second to adjust to the dimness, then moved swiftly in the direction of what she assumed to be his parlor. She found his study instead, and what a marvelous room it was, for through the glow of early-morning sunlight streaming through parted gauze curtains, she was suddenly taken aback by the most glorious collection of foreign treasures she had ever seen.

Paintings, large and small, of every port, city, and landscape imaginable adorned the oak-paneled walls. Bronze

sculptures and Oriental vases of all colors, sizes, and styles
sat upon oak chests, mahogany tables, and stands, and his
grand Sheraton writing desk, now covered with papers,
quills, a crystal bottle of ink, and an ivory-handled blade
for opening correspondence. A magnificent Spanish velveteen portrait in vivid blues, gold, sunset red, and black
hung over the fireplace, from the tall ceiling to the mantel.
Across the polished oak floor lay fine, delicately embroidered Oriental rugs, and on the farthest wall hung an elab-
orate assortment of exotic killing devices.

Natalie raised her hand to suppress a laugh, but truly,
that's what they were.

He had knives and swords of every kind, some with jagged edges, some smooth, pistols with handles of various
shapes and sizes covered with ivory, jade, and foreign let-
tering she had never before seen. And dangling precariously
from the ceiling in front of the wall hung a huge, curved
sword with unusual interlocking black marks across the flat
of the blade.

She couldn't help herself. She had to touch it.

Running her fingertips across the cold metal edge, Natalie considered it peculiar that Vivian had never mentioned
her brother-in-law to be such a very odd gentleman.

With her thoughts elsewhere, she missed the pattering of
feet behind her. Until a ferocious growl pierced the silence.

So sudden and unexpected was the noise, she whirled
around to confront it, slicing her hand with the tip of the
blade.

For a frightful second she glared into the eyes of a huge
German shepherd standing only three feet from her. Then
she felt the warmth of her blood as it oozed down her hand
and dripped onto her midnight-blue traveling cloak, and
immediately she was both awash with pain and completely
incensed.

Taking several deep breaths to control the scream welling
up inside of her, Natalie looked to her palm. The cut was
superficial, though nearly three inches long, stretching from
her index finger to her wrist. She quickly wrapped her cloak
around it to stop the bleeding, then started toward the door.

At that, the animal began a pattern of endless barking as it cornered her under the sword.

"Be quiet, you beast," she whispered nervously, trying to brush the dog aside with her good hand.

It made no difference. The animal growled again, then shocked her beyond belief when he quite suddenly stuck his nose into her gown, between her legs no less, and pushed her back against the wall.

"What are you doing here, Natalie?"

She stilled, eyes bright, cheeks pink with embarrassment as she turned her attention to the door of the study.

He stood there, looking absolutely magnificent as she knew he would, more handsome than memory served, wearing nothing but tight, black trousers molding indecently to his tapered hips and legs.

"Did I wake you?" she asked sweetly for lack of something better to say. "The door was open, and I . . ." Words failed her then as she became increasingly flustered, feeling ever more helpless as the seconds dragged by and the beast of an animal refused to remove his probing nose from between her thighs.

And he was watching the dog. She wanted to scream.

Indifferently he leaned his hard, sleek body against the doorframe and crossed his arms over his chest, relishing, she was certain, her unusual and highly entertaining predicament.

"Sir?" she pleaded, pushing in vain against the shepherd's head with her uninjured hand.

He smiled lazily. "Down, Thorn."

The dog responded immediately to the gruff command, moving back a foot or two to sit and watch her as well.

Natalie could think of nothing appropriate to say, so she simply stood her ground, bravely holding his gaze. Her cheeks burned, but whether it was from utter humiliation or the discomfort she always felt in the presence of this one man, she couldn't be certain.

Finally she could take the awkwardness of the moment no longer. "What a . . . picturesque home you have," she pleasantly acknowledged, chancing a glance around the room.

"Thank you."

"Did you do your own decorating or—"

"Natalie, what are you doing in my home at six o'clock in the morning?"

She almost jumped from the brusqueness in his tone as she looked back to his face. He hadn't moved his body, but the smile had left his mouth.

"The door was open," she replied matter-of-factly as if that explained everything, "and I thought perhaps we could talk."

"You stopped by to chat?"

She nodded and gave him her sweetest smile.

"But the standard social hour doesn't start for several hours, Miss Haislett. What did you intend to do with me until then?"

Her body grew hot beneath her petticoats from his formal, seemingly innocent question, and she clutched her wounded hand with the other, growing noticeably discomfited.

"Do—do you mind terribly if we sit?" she murmured at last.

He continued to stare at her for a moment, then groaned and rubbed his eyes with his fingers. "The coffee's ready by now."

"Coffee is vile," she countered without thinking.

He looked back at her sharply and gave her a cynical smile. "It's coffee or nothing."

"Coffee would be lovely," she returned very quickly, not wanting to chance him throwing her out for ungracious behavior.

"Thorn." He motioned with his hand to a corner of the room where the dog quickly moved to lie with his eyes closed, as if he hadn't a thought in the world other than much-needed sleep.

"He's certainly a large animal," she said pleasantly.

The right side of his mouth turned up almost imperceptibly as he continued to regard her openly. That did nothing but increase the already unbearable tension. "The coffee, sir?"

"I think we know each other well enough for you to call me Jonathan," he drawled.

Natalie didn't know what to say to that, and she was truly beginning to feel not just nervous but extremely uneasy. What was she thinking, walking into his home as if she lived there herself, with no chaperon and at daybreak no less? Suddenly she wished to heaven she were tucked beneath her downy quilt coverlet, or even walking down the aisle of St. George's to marry the boring Geoffrey Blythe. Any banal existence would be better than this.

He must have noticed her apprehension, the thoughts of fleeing outlined on her face, for at that moment he relaxed.

"It's all right, Natalie," he soothed, motioning with his head for her to follow. "Let's talk in the kitchen."

Strangely, she moved toward him without a thought to the contrary, still clutching her now-burning palm with her cloak, hoping the pain would subside and she could get her business done without disclosing the incident. She didn't want him to think her an idiot for touching a sword with no consideration as to the consequences.

She paid little attention to where they were heading, finding it difficult to take her eyes off his bare back as he walked in front of her. He was firm, marvelously muscled, and watching the mere sleekness of his frame, the tightness of his backside, made her feel even hotter in her layers of clothing. Suddenly the absurdity of the situation made her softly laugh.

He stopped short, turning at the unexpected sound, and the movement caused her to tumble into his chest. Grabbing her around the waist, he pulled her against him, to keep her from falling, she supposed, and at that moment her mirth faded as her heartbeat drastically increased from nothing more than his warm touch.

"What's so funny?" he asked, amused.

"I . . ." Nervousness overcame her again as she peered into his eyes, ever so slowly becoming aware of the fact that her breasts were now crushed up against his chest.

She straightened the best she could. "It just occurred to me that my mother would die if she knew you were wearing almost nothing at all."

"Your mother would die if she knew you were here, Natalie," he corrected thickly, tightening his grip on her back even as his free hand came forward to pull the hood of her cloak from her head. Before she could again put a reasonable distance between them, he reached behind her neck and pulled her long hair from beneath the soft wool, allowing it to fall freely down her back.

Natalie's eyes widened. The gesture was far too intimate, and she wanted to kick herself for not taking the time to put her unruly curls in pins. Without thinking, she placed both hands on his chest, pushing against him to free herself.

His gaze hardened, and he released her, turning abruptly to continue walking to the back of his town house. After only several steps, however, he stopped once more and flipped around to look at her.

His expression grew serious as he grabbed her wrists, palms up. "When did you do this?"

She blinked, stunned, for he was nearly shouting at her. She tried to jerk away, but he wouldn't let her free.

"Answer me, Natalie," he demanded.

"I'm sorry," she blurted, unsure of what else to say as she realized that in touching his chest she had inadvertently wiped blood on him. "Your dog startled me, and my hand slipped. . . ."

Her voice trailed off as his face visibly paled.

"It doesn't hurt at all," she whispered up to him.

"Which one?" he asked very quietly.

"Pardon?"

"Which one did you cut it on?"

She almost smiled from his show of concern. "The big one hanging from the ceiling. I'm very sorry." After an awkward pause, she timidly added, "I know touching your bare chest would be somewhat forward, but if you'd like, I'll wash it for you."

He continued to stare starkly into her eyes for a second

or two, then without reply he dropped her wrists, clasped her elbow, and guided her into the kitchen.

"This is probably going to hurt a little," he warned, walking her straight to the sink.

Before she had time to consider what he was doing, he took her injured hand, held it palm up, and poured brandy from a bottle across the cut.

A searing pain gripped her, and Natalie bit down to keep from crying out. She took a deep breath and swallowed, instinctively trying to wrench her hand from his grasp. He wouldn't let her go. Instead, he watched her for a reaction, and that made her angry.

"Was that necessary?" she choked out, clenching her teeth in defiance.

"Yes, it was necessary," he quietly replied, his eyes never leaving hers.

It was finally too much. "Why on earth do you keep staring at me, sir?"

She thought he almost smiled at that. Then, evidently deciding to ignore her question, he turned to his side, reached into a drawer, pulled out a small dishcloth, and proceeded to wrap her hand.

"Why don't you sit at the table and I'll get the coffee. Hold this tightly to the cut."

She did as she was told, grateful his attention had turned elsewhere and he wasn't looking at her anymore. In the momentary silence, she relaxed a little, watching him easily move about his kitchen. She'd smelled the sweet aroma upon entering the room, but what struck her was that he'd apparently made the coffee himself.

"You have no servants, sir?" she asked at last.

He shot her a quick glance. "I have one butler, Charles Lawson, who's away for the week caring for his mother who is in ill health. And I have a part-time cook and house-keeper, Gerty Matthews, who doesn't come in until about eleven." He turned to her. "I'm not in the city much, as I'm sure you're aware."

"I'm sure I'm not," she rebutted too quickly, admiring him openly. Never before had she seen a man so rich of build, so handsome from head to foot, so . . . masculine.

"Why do you keep staring at me, Natalie?"

She blinked, flushing with hot color. Bravely, and congratulating herself for the quickness of her answer, she admitted, "I've never seen a man's bare chest before, and if you weren't so indecently exposed, I wouldn't stare."

"I'll bet you would," he gruffly replied, turning his body to face her fully. He leaned back against the counter, folding his arms in front of him as he gazed at her suggestively.

Natalie was sure that this moment was one of the most uncomfortable of her life. Her mind churned as she considered what she could possibly say to him. Maybe she should run.

"Why don't you explain exactly why you're here."

He had to have noticed the sign of obvious relief that crossed her brow at the abrupt change of subject. "A marvelous suggestion," she agreed, sitting erect as her courage returned. "I need you to help me find someone."

"Really," he stated rather than asked. "Do I know this person?"

"I believe you do, yes."

He turned once more to the counter, poured two cups of coffee, placed them on a silver tray, then carried everything to the table.

"Have you ever had coffee, Natalie?" he asked, sitting in the chair next to hers and handing her a cup.

She shook her head. "My mother proclaims it to be a heathen beverage."

His mouth twisted in a smile. "That doesn't surprise me."

She looked at the thick, dark liquid and shivered. "I usually prefer chocolate in the morning. It's one of my most insatiable desires. I adore chocolate."

He raised his cup to his lips. "And what are some of your other insatiable desires?"

Her eyes grew wide as her pulse began to race. Above everything else, she needed to remember his reputation, to ignore and smoothly glide over every indecent innuendo to come from his mouth.

Finding her voice, she announced levelly, "I'll pay you to help me locate—"

"Jonathan?"

The soft interruption came from the doorway. Natalie looked to her left to see an absolutely beautiful dark-haired woman walk into the kitchen wearing nothing but blue velvet mules and a white, Oriental silk wrap, tied at her waist by a thin silk sash, hiding almost nothing of her body, least of all the outline of her tall, lithe, elegantly curved figure.

Natalie had never been more thunderstruck, and apparently neither had the woman as they both stared openly at each other for one long and extremely awkward moment.

Then Jonathan groaned, and they turned their gazes to him.

He closed his eyes, pinched the bridge of his nose with his fingers, and sank lower into his chair.

"Miss Natalie Haislett, Miss Marissa Jenkins," he said as an introduction.

Natalie wondered for a moment if the woman deserved the title, then decided that was really beside the point. Suddenly made speechless, she slowly came to the conclusion that the exotic-looking creature standing in front of them was the man's mistress. Of course Natalie was a lady, properly bred, but she'd heard rumors and knew many gentlemen of quality had them. She would not, therefore, be shocked. She would not be shocked. But in the course of several long, silent seconds, the poor man seated next to her became so adorably disconcerted, she could hardly keep from laughing. She would positively need to use the moment for all it was worth.

Recovering quickly, she removed her cloak to allow full view of her peach muslin morning gown, cut low across the front to expose the gentle swell of her ample bosom. She originally had no intention of removing her outer garment, but this situation called for the exception. Now she was more than glad she'd worn something a bit revealing.

With a small measure of subtlety she pulled her thick

mass of hair over her shoulder to cascade loosely down the front of her, then gave them both a disarming smile.

"So you must be Jonathan's mistress."

His head jerked up immediately, eyes wide and full of amazement, no doubt stunned to hear such common words from an unmarried lady of her station.

Marissa caught on quickly. "I *was* his mistress, Miss Haislett, until last night when he dismissed me." Gracefully she walked to the opposite end of the table and sat. "Have you ever had coffee? It's quite good with a little sweet cream and sugar."

"I believe I'll try it like that, thank you," Natalie returned smoothly, ignoring the man beside her and reaching for the serving tray. She poured a generous amount of cream from the small pitcher into her cup, then followed it with a large spoonful of sugar. "And why were you dismissed, Marissa?"

The woman sighed. "Well, I do believe Jonathan is ready to find someone a bit more permanent to warm his bed."

"The poor man cannot afford blankets?" she asked with wide-eyed concern.

Marissa placed an elbow on the table, her chin in her palm. "I'm quite certain he's thinking of something livelier and more exciting than blankets."

"Perhaps he should sleep with his huge, warm dog—"

"This is the most absurd conversation I've ever been a part of," Jonathan finally cut in, exasperated and raising his cup to his lips to avoid looking at them.

Both women turned to him as if noticing him for the first time.

"Is she the one?" Marissa asked with calculation.

Natalie quickly came to her own defense. "I assure you, Miss Jenkins, I shall not be warming anyone's bed but my own."

"Of course not," she murmured very slowly, gazing back at her curiously. After an uncomfortable pause, she stood to leave. "Well, I think I'll just get dressed and be on my way. If you change your mind, Miss Haislett, he prefers the left side.''

''The left side?''

''Of the bed.''

''Oh, I'm sure that's no concern of mine, Marissa. But may I say the man certainly has a taste for beauty—''

''I don't believe this is happening in my kitchen,'' Jonathan interjected with growing wonder, tipping his cup to his lips again and draining the liquid with two large gulps.

Both women looked at him innocently, then Marissa moved to kiss his cheek. ''Good-bye, darling.''

He grunted but said nothing as he continued to stare at the tabletop.

Marissa walked to the door, gave them both an amused glance, and quickly left the kitchen.

The room fell still as death. Natalie looked to her lap, clutching the towel with her throbbing hand as she played intently with the fabric of her gown with the other. She knew he'd shifted his gaze to watch her but she just couldn't bring herself to look at him, so engrossed as she was in the quality of fine, peach muslin.

''I apologize for that,'' he mumbled at last.

She shrugged but said nothing.

''Natalie, look at me.''

She raised her eyes to meet his, and it took everything in her to keep her features neutral. ''It's quite all right. What you do in your home is your own business, sir.''

''Stop being so formal,'' he ordered, at once annoyed.

She ignored his outburst and looked again to her gown. ''I only wonder why on earth she was here this morning when you rid yourself of her last night.''

She didn't expect him to laugh, and the suddenness of the reaction made her glance up sharply. He stared ever so intently into her eyes, smiling broadly, then leaned very close to her face. ''Did you expect me to wait for you, sweetheart?''

The question alarmed her, and she certainly didn't know how to answer him. She couldn't just walk out on him for flirting, though, because something larger was at stake.

That's what she had to remember. She was here for a purpose and she needed to get back to the reason for her untimely call.

Keeping her expression completely indifferent, she whispered, "I am not your sweetheart."

His eyes narrowed with lighthearted mischief. "Not yet."

Natalie shivered. Her heart was suddenly beating frantically, but to her total frustration she couldn't find the strength to move. He sat so close to her she could feel the warmth of his body, could see every fleck of blue in the deep grayness of his eyes, could detect the musky smell of sandalwood and rich masculinity.

"I will not be anyone's mistress," she assured him in a measure of defiance.

"You have beautiful hair, Natalie," he whispered seductively, raising his hand to run his fingers through the ends. "Not quite red, not quite blond, and so full and curvy like your—"

"Do you suppose I could have more coffee?" she blurted, jerking back out of his reach, knowing irritably that he would conclude the request to be simple evasion since she'd only taken four or five sips.

For a moment he didn't move. Then finally, with an exaggerated sigh of defeat, he stood with both cups in hand and walked back to the counter. "So, let's get back to the point of your visit."

This was why the man had such a reputation, she mused. He could seduce a lady with words and a smile if he so chose, then casually drop the intensity and turn the conversation into something ordinary with a blink of an eye. Because of his flirtatious nature, she would need to be extraordinarily cautious around Jonathan Drake. Her attraction to him, if considered honestly, was remarkably potent, stunning even her because she had always been so utterly sensible. And she knew to her soul this man would easily break her heart and spread the news of his conquest without a trace of emotion beyond indifference. She could never allow that to happen.

Desirous of moving on and getting home to the safety of her bedroom, she agreed with a nod of her sensible head. "Yes, indeed. The point of my visit." With as much courage as she could gather, she said, "I need you to help me find the Black Knight."

He sharply turned to her, studying her oddly. "*The* Black Knight?"

She straightened. "Yes, *the* Black Knight."

Sauntering back to the table to sit again, he placed her cup in front of her. "What makes you think I know where he is?"

Natalie was slightly taken aback. She had expected the man to be surprised or disbelieving, but instead he seemed only mildly curious. "Vivian told me you know him personally. Naturally, I didn't believe her—"

"I know him," he admitted.

Her eyes flashed with a burst of excitement. "You do? You truly know the man?"

"What exactly do you want with him, Natalie?" he asked cautiously.

She paused to drink her nearly scalding coffee in gulps now, thinking furiously. She realized she had to disclose at least some of her desires, even if the man laughed her out of his home for being completely unbalanced.

Licking her lips, she sat fully erect. "I intend to marry him."

After an eternal moment of looking at her blankly, he leaned back in his chair and stretched his legs out in front of him. "What makes you think he'll want to marry you?"

She had absolutely never expected this reaction. It stunned her into submissive silence, which in turn made him smile devilishly, knowingly.

"You are undeniably lovely, Natalie, but somehow I think there should be more to marriage than attraction, don't you?" He lowered his voice. "Perhaps he'll only want you to warm his bed. Are you prepared to settle for only that?"

She felt color rush to her face once more. "I told you I will not be anyone's mistress, but that's really none of your business. I simply want you to help me find him.''

''Mmmm . . .''

''What does that mean?''

''Nothing.''

She sighed. ''Will you take me to him?''

He gazed at her speculatively.

''Please?'' she begged.

Finally he leaned forward on the table in front of him, placed his arms on the wooden surface, and stared at his coffee cup as he turned it around in his hands.

''What do you intend to do about us?''

Admittedly, she had a fairly good idea of what he meant by that, but in the end decided to play it stupidly. ''About us?''

He pursed his lips but didn't move his eyes from his cup. ''You and me, Natalie. We're strongly attracted to each other, and I don't know if we could be together every day without wanting each other physically.''

Her heart thundered at once from such brazen considerations on his part, and she was certain he could hear it pounding in her chest. Composing herself, she whispered, ''That's absurd.''

He looked to her at last, lifting a brow quizzically. ''I'm quite certain you've thought about it, so don't you think you should be a bit more honest with your feelings?''

She couldn't believe he was talking so intimately about the two of them, as if there were something more to their relationship than a casual acquaintance, and the only thing she could do to take control of the situation was simply to ignore what he'd said.

''I need you to help me locate the Black Knight,'' she maintained, ''and that is the only thing I want from you, sir. Beyond that, there is nothing between us.''

Slowly, thoughtfully, he ran his index finger in circles around the rim of his cup. ''I think you want me for many things, sweetheart, some of which you are probably far too innocent to even understand.''

She stood rigidly. ''I am not now, nor will I ever be, your sweetheart.'' Inhaling very deeply, she asked with surprising smoothness, "Will you or will you not help me find the Black Knight?"

"I will."

The quickness of his words stumped her.

Briskly he raised himself to stand beside her, his expression matter-of-fact.

"I'm sailing to Marseilles on Friday, Natalie, and you're welcome to come with me on one condition."

She was thoughtful for a moment, preparing herself to argue. "And what is that?"

"You do everything exactly as I say. You follow every instruction I give you, keep to yourself, and do not in any way question my authority. Understand?"

She crossed her arms over her breasts. "That's more than one condition."

"Take it or leave it," he returned, crossing his arms over his chest as well.

"And the Black Knight is in Marseilles?"

"He will be when we get there."

"You know this?"

"Yes."

"And you'll introduce us?"

"Yes."

"What's his name?" she asked in a sudden rush of excitement.

He remained silent for a second or two, frowning almost imperceptibly. "I think it would be better if I speak to him first before divulging anything about him."

Her heart sank. Of course it would have to be that way, but it was all she had. "I agree to your terms, sir—"

"You must also start calling me Jonathan."

"Fine," she conceded blandly. "Is there anything else?"

He shrugged. "What about your parents?"

She waved her hand to brush the matter aside. "They're leaving for Italy in two days, to be gone for the season, buying artwork and bathing in the sun." She reached for her cloak. "They'll never know anything."

"Allow me."

His sudden gentlemanly behavior surprised her as he

took the cloak from her uninjured hand and wrapped it around her shoulders. Turning her to face him, he began to button the front.

"Why does this man intrigue you so, Natalie?" he asked contemplatively.

She thought for a moment how to answer such a direct question.

"He's free," she finally confessed. Smiling lightly to his puzzled face, she explained, "I only mean that he's not bound by the mores of society. He's exciting, he travels, he . . . lives for adventure." She leaned toward him even more, eyes sparkling, and lowered her voice to just above a whisper. "I know this sounds a bit odd, but I believe he's also looking for me."

He hesitated, watching her so intensely his eyes seemed to pierce hers. Then he lifted his palm to her neck and slowly began to run the pad of his thumb down from her cheek to the top of her wool collar, stopping at last when he placed it over the pounding pulse beneath her jaw. Within seconds uneasiness returned in full force as she stood so close to him, eyes locked, their bodies nearly touching.

But he was the first to break the spell. Swiftly, he dropped his hand and turned his attention to the table, placing everything on the tray to walk it back to the counter.

"I'm certain you've heard the man's a notorious womanizer," he stated offhandedly.

"I'm sure that's all very much exaggerated," she countered.

He smirked but said nothing else as he placed their empty cups in the sink.

"Is he?" she prodded.

"Is he what?"

She gave an exasperated sigh. "A womanizer."

"I'm sure that's all very much exaggerated."

That made her laugh.

"What's funny now?" he asked, amused, turning to face her again.

She shook her head. "Since you and I have met, sir, we

have had nothing but absurd conversations.''

"Jonathan."

She surrendered. "Jonathan."

He flashed her a smile full of charm and moved toward her. "That's because you are the most unusual woman I have ever known, Natalie Haislett."

"And you've known many, I'm sure," she insisted without thinking.

His smile broadened as he stepped directly in front of her, backing her up against the table and trapping her by placing his arms on each side of her waist to rest his palms on the wooden surface.

"I'm sure that's all very much exaggerated," he whispered huskily.

She swallowed hard and whispered in return, "Vivian told me your reputation for being a rake is accurate."

"Vivian lied."

She was straining so hard to keep from touching him that she was now nearly lying on the table.

"Do you know what I like most about you, Natalie?"

She could feel the warmth of his body penetrate the fabric of her clothing, feel the hardness of his bare chest next to her own, the strength of his arms surrounding her, and still she couldn't look away. "Obviously I don't."

Without warning, he leaned over and brushed his mouth against hers, moving softly back and forth, back and forth. Instinctively, breathlessly, she closed her eyes and succumbed to his touch as he ran his lips across her flushing cheek.

"I like the way you kiss."

Her eyes flew open.

"And ever since that very first time," he whispered in her ear, "I've dreamed of doing it again."

She nearly fainted. In all of her prayers, the one thing she'd asked for the most was that he would completely forget the kiss they'd shared at the masked ball years ago, or at the very least, be a gentleman and never bring it up. That awful night in the garden. How she wished that had never happened.

"I need to leave," she said shakily, pushing her good hand between their touching chests.

Unaffected by her uneasiness, he gradually stood back. "Let me see the cut first."

She quickly moved away from him, removed the towel, and raised her palm to his view. "It's just fine," she said brightly. "What time should we meet on Friday?"

"Come here."

She shook her head.

"I'm not going to ravish you, Natalie, I just want to look at your hand."

Before she could reply, he took two steps in her direction, reached for her, and pulled her against him. With her injured palm in his, he looked at it closely. "It should heal without scarring but it will be quite sore. I'd keep it clean and covered for two or three days."

She nodded and pulled away. "I'm sorry about this."

He frowned. "You could have been killed in there. I should be the one who's sorry."

"I hardly think a little cut like this would kill me, sir."

He raked his fingers through his thick, black hair then put his hands on his hips and stared her straight in the eye. "Several of the knives I have hanging on my wall are from countries you've probably never heard of, Natalie, and several of them were at one time covered with poison that doesn't always come off with a washing. They're made purposely to kill with just a little nick to the skin. I nearly collapsed from fright when I saw your hand because I would never want to explain to your overbearing mother exactly how you came to be dead in my town house at six in the morning."

She covered her mouth with the back of her hand to suppress a giggle.

"Most gently bred ladies would have fainted from that explanation," he said with amazement.

She grinned. "It's not the thought of dying—it's the thought of being found." With shining eyes, she whispered up to him, "My mother is my biggest fright as well."

He gave her a broad, disarming smile. "I'll send you word about Friday—"

"Through Amy, my maid," she cut in. "She's been helping me plan this adventure for two years now."

He raised an eyebrow. "Two years?"

Natalie stopped short. Her excitement was overflowing, and she needed to keep it in check. "I mean, we've been planning what to tell servants and friends, so nobody will question my absence. I'm essentially free as soon as my parents leave for the Continent."

"Ahh . . . well." He scratched his day-old beard. "In that case, I'll send word day after tomorrow, through Amy. We'll need to travel lightly, so don't plan on bringing too many . . . things."

"Thank you," she whispered, touching his arm with her fingertips. "This means everything to me."

She turned and walked to the doorway. Pausing before it, she glanced once more in his direction and graced him with a beautiful smile. "The coffee was delicious," she said sweetly.

With a wave of her hand she was gone.

Three

Natalie stood starboard on the steamship *Bartholomew Redding* in the damp, late-evening air, her forest-green traveling cloak wrapped around her like a comforting blanket as she turned her face toward the setting sun, now finally dipping below the horizon. They were well out of the Channel now, past the Isles of Scilly, heading south into open sea, and the rush of anticipation made her tingle.

Jonathan stood beside her, tall and powerful, dressed casually in midnight-brown trousers and an ecru linen shirt unbuttoned at the neck, his only barrier to the cool sea wind which he didn't seem to mind. It wasn't cold, really, and in a day or two they would be quite hot. Natalie had taken that into account when she'd packed for the adventure, bringing with her only five trunks instead of the usual eight or ten. Jonathan had made a face of disbelief, or perhaps annoyance, when she'd met him at the docks, but what did he expect? She was a lady, and there were just some things one could not do without. Only five trunks for indefinite travel in Europe was incredible by anyone's standards.

Earlier that day, immediately after setting foot on the ship, Jonathan had escorted her to her cabin without so much as a handful of words. The room was square and small, but pretty really, with a round window at the far end

large enough to allow ample daylight to enter, covered with
pale, gauze curtains for appearance rather than decency. To
the right of the door sat a straight-backed chair made of
polished mahogany and crushed burgundy velvet, a small
nightstand and lamp, and next to it was a bed of adequate
size, large enough for one to sleep comfortably, covered
with a thick, rose-embroidered coverlet. To the left, running
parallel to the wall and bolted to the floor, stood an oriental
silk screen, discreetly enclosing a dressing and toilette area.

The cabin was perfect for her, and she made herself comfortable at once, taking time to unpack and settle in for her
voyage as Jonathan, after ushering her inside, left her alone
for nearly three hours, and had only returned a short time
ago with a cold dinner of salmon mousse, cheese, bread,
and fruit which they'd just finished in her room.

From this point on she would need to take care of all
her needs since she'd brought no lady's maid. Traveling
without one was indecent, at least in this situation, although
she prayed nobody would ask why she'd left England alone,
unwed and unchaperoned. She would just keep to
herself until they reached France, which was what he'd
asked her to do anyway.

But now, comfortable at last and thrilled with the adventure ahead, her thoughts managed to stray constantly to her
most handsome traveling companion, now standing quietly
beside her on deck, peering out to the open water as well,
not quite touching her, but there. She was sharply conscious
of his presence, and he was probably well aware of it.

What satisfied her, though, was the growing knowledge
that he would be a marvelous protector of her innocence
while on their little trip. The man was large and imposing,
probably formidable and intimidating when he chose to be,
yet at the same time gentlemanly and gracious. That had
been proven earlier that day when she'd arrived at the dock
and he'd politely nodded to her, directing where her things
were to be taken, offering her his arm and helping her board
the ship with just his palm lightly clasping her fingers.

He'd paid for her passage, she assumed, since she had
yet to give him money. But she would. She'd been saving

every last penny of her allowance for two years now and she had plenty, divided wisely between her trunks, portmanteau, and reticule. She'd even hidden some beneath the soles and hollowed-out heels of a select number of her seven pairs of shoes, where her grandfather, and then her mother, were known to have carried money for emergencies. Natalie didn't know who originally thought of stuffing money beneath one's feet, but she supposed if one were to cross the ocean or foreign land and be put-upon by pirates or gypsies, the hiding place would serve its purpose excellently.

She felt Jonathan shift his body, moving slightly closer, and shyly she realized his gaze now fell on the side of her face, its warmth as stinging as the salty air.

"It's time for discussion, Natalie."

She knew he'd finally suggest a serious conversation. No need to draw attention to it, though. "A discussion?" she repeated coyly. "We've been talking all day—"

"Where does everybody think you are?" he interrupted, ignoring her evasion by coming directly to the point.

Nervously, she looked around. The deck had cleared of people as evening fell, although somewhere in the distance she heard laughter, the hearty laughter of a woman followed by the rumble of a man's voice, words indistinguishable. It was then that she realized Jonathan Drake was her only connection to their homeland. They were now a team, like it or not, and they would need to rely on one another, although admittedly she more than he. She would also need to be a little more forthcoming.

"Natalie?"

Irritated, she turned to face him. He was watching her, smugly amused, and she wanted to snap at him. Every time he said her name it sounded like a silky caress, and she really wished he'd stop. But stop what? Speaking to her? That was silly.

She crossed her arms over her breasts—a useless gesture because she knew her traveling cloak, buttoned tightly against her, really only accentuated them. Already several times that day his eyes had strayed there, lingering inappropriately.

"Everybody thinks I'm visiting my great-aunt Regina in Newburn," she revealed at last.

He cocked a brow and leaned his hip on the railing. "You don't think your lies will be discovered eventually?"

"No. Aunt Regina is seventy-seven, and her mind doesn't work very well. She'll never remember whether I was there or not. And my parents will believe it without question when I tell them, upon their return from Italy, that I went there for a time to contemplate and decide upon whom I should marry."

"You've planned everything very well," he praised her after a moment of thought.

She smiled in satisfaction. "I think so."

He lowered his voice. "And are you?"

"Am I what?"

"Contemplating someone real to marry," he clarified.

She gazed up to him with a purposeful look of confusion. "You mean someone other than the Black Knight?"

"You know exactly what I mean."

She hugged herself against the cool sea breeze. "If you mean a conventional Englishman, no." With a small, impish laugh, she added, "But my parents will believe it, and that's what matters. They're desperate to have me married, since, at nearly twenty-three, I'm a frequent topic of conversation at parties. I've turned four respectable gentlemen down in as many years. Lots of people find that, if not amusing, a bit strange."

He waited again for a second or two, watching her closely. "What about Lord Richard Mydell or Geoffrey Blythe of Guildford?"

She grasped a stray curl blowing across her cheek and tucked it behind her ear. "Richard is a slob, and poor Geoffrey, sweet though he may be, has the personality of doornails. . . ." Her voice trailed off as she looked back to his face. He'd said the names almost distastefully, but what surprised her was his knowledge that both Richard and Geoffrey had asked her to marry them.

"How did you—"

"I know lots of things," he intimated, dropping his voice to an indifferent whisper. He reached for the collar of her cloak and began stroking it with his thumb. "But what I can't imagine is either one of them . . . kissing you to satisfaction, Natalie."

Suddenly she was hot, unsettled from such an impertinent comment. Especially from him.

"But of course they're both rich," he continued matter-of-factly. "Little Richard even has a title, and those two things are usually what a woman wants most from a marriage."

She firmly pulled back from him, and he dropped his hand. "Richard is half a foot taller than you. Hardly little."

He grinned devilishly. "But sickly skinny. A man who would no doubt die of consumption or fever at an early age, leaving you with all the money—"

"I care nothing for riches in a husband," she cut in, rubbing a palm across her forehead in irritation, unsure why she felt the need to defend herself.

"Really," he stated, unconvinced. "Then what are you looking for in a husband, Natalie, sweet? What does the legendary Black Knight have that you could possibly want?"

He was teasing her, and she could scarcely be nasty to him with the almost tender way he approached the subject. But she didn't want it to drag on for their entire trip abroad. She got enough pestering about it from her parents.

He stood silently next to her, waiting for an explanation, and since they were all alone on deck, she organized her thoughts and decided to confide in him, to get everything out in the open now so they could move on.

"About two years ago," she began with a sigh, "I came to the conclusion that if I lived the life my mother wanted for me I would grow old and fat and bored, sitting around at teas, eating cakes and chocolates, chatting idly with other ladies about things like who wore what ghastly shade of red to which ball, and whose daughter suddenly needed to marry within the month to save her family disgrace."

She tossed him a quick glance to see how he reacted to her words, but he held his tongue, expression neutral, giving her his full attention now in the quiet of growing nightfall.

"If you must know, Jonathan," she carried on thoughtfully, "I'm not altogether good at embroidery, or gardening, or choosing the appropriate dessert for a menu, or any of the silly little things a lady of fine breeding is expected to do well or, at the very least, efficiently. That's why my mother and I have been at odds with each other for so long. What my parents want from me is to settle down and have babies with someone boring who expects me to do the boring things I loathe." She snorted with disgust. "My mother *adores* Geoffrey Blythe."

"Go on," he urged huskily.

She raised glowing eyes to his, leaning so close to him the warmth of his body touched her.

Fervently she whispered, "I want to *live,* Jonathan, to travel and see the world. I refuse to marry an average Englishman who will take me for granted, who will expect me to speak only when appropriate, entertain when necessary, and ignore his husbandly indiscretions. I am not a prize to be won and placed becomingly upon a shelf."

Her voice grew with intensity as she fisted her hands at her chest for emphasis. "I want to be in *love,* I want to feel *passion,* like a . . . a fairy princess who meets an extraordinary, handsome prince and is swept off her feet by a tide of powerful emotion. I want to grow old with someone who wants me as a woman, as a person, not as a dutiful wife."

She stood back, composing herself to add determinedly, "Money cannot buy life, Jonathan, and I refuse to waste mine in the desire to possess expensive trinkets my husband provides me to ignore his various childish follies. Even if I become poor as a beggar, I won't settle for anything less than romance with friendship, and a marriage full of joy."

As her voice trailed off to stillness, her face bright with excitement, or perhaps embarrassment at such an open admission, he wasn't sure which, it occurred to Jonathan that she was going to be a good deal of trouble, indeed. He'd known that, in fact, the minute she walked up to him at the dock earlier that day, a dazzling smile parting her lips and her deliciously shaped body wrapped in a cloak that matched her brilliant eyes.

She was spellbinding, really, with creamy, glowing skin and thick, wavy hair the color of a summer evening sunset. And he knew she tried, if not to disguise her figure, at least to downplay it with plain clothing, but with that she thoroughly failed. Natalie Haislett was a frank and total beauty, with a mind of mischief and an adorable, charming character edged with innocence. And what the hell did he think he was doing, carting her along with him to France to meet the mythical Black Knight?

She had captivated him in his town house, he realized now, showing up unannounced, striking him down because she was again doing the unexpected, catching him off guard as she had nearly five years ago in her father's garden. Both times she'd made him do the irrational from sweetly spoken words and a simple naive but candid look from her gorgeous, hazel-green eyes.

But the timing couldn't have been more perfect. He could use her, he decided, although *using* wasn't really a word he liked to describe his actions toward a woman, even in her ignorance. *Assisting* him was probably a better way of looking at it, as it had occurred to him during that same moment of irrationality in his town house that the emeralds he'd been sent to retrieve could very easily be hidden, without her awareness, in her things for transport back to England, if necessary. God knew she'd brought enough of them. And they would surely look magnificent dangling in all their priceless glory from her delicately carved throat if he so chose to indulge her.

Jonathan groaned softly, raking his fingers through his hair as he forced himself to gaze out to the open sea, frustrated with himself and his weaknesses, mostly his weakness for the female sex.

She straightened beside him and smoothed her breeze-blown curls into place inside the knot at the back of her head. "I'm sure you think my notions are ridiculous, sir, but I assure you—"

"I don't think they're ridiculous," he cut in quietly, wiping his face with his palm in mild agitation. "I just—" He paused for a moment and tried again. "You think the Black Knight is going to fill all these idealistic needs for you? What if you don't like him; what if he doesn't like you? What are you going to do when you meet him and find him mean or . . . grotesquely ugly? What if he's a slob like Mydell or boring like Blythe?" He looked back into her eyes. "You're endangering your entire future on a fantasy."

She shook her head. "That's impossible."

"What's impossible?" he returned brusquely.

Pursing her lips, she said flatly, "I've studied this man and his escapades for two years, Jonathan. I know he is dark, sophisticated, charming, intelligent, handsome, and he does good things to help people. There is also a rumor that he has blue eyes, which, as it happens, I like most in a man." She dropped her lashes, as if suddenly realizing she was disclosing too much.

"You've got nice, romantic notions," he murmured thickly after several seconds of silence. "But adventure and eye color are no reasons to risk—"

"I didn't say I would marry him *because* he has blue eyes," she interrupted, glancing back to his face.

Jonathan knew he was aggravating her, but he refused to soften his approach simply to be tactful with her female sensibilities. These things needed to be said now. "You don't understand," he stressed. "I'm talking about your reputation, Natalie. If it's discovered you've left for the Continent with me, you'll be socially ruined, and for life. Have you considered that?"

Those words hung in the air like a dark, menacing thundercloud. He continued to stare down at her from only a foot away, taking note of the crease of perplexing contemplation on her brow; of her shining hair; her long, silky brown lashes; her soft, slightly parted, pink lips, perfectly shaped and lusciously alluring. She had evidently come to a conclusion that day as to the nature of their relationship on this voyage, for she found him neither threatening nor tiresome, but more of a companion. Almost brotherly. Presenting himself as her brother would never be believed by anyone, however, and just knowing that made him gloat inside. He would enjoy the next hour, even the rest of the night, immensely. He was about to clear up perfectly, with no uncertainty, exactly what their relationship was to be. And he had to do it before she pressed him to leave her and go to a room he didn't actually have.

"Then we will have to be extremely careful," she whispered dryly, cutting into his thoughts. "Someone of your reputation . . ."

Her voice trailed off into the clear night sky, as if it gradually occurred to her that she wasn't with her brother, but a man who might very well want her for more than companionship.

"And what do you know of my reputation, Miss Haislett?" he inquired soberly, inching closer to her even as she gripped the railing to her side for additional support.

As nonchalantly as she could, she acknowledged what to her was the obvious. "I know you adore women, and they generally adore you in return. I know you change mistresses as casually as you change your boots. I know you think no woman alive can resist you." She smiled impishly. "I, however, am the exception, and will be for the remainder of our trip. I know you're a trader of fine goods, whatever that means, and that it's made you a wealthy man—honestly wealthy, which is good. I know you enjoy lavishing that wealth on the women you . . . entertain. I know you come from a respectable family and that they enjoy you and discussing your escapades very much."

He blinked, suppressing the urge to laugh at her absurd generalizations, but feeling a stirring heat within of something akin to triumph as she openly admitted her knowledge about him and his personal affairs.

"You've apparently studied me to some depth," he responded with charming smoothness.

She looked out over the horizon, as if taking a sudden great interest in the near-black, lightly swirling ocean. "Not purposely, I assure you, although you as well as other unattached gentlemen come up in social conversation from time to time. Naturally such conversation can't be avoided easily."

"Naturally," he agreed.

"Your brother's wife is also my closest friend," she amended for additional escape. "It would be impossible for me not to hear at least some things."

A most contrived answer, and they both knew it.

"Ahh . . . ," was his only reply.

Seconds ticked by in uncomfortable silence. Then, with keen anticipation of the line he was about to cross, he reached up and cupped her cheek with his palm, turning her face back to his, gazing into wide eyes of instant uneasiness.

"But there's one inaccuracy I must correct," he said softly.

She didn't pull away but batted her lashes in feigned innocence. "An inaccuracy? Which part?"

"The resisting part."

She frowned delicately, as if trying to remember exactly what she'd said. "That no woman can resist you? I hardly think—"

"*You* cannot resist me, Natalie, sweet."

And then he was kissing her, smothering any hint of denial with his lips, pressing tenderly at first, with no real trace of movement, just a touch. He didn't pull her into him, but stood there in the shadow of dusk, the faint sound of waves splashing against the ship beneath them, his palm softly caressing her cheek as his body came eagerly alive from nothing but the penetrating heat of her mouth.

Natalie was so thoroughly stunned she could not immediately react. They'd only been teasing each other companionably, like old friends, and without provocation he'd done the unthinkable.

Instinctively, after several seconds of shock at his daring, she tried to pull away. That's when he grabbed her around the waist and drew her against him, embracing her completely with an arm of solid strength. Her first rational thought was how this wasn't a kiss like the one in his town house only a few days ago—just a delicate brush of his warm lips. No, this was sweet desire, controlling and intense, the sudden taste of him so powerful she was flooded with the memory of their first intimate encounter five years earlier, of what he'd done to her then, both physically and emotionally. And passionately.

Trembling, Natalie reached up and weakly pushed against his shoulders, wanting desperately to break free because she knew she would soon succumb. And she was right. No longer could she think straight as he held to her tightly, caressing her back with one hand, her cheek with the other, as he played perfect music of beauty against her mouth.

Gradually she leaned into him, gliding her fingertips up along his shirt, relishing in the feel of hot skin beneath cool linen, of the hard, flawless muscle mass against her palms. She squeezed her eyes shut, shoving all from her mind but his powerful embrace, parting her lips a little at his insistence. She was breathing hard, her heart pounding in her breast, blood rushing through her veins, echoing in her ears as she tried to get more of him, as she clutched his neck and ran her fingers through the silky hair at his nape.

Jonathan erupted with a nearly uncontrollable inner fire when he felt her relax and mold herself against him, responding so quickly, so anxiously. He'd really expected her to turn rigid with indignation, even slap him—the standard reaction from someone of her upbringing. But he should have known. Their desire for each other was numbing, indescribable, and had been since the moment they'd first come together on the dance floor years ago.

But it wasn't the passion that so startled him. It was the realization that he'd never felt this strongly attracted to a female in his life—to her softness, her smile and eyes, her delicate curves, her scent of soap and flowers and woman. And this seemingly innocent kiss on the deck of the *Redding,* under sprinkled stars and soft moonglow, was the beginning of something he was afraid to acknowledge. He'd hoped that a shared kiss would put an end to his need, but it didn't, it wouldn't, and he was in trouble.

He ran the tip of his tongue along her parted lips, the fingers of his right hand gingerly massaging her neck, his left splayed across her lower back, holding her firmly against his rigid body. She moaned softly in his arms, and as impatient as he was to deepen the magic, to touch her more completely, more possessively, somewhere within he became painfully aware that he needed to stop the encounter before it was carried too far. This wasn't the time or place for this, and she would never end the kiss herself. He knew that now.

With immoderate difficulty, breathing rapidly, attempting to clear his mind from the urgency pervading it, Jonathan did what he'd never done in his life—quelled the passion first.

"Natalie . . . ," he whispered against her mouth, drawing his hands forward to place both palms on her cheeks.

She didn't hear him, didn't respond immediately, and with great reluctance he pulled his lips from hers.

"Natalie," he repeated in a gravelly rasp, lifting his face away. He placed a kiss or two on her brow before he dropped his forehead to rest against hers, firmly cupping her cheeks, holding her to keep her from running, inhaling deeply to subdue his fired nerves.

He didn't want to say anything until she calmed, until her breathing slowed and she regained control. She was probably embarrassed, and he wasn't exactly sure how to handle it, how to explain his actions, to keep her from feeling rejected.

Suddenly she was shaking. She pulled her arms down from around his neck and pushed against his chest.

"Natalie—"

"Stop saying my name like that," she whispered.

He frowned. Like what?

Slowly he released her, waiting, and she stood back, hugging herself, head lowered so moonlight reflected off her hair in shimmering streaks. Even in the darkness he could feel the tenseness emanating from her body. He just didn't know if she was angry at him for initiating the kiss or at herself for showing such reckless desire.

She drew a long, unsteady breath. "Don't ever confuse me like that again," she warned in a murmured rage.

What the hell did that mean? Only a woman would say things that stumped him. "Confuse you?"

"I am promised to someone else," she explained as if he were stupid, seething from every pore.

Enlightenment doused him with pleasure. Now he understood, and in the dimness he allowed himself to smile broadly with satisfaction. Expressing her confusion was completely different from expressing repulsion or shock, or from slapping his face.

He lifted his finger to caress her jaw. "You are not promised to anyone," he corrected in a deep whisper.

Her head jerked up, and she glared at him through furious eyes. "Good night, Jonathan."

She lifted her skirts with dignity and walked past him.

He gave her nearly twenty minutes to compose herself and get ready for bed. Then, with a somewhat guilty rush of anticipation, he knocked on the cabin door twice and opened it without waiting for a reply.

But she wasn't in bed or doing whatever it was women do to ready themselves for it. She was sitting on the edge of it, engrossed in thought, fully clothed, although her cloak was now unbuttoned.

She turned when she heard him enter, staring at him vacantly at first, then with what he could only describe as growing horror.

"How did you—"

"I have a key, remember?" he answered before she could finish.

He shut the door, bolting it, enclosing them tightly inside the small, cramped cabin now filled with her presence, her intimate belongings, the alluring scent of lavender and lilies in creams and powders and perfumes. After only a few hours together he'd come to the uncomfortable conclusion that the most difficult task he'd ever undertaken in his life lay just ahead—not in stealing precious emeralds from dangerous French Legitimists, but in keeping Natalie Haislett's virginity intact.

He heard her stand behind him as he unfastened the top two buttons of his shirt.

"I—I suppose you'll be sleeping in the next room, Jonathan?" she stammered in a soft, shaky voice.

He turned back to her and was nearly brought to his knees by the vivid pleading in her eyes of the hope that he would just go away, from the swell of her full breasts as her opened cloak exposed her form-fitting, tightly waisted gown, from her long, thick hair now free from pins to tumble down the front of her in a luxurious wave of softness.

So innocent and untouchable.

He sighed and confessed the inevitable. "I'll be sleeping on your left, Natalie."

"Oh." The relief outlined on her face was immeasurable. "Then why are you here?"

He placed both hands on his hips, not at all certain how much he would enjoy this explanation, but ready to get it said. Baldly, without expression, he maintained, "I don't mean in the cabin to the left of us. I mean on your left in this bed."

Natalie's first thought was that he wasn't making an ounce of sense. Then the picture struck her graphically, and for the first time in her life that she could recall, she nearly succumbed to a burst of hysteria. Her eyes grew to enormous saucers of disbelief, astonishment. He couldn't possibly be serious.

"You can't sleep . . ." She swallowed, unable even to say it. He was observing her reaction closely as he stood in front of the door, blocking it from her with his large, imposing frame, waiting for the shock to be absorbed.

He *was* serious. And still he didn't say a word.

Her pulse quickened in panic. "You can't stay here, Jonathan."

"I have to stay here, Natalie," he insisted evenly, and very slowly.

Seconds ticked by in deathly stillness before she managed to find enough of her voice to whisper, "Why?"

He reached for the lamp bolted to the small stand to his right, turning it up for brighter light. Then he leaned back against the door, folding his arms across his chest.

"For two reasons, really," he replied contemplatively. "The first is that you have placed yourself in my care, my protection—"

"Protection?" she interjected in wonder, growing more apprehensive by the second. "You're going to protect me after accosting me only hours out of port?"

"I didn't accost you, Natalie, I kissed you," he asserted with a dash of annoyance. "There's a world of difference."

She glared at him. "And who is now to protect me from you, sir?"

"The second reason," he continued, ignoring her question, "is that *my* reputation matters, too. I have serious business in France that will place me in elite circles. If you wish to go with me you must be willing to pose as my wife. Nobody can ever begin to assume I travel with my mistress, and that's the only conclusion people will draw if they know I brought you with me."

"We could pose as—as cousins," she blurted in near desperation, thoroughly appalled at his nerve.

He shook his head. "That would never work, and you know it. We look nothing alike, and the attraction between us will be obvious to everyone. Better to act on it than try to hide it." With a smirk, he added, "It's a challenge, a game to be played, Natalie, and we must start playing it now."

She gaped at him, finding it truly unbelievable that he would talk about them as if they were lovers, that he would want to pose as such to strangers. He was so matter-of-fact, so blatantly devious! He'd planned this from the start, had known about it all day, and had left her to learn of his intentions when she couldn't do anything, least of all run. Where would she go on a ship in the dead of night? Her only option appeared to be overboard.

"Why did you wait until now to tell me we'd be sharing

a . . .'' She gestured with a flick of her wrist. ''A . . .''

He leaned toward her. ''A bed?''

She huffed. ''Why?''

He reached up and rubbed his jaw with his palm. ''I didn't want you to change your mind and walk off the ship,'' he admitted prosaically.

''You . . .'' She faltered at his honest response, flushing ever so softly, closing her arms in front of her protectively and running her fingertips along the lace on her sleeve. ''You . . .''

''. . . need you, Natalie,'' he finished for her again. After a moment's hesitation, he amended, ''To pose as my wife.''

''You planned this,'' she charged vehemently.

He slowly shook his head, his eyes narrowing to sly, gray-blue slits of conquest. ''I believe it was you who walked into my home six days ago in search of help. I'm merely taking advantage of the situation.''

Oh, he was a devil! If he wanted to play games, fine with her. She could act any part magnificently. But woe was him. He couldn't possibly know she was one of the best.

''What of the Black Knight?'' she questioned suspiciously. ''Do you still plan to introduce us?''

He shrugged. ''I intend to, although everything will be on my terms, on my time line, as we agreed before we left England.''

They stared at each other, his expression decidedly blank and unreadable, hers weighing the challenge, calculating possible results of decisions already made, decisions made without thought of what lay ahead between them.

Then finally, with a cunning smirk gently twisting her lips, Natalie turned with resolve and removed her cloak, tossing it over the silk screen. ''You may stay, Jonathan, but no more kissing.''

''Husbands and wives kiss,'' he countered blandly. ''I'm afraid we might have to from time to time.''

She knew he'd come back with that. But he had no idea who he was dealing with. ''Husbands and wives rarely kiss in public. And since we won't be doing it in private, I see no reason to do it at all.''

She faced him again defiantly, elegantly poised, arms dropped to her sides, with full comprehension that he would have to settle for some of her terms as well if she were going to engage in this silly little performance of his. With fortitude, she insisted, "You must also give me your word that you will be nothing but a gentleman should we find ourselves in an intimate position."

He blinked, looking for a moment as if she'd startled him with that statement, as if he couldn't believe she'd said it. She could see him wrestle with a rebuttal of playful arrogance, or perhaps just the desire to laugh. But then his expression clouded, becoming one of serious contemplation.

He leaned back against the door again, watching her, his eyes roving over every feature of her face, her throat and chest and breasts. Cautiously, brows furrowed, he said, "Where you are concerned, Natalie, I've painstakingly been a gentleman since the evening we met years ago." He waited. "Do you remember it like I do?"

Her entire body stilled; color drained from her face. Within seconds the atmosphere became charged, the air thick and crackling with intensity as he continued to regard her provocatively from across the small and suddenly overheated room. Instinctively she grasped her elbows with her palms, feeling hopelessly exposed but unable to look away.

He smiled softly, knowingly. "The evening you innocently asked me to meet you in a moonlit garden for a talk of dreams and I mistook it for an invitation, kissing you until you became breathless." He lowered his voice to a rough whisper, his eyes burning through hers. "I like kissing you, Natalie. Very much. It was good then. It's even better now."

She clutched her sleeves with trembling hands, inhaling deeply to keep from reeling at the intimacy, from the grave, meaningful way the words flowed from his mouth. He was giving her an opening, wanting her to talk about that night. But she couldn't. Not now. Probably not ever.

"Then I can do nothing but trust you," she murmured, mouth dry, eyes still locked with his.

After a long, lingering silence his face went slack. "I suppose that's a start."

He was bothered by her reply, she could tell, or perhaps just confounded by her lack of desire to discuss what took place between them all those years ago. But the topic was too familiar, too humiliating, and she had to get away from it.

With a deep inhale for strength, running her fingers through her mass of hair, she attempted to brighten the mood. "You'll have to sleep in the chair, Jonathan. The bed is small, and I, too, prefer the left side."

Light flickered from the lamp on the table, tossing waving shadows along the dark walls. He hadn't yet moved his gaze from her face, and she was becoming overly nervous about that. He started, as if ready to walk to her, then he evidently changed his mind as his lips turned up to form a lazy grin.

With complete ease, he reached up with one hand and resumed the task of unbuttoning his shirt, looking away at last as he took two steps to the bed, knelt beside it, and pulled what appeared to be his trunk from beneath it.

"I am sleeping in this bed, Natalie," he announced decisively. "And if you prefer the left side, and I prefer the left side, I will have no choice but to sleep on top of you, which, I might add, will be difficult with absolutely no kissing allowed."

She blushed furiously, unable to imagine him on top of her for anything. Disgusted with herself for the reaction he was sure to notice, she turned and walked behind the screen.

"Then *I'm* sleeping in the chair."

It had to be well after midnight when he felt her crawl in beside him. He knew it would happen eventually; it was just too cold in the room.

Jonathan didn't move for fear of making her jump out of bed again. He preferred sleeping in the nude, but with everything else he was forcing her to accept, he could never go that far. So, lying there in worn but binding trousers, he hadn't really been able to sleep anyway. And neither could she as he'd listened to her attempts to get comfortable for nearly two hours before she'd finally slipped between the sheets in defeat.

She curled up behind him, shivering, encased to her chin, fingers, and ankles in a full nightgown of unembellished white cotton, trying to steal his covers, and certainly stealing his warmth. He nearly winced when he felt her feet, now frigid blocks of ice, slithering in between his legs. But as he drifted toward oblivion at last he had to smile at the comforting action, oddly trusting and so very sweet.

Four

Madeleine DuMais was born beautiful. Not in the classic sense, really, for her looks certainly weren't refined, but exotically so. She possessed a quality of bearing unseen in the lower, even middle classes, but perhaps that was because she lived outside one station or the next, if that were possible. Her breeding was mixed, and she knew it; she took advantage of it.

Standing in front of the mirror in her bedroom, a blazing morning sun filtering through parted chintz curtains, she buffed a final touch of color into her cheeks and lips, then rubbed a bit of kohl above her lids and smoothed her chestnut hair back from her broad forehead.

She knew she was exceptionally appealing to look at from head to foot. Indeed, it often proved amusing when men tripped over themselves in her presence, but oddly she wasn't self-centered about her physical qualities. She was proud of them, and over the years they had served her well.

Smiling in satisfaction, Madeleine glided her palms down the front of her silk morning gown, canary yellow with only a touch of pale lace, tightened at the waist and flowing in a thick cascade over whalebone to swish becomingly at the floor when she walked. She took pride in her curves, in her substantial bosom, and a waist that showed no sign of childbirth and hopefully never would. She wanted Jonathan Drake to notice her as well, for he would be arriving at her home in precisely ten minutes for their meeting. And he would be punctual. The English always were when it came to their own national security.

Pleased with her appearance, she turned and left her bedroom, descending the stairs with grace, and entering her parlor where she would await the arrival of the Englishman. The warm atmosphere of the room always lifted her, as it was so enriched by fine mahogany furniture, padded generously and covered with wine-colored satin. The curtains of the same color were divided considerably so the entire room could embrace the sun, which reflected in a hazy glow off delicately flowered wallpaper. Marie-Camille, Madeleine's only maid, had left a coffee service for two on the small, rounded table between two chairs in front of the now-cold fireplace, and the coffee itself would be brought in steaming when he arrived. Madeleine took a seat closest to the door and waited.

From her French mother, a woman of the stage but only mildly talented at best, Madeleine had inherited her unusual beauty, her exquisite figure, her heart-shaped face, and ice-blue eyes. But from her father, a captain in the British Royal Navy, she'd acquired everything else—her smarts, her common sense, her humor, and passion for goodness. He had wanted to marry her mother, but alas, Eleanora Bilodeau, self-centered and common, wouldn't have him, had left him heartbroken, and didn't particularly care for his child, the beautiful daughter she dragged from city to city, from one smoke-filled and stinking theater to the next, not because she felt the obligation, but because Madeleine waited on her like a slave.

For nearly twelve years she begged to be allowed to go to England, to be with her father's very stable family, but her mother had denied her this dream with increasing scorn. Madeleine had only seen him four or five times in her life, but those precious moments had been filled with joy. He had truly loved his illegitimate daughter. Then, in the summer of 1833, she found a note from her English family stuffed into the side pocket of her mother's wardrobe informing them both in a very solemn tone that her father had died of cholera the previous year on duty somewhere in the West Indies. It was that very black day, as her mother paraded across a stage in Cologne, half-clothed and with not an ounce of dignity, that Madeleine's devotion to her homeland died. In her eyes alone, which was all that mattered, she was no longer French.

When she was sixteen she gained her first employment as a line dancer in a hot, crowded hall, where civilized men by day would become sweaty, drunken, lustful animals by night, offering crude remarks as they tossed coins on stage in the hopeful exchange of favors. It was the only income she could maintain by using her natural assets, but not once in four years of dancing did she allow herself to be purchased sexually. Above all else she'd kept her self-respect intact, as her father had always done and expected of her, refusing to fall into personal disgrace like her mother.

At the age of twenty, with plenty of money saved and a gratification she hadn't felt before or since, Madeleine very calmly announced her plans to leave her previous existence as servant girl to her now fat and opium-addicted mother, and turned her back on France forever. The actress had been at first shocked, then enraged, shouting obscenities at her daughter as she walked out on her, shoulders erect and chin held high. That had been eight years ago, and Madeleine hadn't seen her since, nor did she even care whether the woman was alive.

She went to England first, presenting herself to her middle-class, socially refined family who accepted her unconditionally, albeit with quiet reservation, but she didn't expect any more. She was, after all, half French and the illegitimate daughter of an actress. Still, they had treated her with a respect she had never known, and she had relished it, although by that age she knew she would never live the life of an English lady. She had learned their language well enough over time but she could never lose her thick French accent. She could never be one of them. That dream had died with maturity. But with it came the inner discovery that perhaps she could offer something far more valuable to English society, to her English heritage. Her skills could be used to help the people she loved and to the disadvantage of a people she had come to loathe.

So, at the age of twenty-one, she waltzed with grace into the British Home Office and presented herself as she was. She wanted to become an informant. Naturally, as she now recalled with humor, the men in charge had laughed her out of the building. "Good God! But you're French, and a—a woman!" they had blurted in shocked unison. But she would not be discouraged. What better guise could there be?

More determined than ever, and after trying for their attention twice more and getting no response but civility at best, Madeleine changed her approach. She packed her few personal possessions and returned to Paris, there infiltrating government circles on her own by use of her wit, beauty, and her growing skill as an actress—a far better one, she realized, than the woman who bore her. She had, after all, lived her first twenty years with a company of them, and she had learned well.

Several times during the following three years, Madeleine had uncovered secrets which she in turn had forwarded to Sir Riley Liddle at home—nothing ruinous or even scandalous, but little things to help the British cause in Europe. And always did she begin these pieces of information with the salutation, "Warm regards from the Frenchwoman." She never heard anything in return but she knew her investigatory discoveries were being heeded, as information she passed along began to be used, even in subtle ways. That was all the satisfaction she needed for a while, until they grew accustomed to her doing what Englishmen did as a matter of course, and she knew they would in time.

Finally, after fixing herself within the French elite, weaving her way through the upper social arena with charm and sagacity, she had been given the priceless opportunity of earning respect from her English superiors. In July 1843, she stumbled upon the news that two very high-profile French political prisoners were to be transferred without delay directly from trial to dreary Newgate, and a plan was in the works to free them while in transit, with force if need be.

Indeed, on the day of that move, due to the quickness of a Frenchwoman's wit, a small uprising was avoided, as a few stunned, self-serving, heavily armed Frenchmen were apprehended without incident. When she heard the news of victory, Madeleine knew she was in.

Four days later, on August 2, 1843, Madeleine Bilodeau, former line dancer and the daughter of an actress (which many felt was even worse), became a spy for the British government. She was contacted quite informally during a morning stroll up the avenue De Friedland near her Paris home, and within twenty-four hours she had been whisked to Marseilles, with all her worldly possessions in tow, to become Madeleine DuMais, wealthy widow of the mythical Georges DuMais, a world-renowned trader of fine teas, lost at sea. They'd set her up at the breathtaking southern port, in her beautiful city dwelling, so she might be of service to the Crown regarding the ever-growing menace of trade smuggling. During the last four years she'd become socially adored and accepted in all local circles for exactly what she appeared to be, serving her adopted country well, with a sort of glamorous honor attached to her name by those who mattered in England.

Madeleine straightened and smoothed her skirt. The low rumble of a man's voice from the entry hall pulled her wandering mind from the past as she looked to the clock over the mantel. Jonathan Drake had arrived, three minutes after ten, and she was ready to receive him.

He entered as Marie-Camille opened the parlor door, and she was once again awed by his appearance. She'd only met him once, about a year ago, at a gala affair near Cannes, and at the time they were introduced she found herself giggling at the gross understatement of his looks by her superiors. They'd portrayed him as "A right average fellow. Dashing in a good light. Dark hair and all that."

But Jonathan Drake was beautiful, if one could use that word to describe a man. Not in an elegant sense, really, although he dressed impeccably. But rather in a rugged, overtly masculine manner.

Until he smiled, as he did now. Then "beautiful" was most appropriate.

"Madame DuMais." He spoke first, taking her outstretched hand and lifting the back of it to his lips. "Again we meet. How lovely you look. As a breath of morning air."

Madeleine felt herself blushing, as she almost never did in the presence of anyone. But he had taken the time to glance subtly at her figure, which was exactly what she had hoped he'd do when she'd taken the time preparing herself. And how could he not? He was a man, after all, and she'd expected it. His reputation preceded him.

"Monsieur Drake. A pleasure. Please be seated." She gestured to the opposite chair, turned to Marie-Camille who waited patiently by the door, and ordered the coffee to be brought immediately.

She focused her attention back on Drake who now sat comfortably across from her. He looked completely at ease in a morning suit of light dove gray which accented the color of his striking eyes. His white shirt and pale gray neckcloth were made of the finest silk, his midnight-black hair a bit tousled from the removal of his hat, which he'd undoubtedly left on the rack by the front door. He ran his fingers through the ends to smooth it back into place, and Madeleine couldn't help but fix her gaze upon the movement as she spoke.

"I assume your voyage was uneventful?" she asked, more politely than curiously.

He quickly dropped his arm and shifted his large body in the chair, folding his hands in his lap. "I'm here in one piece."

Madeleine's brows arched briefly, but since he offered nothing more she added only, "But certainly no worse for wear."

He nodded once at the remark, staring at her frankly, as Marie-Camille returned carrying an ivory, gold-inlaid china coffeepot atop a silver tray. Because the service had been set earlier, her maid did nothing but pour two cups full, set the pot on the table, and again discreetly take her leave, closing the door behind her.

Madeleine helped herself to warm milk and sugar; he lifted his cup to his lips.

"And how is everything at home?" she questioned nonchalantly, stirring her coffee with dainty fingers.

He shrugged and took a sip. "Fine, I suppose. Except for the matter bringing me to southern France in the dead of summer."

Madeleine's eyes wavered, and she lowered her lashes to stare at the brown liquid at her fingertips, gently tapping her spoon on the side of her cup, a bit dismayed that he would jump so quickly into the concern for their meeting. "I suppose you'll want the details now," she stated quietly.

"At your discretion, madam," he cordially replied.

Madeleine raised her eyes back to his and took a sip of her coffee. He was watching her closely, and this was her opportunity to move forward.

Very smoothly, indicative of her talents, she intimated, "I am hoping, Monsieur Drake, that we shall become more than acquaintances during your stay in France"—she placed her cup and saucer on the table—"so I would be most pleased if you would call me Madeleine."

She was perfectly aware that he might be confused by that subtle invitation, and indeed he appeared to be. He blinked quickly two or three times, then grinned quite charmingly as he placed his cup and saucer on the table as well and leaned back casually to regard her.

"I'm honored, Madeleine," he admitted eloquently. "And you should call me Jonathan. We'll be working together, and I suppose formality could get tiresome."

She smiled beautifully, now nearly certain he was returning the interest but was just being as subtle as she. He was English and a bit more staid than the typical Frenchman. Perhaps she wasn't losing her touch after all but simply needed to be more direct.

Slowly, suggestively, she leaned toward him, her blue eyes sparkling with unspoken thoughts. "I'd be delighted,

Jonathan. In fact, I was hoping that perhaps we could find the time for . . . relaxation together. When the work is finished, of course.'' She ran her fingers sensuously up and down her hair as it coiled over her right breast in a thick, shiny plait. ''I'm sure you'd enjoy the companionship of a woman who knows . . . the area well, and how to entertain a man to the fullness of his time. I'm equally certain I'd enjoy your charms.''

He stared at her openly for a second or two. Then as rapidly as he dropped his gaze to her breasts, he shifted his body in his chair again, uncomfortably, and looked to the window.

Madeleine had really expected him to respond positively at once. He was a man who liked the ladies, and she knew, as any astute woman would, that he found her particularly attractive. But now, as she sat back again to regard his silent form, it began to dawn on her that, although he might have briefly admired her beauty, his mind had been elsewhere since he'd walked in the room. He seemed . . . preoccupied?

Finally he turned his attention back to her and smiled, decisively, eyes focused as he brought his hands together, elbows on the armrests, fingertips touching lightly in a triangle in front of his thoughtful face.

''My dear Madeleine,'' he began with purpose. ''Had I received such a generous invitation from so beautiful a woman only weeks ago, I would have found myself accepting the pleasure of your charming company without reservation.'' He cleared his throat and lowered his eyes to study the thick, inlaid carpet. ''Several things have taken place during the last few days, however, that would make such an acceptance . . . awkward.''

''Really,'' she muttered, completely surprised, not knowing if she should feel dejected or flattered. Never in her life had she been turned down quite so graciously.

He inhaled deeply and raised his gaze to hers once more. ''I am not in France alone.''

Her eyes widened. ''Oh. . . .''

He threw a quick glance to the window again, impatiently it seemed, and Madeleine wondered for a moment if the lady was standing outside. And it had to be a woman, she decided. The Black Knight always worked alone; Jonathan Drake never traveled with anyone. She also knew no man in his prime would turn down such an obvious offer of female affections if his only complication was that he traveled with another man.

Sighing with acceptance, Madeleine reached for her cup, bringing it gently to her lips. "You must trust her implicitly."

For the first time since his arrival, he looked startled by her words.

She smiled shrewdly. "Does she know who you are?"

He hesitated. "Not exactly."

"Mmm . . ." She paused for another sip. "Why you're here?"

He pursed his lips and shook his head. "No."

"I see."

He exhaled loudly and tapped his fingers together.

Madeleine forcefully had to keep herself from laughing. "Perhaps I'll get to meet her," she suggested with honest interest.

He smirked. "I'm deathly afraid you will."

She did laugh at that, placing her cup back on the table. "Then I'm looking forward to it."

With elegant bearing, she stood and walked across the room to a small, mahogany cabinet next to the window. "I suppose, since she alone holds your attention, Jonathan, we should get down to business." She opened a glass door and pulled several sheets of paper from inside a music box sitting within.

"The jewels are being kept in the study safe of Henri Lemire, count of Arles." She turned and sauntered back to him, staring at her notes. "At his seaside estate about twelve miles west of the city. He has four children—three boys and one girl, his oldest—and a simple-minded but lovely second wife of three years who is half his age."

Jonathan reached for his coffee cup, drained the contents in two swallows, then stood as she moved up beside him. He looked down at her face, his dark hair shining in the wavy sunlight, his eyes brilliant and alert, his skin clean and smelling lightly of musk. She exhaled with dismay. Such a shame not to be able to enjoy him.

Handing him the papers, she continued with the present issue. "I've come to know him and his family the best I could over the last few weeks. He's forty-eight, intelligent, has long-time connections, but he's been known to make mistakes. He's well-respected and generally liked by his contemporaries, loves his children—especially his daughter. He dotes on his wife but is quite content to keep her in her place as he attends other issues which he deems more important, including, if rumor has it, an occasional mistress. He's a Legitimist to the extreme, though he doesn't flaunt it. He despises Louis Philippe; feels the king's a weakling underneath, a man who can't control the people. He wants Henri back on the throne for obvious reasons, but I haven't been able to ascertain to what measures he'll go for it, if he's planning any action soon or at all."

She tapped the paper lightly with a professionally manicured nail. "I've included a short report on Comte d'Arles, what history of the family I could find, and a map of the grounds and house, which is fairly accurate. I've been inside twice. You'll also find an invitation to a ball in celebration of his daughter's eighteenth birthday next week. I don't think he'll attempt to sell the emeralds before then. I don't think he's ready. And," she said, dropping her voice, "there is a rumor she may wear them for the occasion."

He looked up sharply. "Really?"

"Just a rumor," she said again, "but something to consider."

"Indeed."

She watched him carefully flip through the information.

"Your assumed identity is relatively simple," she went on. "Jonathan Drake, cultured Englishman who buys French property for wealthy European aristocrats. Comte d'Arles has a lovely twenty-two-room home outside of Paris he's attempting to sell. You'll find information on that as well."

"He needs money?" Jonathan asked speculatively, brows furrowed.

Madeleine toyed absentmindedly with the lace on her collar. "I don't think so. More likely his new wife intends to spend her days lounging on the Mediterranean shore. She adores it here."

"Mmm." He waited, thinking. "And how did I get an invitation?"

"Through me. We've met briefly once or twice in past years. You found a buyer for my late husband's estate in St. Raphael, if you'll recall."

"Ahh, yes." He folded the papers and placed them in his coat pocket. "Do I need another invitation if my traveling companion accompanies me as my wife?"

Madeleine was slightly taken aback. She crossed her arms over her breasts and looked at him askance. "No. Actually it might be better if you did bring a wife." She shook her head in growing awareness of his plan. "If you intend to use her without her knowing who you are, she must be exceptionally appealing to look at—or engaging—for you to risk it. I suppose you're counting on those assets for distraction?"

He grinned in answer.

"Is she clever?"

"Enough to be trouble."

Madeleine bit her bottom lip gently. "If she's that clever she's bound to discover your secrets eventually, Jonathan."

It was a warning laced with amusement.

Chuckling, he confided, "I'm looking forward to it with pleasure you cannot comprehend." He grasped her fingers with his palm, ready to take his leave. "Will you be at the party?"

"Yes, of course," she answered softly.

"Then you can tell me what you think when you meet her." Raising her hand to his lips, he kissed the back of it, his eyes never leaving hers. "I have been most charmed, Madeleine."

Again, for the second time in ages, she felt color warm her cheeks.

"Until the ball, Madame DuMais."

With that he released her and strode toward the door. She followed him through the entryway as he stopped to retrieve his hat from the rack, then stepped out behind him onto the white latticed porch now bathed in bright sunshine.

Suddenly he stopped and turned back to her, his expression contemplative.

"All the invitations I've received this morning have been considered thoroughly," he disclosed in a low voice. "And of course not taken lightly. I am very flattered. I only regret that I cannot accept them all."

She beamed, reached for his hand, and tenderly squeezed it. "Secrets between friends, Jonathan."

Smiling, he nodded just once, then walked down the brick path and across the crowded street.

Five

Natalie sat in the cramped hotel room, on a rickety chair of faded apricot velvet, drumming her fingers on the armrest with impatience. It had been three hours since she'd returned, in a flurry because she was a little bit afraid he'd noticed her following him, and she wanted to appear indifferent and bored instead of curious and, yes, though averse to admit it, even irritated by what she'd seen. Waiting for him, she'd been alternating between pacing the floor and sitting in the chair, fanning herself to keep from melting in the stifling heat, listening to midday traffic outside the open window as she stared at the door.

Until now her trip had been routine, although she couldn't find words to describe her first impression of Marseilles. Enchanting, busy, unique—they all fit. She'd been to France three or four times in recent years, but never to the south of it, and in many ways this southern port city, with its quiet charm and strange mixture of bustling boulevards and vacant, narrow-stepped streets, was completely different from any place she'd ever seen.

Upon arrival, Jonathan had taken them to a small hotel not far from the harbor, and Natalie had followed him obediently, saying nothing as her crestfallen gaze fell upon their assigned room, hoping they wouldn't be staying in it long. It was old and worn, and the hotel itself entertained the oddest assortment of people, though she knew part of her assessment was because of her lifelong shelter from a world outside of piano lessons, gown fittings, soirees, and lectures from her mother.

Their time on board ship had been uneventful after that first day, as Jonathan had either been silent and meditative or talkative and friendly. Underneath, though, he'd seemed distracted, even restless, and she had eagerly obliged his desire for quiet between them. She really didn't mind his moods, but she had to ponder a little what a gentleman without cares could possibly have to worry about.

She really didn't mind sleeping with him either, she had to admit—if that's what one would call it, and she supposed one *would* have to call it that. She had, in fact, found his presence comforting, his body oddly protective, as she had awakened that first morning to find his sleeping form snuggled up against her back, his arms surrounding her and drawing her close to him, his face in her hair, breath on her neck. He hadn't tried to kiss her, or even touch her inappropriately; and since he'd been the perfect gentleman, she instead snuggled deeper under the blankets and into him, for he was protecting her after all, he'd said it was his duty, and she supposed she needed to indulge that distinctly masculine part of him. He seemed somewhat immune to her charms after their talk the first night in the ship's cabin anyway.

But now they'd been in Marseilles for nearly two days, and it was her turn to feel restless. She was ready for more excitement, more adventure. It was true she found some enjoyment in observing the people, but she was fairly well educated in French culture, customs, and history, and she was here for a purpose, had plans to carry through. She wanted more action. Finally, just a few short hours ago, she got what she wanted.

After a light breakfast of pastries and coffee (which she now liked more than tea), Jonathan unexpectedly informed her of an impending appointment, the reason, apparently, for his trip to France. This was the first she'd heard of his plans, which she supposed explained his distraction, but he hadn't, until that moment, really discussed his reasons for journeying to the southern port. If she thought about it, he had been a bit sly regarding his intentions. But that was none of her business, she kept telling herself.

Yet there was something in his darkened eyes, in the light evasion during a simple breakfast, that made her curious. She hadn't mentioned the Black Knight since their first evening together, although she was sure Jonathan knew she was becoming anxious about finally meeting the legend face-to-face. She would consent to his terms but she didn't want to waste her time in France, either. Impatience was getting the best of her. With his odd behavior this morning, if one could call it odd, she was flooded with the excited realization that Jonathan probably intended to meet with the thief today.

So, all good judgment aside, she had feigned an aching head, informed him of her desire to rest, then followed him when he left the hotel room at half past nine. But he hadn't met the thief, he'd met a woman, and a stunningly beautiful one at that, although Natalie had only caught a glimpse of her elegant form from across the street as the lady swished onto her front porch, a slender, graceful figure of shining hair and silk and lace.

Her initial reaction was surprise; she hadn't expected him to meet a woman at her home in the middle of the day. And for what? Then she was filled with thoughts and feelings she couldn't exactly describe—a tangled mess of shock, annoyance, and something she didn't dare put her finger on. She wasn't wholly ignorant. The woman was his mistress, obviously, for the man had lots and lots of them. It just perturbed her so that he felt the need to meet one of them now, on this journey, when he really should have more important things to occupy his time.

Natalie sighed and thumped her fingertips even harder on the shredding armrest, leaning her head back to stare at the paint peeling from the ceiling, feeling incredibly bothered because she very much enjoyed the company of a man with such a nefarious reputation. She nearly smiled, wondering for a moment whether she wanted to be with him because she liked him as a person or because her mother would just be so thoroughly appalled by her lack of judgment.

The sound of a key in the lock brought her immediately upright and alert. He walked in, relaxed and comfortable in his tailored morning suit, with nary a crease or wrinkle in the fabric. Natalie had trouble remaining lucid as it dawned on her all too vividly that of course his suit wouldn't be wrinkled since he hadn't worn it half the morning.

After closing the door behind him, he tossed his hat on the small, narrow bed and turned to her at last, looking her up and down as she sat in the chair, his eyes lingering on every curve he could possibly detect beneath lavender silk. The man had no decency at all, in her opinion.

"I see you're feeling better," he acknowledged flatly.

She squirmed a little, suddenly feeling worse. She was hot and sweating, stray curls sticking to her face and neck, and had to look positively frightful to him.

"Yes, I'm much better, thank you," she returned with a forced smile. "I feel wonderful." She swished her ivory fan in front of her face with one hand while wiping the other across her perspiring cheek, wondering how he could look so cool and composed in such sweltering heat. Maybe it was the offshore breeze he'd just walked out of that couldn't possibly find its way inside the hotel. She should have gone browsing through street-vendor displays instead of locking herself up waiting for him. It certainly would have been a more constructive use of her time.

His features turned contemplative as he stood his ground in front of the door. "Did you do anything while I was gone?"

Natalie bit her lip to keep from blurting out an unbelievable fabrication. He would know immediately if she lied.

"I went for a walk. It's been so warm."

"Mmm . . ."

She averted her eyes to her fan, tapping it absentmindedly in her lap. "And where have you been, Jonathan?"

After a prolonged silence, she lifted her lashes just barely enough to view him. Her heartbeat quickened as she caught his frank gaze.

"I had a business meeting this morning, Natalie."

The deception made her fume. "I certainly hope you completed it successfully," she replied hotly.

With that, he began to saunter toward her, his mouth curving up on one side. "It was very successful, I'm glad to say." He stood in front of her, hands on hips beneath his jacket, now pushed back behind his arms. "And your walk?"

She batted her lashes. "My walk?"

"Don't be coy with me, darling Natalie."

She fidgeted, hardly able to look at him any longer as she glared instead at the ivory buttons on his shirt. "My walk was lovely, although as I said, it was slightly too warm."

"Perhaps you walked too fast," he suggested pleasantly, reaching for her fan which he promptly pulled from her grasp and tossed on the bed to his left. "It's difficult to walk slowly when one is trying to keep up with another."

Her eyes grew round in surprise. Then he grabbed her bare arm and pulled her up to his level, holding her close, almost touching. He scrutinized her face, not angrily, but with vague amusement.

"Why did you follow me?" he asked, clearly puzzled.

His breath touched her heated skin, his eyes bore into hers, and she'd had just about enough of the game. "Why did you feel the need to visit your mistress at ten o'clock in the morning of our second day in town? Your urges must be uncontrollable, Jonathan."

She had trouble defining his expression. At first he seemed stupefied by her words, or perhaps just her boldness. Then his mouth twisted upward again, and he lowered his voice to a cool whisper.

"I'm controlling my urges perfectly, Natalie." Tightening his grasp on her arm, he drew her so close to him her gown bunched between them, and her breasts grazed his chest. "The woman you saw is not my mistress."

She smiled sarcastically but didn't try to pull away. "I'm not stupid, Jonathan."

"I've never thought so," he quickly agreed, "but you are naive."

Her eyes lit with fire. "Not so naive I don't know what goes on between a man and his mistress. You just seem to do it more than necessary."

Jonathan did his best to keep his features slack. She was so unbelievably adorable, sitting in their tiny, hot hotel room, waiting hours for his return, jealous without even realizing it. Knowing he could read her so clearly made his insides boil over with absolute satisfaction. He would always have that advantage, and they both knew it.

She continued to stare at him defiantly, through glowering eyes of displeasure, her skin warm and dewy moist from heat and humidity, looking ridiculously out of place in her summer day gown made strictly for English weather. She had the appeal of an overdressed seductress in a steam bath, teasing him with a calculating look of "disrobe me if you dare." With all her innocence and inability to know what she did to him physically, she'd been making him insane with desire since they'd left England, especially in bed when she snuggled up next to him in her nearly transparent nightgown and he could do nothing but restrain himself.

Jonathan's eyes narrowed mischievously as he continued to hold her against him. "What is it you think I do more than necessary?"

That question she never expected, and he knew it confused her as he watched doubt shade her face.

Nervously she raised her palms to his arms to push him away. "That's irrelevant, and I refuse to discuss your intimate . . . problems when they are none of my business."

Thoroughly enjoying himself, he refused to release her, wanting to hear her attempts to get out of the messy conversation she'd started.

"I think it is relevant," he said at last through an exaggerated sigh. "Tell me, darling Natalie, do you know all of what takes place intimately between a man and a woman, or just bits and pieces?''

She squirmed, turning her attention to the door to avoid his gaze. ''I won't discuss it.''

''You brought the subject up,'' he countered with pleasure.

She wrestled uncomfortably to come up with a suitable answer, or at least just a way to close the topic. Finally she masked her expression and looked back into his eyes. ''I have an excellent idea of what happens intimately between a man and a woman. Now if you will please release me, Jonathan, I'm very hungry and ready for luncheon.''

For all the money in the world, he wouldn't release her now. ''An excellent idea?'' When she added nothing, he continued with the challenge. ''Do you remember how long I was in her home?''

Her eyes flashed brilliantly. ''I remember she was beautiful and hardly the Black Knight, the only person you should have been meeting today. I'm paying you to introduce us. Perhaps you'll try to remember that.''

The urge to kiss her was suddenly overwhelming. ''Answer my question,'' he insisted instead.

She faltered, then sighed and announced, ''At *least* ten minutes.''

He leaned very close to whisper, ''Intimate rendezvous usually take longer than ten minutes.''

She grinned triumphantly. ''But not, I'm sure, for someone of your experience, Jonathan.''

He laughed outright and squeezed her against him, both arms now encircling her waist, relishing in the feel of her supple, perfectly formed breasts against his chest. ''How long would it take you to remove and dress again in these layers upon layers of clothes?''

She gaped at him, made speechless for once.

With the sweet taste of victory, he murmured, ''It would take her just as long.''

Driving that point home, he let her go.

Indignant, Natalie knew he'd won for the moment because she found the topic just too disturbing and foreign to discuss further. She watched him walk to the small bureau of chipped and faded cherry wood, open the top drawer, and pull out a shirt. Realizing he intended to change, she turned her back to him, considering quickly how she could move to a more suitable issue of discussion without him realizing she did so purposely, then ultimately becoming grateful when he did it himself.

"We're leaving here," he said from behind her.

She folded her arms over her breasts. "Going where?"

She heard the rustle of clothes as she imagined him pulling them from his body, and she resisted the urge to peek. For all his faults, and disregarding her virtuous upbringing, she considered his bare chest one of nature's marvels.

"I'm taking you somewhere nicer and cooler," he replied. "That's where I've been for the last three hours, in case you're wondering. Finding lodgings where you'd be more comfortable."

Now she felt guilty. With growing shyness, she mumbled, "I hope you weren't thinking we'd stay with the Frenchwoman."

He chuckled as she heard him sit on the bed. "Her name is Madeleine DuMais, and I think you'll like her—and no, we won't be staying in her home."

"You'll like her" implied a meeting between them, and Natalie couldn't contain her curiosity any longer. Brushing sticky curls from her cheeks, she asked as indifferently as she could manage, "I suppose Miss DuMais knows the Black Knight and that was the reason for your visit?"

When he didn't answer her immediately, she allowed herself to pivot back to him, watching him put his shoes on with concentration, taking in his impressive appearance made casual in dark-brown trousers and a pale, silk shirt, similar to those he'd worn their first day out of port. He certainly didn't bring much variety for clothes.

"Jonathan?" she pressed, tired of waiting for answers.

He cast her a sideways glance, and again she got the feeling he was annoyed, or perhaps just hiding something.

At last he ran the fingers of one hand through his hair, placed both palms on his knees, and pushed himself up.

Hands on hips, he stared at her candidly. "The widowed Mrs. DuMais is arranging a business meeting between the comte d'Arles and me for later this week."

She blinked, surprised. "A business meeting between you and a French count?"

"Yes."

"Arranged by a gracefully beautiful young widow," she stated rather than asked, pronouncing each word precisely.

He spread his palms wide. "Exactly."

That just seemed so thoroughly preposterous to her she wanted to applaud. Restraining herself, Natalie merely tilted her chin knowingly and tapped her fingers on the sleeve of her gown. With mild sarcasm, she charged, "And I suppose, Jonathan, since it's your business to buy and sell things, your intention is to purchase a priceless antique from the man." Her eyes lit up dramatically. "Oooo. Maybe a new weapon for your wall."

For a second or two he watched her with a face void of expression. Then slowly, levelly, he shook his head in wonder. "How did you guess?"

"How did I—" She stopped talking abruptly and gaped at him in mounting disbelief. "You're here to buy a *weapon* from the comte d'Arles?"

His brows rose innocently. "A sword, actually."

"A sword," she repeated flatly, her hands now resting on either side of her waist. "You came all the way to France to buy a sword for your wall."

"Yes, I did."

"From the comte d'Arles."

"Yes."

"And the lovely Mrs. DuMais is arranging it all."

He shrugged. "I think we've covered everything."

"I think I'd like to see this sword of yours," she demanded suspiciously.

He grinned wryly. "If and when the time is right, Natalie, I will allow you a very good look at it."

Even now he was so arrogant. Natalie had no idea what to say to him, if he was lying outright, teasing her, or making excuses to conceal his romantic affair with the beautiful

Mrs. DuMais. She couldn't begin to imagine any man, even him, a gentleman with too much time and money on his hands, traveling abroad simply to buy a sword to hang on a wall. But if he was fabricating an incredible story, she would never recognize it because she just couldn't read him, and that's what truly made her mad. He always seemed to be able to tell what she was thinking.

He turned toward the bed, reaching for his suit. "We're invited to a ball at his estate Saturday," he continued indifferently, moving in the direction of the small wardrobe closet. "I assume you have an appropriate gown hiding somewhere in the piles and piles of things you brought."

It was a statement, not a question, and Natalie ignored it. Her inability to travel lightly was somewhat of a touchy subject between them.

"And before you ask," he went on, now kneeling before his only trunk, "I've sent a message to the Black Knight."

"You waited until now to tell me?" she blurted.

He brushed over that. "He hasn't replied, but there's a rumor he's also planning to attend the party."

"Why?"

"What?"

"Why is he attending this particular function?" she clarified, exasperated.

He lifted his shoulders negligibly but didn't look at her. "I should expect he has a worthy reason, though I really have no idea."

"No doubt to steal the count's precious sword," she offered sarcastically.

He smirked. "Maybe he'll carry you off instead, my sweet Natalie."

His lighthearted words didn't register. Her mind was already racing with possibilities, her heart pounding with anticipation, and suddenly she didn't care about Mrs. DuMais or the count or swords or France. It was now only days until the meeting of a lifetime.

Jonathan walked up to stand before her, gazing down at her face, his excellent eyes turned pensive. Then quite unexpectedly he raised his palm to her cheek, momentarily startling her with the feel of his warm skin against hers.

"Meeting him is extremely important to you," he said softly, thoughtfully.

She inhaled deeply but didn't pull away. "Yes, it is."

He was quiet for a long moment, studying her, gliding his thumb along her jaw.

"You'll like Madeleine, Natalie," he carefully maintained. "She's refreshing and experienced, and those qualities make her interesting." He lowered his voice to just above a whisper. "But your innocence and passion for everything life has to offer make you far more beautiful than she could ever be."

Her breath caught in her chest from the look of honest disclosure in his stunning gray-blue eyes. But before she had the chance to pull away, or to grasp exactly what he'd said, he dropped his arm and strode to the door.

"Pack up your things," he added without glancing back. "I'm going downstairs to find transportation large enough to carry your incredible wardrobe."

With that he walked out, leaving her once again to feel that same tingling inside, that overpowering sense of helplessness and confusion Jonathan Drake had a genius for exposing in her.

Six

The whole Black Knight issue was beginning to annoy him. For years he'd played the part with perfection, if not enjoyment. He'd invented the character himself, and yes, the purely egotistical part of him took pride in the amazing popularity he'd achieved throughout Europe during the last six years. What had always made it nice, however, was that so few knew that Jonathan Drake, second son of an ordinary English earl, was himself the legend.

But for the first time ever he was troubled by his notoriety. It was clear from Natalie that he'd become almost superhuman, at least to her. Because of her obsession with a myth, she'd been detached if not impervious to his presence since leaving England. She was powerfully affected by his kisses, his touch, which he'd held in check at her request. But beyond that she didn't appear at all impressed with *him*—Jonathan Drake, the man. As he thought about it with growing displeasure, failing miserably to charm a woman had never befallen him in his entire life.

For the last three days this irritation had been stewing in the back of his mind. He had an odd notion of trying to please her, a woman he *wasn't* bedding, by making her comfortable and taking her to interesting local places to pass the time. He'd spent a small fortune to find them lodgings upon a cliff on the Mediterranean shore, with a spectacular view of the midnight blue ocean and a continuous breeze to keep her cool. That it was somewhat intimate and located only half a mile from the count of Arles's property was to his advantage, but just watching her eyes light with joy when she first walked inside the cozy, newly decorated bungalow gave him enormous satisfaction. For three days she'd been dazzled by the beauty around her—and totally unaffected by the man who did his best to attract her attention. For all his trouble she didn't exactly ignore him, she just appeared completely consumed with a man who didn't exist. And what did that mean? He was jealous of himself? That was amusing.

But what made him so damn curious was that she didn't act at all like a woman in love, and he very well knew the look of a woman in love. Natalie didn't dream about the Black Knight, she focused on the man like a puzzle, which didn't make sense. Jonathan could understand her passive regard for a male traveling companion if she were infatuated with another, even a legend, but it was becoming clear to him that she wasn't. She'd risked her reputation, which was everything to an English lady, to journey to France to meet a man she didn't know or adore. So was she lying to him about wanting to marry the thief? And what about her reaction the other day when he'd met with Madeleine? At the time Jonathan was so certain she was jealous, but he was now beginning to believe it was simple annoyance at him for wasting her time by not introducing her to the Black Knight sooner. The whole situation gnawed at him because he didn't understand it.

He now had to admit he was becoming anxious to court her affections, but doing so would be very tricky, indeed. He knew he could probably seduce her but only at the risk of his freedom. Until just recently, he'd considered marriage far off into the distant future, if at all. He had female companionship when he wanted, on his terms, and he'd never been interested in being tied to one lady for the rest of his hopefully long life, however beautiful and charming she might be. But now, for a reason unclear to him, he'd begun to give it serious consideration, knowing that if he chose to succumb to that choking estate for the sake of fulfilling his need to stay his growing loneliness, he could choose from any number of women in love with him at the time. If he bedded Natalie he would have to marry her, and she was the only woman he'd ever known who desired him physically but didn't want him for the person he was. And *that* was so irritating and confusing he didn't even know how to digest it. It was true he was probably just as arrogant as the next man, assuming he'd be able to select any woman he pleased, especially with his wealth, excellent breeding, and high social standing. But he also had enough honest pride to realize he didn't want to marry someone who didn't enjoy him, someone indifferent to his personality, no matter how passionate she became in his arms.

Part of him wanted to give up, tell her who he was, and ship her back to her parents so he could forget the entire bit of nonsense. But he couldn't, partly because he was growing increasingly curious about her intentions, and partly because he just plain liked being with her. He found her amusing and clever, warm and comforting in bed, and respectful of his individuality; she was a breath of fresh air.

So this morning, after days of ceaseless contemplation, he drew some conclusions. He was a better thief than a spy, but he could be as deceitful as she. He would learn her secrets. Where that would take them personally, he couldn't guess, but he wouldn't push her sexually until she was ready, if ever, and he wouldn't bed her at all until he was absolutely certain he could trust her. He wanted her very badly, more desperately each time she sashayed by him, smelling of bubble bath and flowers, or in bed when she so sweetly stuck her feet between his legs and pressed her bottom against his rigid erection with little or no understanding. Eventually, if he wasn't careful, she would realize her power over him and she would use it. Women always did, and he could never let that happen. He wanted her to want him first, to desire him for the man he was, to beg him to make love to her. And that, he was beginning to fear, might remain his greatest unfulfilled fantasy. Still, he had to try.

With a clear sense of at least where he stood on the matter, he'd planned an intimate twilight picnic for them on the cliffs above the shore—in a cove, actually—just inside the count's private estate. He was hidden well enough not to be noticed by anyone at the house, but close enough to watch the premises above and study the structure from the outside, which appeared to follow Madeleine's description accurately. He'd purchased them an excellent, outrageously priced dinner of white wine, goat cheese on toast, Sole mousse, veal cutlets in mushroom sauce, fresh oranges, and a surprise he had yet to give her: strawberries dipped in chocolate. If Natalie did nothing else for him while they were in France, she would drive him to the poorhouse.

She sat across from him now, atop a blanket, in a pale lavender skirt and white muslin blouse that reflected a glowing setting sun off her shoulders. She'd finally managed the courage to blend in a little with the locals, working with the hot summer weather instead of against it, foregoing her binding stays and layers of material for a simple, almost peasant look. And she'd pulled her hair from the tight, menacing plaits she usually coiled around her ears and head so that the reddish-gold curls fell loose and free behind her, secured easily with just a simple ribbon at her nape. It was a look he liked immeasurably on her, only to be surpassed, he was sure, by her naked form writhing beneath him.

Jonathan shifted his body and stretched his legs out fully, one ankle crossed over the other, sipping from his glass as he attempted to concentrate on the conversation. They'd finished their meal, she her only glass of wine, and she'd been talking without interruption for ten minutes. He couldn't for the life of him remember a word she'd said but decided her choice of topic—a recent trip to Brighton for a poetry reading by one of England's finest—was altogether boring; silly withdrawing room conversation that had no place on such a gorgeous summer evening by the sea. Finally she paused, smiling at him, and he took the opportunity to change the subject.

"I'm having trouble with something, Natalie," he broached with an intentional air of seriousness.

Her brows arched delicately. "Trouble with what?"

He focused intently on her face. "Trouble believing your story about wanting to meet the Black Knight."

He noticed her eyes widen negligibly, her cheeks pale, and those slight indications of surprise and concern about the comment told him much. She was hiding something, and he had acted foolishly by not being more astute from the beginning.

Looking out over the shimmering water to his left, disgusted at his own inner blindness, he added with daring, "I've been paying attention, sweetheart, and you're very calculating. You're not in love with him, have no idea who he is, and yet you leave everything you know to come to France with a perfect stranger to meet him." He stole a glance back at her. "Why?"

"You're not a perfect stranger."

Her words were husky and cautious, and Jonathan almost offered his congratulations on the decent attempt at evasion. But they also had meaning behind them. He could tell that as she watched him, expression guarded. Suddenly he wanted to dig deeply.

Smiling, he challenged, "Not strangers because we have a past?"

She hesitated, then sat back and dropped her lashes. "We don't have a past."

That irritated him, too, her refusal to discuss their little rendezvous in the garden years ago. Eventually she would talk about that night, about the unusual if not enlightening encounter between them, because he'd force her to. But for now he was content to wait, searching instead for answers to a situation more immediate.

"Do you imagine yourself in love with the Black Knight, Natalie?" he asked more sternly than intended.

She played with the soft wool at her fingertips, quiet for so long his patience began to thin. Finally, through the offshore breeze, she whispered, "Have you ever been in love, Jonathan?"

He was completely taken aback by that, as she knew he would be. She looked up again, staring frankly into his eyes. She was honestly asking, and he relaxed a little.

"Yes," he admitted, grinning sheepishly. "Her name was Miss Featherstone, my governess of two years. I was madly in love with her for seven full months until she left for Brunswick, right before my thirteenth birthday. She was the first woman to break my heart."

Natalie smiled. "The first?"

"The only," he amended quickly. "And I don't imagine it will happen again."

Her lips tightened, not in anger, but to keep from laughing. "Because of age and experience, Jonathan? Or because you think you're so completely irresistible?"

He lifted his shoulders lightly in innocence. "Because I understand women."

"Do you, now?" She tilted her head, eyeing him wryly, and Jonathan knew it was on the tip of her tongue to ask how many hearts he'd broken, which, now that he thought about it, weren't nearly as many as his ridiculous reputation implied.

"So you've never been in love with one of your many mistresses?"

That wasn't at all what he expected, and now he was uncomfortable. He tipped his wine to his lips and finished it off, then began placing items back into the picnic basket. "Why are you so curious?"

She sat forward and curled her legs up under her skirt, hugging her knees with her arms wrapped around them. "Your life and loves interest me."

He fully doubted it. He was now starting to believe she found him rather dull—a tiresome, pompous trader of silly, useless things. She was purposely being sneaky, though to what end he couldn't fathom.

"I've actually had very few mistresses, and never more than one at a time," he defended at last, closing the top of the picnic basket and pushing it from between them to his side.

She looked at him skeptically, but since his explanation was something he couldn't possibly prove, he ignored it and went on.

"I enjoy the company of women, I will admit, but I've been careful not to fall for any of them. So, no, I don't think I've ever truly loved one, at least not as my brother seems to love his wife, or my father seemed to love my mother. But what does my past have to do with you and the Black Knight?"

"If you don't know what love is," she replied instantly, "how can you understand my desire to meet this man?"

It all became clear to him. "Are you saying you love him in a way I wouldn't understand?"

She grinned beautifully. "Exactly. Women often love in ways men don't understand."

That was ludicrous, and now he was totally suspicious. All this shallow talk of love was her way of hiding real motives. He was sure of it.

With his free hand he reached into the basket's side pocket and pulled out the small jar containing four chocolate-covered strawberries. Gingerly he removed one and held it out to her.

She gasped with surprise and resounding pleasure. Chocolate always had a way of succeeding to gratify and delight a woman where a man could not, Jonathan mused. Most of the time that was disheartening, but once in a while an occasion arose where the knowledge could be used to manipulate. As right now.

She cupped the strawberry in one hand, gliding her other palm along her cheek to push aside breeze-blown hair. Then she took one bite and gazed at him tentatively.

"Are you trying to seduce me, Jonathan?"

He almost laughed, attempting in vain to imagine what her idea of seduction might be—or what it led to. "No," he answered easily. Again he sat back a little. "I just want you to like me, Natalie."

She sighed and consumed the rest in record speed, then

licked chocolate off her fingertips—a motion he found particularly sensual.

"I like you very much," she admitted shyly.

His body sprang to life from those innocently spoken words, and with that discomfort the intoxicating image of licking chocolate from her breasts came to mind. He felt like a child who had been given a new toy. "Very much?"

She shrugged and averted her gaze. "You've been generous and gracious, respectful of me and my privacy. And you've kindly brought me to France without argument to meet the man of my dreams."

His face fell. Sexual images vanished. But with dismay came hope—and wariness anew. She hadn't been dreaming, she'd been planning. Her explanation was a flagrant lie.

"I have another strawberry for you if you answer my next question."

She smiled mischievously. "What would you like to know?"

"I want to know exactly why you're so interested in a womanizing thief," he demanded coolly. "And I want the truth. No more talk of love and marriage, because I don't believe it for a second."

She faltered, blinking quickly, sinking into herself and wrapping her arms around her body again in a measure of comfort. Minutes passed, it seemed, with not one word spoken. And he waited, refusing to back down, staring openly into lustrous eyes of indecision and evaluation.

Then at last, in a breath above the sound of lapping waves, she lowered her lashes and began a disclosure of honesty. "I came to France to engage him."

"Engage him?" he repeated, nonplussed.

Now it was she who was plainly uncomfortable. "His services," she clarified huskily. "I need his help."

Jonathan was absolutely astonished. At first he wasn't certain he'd heard her correctly. But after several seconds of consideration, the entire precarious adventure demanded by a cunning but properly bred English maiden began to make sense. This didn't involve her wild infatuation with a myth; it involved something very real and far deeper. At that moment he knew he'd never been more obtuse about anything so obvious in his life.

"But please don't ask me to discuss it with you," she continued quickly, glancing out over the water. "It's— highly personal."

He had trouble finding his voice, or perhaps just the right response to a revelation so staggering. But somewhere inside he was already basking in possibilities laid before him—before them. What fun *this* could turn out to be.

Attempting with difficulty to hide his enjoyment at the turn of events, Jonathan cleared his throat and sat up a little on the blanket. "I think, Natalie, to be fair, I need to understand." He thrust the knife of guilt home. "You've lied to me from the beginning—about everything—and I've willingly trusted you. Tell me something."

She bent her head down. "I can't."

He pushed for detail. "Is this about you?"

"No," was her fast reply.

"Someone you care about?"

She touched her palm to her forehead in frustration. "Someone I love very much. But please don't ask me anything else, Jonathan. I can only talk to him."

That bothered him, though for what reason he wasn't sure. "You're here to help a man you're in love with?"

She stood abruptly, but he grabbed her wrist before she could consider fleeing. "Answer me that, Natalie," he demanded quietly.

A sudden gust of wind blew her lightweight skirt against her legs, making it billow out behind her, and she swatted at it irritably. "If it's any of your business, I'm not in love with anyone."

"I've never met a woman who so totally confused me," he admitted, taking full advantage of the marvelous exposure of her curves from breasts to ankles now outlined for his view. He felt a familiar raw heat as his mind briefly considered running his palm along her leg, swathed in soft fabric. "Explain yourself, and I'll refrain from asking any more personal questions."

"I *can't*," she whispered fiercely. Seconds later she softened her stance. "At least not yet."

He inhaled deeply, calculating his options. She wouldn't talk to him, and that troubled him because . . . why? Because she either didn't trust him or she had something to hide. He knew her desperate attempt to involve the Black Knight couldn't have anything to do with delicate female issues, whatever those might be, because the legend was also a man, and everyone knew it. But more importantly he was a thief, which in itself meant she most certainly wanted him to steal something for her. For the life of him, Jonathan couldn't imagine what that might be—something so incriminating, or revolting, something so personal, which was the word she'd used, or priceless, that she would jeopardize everything for it. Or for the person she loved.

He had to ponder that one. He knew she had no siblings, and if he could believe her insistence of not being in love with a man, it could only mean her mother or father. He didn't think anyone would go to this much trouble, this kind of wild pursuit, for a cousin or other distant relation, and probably not even for a very close friend. The only consolation he had, he supposed, was that she would eventually tell him when she learned who he was. Unless, of course, she was so thoroughly appalled and enraged at *his* lie she refused to speak to him forevermore. But he wouldn't even consider that.

Jonathan pulled gently on her wrist until she consented to again sit beside him on the blanket. Then he released her and leaned forward, elbows on his raised knees, fingertips touching in front of him as he stared out across the expansive blue sea.

"Why did you lie to me?" he pursued with some dejection in his voice.

She stared out at the water as well. "Why do you think, Jonathan? What would an average gentleman believe of a lady in my position? That she desperately wanted to marry or desperately needed something stolen? That she daydreamed of a handsome man's arms around her whispering passionate words of love or that she cleverly needed to manipulate and buy the services of a thief to help an anxious loved one?''

"They're both romantic pursuits," he said cautiously.

She turned to face him. "I didn't know you at all, and consider this absurdity. If I had told you my real motives, you would have laughed me out of your home—any gentleman would have—perhaps even threatened to tell my father of my utter disregard for decency. I'm nearly twenty-three years old; after another season I'll certainly be considered on the shelf. In our world nothing could be worse, and you believed it because you think like any other man. An innocent disclosure of romantic dreams into your realm of circumscribed thought bought me a ticket to France.''

He'd never heard anything so ridiculous and at the same time so logical in his life. Yet he had to admire her sagacity. What she said was very sadly true. Still, he didn't for a moment believe someone so refreshing and physically beautiful as Natalie Haislett would have trouble finding a husband, regardless of age, unless, of course, her virtue were in question. Her dowry certainly had to be adequate if not substantial.

He regarded her, now sitting closely beside him without fear or suspicion. "Do you think about marriage, Natalie, or would you prefer to avoid it altogether?"

That caught her a little by surprise, probably because she really had no choice in the matter. If she didn't choose a husband soon, her father would no doubt force the issue to someone suitable.

"I think about marriage," she replied quietly after a moment of thought. "But not to a fool, or a reserved gentleman who won't allow me to be who I am. I'd rather be a spinster than marry someone just in fear of never finding a husband." The air was still quite warm, and yet she shivered and grasped her elbows with her palms. "I didn't lie to you, either. Everything I said to you on the ship is true, Jonathan. I've studied the Black Knight for years and I find him fascinating." Almost inaudibly, she admitted, "If he finds me at all appealing, I'm hoping he'll consider me."

His brows knitted. "Consider you . . . for marriage?"

She looked down to the blanket, studying the soft plaid intently. "Consider me for a companion, a friend, and a wife."

He just didn't know whether to believe her guarded explanations. In English society a wife was rarely her husband's friend, and most people didn't think twice about it. It wasn't desirable or undesirable, it was just a fact of one's station of existence. What she said she wanted from the thief was extraordinary.

His expression turned serious. "So you came to France to engage his services *and* to appeal to his masculine nature in the hope of a marriage proposal?"

"Yes. I do, however, expect to pay him for helping me with my ... situation, which is more pressing at the moment." She fidgeted, looking totally embarrassed. "And I expect nothing in return if he's not interested in me as a woman."

At any other time, with anyone else, the conversation would have been laughable, and he would have been annoyed at such audacity. But she was just so ardent and determined in expression and voice that Jonathan couldn't help but feel a growing warmth inside, an understanding of risks and unfulfilled dreams, of wishes and pleasures beyond reach. Natalie Haislett, the innocent romantic, slyly put her reputation and future in his hands, and instead of feeling outraged at the deceit, the entire adventure filled him with an unusual blend of excitement and tenderness.

A silence, intimate and comforting, rose between them. There was nobody around, nothing to be heard but gently cresting waves as they splashed against the cliffs, and an occasional squawking gull. The sun had finally set below water, and the horizon glowed with hues of rose, coral, and striking blue.

Jonathan stared at her, lingeringly now, watching as the delicate ocean wind lifted wayward strands of sun-warmed hair, taking notice of her finely shaped, slightly upturned nose, her smooth, flawless complexion, and thick, curling lashes as they formed dark crescents upon her brows and high cheekbones. Her mouth was perfectly sculpted, full

and red and deliciously inviting as ripened strawberries on
the vine. Her chin and jaw were well defined yet feminine,
tapering softly to a long, elegant throat where he could see
her pulse beating rhythmically. He'd never looked at her
features individually before, and taken separately they were
fairly unremarkable. As a whole, her face possessed a rare
and exquisite quality, wherewith he knew without question
the finest painter in the world could never begin to do jus-
tice.

"Do you ever think about marriage, Jonathan?"

The words cut through the stillness, his thoughts, and the
quavering manner in which she spoke unsettled him a little.
"I do. At least I have recently," he answered without pretense.

She drew a long, slow breath and glanced down to her
hands now clutched together in her lap. "Would you give
up your mistresses for a wife?"

He had no idea where her thoughts were leading, but the
sudden turn in conversation made him smile. As did her
timid curiosity.

He reached for the hem of her gown and ran it through
his fingers. "Truthfully, I haven't considered marriage and
all its life changes that closely. But I hope"—he dropped
his voice to an intimate whisper—"that my wife will be so
desirous of satisfying me in every way I won't need one."

"But you can't say for sure you'd give them up," she
pressed, color once again creeping into her cheeks.

He frowned. "I can't say for sure I've given it much
thought."

"I see."

He had no idea what to say.

Another silence ensued until she murmured, "I think,
Jonathan, that a wife will find you pleasing in so many
ways she will do all she can to keep you and make you
happy." Dauntlessly she added, "And I think she will remain faithful to your needs if you remain faithful to your
vows."

He stared at her, then grinned through narrowed eyes.
"You find me that appealing, Natalie?"

She looked back to him with vivid candor. "We aren't talking about me, we're talking about you. I'm advising you as a woman to a friend."

"Ahh . . ." He shifted his weight on the blanket, leaning close enough to see the light dusting of freckles on her nose. "Then you think prospective wives will find me appealing?"

Her brows lifted minutely. "Don't women usually?"

He smiled fully at that. She was enjoying herself, at ease with him again. In a very unusual sense, he found the moment sublime like no other he'd experienced in a long time.

Without a second thought, he reached up and touched her hair, lightly, with only his fingertips, as it fell over her left arm. Her smile faded, but she didn't turn or pull away.

"I want you to find me appealing," he revealed quietly, his eyes grazing her face.

She straightened in an unsuccessful attempt to keep the conversation perfunctory. "I find you exceptionally so, Jonathan, but that hardly matters. I must stay true to my convictions. I won't ever be your mistress, therefore nothing—"

"I want to kiss you," he cut in softly.

Her eyes grew wide with either shock or fear, he wasn't sure which. But she didn't say no; she didn't do anything.

"Just a kiss, Natalie."

"But we're *friends*," she insisted in a confused, wavering voice.

The passionate comment struck him oddly. "Yes, I think we are, and I don't intend to spoil that."

He reached forward and touched her bottom lip with his thumb, and the fact that she didn't pull away in disgust or anger sent a jolt of encouragement and desire through the center of him.

"I won't ever be your mistress," she repeated, her resolve breaking.

"I will never take you as my mistress," he promised in a deep whisper. Then as an indescribable anxiousness filled him, he leaned his head toward her and placed his lips on hers.

Natalie closed her eyes, her body unmoving. Of all the mistakes she'd made in her life, this one would likely be the greatest. But even with a thousand voices of warning screaming within her, she just couldn't pull away. There was really no harm in a little kiss, and he at least had the decency to request before taking. He was just so powerfully attractive and inviting she had trouble saying no. And she desired him beyond question. She always had, and she hoped against hope that he wouldn't realize it from this simple kiss between friends. But everything else aside, she wanted to feel and feel now, to be kissed by the most physically handsome man she had ever known, by the sea in an exotic land, under the purple and golden hue of the setting sun. How marvelous and exciting.

Pressing his lips against hers, he reached around with his hand and grasped the back of her head, holding her a little closer. His mouth started a slow movement of softness, and Natalie relaxed as the expected pleasure began to build. She was used to it now, not afraid as she'd been before. They were quite alone, and she gave in to the enjoyment of the moment. Trusting him.

He began to stroke her hair with his fingers but he didn't pull back from the kiss. If anything, he deepened it a bit, his tongue playing delicately against her closed lips, back and forth, until she opened them faintly. She had to admit she was kissing him back now, and it was obvious by a small husky sigh that he liked it. That pleased her, and out of instinct more than knowledge, sitting side by side, hands still in her lap, she turned toward him and leaned her body very slightly into his.

Within seconds he pulled the ribbon from her hair, and strands of it lifted in the breeze to touch her neck, his face. He ran his fingers through it, cupping her head, holding it fully now as he intensified the kiss. He still wasn't possessive or demanding, being quite gentlemanly in his endeavor, and with that thought reason escaped her, and she let herself go, breath quickening, heartbeat increasing with anticipation. She raised her hand to feel the hardness of his chest through his soft linen shirt, just lightly touching him with hesitant fingers.

He reacted immediately, lifting his free hand and closing it over her knuckles to hold her firmly against him. He was breathing heavily now, his heart beating strongly beneath her palm, and Natalie took an instant raw delight in affecting him so.

She opened a little more for him, and his tongue grazed her lips, sending sudden shock waves through her body. She jolted in reaction, but he held to her, expecting it, making it impossible for her to pull away.

She could feel the tension surrounding them like a physical thing, smell the moist salty air, hear the waves pounding the rocks below, echoing like thunder in the cove beyond. His hard body felt hot against her now, numbing yet comforting, familiar yet strangely new and exciting. He was treating her deliciously, like a fine china doll in his possession, and she wanted more with a sudden, burning ache. It was just a kiss, but so wonderful and perfect.

She reached for him then, gliding her hands along his chest and shoulders until she clasped his neck. He in turn wrapped his arms around her willingly, holding her even closer, nearer now to a full embrace. She opened her mouth completely, and quite by accident the tip of his tongue flicked hers. At any other time, with anyone else, she might have found that revolting. Now she relished in the tingling sharpness within her, whimpering involuntarily from the pleasure of it.

He groaned and did it again, this time with intention, and in a rush of memory, Natalie remembered he'd done that before to her, in a moment of surrendering passion. But she couldn't think about that time. Not now.

In a slow but purposeful motion, he pushed her back to lie flat on the blanket, his mouth still clinging to hers, moving in slow, blissful form, his tongue invading her intimately. He rested his body beside her, his hands in her hair, but he didn't stop kissing her, just continued as he was until she began to feel restless.

Natalie didn't understand it. On the farthest edge of sanity she yelled for him to stop, that it was enough. But it wasn't. And the purely physical side of her wanted it to go on forever.

Then, as if comprehending the ache more than she, in a most gentle touch, he placed his palm on her breast. She didn't notice the faint contact at first until his thumb moved across her nipple in one stroke to cause an exquisite stab of pleasure deep within. She gasped against his lips, but he refused to release her mouth. He kissed her fully now, almost relentlessly, as his hand moved to her waist to hold her there should she decide to run. But she couldn't. Not yet.

Losing sight of the inevitable outcome of their actions, Natalie finally surrendered. She wrapped her arms around him, pulling him against her, her fingers in his thick, silky hair, his broad chest grazing her breasts, his leg folding over hers in one smooth movement.

He groaned again, coming alive with eagerness as she responded to the magnificent torment building within her. He desired her with incredible passion, and that knowledge was a sort of dim power she possessed and refused to relinquish. This was what she'd wanted for years.

He released her mouth at last to begin a trail of fine kisses on her cheek, down her jaw and neck. She leaned back instinctively to allow him access, her mind a whirlwind of confusion and pleasure, eyes squeezed shut, hands holding his head tightly against her in sudden, desperate fear that he might stop. She squirmed and whimpered faintly when his hand found her breast again, urgent in his approach this time, as he began to knead it softly over her blouse, his thumb and finger playing expertly until her nipple hardened to the touch.

He shuddered, his breath coming fast and heavy, and still she clung to him with a wildness she couldn't have imagined of herself only moments before. Being touched like this was exhilarating, a far-extending abandonment.

She was only vaguely aware that he lifted her blouse to reach beneath it, slowly running his palm along her thin chemise, caressing her waist, her ribs, in soft sensuous strokes. Instinctively she lifted her body to him, her hands now on his shoulders as he quite suddenly placed his face between her breasts, still over her blouse, but in such a manner that it shot a powerful shock of raging fire between her legs.

She gasped his name aloud, and he groaned deeply in his chest as he caressed her nipples through only two sheer layers of fabric, back and forth, with his cheek, his chin, his lips. He touched her face with one palm, his thumb on her mouth, and with the other he found the waiting peak of her nipple, circling it over and over with his fingers. He still hadn't touched her skin to skin, with full intimacy, and yet the affect was complete, staggering, and so entirely satisfying at the same time.

Then he was kissing her again, fully and hungrily, with no pretense, and she responded, aching with needs untouched, squirming beneath him, her leg rubbing the length of his with wild abandon.

But he wouldn't let her go. He clung to her, mouth to mouth, chest to chest, his hips slowly beginning to stroke hers as his own acutely felt needs surfaced. He ran his tongue along her lips, his free hand starting a trace down her leg, fingertips grazing the outline with purpose.

She whimpered softly, writhing with a soaring recklessness she didn't understand, holding his face in her palms.

"Oh, God," he whispered against her mouth.

She held him tighter, in desperation to feel, to know, to put an end to the longing.

As if in answer, she felt his palm against her thigh.

"Jonathan—"

"I know."

She pulled at him frantically, her hips lifting to meet the hardness of his, eyes squeezed shut, heart pounding, blood rushing through her veins, throbbing in her ears, drowning all sound.

Then she felt the first very timid contact of his hand between her legs—only one thin piece of linen between his warm skin and the most private part of her. She wasn't certain of it at first because he made no movement. And then there could be no mistake. His intentions were clear, and she arched her back from the instantly sharp sensation.

But he kissed her so deeply, so totally, she lost control, couldn't see the end beyond the action. He placed his left palm against her forehead, fingers weaving through her hair, and with the other he began to stroke her, gently but expertly, not moving the fabric of her clothing away, but leaving it to cover her, the rhythm on top of it, first one finger, then another, then all of them.

Natalie's breath caught in her chest. She couldn't think. Could only feel. Could only react. He was doing something so intimate to her, and yet she couldn't voice a thought or protest because she wanted him like this beyond anything. She gripped his shoulders with rigid hands, aching with need, now moving her hips against his fingers rhythmically as he increased the speed.

He released her mouth, dropping his lips to her neck, then moving his face to her hair. A raspy breath escaped him as he ran his tongue along her ear, grazing the lobe, teasing it, sucking it.

Her legs moved wildly, her body uncontrollably, as she became oblivious to all but his touch at the center of her. She moaned in a feverish surrender, and he silently, relentlessly pursued, placing small kisses on her cheeks and jaw and throat, stroking her, taking her to the ends of the earth.

Suddenly she clutched him tightly. Her eyes flew open, and he lifted his head to look down at her in concentration. And then it happened. Intense and incredible, she exploded within, crying out in wonder, in bliss, at the perfect end to a radiant hunger.

Jonathan swallowed with difficulty, his breathing harsh as he continued to control himself, staring down at her stunned face flushing beautifully as she climaxed from his touch. It had happened so fast he hadn't considered where things were going until he was caught in a rush of momentum that carried her over the edge. But that didn't matter. It was bound to happen—probably meant to—and fighting it was useless.

She shuddered and closed her eyes, turning away from him. He caressed her brow with his thumb, then placed his head on her chest, his heart still thundering as he listened to the steady, quick beating of hers, his body raging with desire he knew instinctively from the beginning would not be fulfilled. He had yet to remove his fingers from between her legs and he could feel her wetness clinging to thin linen, warm and succulent, inviting him to enter and satisfy his pain. He wanted to touch her there with unbelievable need. Just a finger enveloped by hot, moist softness to last him until the next time. But it wouldn't happen now. Without question he knew it wouldn't happen now.

With agonizing acceptance, he lifted his hand and pulled her skirt down to cover her decently, wrapping his arm around her waist, holding her close to him. He inhaled deeply the scent of her skin and hair, relishing in the fullness of her breasts, the curve of her hips. He opened his eyes with resolve, restraint, gaining possession of his senses once more as he gazed out to the water now glimmering in growing nightfall.

She lay motionless, half beneath him, with only her steady breathing to be heard. He said nothing, did nothing, just held her, allowing her to carry the mood as she slowly came to terms with all that had just taken place.

At last she inhaled sharply, and in the quiet night air whispered, "Why?"

It was a question filled with grief, and he knew what she meant. Not why now, why me, why did you. But *why us?*

"I don't know," he murmured after a moment of stillness, honesty rippling through his answer. "Sometimes it's . . . like this—"

Furiously she struggled from under him, moving quickly to all fours, then steadying herself so she could rise. He clung to her for a second, then let her go, following suit, unsure of her reaction until he stood next to her and she faced him fully. Quite suddenly she was shaking with rage, her face, both livid and so very vulnerable, reflecting a dull, shimmering glow from the final traces of daylight.

"You may do this kind of thing with women all the time,

Jonathan, but it does not happen to me," she seethed, hands clenched at her sides.

He blinked, then felt himself pale as comprehension overtook him. "That's not what I meant—"

"Stop it!"

She covered her face with her hands, and just as quickly he grabbed her wrists and yanked her against him. She fought him, but he wouldn't let her go.

"That's not what I meant," he repeated soothingly. He waited, and finally she stopped struggling, shaking her head, eyes tightly shut. "Natalie, look at me."

She ignored him.

"Look at me," he said again urgently.

Reluctantly she relaxed and raised her lashes, glaring at him with huge, vibrant, furious eyes, clear as glass.

He took a long, slow breath, though still clutching her wrists in fear that she would run. "What happened between us just now has never happened to me before."

She gaped at him, appalled. "You're a blatant liar. You've been with so many—"

"Not like this," he broke in gently.

"But isn't it always the same?" she blurted sarcastically. "One woman or another—"

"No," he stated emphatically, his chest tightening because he realized at once that she wouldn't see past the rumors to the man, to the truth as he might explain it. She didn't believe him, and what could he say? That he'd never been with anyone so thoroughly enchanting and delightfully unknowing, so striking to look at, so exciting to satisfy? That he'd never before given without taking in return as he had tonight? Any statement in his defense would sound arrogant and unfeeling, and ultimately would only remind her of those he truly now wished she didn't know anything about. So in the end he said nothing more, which unquestionably made matters worse.

"You lied to me," she wailed miserably, jerking free of him with such force he could do nothing but let her go. She turned her back to him, walking a few feet away, hugging herself, head down. "You didn't want a kiss, you wanted everything."

"I didn't plan this, Natalie, it just happened," he admitted softly, knowing immediately it was a futile thing to say.

She snickered caustically. "As it's just happened to countless others, I'm sure."

His jaw hardened. "That's unfair."

"Unfair?" She whirled around. "What about me? I've never been with a man before, Jonathan."

She said the words as if they'd be some astounding revelation to him. But the fact that this mattered so much to her effectively subdued him. "I know that," he murmured.

She peered openly at him for a long moment, then glanced out over the shoreline, protectively wrapping her arms around herself again. "Oh, God, this is awful," she whispered shakily.

Jonathan rubbed his palm along his neck, then placed his hands on his hips. He knew she was speaking out of confusion and embarrassment, but he felt a trace of irritation just the same.

"Nothing we've done is awful," he began slowly. "It is never awful. It is a perfectly natural act that happened without thought because we have passions between us that are undeniable and, I think, rare. I have never felt this kind of desire for anybody but you, Natalie. And it started years ago when you kissed me in the garden—a sweet act of innocence I have never been able to push from my mind."

She stiffened considerably, closing herself off, and that piqued his anger.

"I don't understand it, either," he continued gravely, "but it's not going to go away. You feel it, too, and each day we're together it gets stronger. Part of me wants to send you packing because it makes me nervous as hell. But I can't bring myself to do that because somewhere inside I believe something wonderful is happening and I for one would like to see where it leads."

She remained silent, unmoving, staring out to the darkened sea. Then slowly she shook her head. "But what about him?'' she asked with a shade of desperation. ''What if this ruins everything I've come here for?''

His first thought was, *What about whom?* Then a gust of wind sliced through the calmness with night-ocean coldness. She shivered, turning her face to him once more, rubbing her upper arms with her hands as she clutched them for warmth and strength. And he knew.

Jonathan, for the first time, felt as if he had been physically slapped for his actions, her callous words biting him with more sting than she could ever produce with the palm of her hand. She showed no reaction to the intensely private feelings he'd only just laid bare before her. Her thoughts were with a dream, a fictional reality centered in her mind, somewhere beyond grasp. A hope she would cherish above everything else until she learned it didn't exist.

His body became rigid, but not with rage. It was helplessness he felt, frustration, defeat, and more understanding for a woman than he'd ever experienced before. He'd just made love to her, partially so anyway, and with anyone else he would have turned and walked away after a comment so burning. Yet right now, reacting as he was, he knew he was more angry with himself—for taking advantage, for losing control, and for giving so much where it clearly wasn't wanted.

''I'm sure the infamous Black Knight will find you innocent and charming and everything he's ever desired,'' he maintained in a dark, acid voice. ''Nothing is ruined. Your virtue is intact. Nobody knows what happened here tonight but you and I, and I will never mention it to anyone.''

Her face went slack, her eyes grew to round pools of shock, probably because she now understood how she'd hurt him. But he refused to acknowledge her thoughts. Instead, he turned and lifted the blanket, packing things quickly and leaving the beach in full darkness, not another word spoken between them.

Seven

Natalie sat at the white wicker dressing table in their bungalow, taking a long look at her reflection in the mirror. Her appearance was decent enough for a ball, she supposed. The bungalow owner's wife had helped her with the tightening of her corset, but she'd had to dress her own hair for the first time in her life, and that had proven quite an adventure in itself. Twice she'd thrown her pearl-handled brush down in exasperation as she attempted to arrange her menacing curls on top of her head in a style that at least resembled an elegant coif. Never before had she really cared about her formal appearance; she merely took it for granted when the maids were finished. Tonight, however, she was a mess—in mind and manner—and her nervous fingers only made things worse.

At last she stood, with forced refinement, appraising her choice of gown—a rich russet silk over full crinoline. She'd only brought two ball gowns with her, so her selection was minimal. Her decision to wear this one had more to do with climate than anything, for it was fairly lightweight for evening dress. The waist was drawn tightly, pushing the bust-line up and forward. The sleeves were short and puffed, off the shoulder, and enhanced by fawn-colored velvet trim along the collar, with matching lace accentuating the full skirt. For adornment she wore only the simplest cameos: two dangling from her ears, one on a gold chain around her throat, and a ring on her right hand. The gown and jewelry did wonders for her coloring, something reddish-brown and ivory usually didn't do for a lady.

This was one of her vainest moments, she considered through a smile. But first impressions were everything, and the Black Knight would see her for the first time this night. She wanted him to be impressed, and she had to admit she looked impressive.

Natalie turned, clutching her shaking hands together, and moved toward the open window to sit gracefully in one of the wicker chairs facing the Mediterranean Sea. Their room was lovely, the view outstanding, especially now with a golden setting sun shining through muslin curtains of sea green. From the minute Jonathan had ushered her inside, she'd adored it.

The furniture was painted white, as were the walls, which were adorned with numerous paintings from local artists. Many were seascapes, rich and colorful, and others were of the surrounding towns and whitewashed buildings distinct to Marseilles. Their room itself was small, but charming in its simplicity. The bed, shrouded in an airy, bright blue coverlet, stood against the far wall. Next to it were the dressing table and stool, beside which stood a muslin screen in coral pink for discreet dressing. The only other furnishings were the two chairs and small wicker table in front of the window, which opened fully to allow the sea breeze to cool the room continuously. It was the most colorful, comfortable place in which Natalie had ever stayed, and she cherished each moment, gazing out to the open sea, knowing she would soon be returning to gray, dreary England.

He'd never said so, but Natalie was sure Jonathan didn't stay in places so beautiful when he traveled alone. That only meant he'd found the bungalow for her. As she came to know him better, she found him to be one of the most thoughtful individuals she'd ever met. And not just thoughtful in a way a gentleman might treat a lady of acquaintance, but in a more subtle, personal manner, as if he truly considered what she might like and how she thought and felt.

The last four days had been interminable. She tried to tell herself it was because she had to wait so patiently to meet the legendary thief after learning he would be at the ball. But realistically she knew it was because it had been four days since her intimate encounter with Jonathan on the beach. The memory of it filled her mind constantly, making her blush and squirm with embarrassment, more so if he walked into the room and simply looked at her. She knew instinctively that every moment they were together he was remembering her reaction to his touch, a reaction unforgivable, in her opinion.

But he hadn't mentioned that evening again. Hadn't, in fact, mentioned much at all. For four days he'd been nearly silent, speaking to her only when he thought it necessary, going about his business as he left her in the bungalow each morning to ride into the city. Or so he said. Natalie really had no reason to be suspicious. He had, in fact, twice on occasion taken her with him. He wasn't in any way rude or devious; it was just that his attention had turned elsewhere, and she wasn't sure how to respond to his sudden impassivity. She was fairly certain it had nothing to do with Mrs. DuMais, but that idea couldn't be disregarded. She only wished she didn't care so much if it did.

Part of her realized his indifference was because of what she'd said to him after their cozy twilight picnic where she'd completely lost control of her mind. She'd sensed his feelings that night, had noticed the look on his shadowed features. He had been totally honest with her—she knew that. And if she considered *her* feelings honestly she knew he was more than accurate regarding their growing attraction to each other. But above it all, more than anything else that mattered in her life, she refused to become one of Jonathan Drake's innumerable conquests. If she gave herself to him to any further extent she'd be the one to lose, and she'd lose everything—her self-respect; her virginity, which was something she truly wanted to give her future husband; and most probably her heart. She'd been consumed, for various complex reasons, with meeting the Black Knight for two years now, and she needed to remain focused on that. She'd worked too hard and far too long for Jonathan, and her confusing feelings for him, to ruin this one night.

This night. And she was ready.

Natalie stood with fired nerves and walked two steps to the window, noting irritably that even with good marks for thoughtfulness, Jonathan obviously hadn't remembered that this was the most important night of her life. She glanced to the silver clock on the dressing table, wringing her hands in front of her. It was nearly seven, and he had yet to return from his city wanderings. What the man did with his time, she couldn't guess.

He entered the bungalow at precisely that moment, as if on cue, and she whirled around to confront him. He carried a cloth bag over one arm, which she assumed contained clothes for the ball that he'd purchased in town since he certainly hadn't brought anything appropriate to wear to such a function in his one small trunk. She faced him, taking a stance of impatience, arms at her sides, chin high, as she watched him close the door.

At last he glanced at her, as he'd done a thousand times, but this time he stared at what he saw. Her pulse quickened, color flooded her cheeks, and that's when Natalie realized she had dressed for him, too. It was a disturbing thought, but she held his gaze, a twinge of a smile on her lips.

"You look beautiful."

The words were those she wanted to hear, but his tone was so matter-of-fact, so bland, she wasn't certain if he was paying her a compliment he truly believed or merely saying exactly what any lady expected to hear from a gentleman of quality.

"Thank you," she mumbled, clasping her hands in front of her to keep them from shaking.

His eyes grazed her figure, from the curls high on her head to the lace at her hem, pausing only briefly at her accentuated bosom and waist. Then he turned and strode toward the screen to change.

"There are some things we need to discuss, Natalie," he said frankly, unbuttoning his shirt with one hand as he walked behind the thin barrier. "First, as far as the Black Knight is concerned, I'll introduce him to you if I see him and if it isn't awkward."

She felt a welling anxiousness in the pit of her stomach. "I'll be very discreet, Jonathan. You needn't worry."

"I'm certain you will, but the meeting still has to be on my terms," he insisted. "The man's identity must be protected. If he's there I'll talk to him, and if he feels it's safe, I'll find a way to introduce you."

She held her tongue of argument, realizing his intentions were all she could hope for.

"The second item of importance is the sword," he continued quickly, rustling with clothing from the bag. "I can't have you mentioning it to the count."

How was that relevant? "Why?" Her expression went flat with comprehension. "He doesn't know he's selling it to you, does he, Jonathan?"

"Not yet."

How men ever survived in the business world she couldn't guess. "Of course," she agreed to the ridiculous. "I won't mention the sword."

He flung his day clothes over the screen. "And finally, we must discuss our marriage."

She swallowed dryly as embarrassment returned, her fingers toying nervously with her cameo ring. It occurred to her at that moment the enormity of the game they were about to play.

"We've been married two years," he continued directly. "We had a usual courtship of six months and live in London proper for the part of the year we aren't traveling abroad. We move in excellent social circles, have plenty of money though not excessive wealth, and as yet no children. The rest of your identity need not be embellished. The count thinks I'm here with an interest in buying his Parisian estate."

"All this drama for a sword?" she asked incredulously.

"It's a very nice sword," was his vague reply.

She paused, thinking. "Is this what Mrs. DuMais arranged for you?"

He was silent for a moment, dropping his shoes on the floor with a clunk.

"Yes, in part," he admitted. "She also knows we're not really married. She's the only one you can confide in tonight."

"Naturally."

He brushed over her rather snide comment, then several seconds later stepped from behind the screen, tying his cravat with expert fingers. And his appearance took her breath away.

He looked magnificent, flooding her with memory of long ago. Another ball. Only this time he was more sophisticated, mature in bearing, more handsome, if that were possible.

His clothes were expensive and perfectly tailored, which partially explained where he'd spent the last four days. A cream silk shirt covered his broad chest, over which he wore an emerald-green waistcoat, and a frock jacket and matching trousers of lightweight wool in deep olive. It was a striking combination, though one she would never expect him to choose. Yet the colors made his eyes, as they bore into hers, an incredibly vivid blue, his hair shiny and dark as polished black onyx.

"Natalie?"

She raised a hand to her throat. "Marvelous," she whispered.

For the first time in days, she caught a semblance of a smile on his lips. "I dress to please you, my darling wife. You've always admired me in shades of green."

She wasn't certain if he was being sarcastic or rising to the moment with a very credible acting debut. She decided to assume it was the latter, playing along as she reached for her gloves and fan on the wicker table. "Have I? How well you've learned my tastes during the last two years, Jonathan."

He straightened his coat. "Indeed, Mrs. Drake. As any husband should." He offered her his arm. "Our hired carriage awaits at the top of the road. Are you ready?''

She hesitated, growing uncomfortable as she considered her next words. Unfortunately they needed to be said before she and Jonathan left to attempt such a crucial masquerade.

Grasping the cameo around her neck, she asked with some reluctance, ''Are we in love?''

He stared at her blankly, then lowered his arm and slowly frowned. ''What?''

She felt hot suddenly, although she continued to look at him levelly. ''As a married couple. Are we in love?''

That bewildered him. He had no idea what to say, or whether to laugh or argue or question her sanity. With all his organization in planning their deception, he'd analyzed them kissing each other—when, how, why, and in front of whom, but not once had he thought of love between them.

Natalie, for the first time since she'd met the imposing Jonathan Drake, knew she had the advantage in the palm of her hand. It was an exquisite moment of triumph, and she could hardly keep herself from grinning.

''*Please*, Jonathan. I have to know how to play the game,'' she returned as innocently as she could. ''Some married couples love each other. Are we one of the fortunate few, or would you rather we avoid each other for the evening?''

It was his turn to hesitate, his eyes narrowing as he continued to watch her. ''I hadn't thought about it.''

''Yes, I know,'' she asserted at once. She realized her face shone pink with discomfiture, but she carried on, hoping to appear bored by a tedious dialogue he should have raised between them days ago. ''As a man you may not have considered it, as the men at the ball surely won't. But the women will notice and respond accordingly.'' She purposely cleared her throat. ''Should I be jealous when you dance and flirt with others, or merely indifferent?''

His mouth twisted in an arrogant half smile. ''You've actually thought about this?''

In the blink of an eye, the advantage was once again his. Now her cheeks were burning as he stared down at her in vague amusement. "Any woman in my position would, Jonathan."

"I see." He dropped his gaze to her breasts momentarily, then raised them back to her face. "What do you think?"

She fidgeted from his shameless regard, never expecting the question and unsure how to respond. She wanted to provoke him by announcing how little she cared, or that she preferred the more plausible relationship of marital aloofness. Then it struck her that *he'd* be more unsettled by her forced loving attention, and instantly that was the game she wanted to play.

"I think we should," she declared confidently.

His brows rose minutely. "Be in love?"

She shrugged. "I think it's more realistic in our circumstance."

"Do you?" He was standing very close to her now, his voice deep and quiet. "As two properly bred members of the English gentry?"

It sounded absurd when he put it like that. He knew as well as she that under such a circumstance love was rarely a motivating factor in a marital union.

She clutched her fan against her skirt. "We're in France, Jonathan. The French are a passionate people and won't give it a second thought. I also think it could be to your advantage with the count."

"Really? How so?"

Her eyes flashed with inspiration. "To keep our stories straight, for one. I can't tell him we spent last summer in Vienna if you've told him thirty minutes before we were in Naples."

"A reasonable thought," he admitted.

"He might also feel you're more respectable, more stable or reliable, with a loving wife at your side." She straightened. "But of course I'm only guessing."

"Of course." He pulled a piece of lint from her velvet collar. After a lingering moment of thought he asked guardedly, "Do you think you can act that well, Natalie?"

He was beginning to annoy her with the endless questions in a conversation going nowhere on his part. She peered into engaging eyes framed with thick, black lashes, to flawless, clean-shaven skin, to his firm, sculpted jaw. The man carried a constant, heady scent of marked masculinity, so rich and potent no woman could possibly resist him. He knew it, too, which had a tendency to make her mad when she thought about it. But right this moment, in the bungalow they shared between just the two of them, she felt a sudden rush of jealousy toward all the women in his life up to that moment. Not a broad disapproval of his libertine reputation like before, but a different feeling. One deep within her, altogether private, vulnerable, and maybe a little bit frightening. Realizing this now made her fume at her own inconsistent, complicated feelings.

Risking everything, she placed her hand on his cheek. Then with calculation, and before she could change her mind, she lifted her face and touched his lips with hers. The contact shocked her more than she thought it would, sending waves of both uneasiness and exhilaration through the center of her. He didn't move, but it wasn't at all what he expected, she knew that instinctively, and by the fact that he didn't immediately react.

She stroked his jaw with a feathery wisp of her thumb, then ran her tongue once, very slowly, along the inside of his top lip. He drew a sharp inhale, and with that she pulled away, beaming in satisfaction, feeling a sudden, marvelous sense of power.

"If it's what you want for the game, Jonathan, I could display a great, intense love for you. I'm a magnificent actress."

For several long, silent seconds he did nothing but stare at her. Then his eyes hardened to blue ice. "I'm looking forward to watching you perform at center stage, Natalie," he said quietly. "Tonight should be enlightening for us both."

She blinked and took a step back, thoroughly confused by his disdain. She'd expected a teasing retort or light rebuff, as was his congenial nature. But as she considered it now, he'd purposely distanced himself since their picnic on the beach, and for the first time since that night she realized she didn't like it at all.

"Love it is, Mrs. Drake," he said coolly, interrupting her troubled thoughts. Then he tightly grasped her elbow and walked her through the door toward their waiting carriage.

Eight

Jonathan was worried. Or perhaps it was just plain, old-fashioned nervousness that plagued him. He'd come to France to do a job, a big job, and tonight everything would be on the line—except he was having difficulty keeping focused, and he knew from experience just how critical that could be to success. He hadn't considered that this might occur when he'd offered to bring Natalie along, which was, if he thought about it honestly, a singularly stupid thing to overlook. Every job he'd done before now had been smoothly accomplished because he'd planned, and planned meticulously. Women were only diversions to assist him, if needed, in the final performance.

But for the first time that he could recall, a woman filled his mind more than the issue at hand, and with irritation at himself he realized this alone could bungle an effort of immeasurable cost to French and English national security. It was that important. He'd already made his first mistake in placing his unusual concern for Natalie ahead of the emeralds. Those who paid him for his services would not be pleased if they knew, and it was surprising that this had not occurred to him until tonight.

They rode the short distance to the count's estate in virtual silence. He stared out the window vacantly, aware of how she squirmed in the squabs from excitement, her beautiful gown billowing over his legs and feet as she smoothed her skirt when she wasn't rubbing her fingers together or lightly tapping her fan in her lap. He didn't have to look at her to be acutely conscious of her presence. She affected him that much.

Every day she confused him more, which he found altogether troubling. Troubling to his rational mind, and more embarrassingly so to his ego. He was growing increasingly suspicious of her, too, and he wasn't sure why. In his experience he'd found women either forward and forthcoming, or virtuous and sweet, but always readable. Not so with Natalie. Each passing day in her presence, he found her to be ever more calculating and smooth, more devious, more of the actress she claimed to be. She was sneaky beyond compare, although she hadn't really done anything outwardly to warrant such feelings in him. It was more intuition on his part that brought this to attention. She just seemed to be in control, and he couldn't quite shrug off the vague notion that she was using *him*. That made him furious.

His anger had grown since their encounter on the beach, and it was mostly directed toward himself for dropping his guard. He felt, suddenly, like all the women he'd taken mild advantage of through the years, women who had fallen in love with him because he'd charmed them with his good humor and attention, his devotion to their needs both innocent and intimate. He had taken nothing from Natalie four days ago, and had been more open with her than any lady he could recall, and yet she had, in a very peculiar way, snubbed him. Her reaction to him physically had been overwhelming as he thought about it now. No woman had ever succumbed to him so easily and quickly, and with so much uninhibited passion. Rationally, though, she just didn't seem to be interested, and the harder he tried, the more oblivious she was to his efforts.

But one thing was becoming clearer to him as the days went on. Suspicions about her motives aside, she was nothing more than a well-bred, lovely, albeit shrewd, English lady. Whatever she was hiding from him, whatever reason she had for coming to France, it couldn't be complicated. So, upon that he'd made this very rational decision: He would take her virginity on this trip as he longed to do, she would enjoy it as much as he, and he would marry her upon their return to England, which he now had to admit was a union he wanted almost entirely because she wouldn't approve of it at all. Only days ago he'd vowed not to marry her or anyone who didn't want him as an individual, but her actions of late had changed his mind. And what was marriage, anyway? Just a contract between families to legitimize heirs, really. He'd have to choose someone eventually, and thinking about owning Natalie in bed and out of it made him smile in the darkness. All her ideas of remaining aloof to his affections would fail her in the end because he would take her and she would belong to him for the rest of their natural lives. He would win, and he couldn't wait for the moment to inform her of this. She would argue that she didn't love him or that her father would never approve. He'd then calmly remind her that she was a baron's daughter, love was irrelevant, and he was a wealthy, unattached, socially admired son of an earl. Her father would approve wholeheartedly, and she would be *bound* to accept him. Jonathan would relish that moment soon to come. It would be a triumph like no other.

But first he had a job to finish.

They arrived at the count's seaside home in lingering twilight, but already the estate was lit up spectacularly both inside and out. It was two stories in height, constructed of polished gray stone chiseled into delicate arches and sharp angles of contrasting design. It sat only a short distance from the edge of the cliffs and was surrounded by a large, immaculate garden of various trees, shrubs, and flowers. The party guests were made to stroll through it on a winding brick path to reach the front door, and Jonathan was immediately struck with the pungent, weighty odors of honeysuckle and roses clinging to the balmy night air, flying insects buzzing as they circled the foot lamps along the walk.

Natalie stood very close to him as he handed their invitation to the footman. Then he placed his palm on her back and guided her into the foyer.

The inside was typical of design, and he had studied it well. The ground floor consisted of a morning room to the immediate right, followed by a music room and other various rooms for entertaining, all leading toward the kitchen, and finally the servants' quarters and their staircase to the second floor in the back of the house. To the left was the grand ballroom where they would spend most of the evening, behind which was the ladies' withdrawing room, then the smoking room and dining room, in that order. Straight ahead loomed the wide staircase of dark oak leading to the second floor—the family sleeping quarters to the right, various guest rooms to the left, followed by the family library and finally the count's study at the end of the hallway.

Six doors down to the left, in the southwest corner, with the greatest view of the evening sun and picturesque Mediterranean Sea, the emeralds contained in a relatively easy-access safe behind a small, romantically frivolous Fragonard oil above the mantel. The evening was starting, and Jonathan relaxed as he considered the plan, a very good one indeed. This was what he did, and did best, and in only hours the priceless emeralds that once belonged to the empress of Austria would be back on British soil where they belonged. That aside, Natalie was soon to encounter the greatest shock of her life. Yes, indeed, it would be a night to remember.

Grasping her elbow, he ushered her toward the ballroom, standing alert to the atmosphere and the mood of other guests as he followed them to the receiving line. Already her gaze darted from one man to the next, calculating, estimating age, bearing, description, and how each one matched the Black Knight and rumors of his appearance. Jonathan watched her, feeling power coupled with mischief and an odd sense of enjoyment at her frustration in waiting.

Moments later, as they neared the count and his bride of three years, Jonathan leaned toward her and broke the silence between them. "Here we go, my darling wife," he whispered in her ear. He felt her stiffen, although whether from the implication of his words or from the knowledge that the game was beginning, he wasn't sure. Spontaneously he rubbed his thumb along her elbow in a measure of comfort.

"Monsieur et Madame Drake," came the presentation from the man to the count's right. "The Englishman," he mumbled as an afterthought, though purposely forgetting to add, "who buys properties," which would have been indelicate during an introduction but was undoubtedly understood by all parties.

"Monsieur Drake," the count boomed in thickly accented English. "How nice of you to join our celebration for my daughter Annette-Elise. I am hoping we will be able to talk at length of your travels and stay in our country. Madame DuMais holds you in the highest regard."

Jonathan swiftly took in the count's appearance. Average in height, balding on top as thick, coarse hair receded from his expansive forehead in the most unusual color—not quite brown, not quite gray, yet not exactly a salt-and-pepper mixture of the two. His jaw, probably square and hard in youth, was now fleshy, and he attempted to hide this with long, full side whiskers. His cheeks were ruddy and nose was pink, as if he had imbibed a good deal of wine. His mouth, wide and drawing and somehow unbefitting his face, was soft and full of humor, quite unlike the rest of his bearing, especially his eyes. They were shrouded by dark, heavy brows, the clear circles striking and nearly black in color, sly and deep set, exuding intelligence.

The man was dense of build though not quite fat, perceptive of mind, overindulged in life's pleasures, but was probably pleasing to the gentle sex and not unattractive for his middle years. Women would no doubt find him so, regardless of his physical assets, if this one great home was any indication of his wealth. Tonight he wore a perfectly tailored dark-blue tailcoat of superfine over a blue-and-white silk waistcoat, dark trousers, and a black cravat over pointed collar. Quite fitting for the occasion, albeit conservative, but then his political ties would suggest that.

Jonathan smiled and bowed ever so slightly, though his eyes, lit with charm, never left the Frenchman's. "Comte d'Arles. Thank-you for your gracious invitation. It would be my pleasure to spend time in discussion this evening."

"I am looking forward to it," he replied readily. Turning, he added with pride, "My wife, the countess of Arles."

Jonathan's gaze shifted to the man's immediate left where his wife, Claudine, stood rigid and grossly thin in a gown of pale pink taffeta covered with large, white bows that did nothing but make her look older than her twenty-six years and her bronzed coloring unnaturally orange. She was a pretty woman but far from feminine, her blond hair now piled on her head, faded from hours in bright sunshine which also undoubtedly accounted for the deep grooves already appearing on her face. Her eyes were hazel and fiercely penetrating, though somewhat lacking in wit and trust, and she stared at him with lips pulled into a thin, pink line.

With his most disarming smile he grasped her gloved fingers lightly and brought them to his lips. "I am enchanted, madam."

"Monsieur Drake," she said formally.

Already the count had shifted his gaze to Natalie with obvious appreciation, and Jonathan took the cue. "May I present to you both my wife."

"My dear lady," the count addressed her smoothly, his eyes grazing her throat and bosom in an almost indecent manner. "How lovely. Your husband is a very fortunate man, if I may be so bold. Welcome to France and my home."

The man not only took occasional mistresses but was also an open flirt, Jonathan mused, which his wife obviously did not appreciate by the look of her ever-narrowing lips as she stared at Natalie with hard assessment. Madeleine had left that out of the equation, but it could be useful. He watched in amusement as Natalie recognized it, too, and came alive with radiance.

"I am most charmed, sir," she replied through a gracious smile, curtseying gently. "My husband and I are delighted and honored to be a part of this festive occasion."

"Indeed, madame." The count's smile deepened, and he had yet to release her hand. "Perhaps we can share a dance or two later, hmm?" He glanced to Jonathan abruptly as if he'd only just recalled he was there. "With your permission, of course, Monsieur Drake."

Jonathan nodded once. "And your lovely wife's?"

He expected Henri or Claudine to speak, but it was Natalie who took the lead, with keen observation of what needed to be said at the moment. "And what a beautiful home you have, Madame Lemire. You have such grand taste."

"Thank you," Claudine replied tightly.

Natalie carried on, glancing around the entryway and into the ballroom. "It's marvelously decorated, but I knew it would be the minute we stepped through your garden, so lush and well tended."

Claudine gave her a brittle smile. "Is your home in England rather too small for a garden, Madame Drake?"

It was a direct insult given without the intelligence for subtlety, and Jonathan wondered if it stemmed from simple jealousy or her dislike of the English as a whole.

Natalie rose to the occasion with wide-eyed innocence. "Oh, we have lovely gardens in England, of course, but not with such sweet aromas brought out by daily sunshine and warm, offshore breezes. And may I add that your steady exposure to sunshine has brought out such a healthy glow to your skin, Madame Lemire, unlike those of us who remain pale from lack of it."

She touched her cheek, eyes narrowing with light mischievousness as she leaned toward the Frenchwoman, pretending a whisper like old friends discussing their beloved husbands in their presence. "Perhaps I'll someday persuade my dear Jonathan to buy us a home on the shore, or maybe you can persuade him for me tonight with your good charm. How you must adore it here, as I'm sure you have for many, many years. And how I envy you!"

She was perfect and enchanting, and Jonathan swallowed a laugh.

Claudine blinked quickly, unsure if she had been com-plimented by a beautiful woman or completely duped by one more astute than she. Henri simply watched the exchange with half an ear, implying that talk between la-dies, whatever the topic, was unimportant, even bordering on the silly. Something that could also, if needed, be useful.

"We're very happy here," the Frenchwoman affirmed with growing confidence. "Tonight we are quite engaged, but perhaps you'll visit us later in the week when you can view our home and grounds by daylight, Madame Drake."

It was a frank dismissal, and Natalie responded accord-ingly. "That would be lovely, and I look forward to it." She turned to Jonathan and grasped his arm. "But come now, darling. We're holding up the line."

"Yes, of course," he agreed, nodding once to his hosts.

From there they moved down the line, introducing them-selves with light conversation to relatives and other local notables. Jonathan found it of interest but not unexpected to meet several men of old nobility from as far away as Anjou and Brittany, whose families dated from long before prerevolutionary days and whose political ties paralleled those of the count, at a ball to celebrate the eighteenth birth-day of his daughter. There was much going on behind the scenes, in anticipation of another revolution if Sir Guy was correct, and Jonathan was now convinced this party was a front for strategic planning. Those involved were ready to sell the emeralds. A triumph for arrogant minds that would be very short-lived. He was counting on it.

At last they wandered into the ballroom proper, already filled with people dancing and mingling, with music and laughter. Men in formal attire and top hats, and ladies in fine silks, taffeta, velvets, and lace of every color stood in small groups of deep discussion over politics and social issues, trivialities and gossip. Footmen in scarlet livery car-ried trays of steaming food to buffet tables, the aroma of it permeating the air along with heady perfume and the scent of a thousand burning candles. Four magnificent crystal chandeliers hung in line above their heads. Two of the four walls were adorned with enormous paintings and tapestries, the others with long, gilded windows, floor to ceiling, all lavishly decorated with drapes of red velvet, drawn back by golden ropes and tassels, golden cherubs sitting atop them as they stared down at those present with frank regard.

On the surface, a party like any at home.

In silence Jonathan guided Natalie through the crowd to a refreshment table and handed her a glass of champagne.

"You were marvelous," he said in praise.

She eyed him carefully and took a sip. "The count is sly and somewhat charming, but she's rude and jealous of him unnecessarily. Simpleminded and tactless."

Jonathan smiled wryly, taking notice of the rosy hue to her cheeks, eyes shimmering from irritation. "Very observant, but perhaps she has reason," he offered. "You outshine her beautifully from head to foot, and she knows it."

Natalie huffed, brushing over his compliment as she began to search faces in the crowd for a resemblance to the thief. Irrationally that piqued his anger.

"And like most members of the nobility," he added, "he's taken mistresses, and I'm sure she's aware of that. He probably has one now. Maybe more than one."

Jonathan had no idea why he said that, it just seemed the perfect remark to grab her attention. It worked, too, for she quickly looked back to his face, her brows pinched in a light frown of disapproval.

"This might come as a complete surprise to you, Jonathan, but not all gentlemen of breeding have adulterous affairs. Many obviously consider it a right of good birth and take advantage of wealth and opportunity, flaunting their paramours for all to admire." She drew a long breath and raised her chin stubbornly. "But there are others, regardless of the fact that they are few in number, who are wonderful men with keen moral judgment, rigid self-control, and sufficient love for their wives and families to remain faithful."

He lifted his glass to his lips, curious as to how and where she acquired this information, but refusing to ask because that was exactly what she wanted. Instead he lowered his voice and returned candidly, "You're really passionate about this, aren't you, sweetheart?"

Her cheeks warmed a deeper shade of pink, but she stared at him levelly, ignoring the sweetheart comment either by choice or because she was already fuming. He hoped it was the latter.

"Perhaps it's something you should take note of, Jonathan," she advised a bit derisively. "How positively tragic it would be for me to learn that your future wife stabbed you through the heart with the count's mighty sword due to your lack of self-containment. Knowing your particular reputation, I suggest you reconsider buying it." She grinned in speculation. "Come to think of it, if you marry a feisty, jealous lady, she'll have a wide range of weapons to choose from already hanging on your study wall. If I were you I'd sell them all."

Jonathan felt the urge to pull her into his arms and kiss her senseless, to hold her tightly and relish the feel of her breasts against his chest, to run his fingers through her hair, and to hell with everyone present. He restrained himself, however, by taking another large swallow of champagne, his gaze never wavering.

"I'm delighted to hear how much you care for my well-being, Natalie. But considering how much I cherish my existence, as well as my extensive and priceless collection of weapons, I think I'd rather give up my pursuit of the ladies. Particularly," he added in a whisper, leaning close so only she could hear, "if I marry someone as beautiful and challenging as you, my sweet. You would undoubtedly keep me in fear of my life should I break my vows."

She stared at him, eyes large, measured alarm gracing her features as she considered a binding, permanent union between them, probably for the first time.

"But then again I shouldn't worry," he continued off-handedly, raising his free palm to cup her chin, tracing her jaw with his thumb. "You'd have me so exhausted in the marriage bed I would never have energy enough to go elsewhere for a pleasure that couldn't possibly compare to what I get from you anyway."

Now she gaped at him, thoroughly startled and speechless. There was nothing he enjoyed more than teasing Nat-

alie Haislett into shocked silence, and he grinned broadly,
knowing she understood this as well and that it infuriated
her to acknowledge it.

Before she could verbally attack him in response, he
pulled the champagne glass from her fingertips, discarding
it next to his empty one on a side table, and lightly gripped
her arm. "I see Madeleine. It's time for an introduction."

For the most part, Natalie adored parties of all kinds. At
the age of five she'd been allowed a peek at her first—
something her mother had called a small gathering, which
actually turned out to include more than ninety people. She
had been overawed by the glitter, the laughter and music,
the color of coattails and skirts, tables upon tables of food,
the flowing champagne. Twice more in her childhood she'd
caught a glimpse of the glamour, until 1842, the season of
her debut, when she'd finally been allowed to attend. That
was the summer of the masked ball where she'd met Jonathan.

She wanted to cringe from the memory of that first dance
so long ago. That first kiss. Oh, God, how that one small
event had turned her life upside-down!

Tonight he was her escort, handsome and sophisticated
and smooth as new satin, astounding her with his ability to
charm, to coerce, to lie with ease and perfection. Her
cheeks burned from his suggestive comment, but regardless
of the attempt she couldn't think of a suitable thing to say
in response to something so presumptuous. And ridiculous.
So she kept her mouth shut, moving in step with him like
an obedient puppy.

Quickly he guided her toward the edge of the dance floor
where a group of ladies stood talking, wildly animated. So
like the French to be enthusiastic when they were no doubt
discussing how the count's wife dressed like a child ready
to walk the Easter Parade. The English would discuss her
lack of taste, too, but they, at least, would be staid and
discreet about it.

Then her eyes fell on Madeleine DuMais. Natalie recognized her immediately, a stunning woman, tall and elegant, with chestnut hair parted down the middle and pulled

up high on her crown to cascade down her neck in soft ringlets. She wore a rich satin gown of modern cut in striking royal purple, with bold yellow rosebuds on the bodice and hem, and accentuating black lace flounces covering the low pointed neckline, enhancing her full breasts and tiny waist. In one hand she held a half-parted black-and-gold fan; a long, sheer black shawl flowed over the opposite wrist. Speaking to the ladies beside her, she was fluid and graceful, and stood out above them all. She was the kind of woman Natalie perceived as taking a country by storm, as one who would live on through the ages because men in love with her dream would die to possess her, writing poetry and stories of battles to defend her honor. She was that beautiful.

Jonathan walked up beside her, and she turned, a look of delight brightening her face and filling her bold, light-blue eyes as she recognized him.

"Monsieur Drake, I'm so pleased you could attend this evening," she said through a shining smile, staring at him openly, brushing aside the other ladies who carried on their conversations without notice.

Jonathan took her long fingers in his, bowed, and kissed them. "Madame DuMais, it is always a pleasure." He turned. "May I present to you my wife, Natalie."

A most uncomfortable moment seemed to stretch for hours as Natalie, feeling suddenly small and homely, stood stiffly by his side, squeezing her fan with tight fingers, while the Frenchwoman's gaze fell upon her at last.

"Madame Drake. At last we meet," she addressed her in heavily accented English. "Your husband has spoken so well of you I feel I know you already, although to be truthful"—she looked her up and down—"he was somewhat lacking in complements as husbands usually are. What a beauty you are!" She glanced at Jonathan, shaking her head in feigned disgust. "My late husband was the same. A dear man who described me to everyone as 'tall with dark hair.' Nothing more. A pity we go to such trouble with our appearance—expensive   gowns   and   perfumes   and years of practicing the finer graces—when no one really notices but other ladies.''

Natalie grinned, liking her instantly, with no real idea why. Up close she spotted the subtle traces of false color on the woman's face—lips redder than natural, a touch of kohl outlining her lids to make her eyes stand out, and rouge to pinken her cheeks. Her mother's voice thundered at once into her otherwise pleasant thoughts: ''A lady of quality does *not* paint her face. She enhances that with which God has blessed her by adding only a delicate pinch to the cheek or a gentle bite to the lip for soft color.'' No, her mother wouldn't care for this woman at all, and Natalie liked her all the more for it.

Confidence returning, she relaxed. ''Indeed, Madame DuMais, I understand perfectly. Gowns in all colors and cuts for every function line my wardrobe, and yet my dear Jonathan no doubt described me to you as 'short and rather pale, but of good family.' '' She tapped her fan against her free palm. ''So typically English; more typically male.''

Jonathan looked amused, hands clasped behind his back, mouth twisted in a half smile. ''I suppose I did forget to mention your beautiful assets, my darling,'' he replied conversationally, though peering straight into her eyes. ''Deliciously curvy, hair the color of a sunset, eyes like jewels, a smile to light a room.'' He pursed his lips, brows furrowing. ''But of course I tell everyone you are of good family. Why else would one marry?''

Natalie flushed from his blunt statement and open regard, but her eyes sparkled with pleasure as she answered dramatically, ''Good breeding aside, I married you for your money, Jonathan.''

He bowed fully, and Madeleine threw her head back in a small laugh. ''Goodness, such honesty between you. And my dear Natalie—may I call you Natalie? And you must call me Madeleine. I married my late husband for the same reason, and may I say I have been able to enjoy every minute of his death.''

Natalie stifled a giggle, watching Jonathan, who appeared captivated by the conversation.

"I shall take that as good advice, Madeleine," she noted brightly. "Perhaps I'll be as fortunate."

"Let's hope so." Smiling, Madeleine took her by the arm. "Now, I'm sure your husband would like to wander into the smoking room, or do whatever it is men do at such functions." She looked to Jonathan. "If you do not mind, Monsieur Drake, I will take your wife and introduce her to a friend or two. And I'm certain she and I have many things to discuss."

"I've no doubt," he replied dryly. "Just please don't change her mind about how much she adores me."

Madeleine's grin broadened for him. "Impossible to do, I'm sure."

Natalie fidgeted and for the first time caught a glimpse, an impression really, of something more between them. Not suggestive, or even implying closeness, but a kind of . . . understanding. As if they knew a secret she didn't.

"And Natalie?"

She shook herself from that uncomfortable thought and gazed back to his face.

His eyelids thinned when they met hers. "We'll dance later."

It was a simple and innocuous statement, and yet anxiousness flourished from the look he gave her—intense and full of meaning. As if they were the only people in the room.

She nodded minutely. Then Madeleine pulled on her elbow, and he swung around and disappeared into the crowd.

For twenty minutes the Frenchwoman introduced her to various acquaintances, most accepting her presence there indifferently if not a bit coolly. Natalie was as gracious and attentive as she could be under the circumstances, her face and manner expressing an easy consideration to those around her, while inside she boiled with apprehension. She wanted to follow Jonathan, not exchange pleasantries with the French elite. She wanted to observe from the shadows when he met the Black Knight, to see the legend for the first time unnoticed. She was almost beside herself, knowing the thief might already be at the ball, that he might already have spoken to Jonathan, that he might even now know of her presence.

"Why don't we talk a little," Madeleine suggested, leading her toward a group of mostly empty straight-backed chairs in the far corner of the ballroom.

"I'd like that," Natalie returned absentmindedly, eyes skimming the crowd as time seemed to drag while her restlessness steadily increased.

After gracefully sitting beneath a large, lovely portrait of a child kneeling in a blooming rose garden, and after taking the necessary time to straighten skirts to avoid wrinkles and entangled hems, Madeleine asked directly, "What brings you to France, Natalie?"

The question took her by surprise, forcing her to focus her attention back on the woman beside her instead of each dark-haired gentleman of the Black Knight's vague description within her view. "I beg your pardon?"

Madeleine opened her fan and began lightly to brush the air in front of her face. "I'm wondering what brings you to France since I do understand perfectly your relationship with Jonathan."

Natalie's first thought was that she hadn't realized her faux husband and this woman were on first-name terms. But of course they would be. They actually appeared to be more than acquaintances, and had, after all, spent some time alone together in the lady's home discussing their business arrangement, which, on the whole, still sounded suspicious to her.

She sat a little straighter in her chair, hands placed properly in her lap, annoyed that the reflection should bother her. "Jonathan has agreed to introduce me to a friend."

Madeleine's brows rose. "Really."

The simple comment implied disbelief, or at the very least suspicion in her own right. The air began to feel unpleasantly warm with the growing number of people filling the ballroom, and Natalie raised her opened fan as well, steadily swishing it in front of her.

"May I be candid with you, Madeleine?" she asked after a moment of silence.

The Frenchwoman breathed deeply and leaned gingerly on one padded, velveteen armrest, eyeing her with calculation. "I hope you will be. Please believe I can be your friend, too, Natalie."

Again, a simple statement saying little, and yet Natalie felt the woman's honesty, and her own urge to confide. She shifted her body in her chair, angling closer and lowering her voice. "Have you heard of the English thief called the Black Knight?"

The only noticeable sign that Madeleine heeded her words was the slightest pause in the movement of her fan. Then she murmured, "Yes."

Natalie gathered her courage. "I believe he's here, in Marseilles, and that Jonathan knows him personally. I'm paying him to introduce us."

A shot of rolling laughter broke out in a small group of ladies to their left. Madeleine's concentration, however, remained transfixed on her, with only the barest flicker of puzzled amusement crossing her features.

"I wonder how he intends to go about this introduction," she said very slowly.

Natalie considered that a rather odd thing to say when she expected questions. "I–I'm not sure," she stammered, straightening. "He's supposed to be at the ball tonight."

Now the Frenchwoman appeared enthralled, dropping her fan to her lap and sitting forward. "Is he? And why, do you suppose?"

That thought had only occurred to her once before, in their hot hotel room by the harbor, and even then Jonathan hadn't been forthcoming regarding his guess as to why the thief would attend this particular party. She assumed it related to the sword Jonathan intended to purchase, but now this seemed far-fetched. The Black Knight was an expert at intrigue and deception, working for the good of governments, the underprivileged. What would he want with a sword? And how could he steal it in front of five hundred people and out from under the count's crafty, observant nose? He couldn't, wouldn't, and now she felt her confidence abating as her confusion grew. If he appeared at all, it would be for something else, something she hadn't yet considered.

"I can't imagine that he would attend a ball in honor of the comte d'Arles's daughter because he's a family friend or acquaintance," Natalie conceded at last. "That just seems too incredible. Logic then suggests he'd be here on business, more exactly to steal something. And if he came all the way to the south of France to steal, the object of his interest must be of great value." She sighed and shook her head. "But this is just guessing on my part. I really don't know."

Madeleine didn't appear to notice her stupefaction. Instead, her entire countenance flashed with levelheaded fascination. "The only thing I can think of small enough for a thief to steal at a ball would be . . . oh . . . documents the count might possess somewhere in his home, or more likely a lady's priceless jewels. Something he can hide in a pocket—perhaps a diamond brooch or a ruby ring."

Natalie frowned. "But why come all the way to France to steal a brooch? He could do that in England."

Madeleine pursed her full, red lips, forehead crinkling in prudent thought. "Unless this particular brooch has priceless value of a different sort."

Without trying to sound too terribly ignorant, she asked, "In what way would jewels have value beyond what they're worth in sale?"

The Frenchwoman began fanning herself again. "Well, imagine for instance they could be traded for important documents that might be of some use to the British government."

"Trade a stolen French brooch for French documents . . . ," she thought aloud.

"Or maybe the Black Knight is here to confiscate jewels originally stolen from a British subject," Madeleine proposed instead.

Natalie contemplated that one and had to surmise it made the best sense of all, given the man's penchant for returning items he steals.

Madeleine leaned very close again, eyes sparkling.

"Every good thief must have a reason behind his actions," she concluded in a whisper. "And the Black Knight especially isn't known for stealing items for money alone. If Jonathan expects him here tonight, I think I will watch those ladies wearing priceless jewels. This could turn out to be a very eventful and entertaining evening."

Natalie glanced out at the party guests once more, observing ladies dressed in finery mingling, gentlemen idling around buffet tables, couples laughing, whispering, dancing to a beautiful Viennese waltz being expertly played by a twenty-piece orchestra. Nearly every lady she could see wore diamonds or sapphires, or something just as valuable displayed for all to admire. The target could be any of them, providing Madeleine's conjecture was correct.

"May I inquire why you've come all the way to Marseilles to meet him?"

Her eyes shot back to Madeleine's.

The Frenchwoman smiled perceptively, pushing a dark curl from her temple with the back of an elegant hand. "It is a somewhat daring pursuit, don't you think?"

For the first time that night, Natalie considered lying. Her reasons were so personal, even embarrassing, and confiding in anyone might actually be risky, for many complicated reasons. She could also never admit to anyone that she had bright visions from time to time of herself in the arms of the Thief of Europe. That was just too silly, though it would probably be believed considering the standard romantic nature of most unmarried ladies her age. Still, as much as she enjoyed this woman's company, and although she needed to say something, it behooved her to divulge as little as necessary.

Absentmindedly she touched the cameo at her neck, rubbing it between her fingers. "I'm very much interested in him professionally. I need him to help me locate something quite important and—personal."

Madeleine stared hard at her for several silent seconds. "Oh, I see. . . ."

Natalie started to feel agitated again, uncomfortably warm. This wasn't where she wanted the conversation to go and she hoped Madeleine wouldn't be so unmannerly as to delve deeper into her private thoughts and plans. She decided not to let her by changing the topic of conversation herself.

"So tell me, how did you arrange for Jonathan to purchase the comte d'Arles's priceless sword, and I assume it's priceless?"

Madeleine's expression never changed. For a long moment she looked at her boldly, features neutral but eyes vividly alert. Then with care she pulled her shawl from her arm and draped it across her lap.

"Yes, it's priceless," she acknowledged, "which I believe is the only reason he traveled so far from home to acquire it. The interest in the transaction came to me by rumor because my late husband was a trader and knew various men of importance in the Paris area. The count lives there for part of the year. But I didn't ask Jonathan why he wanted to buy it, and I really don't know the details. I merely set up the meeting."

Natalie smiled. "It does sound a bit ridiculous, but to be fair the man collects weapons, both modern and antique, as a hobby."

Madeleine studied her critically again. "I assumed he must."

She felt warmth creeping into her cheeks and decided it best to clarify. "Of course, I've only been in his home once, in his study, but he has one wall covered with swords and pistols and other sundry munitions. I suppose they're probably worth a small fortune."

Madeleine softened, gracing her with a knowing grin. "Really? I suppose collecting is a common diversion for a gentleman, though, is it not?"

Natalie closed her fan, placing it in her lap.

"It's certainly a diversion for him," she acquiesced, a trace of amusement coloring her tone. "And it is an extensive collection in which I know he takes a great deal of pride. I would just find myself more impressed if a gentleman as sharp and impassioned as Jonathan better spent his time on more worthy or notable causes, perhaps addressing government issues or social problems. Instead, he seems to spend much of his life in frivolous pursuits of personal enjoyment, traveling the world at his leisure, spending his money on insignificant treasures." She shook her head. "So much time . . . playing."

It occurred to her at that moment, with some surprise, that she'd never thought of him in such detail before, considering the fine points of his personality with no knowledge of childhood factors that might have shaped him, molding him into the man he was now. And she'd also just described almost exactly the type of unconventional man she'd told Jonathan on the ship she wanted to marry—a man not tied to stiff society and its stifling mores, but free and adventurous and filled with the desire to experience the joys and excitement of life. Irritably she also realized he would have caught this blunder of hers at the time.

"You like him, don't you?" Madeleine asked quietly, eyes intense and full of insight.

"Yes, I do," she admitted through a sigh, slumping a little into her corset. "He's very charming and considerate, as I'm sure you're aware. But our relationship is strictly one of casual friendship. Nothing more."

"Of course not," Madeleine agreed appropriately with a slight drop of her chin.

Natalie's voice tightened as she added, "All women seem to be aware of his attractive personality. They adore him, and he knows it. He thrives on it, which is *not* one of his better qualities. But naturally that's none of my business."

Madeleine chuckled softly, studying her for a second or two, head tilted. Then she reached for her hand and squeezed it gently. "I wouldn't judge him so severely, Natalie. The man has more depth and devotion than you probably realize."

For a moment she wondered how the Frenchwoman would know this. Before she could comment, however, Madeleine's expression thinned as her gaze shifted to a group of ladies strolling in their direction.

"Oh, dear. Madame Vachon and her tiresome daughter,

Helene.'' She sighed, grasped her fan and shawl, and gracefully stood. ''Helene does nothing but talk of the gaieties of Paris and how she married above us all—a financier, I believe, of noble blood, who died unexpectedly on the honeymoon and left her a fortune. I suppose I should intercept them first and say hello.''

Natalie took the opportunity, standing as well and swishing her opened fan again, attempting to keep the eagerness out of her voice. ''I think I'll walk a little, then. Maybe wander into the foyer where it isn't quite so stuffy.''

''A good idea,'' Madeleine agreed. ''And it's probably time you looked for Jonathan. The count's daughter will be down shortly.'' She stepped forward, then paused and turned back. ''Do not be blind to his admirable qualities as a man, Natalie,'' she admonished quietly. ''Everything you want for yourself is available to you here, although your greatest desire may not be wrapped in the package you would choose to open first.''

That bold statement confounded Natalie, leaving her uncharacteristically blank of response. Again she sensed that Mme. DuMais knew something she did not, that she and Jonathan were guarding secrets within secrets, of people and events of deeper meaning. But it was a troubling thought so vague she could do nothing about it, least of all put it into words.

Madeleine smiled again as if reading her mind. ''Remember, you can always confide in me, about anything. Find me later and we'll talk more.'' With that she lifted the full skirt of her beautiful gown, pivoted smoothly, and walked away.

It took Jonathan nearly fifteen minutes just to meander through groups of people, into the foyer, and up the stairs. Of course, if anyone asked, he'd say he was looking for his wife, or that he'd heard the count had an outstanding private art collection in his study and that he thought several acquaintances had mentioned they'd be viewing it momentarily. When he was consequently informed he was mistaken, he'd stress that he only knew a little French and perhaps he'd misunderstood. His charm would get him through if he were caught. If Jonathan was anything, he was experienced with deception.

But he didn't get caught, and he wasn't seen once he slipped out of the foyer and up the staircase, and in actuality he spoke far better French than anyone would ever guess. He was a master of his craft, but what made him great was that he was never pompous. He was humble enough—or perhaps smart enough was a more accurate phrase—to realize he could never afford the luxury of arrogance. Every time he left his home to do a job, he calculated the different ways of being exposed, of someone learning his intentions and discovering his identity. He knew that without caution and an alert mind ready for immediate change in action, always, he could end up jailed or more likely dead. Neither was a possibility he liked to contemplate.

Quietly he made his way along the hallway. The lights were low, though not unusually so for a private home this time of night. Naturally neither the family nor staff felt it necessary to illuminate brightly an area that really wouldn't, and shouldn't, be traversed by a party guest.

His shoes made a soft padding noise on the dark carpet, but the gaiety of the ballroom below muffled any echo he might have made with his stride. Annette-Elise and her maids were on the same floor, though at the other end of the house, getting ready for an entrance less than twenty minutes away, but his greatest concern was stumbling into servants. As in all grand households, they were everywhere—in the shadows and corners and otherwise vacant rooms. Like furniture, as some without consideration tended to treat them—with function but lacking minds or feelings. Jonathan knew better and deemed them as threatening as Lemire himself.

He needed to hurry. He was beginning to feel an almost unnatural ache to be back in the ballroom by Natalie's side. She would become suspicious if he didn't return soon, and he trusted Madeleine to keep her entertained for only so long before her mischievous nature took over and she considered looking for him.

At last he reached the study door. He paused, listening, ear pressed close to the panel for any sound coming from the other side. Nothing.

He placed his palm on the knob, turned it until it clicked, and pushed the door open.

The room was dark. Moonglow through the windows added little brightness, but it was too risky to find a lamp. He would have to do without, he decided, closing the door behind him.

He knew the layout well. Desk to the right, two chairs sitting opposite, cold fireplace along the west wall, the safe above the mantel. He waited only seconds for his eyes to adjust, then promptly felt his way across the room, ears sharp, mind alert should he need to prevaricate.

At last Jonathan stood before the safe, the Fragonard now lowered from its hanging position on the wall. He reached out and touched the cold metal. The safe was wide open and empty. Annette-Elise would be wearing the emeralds tonight, as rumor foretold.

Nimbly he stuck his fingers into the folds of his breast pocket and pulled out a small velvet pouch. Then with care, he set it inside, easily seen and ready to be discovered.

He grinned broadly in the blackness.

His plans were falling into place.

Nine

Henri Lemire quietly stepped inside his private library on the second floor, tumbler in hand filled to the brim with excellent whiskey, and closed the door behind him. Less than twenty minutes until Annette-Elise's debut, and he would need to be present. Decisions would have to be made quickly here now, as time was critical, and this would likely be their only opportunity tonight.

Alain Sirois, vicomte de Lyon, had already entered, squeezing his rotund frame into one of the two brown leather chairs. He had arrived only late last night, making this their first opportunity to speak privately, and unfortunately it would have to be in haste. Michel Faille would be here as well, any second now, and finally they would get down to the business of saving France.

Alain began to chatter about his annoyance with his wife, an obnoxious woman, loud and round and ugly. Henri leaned against a bookshelf, smiling and nodding attentively when necessary, sipping his whiskey while his mind wandered to much more pleasing issues, like Madame Quinet's large breasts rubbing his chest during a dance promised him later, or serious issues like the precious emerald necklace to be dismantled with care and sold tomorrow at noon. Alain, with his white, thinning hair, long pointed nose, and dark eyes like a crow's, was nearly as irritating to look at as he was to listen to. But he had excellent connections in Paris and was extremely useful to their cause, so Henri treated him like an old family friend, which of course he was not. Everything else aside, however, Alain loathed Louis Philippe, and that was their common thread.

Alain fell silent, to Henri's relief, as the door opened for a second time and Michel Faille, vicomte de Rouen, entered without pause. An outrageously tall man, he stood at nearly six and a half feet and was thin of build but carried himself awkwardly for someone who had possessed such a body for more than fifty years. He maintained a harsh, shrewd personality, often cruel and coarse to his inferiors, but had features like those of a dove—pale complexion, graying hair, unnaturally soft skin like that of a woman's, and large brown eyes with droopy lids. His looks had served him well through the years because they caught people unawares. One would treat him like a sweet, gentle man only to learn he could be brilliant and almost evil in thought and action. Henri actually admired him for that.

"Lovely party, Henri," Michel noted with sarcasm, strolling to the only empty chair in the room. He sat clumsily, his huge feet planted on the plush Aubusson carpet, which naturally placed his knees above the armrests in height. "I assume we can talk candidly here."

It was a statement, not a question, and Henri ignored it. "The sale is set for tomorrow noon," he began after a long swallow from his glass. "I'll ride into the city about ten and should be back here by one or two, cash in hand. We'll divide it evenly tomorrow night after which you two will return home. The affair in Paris is two weeks from tonight. Our gracious king plans to attend, at least for now, and we will go with that—"

"Not enough time, Henri," Alain interjected with a snort, attempting in vain to adjust his enormous body in the chair.

"Of course it's enough time," Michel snapped irritably. "Don't be stupid. Starving men walk the streets of Paris by the thousands. Any one of them will do it tomorrow for a price. Hiring a professional instead is just better business, and this is business, Alain. We must be diligent and careful, but act fast.'' He shifted his supple, feminine gaze to Henri, turning his attention to a matter more urgent. ''Where are the jewels now?''

Henri drew a long, steady breath, stalling for thought as he began to pace in front of bookshelves lired floor to ceiling along the wall, snugly filled with leather-bound volumes of literature, poetry, and history. They weren't going to like his answer at all, but it was his house, his beloved daughter, and by all rights, his emeralds. He was the one to devise the plan, and he was the one who paid to have them stolen in the first place. Any argument on their part would be moot at best.

''Annette-Elise is wearing them as we speak—''

''What!'' Michel nearly jumped from his chair, his features turning from their natural look of mild weakness to controlled rage.

Henri's head flipped around. ''Be quiet, Michel!'' he said vehemently in a whisper, face taut. ''A servant will hear, or perhaps someone walking the halls.''

Alain reddened and began to sweat profusely. He mumbled under his breath and reached into his breast pocket for a handkerchief, using it to pat his face with shaking hands. Michel sat again, staring rigidly at his host, raising one gangly arm to rest the elbow on the back of the chair in an unsuccessful attempt to find a comfortable position.

Henri gave them both a second or two to calm, finishing off his whiskey with three large gulps. ''The emeralds are secure,'' he insisted. ''They've been locked in my personal safe for weeks until thirty minutes ago when I clasped them about my daughter's neck myself.'' His eyes grew bright and round as he confronted them both with logic. ''Who, do you suppose, is going to steal them from there, hmm? At a party of five hundred guests? Ridiculous thought! Half the women invited are wearing precious gems—''

''Not like these,'' Alain cut in once more, his voice choked.

Henri placed his empty tumbler on a shelf and leaned

toward them, his impatience brewing as he forced his voice to drop to just above a whisper. "They are exquisite jewels, made to be worn by queens and empresses. It is only fitting they should be worn for the last time by my beautiful, innocent daughter at her only debut."

"Arrogant bastard," Michel sputtered between velvety soft lips and strong, clenched teeth.

Henri smirked boastfully. "Perhaps I am. But tonight they are still mine, gentlemen. I have been the one to take the risks, not either of you, and certainly not others who are only half inclined to agree with our policies to protect a rightful king." Pulling himself up to stand erect, he smoothed his tailcoat and grumbled in light warning, "Tomorrow they will be sold so that legitimate French nobility, who have waited decades to reclaim the throne for Louis's heir, can also regain their deserved power and position given them centuries ago by church and God himself. Tonight is a prelude. Tomorrow it begins."

It was a bold statement, grossly exaggerated, filled with uncertainties, and they all knew it. Still, it had its dramatic effect, as the three men, for a static moment, all looked at each other, weighing decisions, the cost to reputations and bank accounts, the pleasure of the pursuit, and victory overriding the grave situations that might arise if they were wrong, if they were discovered. But they had been planning for far too long to turn back now. And not one of them would admit they wanted to.

Faint music and muffled laughter filtered through the floorboards from the ballroom below. Then Alain swallowed hard and pursued the essentials. "Time is short. If we are to be on guard when your daughter makes her debut wearing priceless jewels, you'd better tell us quickly about Paris, Henri. . . ."

Natalie climbed the stairs to the second-floor landing, arranging her wide skirts with purpose to keep from tripping. Nearly everyone was in the ballroom; only one or two guests lingered in the foyer, most of them making their way down the hall to the smoking and withdrawing rooms. Nobody appeared to notice her, and if they did they would think her only a mere woman lost as usual, or looking for her wandering husband, perhaps herself intent on meeting a lover for a few passionate kisses in the darkness. All very common occurrences at parties.

Her intent was to find Jonathan, who was undoubtedly engrossed in some escapade or another, probably searching for the count's personal antiques, which the Frenchman likely kept in his study or personal library. Or maybe, with any great hope, he was even now engaged in conversation with the Black Knight. These were the two things that could best explain his disappearance, other than his own involvement with a woman in the shadows, and that she refused to consider at all, even knowing his personal inclinations. She couldn't imagine Jonathan lounging away the evening in the smoking room, discussing politics and the hunt with other men. It wasn't his style. He would more likely be dancing and charming the ladies who were so neglected by their own. *That* was Jonathan, but she knew he wasn't in the ballroom right now, nor in the rooms on the first floor, where she'd already quickly peeked.

Standing at the top of the stairs at last, she found herself unsure. She would have to make a choice—right or left—and one guess was as good as the next. Then she saw a thin, brown-haired girl in a smart, starched gray gown and white apron and cap step onto the landing from the nearly invisible servants' staircase, pressed gentlemen's shirts in hand, who turned toward the north hallway and disappeared around the corner.

She was heading to the family's private quarters, Natalie speculated, which meant the library was probably to the left. Not necessarily, but a decent guess.

Natalie turned the corner, chancing one last glance behind and down the stairs to make sure she wasn't being followed, and fairly tiptoed through the deserted hallway, feeling a bit guilty for trespassing on private ground. In her mind, however, her excuse was valid.

Unexpectedly she heard voices, rich and deep, though cushioned enough from thick paneled walls to hush the words. She stopped in the center of the corridor, intending only to listen long enough to decide if Jonathan's voice was one of them, then the intrigue enveloped her, and she pressed her ear against the door.

Jonathan heard the voices, too, as he stood in total darkness, coming from the count's library in the room behind the wall safe.

It took him by surprise, as all was silent until the muted conversation started. He waited several moments, trying to distinguish words and phrases or if the discussion was of great importance, but ultimately he couldn't understand anything from his location. More to the point, if he couldn't learn anything by eavesdropping, there was no reason to risk being found in the count's darkened study. He would be better caught in the hallway if at all.

In four strides he was once again at the door. Then he heard rustling from the library—a clunk, a raised voice.

It was possible they were leaving, and if true he would be stuck in the study until they were gone. With any luck they would head toward the ballroom and not his direction, but he had to be prepared for the possibility of being dis- covered.

Calmly, his quick mind shifting into alert as he prepared a plausible scenario for his being there when there really wasn't one, he reached for the knob, opened the door a crack, and peered down the hallway. What he saw both startled and unnerved him.

Natalie was there, hips swaying in her full-skirted ball gown as she walked swiftly toward the main landing. Just as she rounded the corner, the count emerged from the li- brary followed by two men, one average in height, the other incredibly tall and ungainly. All French nobles; all with common interest in deposing the current king of France.

What the hell was *she* doing there? Listening—or look- ing for him? It was possible she knew the French language to some degree, as most English ladies were so taught, but it was unlikely that she spoke it fluently or she would have used a few words in his presence while they were in France.

Most chilling of all, he realized in that instant, was the consideration that she might have been observed in the shadows or rounding the corner by the count himself. In that case, knowledge on her part was irrelevant. A very powerful and wealthy French count, if he had been discussing national security issues, and by all accounts they were discussing precisely that, would have to assume she knew something and would be inclined to take action.

Jonathan sucked in a breath, standing motionless, door opened to a crack only the width of his eye, as the count glanced in his direction. Then with haste the three men turned and strode in the direction of the ballroom.

He waited nearly five minutes, which dragged immeasurably slowly. But he couldn't chance one of the Frenchmen noticing him following. Finally time grew critical, and he had to move.

Smoothly he opened the door and stepped into the deserted corridor. With haste, and without observing a soul, he walked to the center landing, down the stairs, and into the ballroom. Already the noise level had risen as the area had become more crowded. It took him another five minutes to find Natalie, standing with Madeleine near one of the long windows, now opened to cool the room with a more imagined than obvious breeze, her side to him as she fanned herself while listening to an enormous woman, pink-cheeked and perspiring, bellowing with laughter at herself and a comment she was making.

Then slowly Natalie turned to him, as if feeling his presence more than realizing it, a delicate, almost indistinguishable smile parting her lips when she looked into his eyes.

Jonathan felt ridiculously like an adolescent, his heartbeat increasing, mouth drying from nothing more than staring at her beautiful face softening for him alone. He saw neither fear nor anxiousness in her gaze, but rather yielding warmth and questions she was aching to ask. Whatever she'd heard in the count's private library, if anything at all, either wasn't enough to concern her—or she was hiding it flawlessly.

Clasping his hands behind his back, he sauntered up to

the ladies, who stopped talking as he approached. "Walk in the garden with me, Natalie?"

Madeleine looked at him. "Oh, yes, go," she insisted.

"But the count's daughter is expected now. It would be rude," Natalie argued without conviction.

Jonathan leaned toward her and lowered his voice. "What better time could there be? Everyone will be in here."

He watched her hesitate, eyes shifting over the crowd, weighing the possibility of learning something from him that perhaps he couldn't divulge in the presence of others. Madeleine had turned her attention to the large woman again, both in discussion once more, this time in French, which meant they'd already taken note of their impending absence. He took Natalie's arm and, without another word, led her by the elbow into the foyer, out the front doors, and into the garden.

They weren't alone, as yet. Three or four other couples strolled along the brick path that meandered through the grounds, most arm in arm, communing in muted tones, laughing softly. The scent of flowers and freshly cut grass filled the calm night air. Lamplight brightened the walkway in hues of dimmed yellow; music and conversation from the ballroom filtered through the partially opened windows to mix with the buzzing insects of nighttime and the far distant sound of the sea.

The warm, serene atmosphere enveloped them both, as Jonathan laced his arm through Natalie's, drawing her closer without confrontation on her part. She hadn't spoken since they'd walked outside, but she wasn't rushed or bothered, and in fact seemed quite comfortable alone with him in the somewhat intimate atmosphere.

"Enjoying yourself?" he asked politely.

"Enough. It's beautiful here." She glanced at him sideways. "And you?"

He watched her face, half in shadows, half illuminated by the golden light of the house behind them. She was smiling, though her eyes pierced his for enlightenment. "I suppose. I especially like that you're here with me."

It was the manner in which he said the words—subdued and serious—that took her aback. Her smile faded a little, then she turned her head so that she faced the garden once more. They walked in silence a few more steps, until he spied a wrought-iron bench near the southeast corner and directed her toward it.

"Jonathan—"

"I have something to ask you, Natalie," he cut in pensively.

She hesitated, then allowed herself to be seated, straightening her skirts once more as he stood slightly to her side, arms crossed over his chest.

"Please," she acknowledged with a wave of her palm.

He knew she was anxious to delve into matters of her concern but was purposely holding her abrasive tongue in check lest he decide to forgo the all-important meeting that had brought her to France. He felt another surge of modest power over her at that moment as he stared down at her face, illuminated dimly by golden lamplight.

Tilting his head, he asked cautiously, "How well do you speak French?"

That surprised her, as he knew it would, and her expression of mystification was what he wanted to see. She had no idea where the conversation was heading.

She squirmed a little, wringing her fan in her lap. "That's a rather odd thing to ask."

He looked to the brick pathway, rubbing his leather-soled shoes along the pebbles. "It's not an embarrassing or even unusual question, Natalie."

She waited several seconds, then sighed and relaxed against the back of the bench. "I speak fluent French, although I can't imagine why it should matter to you that I do."

He wasn't amazed by the answer, and yet somewhere in the back of his mind he began to heed a caution, as yet unclear. Looking into her eyes once more, he reasoned, "And you learned the language from a fastidious governess?"

She gave him a flat smile. "My mother made it imperative. She insisted I not lose my heritage, for what it's worth.''

His brows rose. ''Lose your heritage?''

Her features grew serious, and she hugged herself at the elbows, causing her breasts to flow together into swells of creamy softness. He tried not to glance down at them as he concentrated on her face.

At last she murmured, ''My maternal grandfather was the count of Bourges.''

The air stilled around them as Jonathan suddenly became absorbed by her words. He stared openly at her as the seconds ticked by, but she continued without notice.

''Actually, he was a wealthy and well-respected count before the Revolution of ninety-two. In one night he lost everything as peasants stormed his country home. Through a bit of luck he paid off a jailer with bits of gold he had hidden on his person, and two days before he was to be shipped to Paris for trial and certain death, with the help of the bishop of Blois and various hard-line clergy, he managed to wade his way through the country until he found passage to England, as did a few other lucky French nobles. A few years later, after building a small fortune in trade, he married my grandmother and had three daughters and a son. My mother was the youngest.''

Jonathan's mind raced from her disclosure. Possibilities were innumerable now. ''Why didn't you tell me?''

''Goodness, Jonathan. You make it sound as if I'm keeping deliberate secrets.'' She sat forward, dropping her arms as she reached for her fan again. Absentmindedly she began tapping it in her lap. ''It's not really information one goes around spreading in polite society.''

He couldn't argue that. Being one-quarter French wasn't necessarily bad. On the other hand, it didn't speak well in making a good marriage when one wasn't completely English, or when one's grandparents and distant relations were Catholic. Though unimportant, these incidentals could have an effect on some in the social whirl, for nothing else but gossip. This said nothing of the English view of the French and sexual promiscuity and culture. Now that he thought about it, he supposed not mentioning a French count for a grandfather was probably well advised for those other than family or close friends.

He leaned against the lamppost. "Why haven't you spoken the language here?"

Now she grinned in droll merriment. "Doesn't it seem more logical to act the innocent in the exchange?"

His forehead pinched in confusion, and she leaned toward him so closely her face was nearly to his waist.

"Remember shopping Thursday, in that little boutique near the waterfront?"

He snickered. "I remember the offensively priced, ugly brown bonnet you bought to add to your scant wardrobe."

She ignored the sarcastic comment, though her lids thinned with feigned disgust. "It was a chocolate-colored silk and quite fashionable, but that is beside the point. I purchased the bonnet although I didn't need it—"

"You're joking," he interjected, straight-faced.

"You don't understand," she insisted patiently, sitting back a little. "I *wanted* the pink parasol. While I was considering the parasol, however, the saleswoman began speaking in French to two other French ladies about how the English had no taste at all, and always wanted things pink regardless of their individual skin coloring which was usually ghastly." She flicked her wrist in indignation. "Then they carried on about how the English never seemed to dress boldly and elegantly like the ladies in France. I couldn't allow that to pass without response."

"Of course not," he replied accordingly.

She eyed him carefully, not certain if she should take his sudden smile of amusement for condescension toward the female mind and its trivialities, or enjoyment at such a ridiculous predicament. When he said nothing more, she brushed over it.

"In any case, they then began to discuss the bonnet, it being of the latest fashion in color and cut, quite stunning and from Paris. When I heard that, I picked it up. The other ladies wanted it, but it was in my hand."

"So you purchased something you don't need."

She breathed deeply and jutted her breasts out fully,

straightening in defiance. "But they thought twice about my lack of taste."

"You'll never see them again," he enunciated blandly.

"That is irrelevant."

He stared down at her smug expression for a long, quiet moment, then rubbed his eyes with his fingertips. Women. He would never understand them.

"This is why you haven't spoken French since you've been here?" he asked, attempting to return to the point.

She shrugged. "I suppose if I needed directions I would call upon it."

He lowered his voice. "But pretending the innocent allows you to listen to otherwise private conversations."

Her smile faded most abruptly. "I'm not being malicious at all. It just puts me at a little bit of an advantage when others are talking rudely about me—as they have once or twice here tonight—because they don't realize I know what they're saying."

Jonathan paused, his eyes grazing over the low garden wall and out toward the open sea, black but for a long, shimmering stream of moonlight. The eavesdropping really didn't bother him, mostly, he assumed, because he'd been doing the same since he'd arrived in France. What troubled him, however, was learning that her grandfather was a deposed French noble. And what did that mean? Probably nothing at all. She was correct that many nobles escaped to England during the time of the Revolution, a few of them providing for themselves as her grandfather had done, most expecting the British gentry or government to sustain them.

But something more disturbing was slowly taking shape in his mind. Could she possess some loyalty to the Legitimist cause, to those who intended to unseat the present king and replace him with the line of long ago—of the time when her grandfather had had power? This seemed extremely far-fetched, though not impossible to ignore, especially after his consideration earlier this evening that her motives went far deeper than she admitted, that he felt she was subtly using him or hiding things. To be fair, she had a life of relative wealth and ease in England and didn't speak of her French connections to anyone, so why would she care who was king of France? She was also a woman. Women generally didn't take notice of political issues, as it certainly wasn't a feminine pursuit and was frowned upon by society as a whole. Then again, Madeleine was a woman, and she believed in righting political wrongs and working for government issues *because* she was female and would therefore be unsuspected by all. Natalie, for all her youth and naivete, could very well think the same. She was certainly smart enough.

What unsettled him the most was this: If she was hiding real motives, she had no reason to tell him of her ancestry, but learning her grandfather was once the count of Bourges seemed extremely coincidental to the moment and his reason for journeying to France in the first place. It would also firmly account for her eavesdropping on the French elite, without any reaction or concern, as they planned to rid themselves of the current king. Perhaps she'd heard nothing in a conversation about gaming or hunting or other gentlemanly endeavors. This was entirely possible and yet seemed unlikely given the knowledge of who exactly was behind the closed library door. But above it all, Jonathan had to admit that knowing she might now be aware of a political turmoil to come made him apprehensive.

"What are you thinking?"

Her huskily murmured words sliced into his thoughts. He turned to her, looking down at her face glowing softly in the lamplight, and the gaze of genuine question emanating from her eyes.

He gave her a half smile and tugged at a bougainvillea leaf clinging to the white trellis on his right. "The Black Knight is here tonight, Natalie."

He watched her eyes widen with at first stunned disbelief, then almost instantly narrow with titillating excitement. "Did you speak to him?" she asked in a rush.

He looked at the leaf between his fingers. "Yes."

She sat forward on the bench, palms clinging to the iron seat. "And?"

He hesitated with pleasure, making her wait, enjoying the moment for all it was worth. Then he dropped the leaf, reached for the fan on her lap, tossing it on the bench to her side, and lightly grabbed her arm to help her stand, which she did without thought.

"Before we get into that, there's something I need to know," he said vaguely enough to cause a flicker of doubt on her brow.

A sudden cheer, then applause and commotion erupted from the ballroom beyond. Annette-Elise had arrived, the emeralds no doubt gracing her throat, and hopefully he and Natalie were the only ones missing the debut.

Jonathan glanced around. They were alone, and the timing was perfect.

"Walk with me, Natalie." It was rather unlike a question, more of an insistence, and she really had no choice. Her mind wasn't on him and being alone in a moonlit garden, it was on the intrigue to come. Quite an advantage for him, and he would use it, naturally.

"Are you hiding something from me, Jonathan?"

That stopped him short. "What?"

She gazed into his eyes, concentrating. "About the Black Knight. I mean"—she shook her head to clarify, lips thinned—"I know he exists. That evidence is conclusive. But he's also a man and he must have a life besides thievery. How do you know him? Why is he here?"

Without hesitation, experience took over, and he began to walk again slowly, his arm linked with hers, frowning in remembrance exactly as he should. "I met him four years ago during a gentleman's card game in Brussels. He was playing terribly, losing every hand, wagering more than he probably should have, and I assisted with a small loan, between Englishmen of course, before he could be called for cheating or betting what he couldn't pay. That incident began a friendship that has endured to this day. We're close in age and we both have the same sort of . . . wandering spirit."

He noticed her features change. He was taking a gamble on the fact that she didn't know the first thing about what went on during card games, but in the dimness he couldn't tell if she was aghast or captivated. Maybe just plainly disbelieving. He carried on before she could question something more and interrupt.

"As to why he's here tonight, I don't know. I didn't ask him. But he is here, and I assume for a very good reason." With pure amusement, he leaned toward her and added, "I gave him your vague description; told him you needed his help, nothing more. And he does indeed want to meet you, and has probably laid eyes on you already."

She was thinking intricately now, brows wrinkled minutely, mind calculating coincidences, suspicion building. The deception wouldn't go on much longer; she was piecing together too much. But he couldn't afford a scene between them now, not when the final act was to take place in the ballroom in less than an hour. He needed her to remain unknowing for at least one more night.

In silence, he guided her to the farthest corner of the garden, where darkness prevailed as lamplight faded, where only grass lay beyond to give way to jagged cliffs and open sea. They stood quietly for a second or two—he studying what he could see of her face, she staring intently into his darkened eyes.

"Jonathan—"

He touched her lips with his fingertips to quiet her, and he felt her physical jolt of surprise. But he didn't remove them. Instead he glided them along the soft, full line, enjoying the stirring heat it created within him, wishing suddenly she would kiss them with her own charge of need. Instead, she reached up and seized his wrist, pulling his arm away.

"I think we should go back to the ballroom."

She attempted to sound stern, but her quavering voice exposed the battle she was losing inside.

"This brings back memories, doesn't it?" he pursued, lowering his tone with intensity. "Of a night long ago, of another moonlit garden, of the scent of flowers in full bloom. Of hearing your sweet voice in shadows, of the desire I witnessed in your beautiful eyes when you looked at me, of touching you—''

"Please, Jonathan, don't do this," she begged in aching softness. She stepped back, lowering her head and running her palm across her forehead in irritation.

"Why?" The word was almost inaudible, and yet he knew she heard it. "Why won't you talk about that night?"

"I'm here for a reason, and it's not about us," she maintained anxiously. "I'm not here to be with you."

That stung him, but he wouldn't let it go. "You *are* with me, Natalie."

Her head shot up, and she glared at him through blazing eyes. "Only for a short time and only because I have to be—"

"You want to be."

"That's not true," she insisted, jaw tight, body stiff. "And I don't understand how you can keep thinking this way when I've made it so perfectly clear that I don't want you."

He smiled and slowly shook his head. "There's nothing to think about and there never has been. We're going to be together."

It was a statement of fact made so profoundly, so intimately, and with so much finality, she couldn't counter it. For moments she stared into his eyes, radiating unsureness and anger, even inexplicable awe at his confidence.

"It's not worth fighting, sweetheart," he gently persisted. He reached up and placed his palm on her chest, his wrist touching the tops of her breasts, feeling the quick beating of her heart beneath her warm skin. She didn't move.

"I won't be your lover, Jonathan," she disclosed in a thick, fervid whisper. "I can't be. I will never stoop so low in morality and self-respect to become another one of your conquests."

He drew a long, full breath, allowing himself to admit openly what he already knew. "You don't have to. You are *the* conquest, Natalie."

She faltered with that, blinking away incredulity, her features going slack, body sagging in erupting confusion.

He calmed completely, understanding himself at last and the incredible power between them that had been there since the night they met.

"It's all right," he whispered, running his thumb along her neck in soothing strokes. "Everything will be all right." He reached around her with both arms and pulled her into him, lowering his mouth to hers in a soft touch of warmth. She didn't respond at first, but he pursued, gliding his tongue along the crevice of her closed lips until she opened her mouth for him.

She put her hands against his chest in a defensive measure that allowed her to touch him, and he savored the feel, tasting her completely, tongue against hers, listening as her breathing quickened to match his, as the waves crashed against rocks in the distance, as music from the ballroom became an echo of another time.

Slowly she began kissing him back with growing surrender, knowing as he did that it was useless to resist. He ran his fingers down then up her spine until they relaxed through the ringlets of her hair at the base of her neck, feeling the softness, reeling from the scent of lavender on her skin. She was more than a fantasy, real not imagined, wanting him with vigor and loveliness she didn't even comprehend. That was what made her more beautiful than all who were gradually fading from memory. She was a brilliant jewel shining in a lonely desert of unfulfilled dreams. At last he understood, even if she didn't.

She moaned deliciously, barely enough for him to hear. But hear he did, and he knew instinctively she was losing herself to the moment. From his own engulfing need he could wait no longer to caress her as he'd longed to do seemingly for ages. He brought his hand down, grazing his fingertips over her satiny neck and chest to run his knuckles lightly along the tops of her breasts, across warm, sensitive skin, aching for his attention as she pushed them into him. His hand closed over her fully then, his palm and fingers lightly massaging her through the bodice of her gown, his thumb flicking across her nipple until he felt it harden for him through thin fabric. This was the torture—the wait, the longing, the beginning vision of the rapture yet to come. For both of them.

She gasped against his mouth, but she didn't pull away. She wanted him, more with each passing second. And that's what he needed to know. Natalie wanted *him,* not a myth, deny it though she might, and fulfillment would eventually be theirs. He knew it as surely as autumn followed summer. The day she resigned her sexuality to him at the beach was not chance, nor a momentary heat or loss of control. The force between them was there in the garden of long ago, and would be a part of them always. There was no stopping it now, no going back to the individual lives they knew before. Fate had brought them together again, for the second and final time, and eventually she would accept it.

Gradually, with more reluctance than he could ever recall feeling, he drew his hands up and placed his palms on her cheeks, pulling his lips from the embrace, resting his forehead against hers. She began shivering, from desire not cold, and he inhaled heavily to control his own aching need.

He clung to her like this for minutes, until she calmed, feeling her breath on his cheeks, her palms still warm against his chest. "I need you, Natalie."

She shook her head in small, violent movements, but he persevered.

"I want to touch you skin to skin, to feel you lying naked beside me, to take you as mine alone and watch when the passion explodes inside of you as it did days ago on the beach—"

"No—"

He tightened his grasp on her face, afraid she would jerk free and run. "We're not playing anymore. Not now. Not here. This is real, Natalie, and you want it, too. I can feel it in you when I touch you, when I hold you, when I look into your eyes." Slowly, fiercely, he whispered, "It will happen."

He'd never seen her cry before, but now he could feel wetness on her cheeks, brought out, he was sure, by frustration, anger, and confusion. He wiped them away with his thumbs but he wouldn't release her. Not yet.

"Why do you continue to fight this?" he asked huskily. "Why won't you let it be what it is?"

"Because I *can't,* Jonathan," she answered through a forceful breath. "Not with you. This is *my* choice, and I don't want you like that. You are my friend, not the man I will lose myself to."

At any other time in his life, he would have been offended or disheartened by such a passionate statement made to be a cold dismissal. But he knew she was lying, even if she hadn't yet admitted it to herself. Her words of negation also made him smile inside as he really thought about them. She insisted on thinking of him as a friend, even after he took advantage of her feelings on the beach, even after forcing himself on her emotions now. Friendship between the sexes was unusual at best, and yet it was now becoming clear to him that this was how Natalie was dealing internally with her awkward and inexpressible fondness for him—an attachment growing by the hour. And this fondness, he decided as he acknowledged a first real hint of relief, would be the advantage he would need when she finally discovered who he was.

Tenderly he kissed her forehead and stood back a little, gazing down to her face still resting in his palms, though partially hidden in shadow. "Perhaps you'll think differently about men and attraction after you meet the Black Knight."

She breathed deeply and opened her eyes, gaining better control of herself as he eased his approach and manner and turned the conversation away from them.

He grinned, attempting to lighten the mood. "It would take me hours to discard all these clothes to take advantage of you anyway. I just can't do that here, not when the fun is about to begin and we haven't even danced."

For every ounce of compassion and strength, intelligence and reason within her, Natalie simply could not understand him—his moods, his feelings—if he had any beyond lust—his reasons for being there and doing what he did, why he expressed such words of longing when she was just another

woman to spend a few weeks in his company. Every day
she found him more beautiful to look at, warmer and kinder
than the day before, so increasingly exasperating and dar-
ingly masculine, kissing her boldly even after she'd insisted
he not, caressing her as if they'd been intimate for years.
He got the best of her with each round, and somewhere
deep in her mind, as an almost unconscious ripple, she
knew he was winning the game he played with her good
judgment and body, her heart and soul. She wanted to be
harsh, to make him understand how she felt about him and
his past, how she'd made up her mind long ago about which
path she would follow. Her life just did not include him.

She knew she was blushing as he stared down at her,
though the darkness covered it well. She wiped her cheeks
with her palm, angry at herself for reacting so wantonly
each time he touched her, but more so for succumbing to
tears he'd noticed. She hated weepy women who sniveled
over men for every minor catastrophe, real or imagined,
and she'd never really cried before in the presence of anyone. It didn't become her, and she knew it. Yet Jonathan
brought out her passions with the greatest of ease, though
the tears hadn't appeared to annoy him, which she supposed
was a good thing.

Striving to keep the choke out of her voice, she stepped
back from him a foot or so, folding her arms in front of
her. "Are you going to introduce us now?"

Seconds passed, and he said nothing, just watched her
intently as she fought a swirl of emotions within. Then,
without any physical touch, she could positively feel his
gentleness envelop her.

"Tomorrow. It's too risky for him tonight, and I'd rather
you spend it with me anyway."

She opened her mouth to protest, but the words wouldn't
come. She heard laughter in the distance, the violins and
French horns and oboes through the partially opened windows, smelled honeysuckle in the balmy night air. Reality
had returned, and she hadn't given in. She was in control,
or would be again when she finally met the thief. At that
point the masquerade with Jonathan would be over, and her

life would begin a new, far more exciting and challenging twist that would not involve him. It was a somewhat painful thought, she finally admitted, but then many times in adulthood the right choices came with heartache.

"I need to see him, Jonathan, and I can't wait much longer."

"I know." He turned toward the house and offered her his elbow. "Dance with me?"

She hesitated briefly, but the lamplight in the distance once again reflected his smile of assurance, even comfort and honesty, and at this point she could do nothing but trust him.

Smoothing her skirts, feeling composed once more, the gravity of the moment gone, she grasped his arm, walked to the bench to retrieve her fan, then strolled gracefully beside him along the garden path and back into the house.

Ten

The ballroom had grown from warm and stuffy to hot and stifling, but Natalie hardly noticed. She opened her fan, swishing it without thought, studying the gentlemen guests with returned interest. Jonathan walked beside her, cool as usual, or at least not openly sweating like the others. But many people were already wandering outside again, and the windows had been opened fully now, so perhaps there would be a reprieve from the heat after all.

Then she saw Annette-Elise, in the center of the dance floor waltzing with her father, and her mind began to race. She stopped and stared, which forced Jonathan to do so as well. He shifted his gaze to the place where she fixed hers, then leaned over to whisper in her ear.

"Stunning, isn't it?"

Natalie knew he meant the necklace. Annette-Elise, as a woman of eighteen, could only be described as modestly attractive, with light-brown hair piled high on her head and a ruddy complexion she tried to hide with ringlets about her face. Her body was thick, though not fat, just . . . shapeless, with no breasts or waistline to speak of, and unfortunately from lack of experience she actually tried to draw attention to both from the cut of her gown. And her choice of clothing for the occasion had obviously been made with the supervision of her stepmother, as she wore the most unbecoming dress of mint-green satin, accented by huge, emerald-green bows and yards of white lace along the full skirt. But everything about her went virtually unnoticed after only one glimpse of the necklace.

It was magnificent—breathtaking—and Natalie couldn't help but stare. Its design was angular and sharp, not round and soft, and quite unusual. The thick chain of gold was likely only fourteen inches long, and yet at least one dozen emeralds covered the entire length of it, spaced about a quarter of an inch apart from each other, and cut into thick sections, each about one-half-inch squared. But what made it so unique was that the emeralds didn't hang in a circle attached to the gold necklace at the top of each gem. An experienced jeweler had taken an enormous amount of time in sectioning each emerald perfectly, then attaching each one individually at the exact place on each jewel, whether it be at corners, to the sides, or somewhere at the top or bottom, adding gold if needed, so that each one hung absolutely straight at right angles to the others and the ground when worn. The emeralds themselves were probably worth a fortune. But the necklace, intact as it was like this, was unquestionably priceless, and she had never seen anything like it in her life.

"That's what he's here for," she whispered with growing wonder. She glanced up to Jonathan who was once again watching her, faintly amused. Then without response, he led her onto the dance floor, only giving her time to grasp her fan against the soft wool on the arm of his frock coat and lift her skirts with the other hand as he took it in his.

The contact shocked her as they began to move rhythmically in time to the music, not because he held her closer than appropriate, but because to her the memory of waltzing with him years ago was the most vivid she possessed. Perhaps he recalled the kissing and touching to the particulars, but she remembered the dance, his eyes, strikingly rich, piercing hers from a face and soul hidden behind a black satin mask. In five years she'd thought of that night often, sometimes dreamily, sometimes with extreme discomfort, but always with a detail as fine as if it had all happened yesterday.

"What are you thinking?"

His words cut into her thoughts, and she caught herself, blinking quickly to reality. "That I want to be there when he steals them."

He laughed softly, though his gaze never wavered, tightening his hold of her waist to draw her closer as he expertly twirled her around on the floor. "You think that's what he wants tonight?"

"Don't you?"

"I suppose it's as reasonable an assumption as any," he admitted.

She ran her thumb back and forth along his as he held her hand. "But I also think there's more going on," she disclosed with the briefest spark of excitement. "I think the reason he's here is political."

That comment grabbed his full attention. "Really? Why so?"

She lifted her shoulders negligibly. "The Black Knight isn't known for stealing items for money, and if that's all he wanted he could just as readily steal from the English. Madeleine and I had a discussion about this very thing earlier tonight, concluding that if the Black Knight does indeed make an appearance, he will steal jewels worth something more than their monetary value." She leaned very close to his face to whisper, "I believe those emeralds are priceless, likely stolen, and probably worth something politically, either to the French or English government."

Jonathan stared into her eyes for a moment or two. His expression never changed as he gauged whether her spoken thoughts were from knowledge or conjecture, as the hem of her thick gown hugged his legs while their feet traced the parquet floor in a soft click of rhythm to the crescendo of music and the murmur of conversation around them.

Finally, in a voice low but firm, he asked cautiously, "Did Madeleine tell you this?"

It irked her at once that he wouldn't think she could

deduce this on her own. She pulled back a little, feeling color creep into her cheeks. "We talked about it at length and concluded it together."

"Oh, I see."

It was a pat acknowledgment revealing nothing. He was pacifying her, and she didn't like it at all. Of course, stealing the jewels could also have something to do with the discussion she'd overheard upstairs in the library less than an hour ago, but that seemed unlikely, and she wasn't going to mention it to Jonathan. The French were always considering ways to oust the current king from power, and most of it was just impractical and boastful talk brought out by too much drink, especially at a function like this one. What she'd heard was interesting to note, but not serious, and telling him as if it were something significant would likely make her look foolish. Still, she refused to let the subject end there.

"Can you think of a better reason for him to be here, Jonathan, darling?" she asked through batted lashes. Then her eyes grew round with exaggerated innocence. "Maybe he's after my cameos!" she whispered with a surprised gasp. "I certainly hope you'll protect my sensibilities as a devoted husband should he come after my jewels in one of comte d'Arles's darkened hallways."

His eyes flashed with a sort of admirable regard for her comeback, and he almost laughed, making every attempt to keep his features neutral, which she noticed with not too much difficulty.

The waltz ended, but another began immediately, and he never let her go, just danced with her as if he didn't hear the change in music at all.

"Cameos are semiprecious at best, Natalie, and hardly worth his time." He cocked his head slightly, his gaze traveling intimately over every section of her face. "Perhaps after one good look he'll rather have you."

She tossed him a somewhat mocking smile. "And you'll protect your precious wife from his ardent advances?"

"Oh, with my life, Natalie, darling," he avowed in fast response.

Although she knew he was now being as sarcastic as she, the words melted her within, satisfying something she couldn't exactly put her finger on.

Abruptly he changed the subject. "What else did you and Madeleine discuss?"

Perhaps it was simple intuition, but Natalie was certain she detected in his question a slight note of . . . anxiousness? She absolutely had to play that for all it was worth.

"We discussed you, Jonathan," she revealed sweetly.

"Did you?"

She knew he was more than intrigued, though unwilling to admit it or pry for answers.

"Actually, Madeleine seems to like you, as all women apparently do." She shot a quick peek at the gilded ceiling, forehead creased in recollection. "Together we decided you are charming and quick-minded, self-confident, and agreeable to look at."

Her eyes returned to his face, and he was smiling fully, whether because these were positive traits or because he simply enjoyed being discussed by women, she wasn't sure. But she refused to stop there.

"I also said I thought you were a bit too sportive and frivolous with your wealth, roaming the world at your leisure for nothing more than little bits of unimportant items and the opportunity to play. But then Madeleine defended you by insisting you have more depth than I give you credit for."

"I do," he stressed with a sudden serious air, smile fading just enough to imply he was no longer being quite so whimsical with her.

Uncertainty hit her in a dousing wave. It wasn't jealousy she felt exactly, but a kind of mild resentment that the Frenchwoman might be more closely acquainted with him than she was. And it made her hot with anger that she should feel this way. Curtly she said, "I wonder how she knows this, Jonathan."

"Her eyes are open, Natalie," he returned baldly.

Somehow that was the most hurtful thing anyone had said to her in a long time, and he knew it affected her that way, too. She could see it in his now-penetrating stare, his rigid brows, the tightness of his jaw, and his thinned lips— not quite smiling anymore, but daring her to respond with a wry, almost noticeable smirk.

"Perhaps you'd like something to eat," he said as a statement of fact, releasing her as their second waltz together came to an end.

Before she could respond, he took her by the elbow and guided her through the crowd toward one of the refreshment tables. Madeleine stood beside it, tall and elegant in her beautiful gown, conversing congenially with a middle-aged gentleman. Several feet from Madeleine, also next to the buffet table, stood Annette-Elise, eating chocolates with dainty fingers, her stepmother and father beside her, and all of them surrounded by four or five acquaintances of the local affluent class, either discussing the emeralds or perhaps guarding them. Stealing them like this, from around the lady's neck and in front of hundreds of people would be an incredible feat. For the first time, Natalie felt a shred of doubt in the Black Knight's abilities.

Madeleine turned to them as they approached. "How was your walk?" she asked with genuine interest.

"Lovely," Natalie replied levelly.

"But of course too short," Jonathan added without hesitation, tightening his grip on her elbow. "All alone as we were, I think my wife would have liked to . . . linger."

She couldn't believe he'd said that. Her cheeks warmed again, and she opened her fan, desperate for air movement, unable to look at him. She didn't need to when she felt his burning gaze on the side of her face.

"And a most romantic setting for lovers," Madeleine offered with a slight twist of her mouth. Then she tactfully dropped the subject, turning to the gentleman standing on her left. "Monsieur et Madame Drake, may I present Monsieur Jacques Fecteau, a longtime acquaintance of my late husband, Georges. He is a jeweler from Paris, traveling through Marseilles on business. I haven't seen him in, oh"—she looked at the Frenchman—"five years?"

"At least that long," he confirmed brightly in excellent

English. "But now we meet again. What coincidence, *non*?"

Natalie offered him her hand. The man was about Madeleine's height, stout yet expertly clothed in a dove-gray frock jacket and trousers, white shirt, and black cravat. He sported thick side whiskers and oiled hair the color of wet bark, a large jovial mouth, and eyes that crinkled in delight when he smiled. He gave her his full attention as he clasped her fingers with his palm, lightly kissing her knuckles.

"Madame Drake. A pleasure."

"Monsieur Fecteau."

He glanced up at Jonathan. "And Monsieur Drake, Madame DuMais has told me of you already, and your interest in European estates. Are you enjoying your stay in Marseilles?"

"Oh, indeed, Monsieur Fecteau. And you?"

Natalie played her part well as they all exchanged pleasantries, learning the man had traveled extensively abroad for several years while mastering his trade, which accounted for his firm grasp of their language. But for all her effort, she had trouble focusing on the conversation, which, on the whole, seemed remarkably stilted and mundane, although Madeleine and Jonathan remained particularly attentive. For more than five minutes Jonathan stood erect at her side, hands behind his back, engrossed in Monsieur Fecteau's account of what he described as a harrowing trip south the week before; something about his coach losing a wheel and plunging into a muddy embankment, forcing him and two ladies to wait in smothering heat for hours before they could continue their journey, one of the ladies fainting, which consequently forced their driver to revive her with a splash of cold water from a nearby creek.

It was the most out-of-place discourse going nowhere that Natalie had ever been a part of, and she wasn't sure why. It just seemed so superficial to her. Contrived. They should have been dancing, mingling, drinking champagne, basking in the excitement, and still Jonathan and Madeleine nodded and commented accordingly, standing by the food table, listening intently to a Parisian discussing the differences between the dry heat of northern France and the moist heat of the south.

And then it happened. Madeleine stepped subtly to her right toward a plate of sweetmeats and nut bread, leaning ever so gingerly behind Annette-Elise who was now eating at her side, and Jacques Fecteau stopped talking in mid-sentence as he stared openmouthed at the emeralds, now quite plainly in his line of sight and only several feet away.

"Good heavens, that's a marvelous piece," he sputtered in awe, switching to his native tongue.

Silence fell around them while Fecteau moved closer, suddenly absorbed by the craftsmanship of the necklace, the glitter from the jewels and the luster of gold.

Natalie felt an immediate change in atmosphere. Music, dancing, and festivity continued around them, but none in their vicinity took notice. Jonathan continued to stand beside her, quiet and watchful. On her left, two feet away, stood a very tall man with unusually sensitive features, Michel Faille, vicomte of . . . something, she couldn't recall, followed by Alain Sirois, vicomte de Lyon. She'd met both of them through Madeleine earlier that evening. The comte d'Arles stood between Alain and Claudine, his wife, who leaned one hand on the edge of the buffet table. And all were surrounding Annette-Elise and her priceless emeralds.

Fecteau moved closer, concentrating on the jewels, oblivious to everything else. "Stunning," he whispered. "Excellent workmanship."

Henri straightened, a boastful smile tugging at his mouth. "A family heirloom. We are quite proud that our daughter wears the emeralds so beautifully on this occasion."

"Indeed," Fecteau mumbled.

Henri's eyes narrowed. "I do not believe we've been introduced, Monsieur . . . ?"

"Fecteau," Madeleine finished for him, her voice and manner light and charming. "He is a former acquaintance of my late husband, Comte, and a jeweler from Paris. He arrived in Marseilles only yesterday, much to my surprise, and I asked him to escort me this evening." She reached out and touched Henri's arm, eyes sparkling with a delicate familiarity. "I hope you do not mind that we somehow missed introductions before now."

Henri looked stumped, blushing and uncomfortable, yet enjoying perfectly the rather candid approach of such a lovely woman.

Claudine cleared her throat, returning brusquely to the point. "You are knowledgeable where *priceless* jewels are concerned, Monsieur Fecteau?"

"Oh, I've been in the business for more than twenty years," he answered graciously, dismissing the note of doubt in her words and her indelicate manner. Then he looked back to the necklace, his eyes round pools of wonder. "My experience is in forgery—paste—and never have I seen a better one than this."

Someone gasped, and Fecteau, without notice, looked directly at Henri for the first time, smiling confidently. "Outstanding work. You paid a great sum, did you not?"

Natalie's first inclination was to applaud at the rejoinder, appropriate and tactful, and probably not something Claudine and her simple mind would even grasp without explanation. Then she felt an unmistakable shift in mood. Tension became a tangible thing surrounding them, hot and pressing, the reason unclear but unmistakable even to those innocent of its meaning.

She stood motionless, heart pounding suddenly, the moment becoming illusory like no other she'd experienced. For seconds nobody said anything. Then Annette-Elise went pale as she raised her fingers to her throat.

"Papa?"

Henri blinked quickly then seemed to recover himself. "You are mistaken, Monsieur Fecteau. Your experience is lacking. I assure you these emeralds are real."

The orchestra stopped playing in that instant, turning small discussions above music in the ballroom into a level drone.

The jeweler seemed taken aback. "I-I am terribly sorry." He licked his lips, eyes wide and confused. "I assumed you knew."

"Knew?" bellowed Michel Faille, his full mouth thinning as the muscles in his neck strained against his shirt collar. "What we know is that these emeralds are priceless and that they once belonged to the queen of France. What we do not know is who you are, exactly, and what your purpose is in spreading false information regarding jewels about which you know nothing."

His voice rose with each word, and Natalie recognized the growing offense taken by the jeweler in response. At that point other party guests in their immediate surroundings quieted and began to take notice of the exchange.

Fecteau raised his chin a fraction, inhaling deeply and eyeing Henri with conviction. "Forgive me, Comte, but I know my craft. I have been a professional jeweler for more than two decades, have myself made paste jewelry from originals for those of the middle classes as well as aristocrats, and I know forgery the moment I see it." In a deep, solemn voice, he enunciated, "This necklace is a forgery."

Natalie felt Jonathan take her hand, lacing her fingers in his, squeezing them gently, and her mouth went dry.

The blood drained from Henri's face. "Impossible," he said in a raspy breath. "It's been locked in my safe for weeks."

A heavy stillness spread over the room. Fecteau clasped his hands behind his back resolutely. "Then, Comte d'Arles, if you believed these emeralds were real, I submit to you that your safe has been compromised and you have been cleverly duped. If you will only take a knife or sharp object to the gold, you can scrape it off. The green is nothing more than glass."

Alain began to sweat, his forehead beading profusely; Michel became red with rage; Annette-Elise clutched the emeralds, her ruddy complexion now white as graveyard lilies. Nobody did anything for seconds, then Claudine muttered, "The safe, Henri, check the safe."

It was a useless thing to do, given that the jewels, if Fecteau was correct, were already stolen. But he turned and walked quickly to the ballroom door, then out into the foyer.

Everyone began talking at once—the noise a clatter, heat oppressive. Natalie stood silent, basking in the thrill of the moment as it coupled strangely with tension, knowing the Black Knight was there, probably watching. Jonathan ran his thumb back and forth along her knuckles, and she peeked up cautiously to note his expression of mild curiosity. He didn't have to know the language well to grasp what was taking place, or the enormity of it all.

Madeleine began a fierce, animated exchange between the jeweler, Claudine, and the other two men, and Natalie felt Jonathan very casually pull her back a foot or two to the side.

"He did it," she said softly.

"With his usual style," he whispered in return. "But it's not over yet."

Seconds later, Henri reentered the room, and everyone turned, a hush falling over the crowd again as they witnessed the astonishment in his expression. He looked physically ill now as he stumbled back to the buffet table, skin pasty gray, dark eyes wide with horror, beads of perspiration rolling from brow to chin.

"What is this?" he demanded in a harsh, choked voice, holding out a black, velvet pouch with shaking hands. "What is this!"

Silence boomed. Movement stopped. Fecteau guardedly reached for the pouch, his countenance embracing a flat, knowing pessimism. With agile fingers he reached inside and carefully removed the contents.

"Oh, my God . . . ," someone whispered.

Sitting daintily in his palm was a replica of the necklace, but made of black stones and cheap metal, and only about half the size. It was a demoralizing hoax; a mocking tribute.

Fecteau bristled. "This is a low-grade silver, Comte d'Arles, and the stones are black onyx. Semiprecious. Quite ordinary but a nice piece, and probably worth more than the emerald forgery." He turned it over in his hands. "Unusual, really. One normally makes, oh . . . cameos from onyx."

A gust of ocean wind swept through the opened windows

for the first time that night, severing the collective shock with chilling reality. Then the low rumble began to ripple through the crowd again—outrage for those enlightened, whispered confusion and uncertainty for those still ignorant.

Suddenly Henri was red-faced and seething, fists clenched at his sides, eyes watering with a rage he couldn't begin to place, his Adam's apple convulsing as he swallowed, unable to speak.

Michel grabbed Fecteau by the collar, glaring at him, ashen but for bright red cheeks. "Did you steal them?"

"Monsieur Faille!" Madeleine gasped, moving between them.

He ignored her. "How coincidental that you are here tonight—"

"Shut up, Michel!" Alain spat, pulling at the tall man with quaking hands until he released the jeweler. "Unwarranted insults will only cause greater trouble and attract outside attention."

Fecteau looked appalled, stepping back, still clutching the onyx necklace with the fingers of one hand while smoothing his frock coat with the other. "I did not steal anything," he insisted, his voice cracking nervously. "I cannot imagine how I or anyone could have stolen such a necklace from around your daughter's neck *during* this ball. And if I had stolen it before today, I assure you, monsieur, I would not be here now."

Perfectly logical, and everyone knew it.

Alain turned his corpulent figure to Madeleine and her escort. "You are undoubtedly correct, Monsieur Fecteau. Our profound apologies to you."

The commotion grew to a thunder with that, and Annette-Elise began to cry, still clinging to the worthless glass. Then Henri grabbed the necklace, yanking hard once. The clasp broke easily, and they fell away from her throat into his hand.

"They'll search us," Natalie said dismally.

Very slowly, Jonathan murmured, "No, they won't. They can't."

She looked up to his face in question.

''Searching anyone here tonight will ruin them socially, and they can't call the authorities when they stole the necklace in the first place.'' In a vaguely arrogant assertion, he added in a whisper, ''They've lost the emeralds and they know it.''

She watched him as he continued to stare at the count with hard, clear, observant eyes, a wisp of near-black hair falling low over his forehead unnoticed. But it was the certainty in his voice and stance, the expression of his mouth that made her hesitate—not exactly a smile, but a barely upturned line, a poetic smirk of quiet satisfaction, of bland but ultimate triumph. As if he'd just won the prize in a challenging and enormously reckless game of chance.

As if he'd stolen the necklace himself.

Natalie stilled completely, transfixed in time as a gradual breath of comprehension began to form within her. Somewhere in the very far distance she heard the music resume, awkwardly played. Henri and several others quickly left the ballroom; Madeleine talked with Fecteau in hushed tones, and yet Natalie's thoughts went beyond them now. To another place, another moment that now seemed like so long ago.

. . . he is dark, sophisticated, charming, intelligent, handsome, and he does good things to help people. There is also a rumor that he has blue eyes. . . .

A chill, so cold and numbing, blanketed her and she started to shake.

And the Black Knight is in Marseilles? she had asked him.

He will be when we get there.

''Oh, no . . . ,'' she whispered.

Jonathan looked down at her, his vibrant eyes searching hers as he noticed her expression.

He's exciting, he travels, he . . . lives for adventure. I know this sounds a bit odd, but I believe he's also looking for me.

Beyond doubt, as forceful as a punch to the stomach, it was there in front of her. All the questions and understandings, all the hope in her future rapidly dying in her heart, all her dreams shattered by one incredible stroke of realization. Why hadn't she seen it before now? How could she not have known? Because even the thought was something she could never imagine; a nightmare realized she could never accept.

"Natalie?"

She was freezing, trembling inside, staring into his magnificent eyes now pulled into a slight frown of curiosity. Suddenly she felt a powerful sense of rage and the crushing embarrassment of the things she'd confided in him, the consuming humiliation of being lied to repeatedly, of being used.

He still held her hand, the touch now as scorching as burning oil on skin. But with an almost instantaneous insight into what lay ahead she didn't jerk it free. Reason flooded her in a torrential wave, stopping her from immediate, irrational action. The answers were there before her, making clear and obvious sense as she began to put the pieces into place, but the proof was not. Call it sharp knowledge or an almost overwhelming instinct, her mind took control at that moment, and for good or bad, it made her pause.

She couldn't let him know. Not here at the ball in front of hundreds of people. He had played her for a fool, and she would hate him for that. But he had stolen the emeralds for a reason, and now she was intensely curious as to what that was, where they were, how he'd done it, and most of all why he'd brought her along on this journey. If she confronted him now she would embarrass them both, but even more than that, he would win. And she couldn't let him win.

He could not win.

Calming, her mind working frantically, eyes thinning with a broad smile of hidden intention, she murmured, "I-I'm just . . . shaken."

He ran his thumb softly along her fingers again, and she fought the urge to slap him with all of her strength. Instead she squeezed his hand tenderly. "I think I'd like champagne now."

For moments he stared into her eyes. "Would you like to go?"

She lowered her gaze, scanning the crowd. Two or three couples took to the dance floor, boldly attempting to ignore the unpleasant moments just passed as silk and satin once again swished in rhythm to the too-brightly played music; small groups of people whispered in corners, at refreshment tables, eating or drinking; some discreetly took their leave.

With resolve, and a warm smile of excitement she no longer felt, she looked back into his beautiful, deceitful eyes and began the best performance of her life.

"Not now," she said effortlessly. "I'd like to . . . see how things play out."

That appeased him, and he seemed to relax. "Then champagne it is." He released her hand at last and reached up to cup her chin. "We might as well enjoy ourselves while we can, and I think you owe me at least one more dance before I turn you over to the thief."

She did hate him for that—for his smoothness, his irresistible charm, his attention to her, and the unquenchable desire between them he'd expertly used to his advantage. And what did Madeleine say? *I wonder how he plans to go about this introduction?* He'd said it would be tomorrow, and that gave her time. Time to think of something that would place the advantage in her hands. And she would think of something. She had to. Then she'd have control and she would win.

She would win.

Eleven

It took Natalie nearly ten minutes of staring at his trunk before deciding it was time to open it and check the contents. Naturally, searching his personal items would be a most embarrassing thing to do, but she had no choice. It was the only way to know absolutely. Jonathan had just left the bungalow to purchase them a cold luncheon in one of the nearby villages, leaving her with the promise of an extensive discussion when he returned. Such a discussion would no doubt be about the emeralds, about the Black Knight, and she wanted to be ready for it. She had to find the jewels first, though, for any leverage at all, and she was fairly certain he didn't have them when he left. Carrying them in a pocket would have been noticeable probably, and she just couldn't imagine him selling them anyway, which would be the only reason to risk carrying them at all. That meant they were still here. And the only place they *could* be was tucked somewhere beneath his personal belongings.

They'd returned from the ball shortly after two in the morning. The party had continued to some degree after the forged emeralds had been discovered, although the mood had changed to one of quiet static. Most guests left early, but she and Jonathan had remained at her insistence, danc-ing occasionally, mingling socially, being nearly the last to

leave. The comte d'Arles had not returned after the fiasco
with Fecteau, but Claudine had done her best to keep the
party alive for the sake of Annette-Elise. It was all she
could do, really, and Natalie felt sorry for both of them.
One could hardly call the ball a success, but it hadn't, at
least, ended disgracefully.

She was, however, extraordinarily proud of herself. Her
acting had been superb, as Jonathan had remained completely blind to her sudden discovery of his identity. That
gave her power, something that would serve her well in the
days ahead. During the last nine hours she'd done nothing
but fidget internally, sleeping little, hiding her intentions as
best she could, almost wanting to murder him, but deciding
to get even instead. At six this morning, lying next to his
carefree, slumbering form in bed, it had come to her. She
now had a plan, and a way to use him in the manner in
which he'd used her from the moment she'd walked into
his town house.

So, with dignity, and before she could change her mind,
she knelt at last beside his unlocked metal trunk, smoothed
her lavender skirt around her, released the brass latches,
and opened the lid.

If she expected to be surprised at the contents, she was
mistaken. Of course, she'd never done anything so obtru-
sive in her life, nor had she ever been so closely exposed
to a man's underthings. But her first impression upon opening the lid was amazement at how neatly everything was
folded and placed within. From shirts to shoes, it was perfectly tidy. Oddly, she'd never expected that from Jonathan.
In personality he seemed so capricious, and yet his manner
of dress and style ran more to the elegant, reserved tastes
of a gentleman, which, she had to remind herself, he actually was.

Carefully, starting on the left side of the trunk, she lifted
his shirts, one by one, and placed them on the floor beside
her. Trousers followed, three pairs, and these she also removed with care. Beneath them, on the bottom, were two
pairs of shoes. No emeralds, although she gingerly stuck

her fingers into the toes to be sure they weren't stuffed inside.

Then she moved to the right half of the trunk. She'd purposely avoided this side at first because she'd noticed his more personal items—comb, razor, toothbrush and powder, underwear—which was none of her business. But still, to reach the bottom, she had to go through it all.

With anxious hands she removed the toiletries, setting them to her side. Next, and quickening her pace, she began to lift his folded undergarments, growing increasingly uncomfortable as she touched each one, but reminding herself of her purpose. She needed the emeralds and she needed to hurry.

Then finally, as doubts began to seep in, she discovered the object of her search. A black velvet pouch, exactly like the one that contained the onyx necklace, sat conspicuously between the last two garments.

Her first thought was that he'd left it in such an obvious place because he knew she'd look for it. But after only seconds of speculation, she realized this conjecture was wrong. He didn't yet know she'd discovered his identity. It did seem a bit foolish for him not to conceal the jewels in a hidden pocket or within a shoe, but she really didn't have time to speculate about his tactics as a thief. The only thing filling her mind was the scrumptious thought of the shock she would witness on his face when she confronted him.

Her heart beat fast as she took the pouch in hand, to some surprise finding it to be lighter than she'd expected. With a rush of exhilaration she swiftly opened it to stare at the contents.

The sparkle and shimmer of green and gold took her breath away. The necklace was even more magnificent up close—not at all a feminine piece of jewelry to accent a woman in her gown, but a work of art to be displayed only on the canvas of warm skin, everything else fading behind its brilliance.

She dropped the pouch to the floor unnoticed and slowly glided her thumb along the emeralds, cold yet vibrantly beautiful, allowing them to fall between her fingers, a smile of ultimate satisfaction growing on her lips. The stolen, priceless necklace was now in her possession. All doubts faded. She had the power at last and she would use it. She would win.

Natalie glanced briefly over her shoulder to the clock on the dressing table. It was nearly noon. Jonathan would be returning at any moment.

Tucking a menacing curl behind her ear, she returned the emeralds to their protective, velvet casing, rested the pouch in her lap, replaced each of his items perfectly in his trunk, and closed the lid.

Then with speed and newfound determination, only vaguely becoming aware of how things were about to change between them, she moved to her own trunk near the wardrobe. Quickly she opened the lid and reached deeply inside until her hand found one of her tall, black leather boots. She pulled it out from beneath shoes and other miscellaneous items, then sat fully on the ground and went to work.

One of the greatest stories her mother ever told her about her grandfather was not just of his escape from France but of how cleverly he'd accomplished it. He never would have made it out alive had he not paid off the jailer. And he never would have been able to do that if he hadn't hidden several gold coins beneath the soles of his shoes, which he'd hollowed out for that specific purpose. When the peasants searched him, they found nothing on his person but they didn't think of looking closely at his shoes. Neither would Jonathan, for she'd heeded the advice of her mother and had, over the years, hollowed out various shoes of her own to hide money should that ever be necessary when she traveled. Call it pure nonsense as many would, but doing so had now finally come to serve a purpose of her own. She would hide the emeralds in her boot, where they would be secure and never discovered by anyone.

With a good deal of prying, cracking a nail in frustration, the bottom leather sole of the tall heel finally came loose. Her initial idea was to stuff both emeralds and pouch inside to keep them well protected, but it was immediately clear that she didn't have the room, and only the jewels themselves would fit. And just barely.

After once again removing the necklace from its velvet covering, she cushioned it as delicately as she could inside the heel, and with a great deal of pressure from her hand, closed the top leather just enough to secure the contents. Grinning from a great sense of accomplishment, she turned the boot over in her hands. It would take close examination to notice that the leather sole didn't quite meet the wood, and who would think to look? The hiding place was perfect.

Natalie placed the boot back inside her trunk, tucking it under several pairs of shoes just to be safe, and closed the lid. It was then that she heard his footsteps on the stone path outside.

She stood rapidly, clasping the empty pouch with her hand, and raced to the other side of the room, sitting in one of the wicker chairs just as he opened the door.

He stopped to stare at her, his mouth twisted in a half smile, head tilted a fraction, and intuitively—either from her nervous breathing or perhaps just the charge in the air— he sensed that something was different, something had changed. Then the look vanished as he stepped inside the room, basket of food in hand, and closed the door behind him.

"I found a good price on roasted hens," he said pleasantly, walking to the table next to her and setting the basket on top. He glanced at her face, his eyes narrowing with just the slightest trace of suspicion. "Anything happen while I was gone?"

Her heart began to race. As always, he overwhelmed her with his presence, standing before her, informally dressed once more in a cream linen shirt and dark-brown trousers, hair tousled from his walk in the breeze, his skin bronzed from just their short time on the Mediterranean coast. But the moment for confrontation had arrived, and she refused to allow him to think he had the advantage simply because of her obvious discomfiture, of which he was usually clearly aware.

So with fortitude, and timing the exposure expertly in her opinion, she reached for his hand, turned it flat, and placed the empty velvet pouch in his palm.

"I found your necklace, Jonathan," she confessed in a sultry whisper.

She heard him suck in a small, sharp breath, but his eyes stayed transfixed on hers, and he didn't move his hand. The unsureness she felt from him at that moment filled her with confidence and extreme gratification.

In one fluid motion, she reached around and pulled the ribbon from her hair, letting her thick curls fall free, then gently kicked her shoes from her feet. Rather unbecoming for a lady in the middle of the day, but she wanted to appear comfortable and self-assured for the discussion ahead. She shifted her body in the chair, pulling her legs and feet up under her gown to rest them on the seat, grinning triumphantly, waiting.

Finally he glanced to the pouch, running his fingers over the velvet. "What do you think you know, Natalie?" he asked quietly.

She folded her arms casually across her belly. "I know I have the emeralds."

For moments of unbearable silence he did nothing. Then he raised his gaze to hers once more, but instead of the anxiety or anger she expected to see in his expression, he instead smiled, eyes flashing in a sort of prideful amusement. That unnerved her so suddenly, she faltered, which she was sure he noticed.

"You looked through my trunk?"

Now she squirmed in her chair, sitting up a little as warmth flooded her. "How else was I to confiscate them?"

His brows rose. "How else, indeed."

He tossed the pouch on the table, then sat heavily in the chair next to hers, folding his hands politely in his lap, eyeing her with what she could only describe as pleasured calculation. "I trust you didn't steal my razor."

She almost laughed, restraining herself with difficulty. "For a moment I considered it, Jonathan, but then I recalled the thickness of your skin."

He did laugh at that. Very softly. Watching her. "And did you replace all of my personal . . . apparel?"

Her cheeks burned, and from nervousness she reached up and ran her fingers through her hair. That was a mistake, as his eyes traced the movement with gross familiarity.

"I believe we're straying from the point, Jonathan," she maintained sternly.

"Mmm. The point." He relaxed a little against the wicker back, tapping his thumbs together. "What do you want to know?"

"Is Madeleine a spy?" she asked pointedly, her voice flat.

"Yes," he replied without evasion. "She's employed by the British government for that purpose and was deliberately set up for this job as my contact in Marseilles. She's very good at what she does and is exceptionally loyal to the British cause."

Natalie blinked, surprised by his quick, candid answer. "You work for the government?"

He pursed his lips, brows furrowed in concentration. "Not precisely. I work for three individuals: Sir Guy Phillips, Lord Nigel Hughes of Cranbrook, and most directly for Christian St. James, earl of Eastleigh. They are all my friends, although Sir Guy is my official contact, and I go through him as the Black Knight. We—the four of us—are the only ones who know of their involvement in my work. Should I ever be caught or arrested, they can never be implicated except by me, and that won't happen. I am not involved with political issues exactly; I work independently of them, although there are several men in high government circles who know who I am. Sir Guy is one of them, and he arranges my contacts throughout Europe—for any help, should I need it."

Natalie stared at him, stunned. "I can't believe you're telling all of this to me so readily."

He breathed deeply, scrutinizing her with intensity. "I trust you, Natalie."

Never had four simple words melted her so completely. But it wasn't just what he'd said, it was the meaning behind it, the gentleness in his deep voice, in his eyes.

"So why do you do it?" she continued softly.

He thought about that for a moment. "I strive to right wrongs, but there's more to it than that. In many jobs I do, I think of my work as rather a way to . . . fix things. Things that can't be fixed in any other manner. I expose illegal trade or people who are so clever they cannot otherwise get caught doing illegal or unscrupulous acts—both personal and political. Sometimes I work for government issues, although those in government, aside from a select few, don't know at all I'm involved in . . . oh . . . setting up political criminals to be discovered and arrested, or locating the whereabouts of extorted money or stolen weapons. I'm not technically a spy; I've had no formal training for anything. I work instead for myself, by doing. I'm given detailed information about a specific situation, and it's up to me to do the rest, at my discretion. Once in a while I need help and I get it unconditionally, as is the case with Madeleine. Most of the time I work alone, and most of what I do is simple thievery designed to affect the outcome of a broader situation. When the job is completed, I'm paid, and paid very well."

"By Sir Guy."

"Yes, and my other two benefactors. I'm paid with private funds, not money from the public treasury." He paused, his eyes growing dark as they pierced hers. Then leaning forward, elbows on knees, hands clasped together in front of him, he lowered his voice to a deep whisper. "I invented the Black Knight six years ago, Natalie, and although my work has made me wealthy, what I do as the thief is for the betterment of society and my own personal satisfaction. Not for money. It's each of these accomplishments that makes me who I am as a man, and even if I were never paid again, I don't know that I could give it up completely. I enjoy what I do and I hope to continue working in this capacity, to some degree, for the rest of my life." Very cautiously, he added, "Do you think you can accept this?"

She had no idea what to say, or what specifically he

wanted from her with such a direct question. He was profoundly serious in manner and tone, his eyes locked with hers, waiting for a response. And then she understood.

A strong gust of cool, ocean wind swept through the open window behind him, making the curtains billow around him in a dazzle of sea green against the blackness of his hair. But he didn't appear to notice the intrusion, concentrating as he was on only her and the importance of her reply.

With total depth of her own honesty, knowing just how much this mattered to him, she murmured, "If you're asking me to remain silent about this and your identity, Jonathan, of course I will. I swear to you I will never tell a soul." Then she purposely twisted her mouth into a knowing grin in an attempt to brighten the mood and return to the most immediate issue. "Besides, I couldn't expose you now even if I wanted to. I have my own agenda."

He stared hard at her, calculating her motives, searching her face for answers he couldn't yet perceive, or perhaps just weighing the challenge to come. Then slowly he sat back again, placing his elbows on the arm of the chair, chin resting on the tops of his fingers, studying her.

"It appears you also have my emeralds."

Eyes sparkling, she swallowed a giggle of triumph. "Yes, I do. And before you get any ideas about stealing them from me, let me assure you now that you will never find them."

He lowered his eyes blatantly, first to her breasts, then to her hips and legs, outlined for his view by a modest white blouse and a skirt without stays. "I don't suppose you'll allow me the pleasure of a search through *your* personal items."

Never had a man made her so thoroughly uncomfortable from a look, a simple phrase, as Jonathan did, and did continuously. Embarrassment returned, but she ignored the feeling as she ignored his brazen comment, pulling her knees up, bare feet flat on the cushion, wrapping her arms around her legs to hug them against her protectively.

"When did you steal them?" she asked a little too harshly.

He looked back into her eyes. "Wednesday."

"Wednesday?"

"Actually it was probably Thursday morning," he amended with a shrug. "While you slept, anyway."

She shook her head in amazement. "You left me here alone in the middle of the night, walked into the count of Arles's home, then his private study, broke into his safe, stole priceless emeralds, then returned here and climbed back into bed?"

"That's . . . a fairly accurate description of events."

She didn't know whether to be shocked at his daring or proud of his accomplishment, but the intrigue was certainly building. "How did you do that?"

"Quietly."

She grinned in spite of herself, biting her lip to keep from laughing.

He stretched his legs out in front of him, crossing one ankle over the other. "I didn't break into his safe, though, I unlocked it. And I didn't steal the emeralds, I exchanged them."

"For forgeries."

"Yes."

"How on earth did you learn to unlock a safe you'd never seen before?"

"With practice."

"You're being evasive."

His brows rose in innocence. "I'm being truthful."

She rested her chin on her knees. "What if I woke up and found you gone?"

That made him laugh. "You'd sleep through a chariot race, Natalie."

The statement shook her a little, making her feel both offended by his vigorous rebuttal and oddly warmed by the fact that he'd actually paid attention to how she slept.

She moved on without response. "Why did you bother going to the ball if you already had them in your possession?"

Mischievously he challenged, "Why do you think?"

She shouldn't have asked that. He knew she would know. He understood how well she'd studied the thief, admired him, wanted to be a part of his life. It was unnerving, mortifying when she thought about all the things she'd said to him, disclosed in confidence. But what kept her from cowering in that mortification, or running from it, was her determination to even the score.

"It's his style," she said levelly, though dropping her gaze to study the fine, silk weave of his shirt. "The Black Knight is not a conventional thief. He does things to make a point, wanting to be a part of the action, to be acknowledged in a different way from all the others." She looked back to his charming, beautiful, arrogant face. "Quite frankly, Jonathan, I'm surprised he didn't leave a calling card."

"*I* didn't need to. The rumors will spread on their own."

Her comment was meant to be a subtle insult, but he didn't seem to take it that way. "You're rather pompous about the whole thing," she said brusquely.

He shook his head very slowly. "It's neither pompous nor foolish for one to work the way he works best. That is, instead, the smart and very cautious thing to do."

She smirked disgustedly. "Waiting around to be suspected hardly seems the best way to work, or the cautious thing to do."

He pulled a face of genuine surprise. "Why would they suspect me?"

"You're English," she said, exasperated.

"With an impenetrable false identity."

She straightened. "Arranged by Madeleine—"

"Who has never been, is not now, nor will ever be my mistress."

That bold statement absolutely startled her. It had come from nowhere; an explanation certainly wasn't required at her request this time. He had thought of it, and for reasons of his own, had stressed it of his own accord with the firm intention of making this perfectly clear to her. What she wasn't sure of exactly was why he bothered to do this.

Irritated, she ran the fingers of both hands through her hair. "I don't care."

"I think you care a great deal," he replied softly.

It was a lightness of the assertion coupled with the huskiness of his tone that flustered her. But he wasn't being at all careless with his choice of words. They were evaluated; she could see the determination in his features, in his eyes as they once again bore into hers.

Voice quavering with sharp anger, she whispered, "I hate you, Jonathan. I despise you to the center of your soul."

He grinned wryly. "I don't think so. If you hated me that much you would have murdered me. Or left."

"You're so arrogant."

"No, I'm positive," he countered.

"You made me a fool."

"You are no fool, Natalie. You're one of the smartest women I've ever known."

That hardly registered as she pounded her fists once on the armrests, refusing to give in. "You lied to me, humiliated me—"

"I had a job to do."

"You could have told me," she said fiercely.

He sighed, rubbing his jaw with his fingers. "If I had, you either wouldn't have believed me or you wouldn't be here with me now. I didn't like the thought of either scenario." He dropped his arm and lowered his voice. "I like to look at you, Natalie, to talk to you every day, to feel you in my arms." He hesitated for seconds, then whispered huskily, "I like the thought of you beside me."

Natalie actually had to sort through and purposely contain her emotions, careful not to expose her confusion to his watchful eyes. She wanted to hate him passionately; she wanted to lean over and kiss his lips with all the softness and desire she possessed. She wanted a magnificent revenge; but with a melting of her soul, she also realized she wanted him more. To look at, talk to, feel. Beside her.

Quite unexpectedly he reached for her toes as they peeked out from the hem of her gown. Tenderly he caressed them with his thumb and fingers, sending a marvelous jolt of tension through her body. He knew perfectly well just how much she *didn't* hate him, even after everything he'd done, but she wasn't ready for him to stray from the all-important conversation of the emeralds so easily. He could probably seduce her right now; he probably knew it, too, and that infuriated her. She needed to get to *her* point of attack.

Abruptly she pulled her feet from his grasp and stood, walking to the window and resting her hands palm down on the sill as she stared out at a cloudless, silver-blue sky. "Fecteau was in on it, too."

"Of course," he acknowledged quietly. "The comte d'Arles, or more precisely someone working for him, stole the necklace from the duke of Newark several months ago, Natalie. It's priceless, once belonging to Maria Theresa of Austria, and he and other members of the French gentry believe it should have gone to her daughter when she married their king. The English purchased it legally—this is documented to the best of my knowledge—but there were several in this country who wanted it back for selfish reasons. They stole it from us; I stole it back." He cleared his throat. "Now it appears you've stolen it from me."

It was an open-ended statement. He wanted her explanation but was unwilling to ask outright, or perhaps pry into what he now began to perceive as a very private matter.

A deafening silence enveloped the room, the disquiet in the air invaded only by the sound of crashing waves on the distant cliffs, the whistling of a bird. The rich aroma of food made her stomach growl, but she didn't feel like eating. She was too anxious, sensing his eyes on her back, her nerves prickling with the thought that she was about to reveal to him exactly why she'd come to France.

Finally she turned to face him squarely. He continued to regard her, cautiously, sitting comfortably in the wicker chair, chin in palm, one leg crossed over the other, waiting.

"I'll give the necklace back, Jonathan."

"I never doubted that, Natalie," he returned almost at once.

Her skin felt hot, her mouth dry, and she clasped her hands in front of her, wringing them tightly in anticipation. It was time for truth.

"I-I suppose you'll recall that I mentioned needing the Black Knight's help."

"Yes, I believe I recall that."

His casual tone and flat expression made it excruciatingly difficult for her to get to the point. He wasn't helping her along, either, by asking questions or showing even the slightest trace of curiosity.

"I need him to steal something for me," she revealed through a shaky breath.

He never altered his features. "I think you mean you want *me* to steal something for you."

She knew she blushed fully with that but she kept her eyes locked with his. "Yes, I do."

He waited, eyebrows raised expectantly. "Are you going to tell me what it is?"

"Will you steal it?"

He looked at her strangely. "How can I answer that if I don't know what it is?"

That made perfect sense, and yet it was the most difficult part of all. For months she'd thought about how she would disclose this to the Black Knight—a man she assumed would be impartial, unknowing, rational, and concerned for payment. *Never* had she remotely considered that the matter would involve a friend, and one for whom her feelings ran the gamut and yet were so difficult to define.

"It's extremely important to me, Jonathan," she confided faintly, "and highly personal."

"I gathered that, or you wouldn't have risked so much."

His words were totally sincere, touching her because she knew he meant them. She grasped her elbows in front of her, rubbing them with her fingertips. "The situation could result in serious social consequences."

He warmed from her troubled expression, the graveness in her tone. "Just tell me, Natalie," he pushed soothingly. "I can't help you if I don't know what you're talking about."

The time had arrived, and she had no idea where to start. Pulse racing, she looked directly into his eyes. "My mother has not always been so . . . honest with my father."

"Really," he said blankly. Seconds later he added, "I imagine that's common in many marriages."

She fidgeted, shifting her weight from one foot to the other, leaning against the windowsill for support, hugging herself. "You don't understand."

His eyes widened, but he said nothing more.

Keenly embarrassed, she finally whispered, "I mean faithful—honest in the marriage bed. My mother has . . . been with someone else."

She hadn't felt so disconcerted in ages, standing five feet away from the man of her desire, exposing family secrets of an intimate nature. But he didn't appear shocked; his expression remained neutral.

"I see," he murmured at last.

She glanced at the wall, her eyes grazing over paintings, large and small, each an artistic mastery of color and charm, her gaze finally settling on a luscious landscape, expertly painted in watercolors of teal green and chocolate brown. "I'm not sure when this indiscretion began," she continued, "but I do know it took place several years ago and went on for some months. I-I think it was a love affair."

"Perhaps your information is inaccurate," he said very quietly after a moment of consideration, "or nothing but a rumor overstating an innocent flirtation."

She knew he was trying to be delicate with her sensibilities; how she wished very much that he were right.

"It's not inaccurate, Jonathan," she corrected, turning back to him. "Nor was it just an innocent flirtation. If I wasn't so absolutely certain about this I never would have come to France to engage you."

The wicker beneath him creaked as he placed his palms on his knees and pushed himself up from the chair. But he didn't move toward her. Instead he crossed his arms over his chest, standing erect, regarding her thoughtfully. "Engage me for what?"

She inhaled deeply, raising her chin in a measure of obstinacy.

"The man of her improper affection was Paul Simard, a Parisian and an officer in the National Guard. My mother met him during the social season, on one of her many visits to the Continent, and they became enamored of each other. Eventually they . . . carried on."

She didn't know how else to describe it, and he was probably laughing inside. But she couldn't think about that. The moment of truth had arrived. She had nothing to lose now.

"As I said, the affair went on for some time, after which my mother returned to England—and my unknowing father. But the problem, Jonathan, is that it didn't end there. If it had, there would be no proof. As it was, there was."

Now he looked confused. "There was what?"

"Proof."

"Proof of . . . ?"

Her lips thinned irritably. "Proof of the"—she flicked her wrist—"liaison, the romance. That she was his willing mistress."

He stared hard at her. "Natalie, what are you saying to me?"

She dropped her hands to her sides, forcing the calm within her. "Paul Simard died three years ago, in Paris. Roughly two months later my mother began receiving requests for money. It seems she and her French . . . lover had corresponded with each other for a while after her return to England, and now Paul Simard's son, Robert, has the love letters in his possession and is blackmailing her with the threat of exposure. These letters are of an explicit nature, and she is in great distress over this, paying when she can, unsure what to do next, afraid to confront my father. I think you know, Jonathan, that this could be ruinous for her, scandalous to my family, and devastating for my father if the letters are read by others, or her indecent behavior is ever made known within society."

She took a step toward him, lowering her voice to an impassioned whisper. "I need you to escort me to Paris, find Robert Simard, and steal my mother's letters from him. Six of them in all. When that is accomplished, I will return the emeralds to you.''

Jonathan gaped at her, utterly incredulous. If he had been with any other woman he would have laughed himself silly at such a command. What had his life become that he now found himself in a situation so ridiculous, a farce of such unbelievable proportions? He was Europe's most famous thief. Legends had been built around his cleverness, his unique style, his successes. He'd held priceless Chinese artifacts in his hands, smuggled thousands of pounds worth of diamonds from one country to another, helped right social wrongs, hunted and found political criminals, was even indirectly responsible for saving national governments from possible collapse. Yet she stood before him, elegantly poised, shiny, sun-warmed hair spilling over her shoulders, her exquisitely curved body tense with determination, demanding he take her to Paris to steal *love letters*? He'd underestimated her. She was devious in approach, beautiful of face and form, and most assuredly insane of mind. She was also deadly serious, and he was in trouble.

But it was Natalie herself, not her laughable request, that gave him pause. Jonathan could not recall a time in his life when he'd gazed upon anything so incredibly sweet as this innocent woman divulging her mother's infidelity to a man she knew had been with many women. Her cheeks flushed pink from a shame she couldn't even verbalize, her eyes vibrant with trepidation as she tried to put the action of sexual misconduct into words like ''carried on.'' She possessed a great bearing, an honesty of will he didn't think he'd ever seen in another, a devotion to goodness and faithfulness in marriage rarely witnessed. And it moved him in a manner he didn't exactly understand. He wanted to reach for her suddenly, to pull her against the hardness of his body, to comfort, to draw the warmth and sweetness from her lips in a breathless pursuit of passion. To feel her.

''What are you thinking, Jonathan?'' she murmured with only the slightest hint of apprehension.

For a long, silent moment he looked into her eyes. Then

he smiled faintly, acknowledging defeat, and raked his fingers through his hair. "That I really don't want to go to Paris."

She bristled, fisting her hands at her sides, her eyes flashing with hot anger. "I thought certainly you'd do it for the emeralds," she charged, "but I was also prepared for the fact that you'd find my situation foolish and unimportant—"

"I don't think it's foolish or unimportant," he cut in frankly. "I think this is just another form of blackmail."

That stopped her for a second or two. Then her lids thinned with deliberation anew, her mouth twisting in a smile of ultimate triumph, and she began to saunter toward him. "If you take me to Paris, I'll give you something more, Jonathan."

She'd misunderstood him. He hadn't exactly said he wouldn't go. But now he found himself intrigued, which in turn compelled him to keep his intentions silent.

"More?" he prodded.

She stood directly in front of him now, her breasts nearly touching his chest, her expression exuding shrewdness with the thought of her objectives.

"If you take me to Paris and retrieve my mother's letters," she intimated guardedly, "I will give you something you can use. Something you want. Something priceless to you and your . . . convictions."

It wasn't her manner but her unusual words that dazed him. "What could you possibly have that would be more valuable to me than the priceless emerald necklace?"

Her brows pinched negligibly, whether in speculation or confusion he wasn't sure. Then her entire countenance became grave. "I think that's for you to discover," she said in a most sensual whisper. "But I won't disappoint you, Jonathan."

Perhaps it was her tone of absolute certainty, perhaps just the expectation in the air, the anticipation of things to come, but with a raw surge of an indescribable physical hunger, he understood her at last, dared to imagine the possibilities. He knew, and it shook him deeply.

"These letters are that important to you?"

"They mean everything to me," she replied resolutely.

His eyes skimmed over every feature of her face—from her long, thick lashes and arched brows, to her forehead, temples and high cheekbones, to her perfect lips and the gently carved line of her chin and jaw. Then he reached out and touched her hair, running his fingers through the silky strands, marveling in the softness, the texture of it, longing to feel it against his cheek, his neck, and chest. Taking her at her will, cradling himself inside her warmth, holding her against him in the heat of rapture would mean everything to him. She knew this, too.

"How can I trust you to keep your end of the deal?" he asked in a raspy, quiet voice.

Her eyes melded with his. "Because you said you already do, and I believe you."

It was the cleverness within her that enchanted him, he realized now, her quickness to take matters into her hands, to experience the adventure that was life.

Smiling vaguely, Jonathan dropped his arms to his sides. "Maybe I can't accept that, Natalie. Maybe I'd rather just search you for the emeralds."

She knew he was teasing her, and still it wasn't what she'd expected him to say. She pulled back from him a little, unsure.

"You'll never find them in my trunks—"

"I've no doubt," he cut in pleasantly. "It would take me weeks to go through them all anyway."

Stiffening, ignoring that, she asserted, "And naturally you wouldn't dream of searching my person. I think, then, Jonathan, you really have no choice."

Her confidence thoroughly amused him. But he didn't have to comment verbally. The look he gave her implied most certainly that he would indeed search her person, slowly, caressingly, enjoying every second of it with indescribable pleasure.

"I will take you to Paris," he whispered richly, "and once there you will give me everything of value you've promised me."

It was a demand, and she understood the significance of it, wavering a little as relief visibly flooded her, as she stared into his unyielding eyes so expressively conveying his desires.

"I agree to your terms, Jonathan," she said in a sudden rush of eagerness. "We'll leave this afternoon—"

"No, we'll leave tomorrow."

That stumped her. "Why?"

He took note of the defiance in her stance, the subtle swell of her breasts and hips. She would give him all in Paris, but he wasn't ready to let go of the innocence so quickly, of their time alone in their intimate bungalow on the shores of the Mediterranean Sea.

"Because I am still in charge, Natalie, regardless of the power you have over me. Remember that."

She glared at him, a firm rebuttal on the tip of her tongue. He disregarded that entirely, turning away from her at last and striding once again to the table where their lunch, probably now cold, awaited them. "Let's eat. I'm starving."

Fuming, and without another word, she gracefully walked to his side and sat again.

Twelve

Natalie ran her brush through her hair one final time, placed it on the dressing table, and stood. She pulled her robe tightly around her, clasping it at the neck with her fingers, at last turning toward the bed.

Jonathan already lay under the coverlet, facedown, head buried in his pillow, arms beneath it, probably asleep, which was the way she liked it when she finally rested her body beside him. The room was dark save for a small lamp next to the bed and a strong full moon reflecting off the distant water to shine through the windows.

They'd spent their last day in Marseilles together, relaxing on the shore, talking of trivial things as well as some of Jonathan's Black Knight escapades about which she'd always been especially curious. She had laughed with him over several of his stories, enjoyed his company with a growing respect and admiration for his various accomplishments, many of them incredible to her, and now she was thoroughly glad they hadn't run off to Paris immediately. Aside from her initial anger when she'd confronted him about his identity, the moment when deception and secrets had given way to openness between them, the day had been, well . . . perfect.

Natalie walked to the edge of the bed, removed her robe,

which she placed across the foot of it, dimmed the lamp, and crawled in between the sheets. There was hardly enough room for both of them, and each night it took every effort on her part not to touch him somewhere. Usually, though, she woke up at some point to discover her feet against his legs or her arm against his bare chest, but thankfully he didn't seen to notice this, or care, anyway. He wore no sleeping attire beyond a pair of old trousers, which she considered odd, but that was really none of her business. She, of course, was always decently covered.

Jonathan stirred and turned on his side, facing her. She lay flat on her back, arms folded neatly across her stomach, knowing intuitively he wasn't sleeping after all but looking at her in the moonlight.

"What do you do with your dog?" she whispered, staring at the blackened ceiling.

"What?" he replied in a gruff, low voice.

"Your dog," she repeated. "When you go on your little Black Knight journeys, what do you do with him?"

He inhaled deeply and readjusted his body to lie more comfortably. "If I'm only leaving the city for a few days, my housekeeper and butler look after him. If I actually go abroad, as on this trip, my housekeeper and butler are dismissed with pay, and I leave my dog with my brother at his estate near Bournemouth."

She turned her head to look at what she could see of his face. "You take your dog all the way to the coast?"

He smiled faintly in the shadows. "Every time." Sheepishly, he added, "I love my dog."

That made her smile, which she was sure he could see as moonglow cast a strong light on her features. "Why do you call him Thorn?"

"He's a thorn in my side."

"But yet you love him enough to take him nearly a hundred miles away from home, when you already have household employees who can feed and walk him?"

"It isn't the same," he returned quietly. "Vivian and Simon love him, too; their son loves to play with him. It also gives me a chance to visit them."

She paused for a moment, then her voice became serious as realization washed over her. "Vivian and Simon know who you are."

It was a statement made in sudden awareness, and he actually laughed a little, softly. "Of course they do. I like my brother to know where I am and what I'm doing. I trust him and his wife. They're the only people aside from those I work for—and now you—who know about me, though. And they'd never tell anyone."

That made her absolutely furious. Vivian was the one to suggest she talk to Jonathan in the first place, the one who confided in her that Jonathan knew the Black Knight. Vivian also knew of Natalie's infatuations with both the myth and the man, and had still sent her on a wild adventure of uncertainty, with full understanding of what embarrassment it could eventually cause.

Her lips thinned as she turned her eyes once more to the darkened ceiling. "I'll kill her for lying to me and sending me to you like this."

Jonathan sighed. "I think she knew what she was doing."

His whispered words were meant to soothe, but instead Natalie's mind succumbed to the most devastating notion of all. Voice flowing with hesitancy, she murmured, "Did Vivian tell you about me?"

He was quiet for a moment, a moment so long, in fact, that she finally turned to him again. He watched her pensively, but even that was more perceived than obvious, as the expression on his face, only a foot away from hers, was no more than dimly noticeable.

Finally he sat up a little, resting his elbow on his pillow, his chin and cheek in his right palm, his left hand flat on the sheet next to her shoulder.

"I've inquired about you once or twice during the last few years, Natalie. That's how I knew who was courting you from time to time." He started to rub the sheet with his fingertips. "But Vivian didn't really tell me much about you, and no, before you ask, I didn't know she'd be sending you to me."

His acknowledgment made her grin in more than mild relief and with a certain satisfaction to learn he'd actually asked about her.

"Then I'll still consider her my friend," she said somewhat deviously. For clarification, she added, "And nobody courted me, either. I've never been the least interested in any of the stuffy gentlemen acquaintances to walk into my parlor."

"Except me," he countered in a deep voice.

"You've never walked into my parlor," she innocently reminded him.

He knew she was sidestepping the issue and he smiled again. "No, and I think it would also be accurate to say I'm more than an acquaintance."

"We are certainly nothing more than acquaintances, Jonathan," she corrected, gazing back to the ceiling.

He leaned so close to her she thought for a second he might actually kiss her temple. With lips nearly skimming her ear, he whispered, "Acquaintances of opposite sexes never sleep together, Natalie."

The warmth of his face touched hers; she could smell the lingering traces of soap on his skin, and as much as she trusted him to be a gentleman, nervousness crept in of its own accord. "But this is all by chance—a business arrangement, if it must be named something."

"I wouldn't call it chance or business," he replied. "I would call this fate."

He let the statement linger in the quiet night air. And finally, when she knew he would add nothing more until she did—or looked at him again—she tilted her head fractionally, just enough to gaze into eyes too hidden in darkness to read.

Bravely she contended, "This has nothing to do with fate. I'm here of necessity. I've never been remotely interested in you except for your skills as a thief. Attractiveness aside, you've not one husbandly trait in your body."

"Many women would think otherwise," he stressed with mock formality.

"Precisely my point, dear Jonathan."

That amused him again. She could feel it more than see it, although he didn't argue. He watched her, his face inches from hers, his fingers grazing her upper arm through light cotton as they moved back and forth along the sheet.

"Yet you wanted to marry a thief," he persisted softly. "Certainly you expected to find nothing domestic about him. Or was that whole notion just a made-up story for my benefit?"

He'd let the words sort of . . . spill out of his mouth, and yet she knew by their serious intonation that he was really asking. She couldn't talk about that, however, or disclose just how deeply her dreams had run.

"You're right," she admitted sweetly. "I lied."

He waited a moment, then grasped her arm with his hand and squeezed it gently. "And you're horrible at it."

Her pulse began to race from both the close contact and the implication of his words. He knew she was lying now, that her original intentions were exactly as she'd confessed. But alas, he played the gentleman by not dwelling on her embarrassment, although from instinct, and perhaps because she was growing to know him so well, she realized just how much he wanted her to admit and explain her innermost feelings.

And yet she couldn't. Twice in her life now she'd been humiliated by her candid disclosures to Jonathan Drake, and that was enough. Things were too intimate between them as it was, lying next to him in bed, feeling his warmth, smelling the salty, sea air mixed with the alluring masculine scent of him. Quietly she changed the subject.

"You were the one to donate hundreds to Lady Julia Beverly's home for unfortunate girls, weren't you, Jonathan?"

She could sense his surprise at the turn in conversation, and perhaps even his dismay that he no longer wanted to talk about them. For seconds he said nothing, just continued to stare at her in the moonlight, caressing her arm without apparent thought. But this was something she was aching to know; it was one of London's greatest mysteries, and at the time of its occurrence had created scrumptious gossip

around the city. Most were certain the act had been insti-
gated by the Black Knight, but it was one of those inci-
dences that hadn't led to him directly.

Finally he breathed deeply and nodded in acknowledgment. "About two years ago," he started thoughtfully, "I
was asked to look into the theft of an antique diamond-
studded pocket watch, reported missing by Sir Charles Ken-
dall. Sir Charles had said it was stolen at his club during a
high-stakes card game between several members of the gentry. I became involved because the watch's description
matched that of one stolen nine years earlier from a Mr.
Herold Larken-James, a barrister and collector of fine an-
tiquities, who died in a fire before his watch could be found
and returned to him.

"The job took me weeks, actually, one of the longest
I've ever done, because I had to risk entering the home of
every man who had attended that card game. But my search
eventually proved fruitful when I located the watch in the
wardrobe drawer of Walter Pembroke, a retired navy ad-
miral, who had swiped it himself during the game, where
everyone was betting heavily and drinking too much to notice. In the end it turned out indeed to be the watch of Mr.
Larken-James, as his initials were carved very delicately on
the inside, and because he was dead with no family to
whom I could return the watch, I decided to give it to a
better cause. Technically, at that time, since it wasn't rightfully anyone else's, it belonged to me."

Intrigued, intimacies forgotten, Natalie turned on her
side, facing him fully, which forced him to let go of her
arm. She rested her elbow on the pillow exactly as he did,
cheek in palm, and dropped her voice to a whisper. "Perhaps Sir Charles bought it from the person who stole it from
Mr. Larken-James, and he felt he owned it legitimately?"

He shook his head faintly, his mouth turning down in a
slight frown. "I'd wondered that myself at the time, then
came to learn Sir Charles had sought the barrister's services, in the man's office, roughly two weeks before the
watch was reported missing. It was later stolen from his
office on a day when Sir Charles had conveniently held an

appointment; this was documented. Mr. Larken-James didn't suspect him of course, but I've learned over time that class has no bearing when it comes to the negative tendencies of human nature.''

She thought about that for a moment, fascinated. "So why did you choose Lady Julia's cause?''

Without hesitation, he replied, "Because Sir Charles, a not very decent character, had a nasty habit of getting his servant girls in that particular unfortunate condition from time to time, then dismissing them without reference to live, essentially, on the street. I found it fitting that he should help support others who had perhaps fallen into disgrace in a like manner, so I sent the watch to Lady Julia suggesting she discreetly sell it if funds were needed for her home. A month after she did so, I sent another anonymous letter to Sir Charles informing him in detail of what exactly had become of his watch.''

Natalie felt dazzled, touched by the excitement. "Who paid you, then? Certainly not your benefactors. They'd have no reason.''

He lifted his left shoulder minutely. "I wasn't paid for that job.''

She blinked. "You risked exposure and possible arrest for nothing?''

He leaned toward her to murmur, "Once in a while, Natalie, I do my work simply because it feels good.''

It had been an act of kindness, of unselfish service to those less fortunate, she realized, not a deception about which to boast as when he'd stolen the emeralds, and she couldn't help but smile into his eyes.

"How noble you are, Jonathan,'' she teased.

"I can be on occasion.''

"You could have at least taken credit for it,'' she added softly.

Very gently, he admitted, "I had nothing to prove to anyone.''

She gazed at his face only inches away, feeling warmth and contentment encircling them, the serene sense of friendship between them. She longed to reach up and brush the hair off his forehead with her fingers, to touch the stubble on his jaw, the curls on his bare chest. It took all that was in her to hold back. Quite suddenly, lying there so close to him physically, connecting with him confidentially, it occurred to her that she'd not asked him the most personal question of all.

"Why do you do this, Jonathan? What made you decide to become a thief, to invent such an incredible . . . personality of deception?"

He reached for the string ties hanging from the collar of her nightgown and began to twist around his fingers one. He said nothing immediately, which prompted her to press for detail as she moved her right foot forward just enough to rub his shin with her toes.

"I won't tell a soul," she whispered.

He exhaled a small, contented breath. "It's not a secret. I've just never told anyone."

She continued to stroke his leg, saying nothing in reply, hoping he wouldn't now decide not to confide in her.

At last he dropped the arm propping up his head, adjusting his body comfortably beside her, resting his cheek on the pillow once more, eyeing her directly.

"You're an only child," he began, "and female, so maybe you'll not understand this. But I'm the second son of an earl."

She laid her head down beside him, pushing her hands up under her pillow, smiling. "I know that, Jonathan. You're not shocking me yet."

He smiled in return. "Don't take that statement superficially, Natalie. Think about what it means. There are only two of us, Simon and me, nineteen months apart in age. My father was overjoyed that his wife bore him two sons, but I probably would have been better off had I been born a girl—"

Her scoff of the ridiculous cut him off. "That's nonsense talk coming from someone who won't ever have to be one," she scolded. "You have options, the entire world available to you; I'm expected to marry and have babies and bow to my husband's whims."

He tenderly touched her cheek with the back of his fingers. "You don't understand. I'm talking strictly of the attention given girls by their parents. Yes, as a man I can make my own decisions, go places and do things at my discretion. I know society allows me things it doesn't allow women." He lightened his voice. "And of course I enjoy women far too much to ever want to be one. I'm very much thankful I was born male."

She tensed a little at the remark, but he didn't appear to notice, carrying on before she could comment, reaching again for the ties holding her nightgown together at her neck.

"I'm referring to me as an *individual,* Natalie," he explained, subdued. "My parents cared for both Simon and me, there's no question there. But my brother was raised to be an earl; I was raised to be one 'just in case.' My brother was expected to be educated; I was expected to do less because it didn't really matter since I wouldn't be managing the estate. My brother was groomed for importance; I was allowed to do as I pleased most of the time. My brother was the serious one, taking on his duties efficiently and at a young age; I was far more gregarious and teasing by nature, more . . . tolerated, for lack of a better word."

"I should think there are many noblemen wishing they could be second born," she offered. "Where choices and opportunities would be theirs, where the pressures to succeed didn't weigh so heavily on their shoulders."

"I suppose there are," he agreed. "And maybe if I had several brothers and sisters I wouldn't feel this way."

She frowned. "Feel what way, exactly?"

He paused, brows creased in remembrance, concentrating on hidden thoughts. "When I was fourteen I stumbled upon a private conversation between my parents. They were arguing about me, about my carefree nature and lack of application to my studies." Hesitantly he added, "My mother mentioned that I paid too much attention to girls and having fun."

"It seems you haven't changed," she acknowledged without expression.

He smiled faintly again but ignored that, adjusting his head and body so that he moved even closer to her—so close, in fact, that she could feel the warmth emanating from his skin, his soft breath on her cheeks as he talked.

"They were deep in discussion about sending me away," he disclosed huskily, "about sending me abroad—to a boys' school in Vienna. My mother was reluctant, but she and I were very close so this was not surprising. My father felt I lacked refinement as a child of good breeding and that a strict environment designed to instill good moral conduct was what I needed to correct my tendency toward what he felt was irresponsible behavior. In the end, though, due to my mother's determination and my father's adoration for her, I was allowed to remain in England. As far as I know, they never again mentioned it. They never told me of their discussion, and they never knew I knew."

He lowered his tone to a sullen whisper. "The idea of being sent away didn't surprise me, or even really upset me all that much. But it was the actual exchange between them on that day that changed my life, Natalie, and I will never forget it. My mother, crying, said, 'I always thought Jonathan would be the clever one.' To which my father said, 'He's not clever, he's devious. He's an ill-behaved boy who will never amount to anything but a social rake, who will run up debts that will need to be paid by Simon. Simon will be the one to make us proud. Jonathan will be the one to ruin us.' "

Natalie felt a powerful wave of compassion and sympathy course through her as she considered how such a conversation, even spoken with good intentions, could devastate a child if overheard. There was no one in the world who better grasped the feelings of not living up to set ideals, of being underrated and unappreciated.

"I know what it's like never to quite meet parental expectations, Jonathan," she whispered in a silky breath of deep reassurance.

He stared at her as he answered intensely, "I know you do. You're the first person I've ever revealed this to, Natalie, and I did so because you're the only person I've ever known who would so totally understand.''

She felt drawn to him from that simple statement, uttered in absolute honesty and with such depth of emotion, of trust. She lay beside him, alone together in a small, warm bed, in a beautiful bungalow on the seashore of an enchanted land, and right now, for her, they were the only two people in existence.

''So why did you choose to become a thief?'' she asked, looking into his blackened eyes. ''Doesn't that mean they've won?''

He placed his palm over her nightgown, flat on her chest though just under her neck, and for the first time ever, the forward action didn't bother her at all. It felt marvelously natural.

''Think about it, Natalie,'' he suggested in a smooth, rich voice. ''We've all won.''

That's when she fully understood. He lived the life expected of him and his station, a life carefree but with the underlying stability of honest work, his amazing cleverness and achievements as a fantastic thief concealed beneath the guise of a frivolous air of gaiety within fashionable society. Most of all, he had grown into the man he wanted to be with the integrity his parents had never foreseen.

''But they've been dead for years, Jonathan,'' she argued carefully. ''They never knew you as the Black Knight. They'll never know of your successes.''

He smiled again. ''*I* will know.''

She grinned in return. ''And Simon.''

''And Simon,'' he concurred.

Silence grew around them, calmness filling the room, and neither one of them moved. Jonathan had a better view of her than she did of him, he realized with a slight acknowledgment of the advantage. The full moon behind him cast a glow to her vivid eyes so full of expression, to her face and shiny hair as it tumbled in waves over her shoulder and breasts. Since she'd crawled into bed, he'd wanted to reach for her, to wrap his arms around her and pull her close, but as always, because he knew how she'd react, he held the desire in check. So naturally it came as a complete surprise when she reached up with her hand and gingerly touched his face, cupping his jaw, the pads of her fingers caressing his cheek as she studied what she could see of his features in the dimness.

He watched her, saying nothing, unmoving for fear she'd back away. It was the first time she'd ever purposely touched him expressing tenderness, flowing from her in radiance, embracing both of them tightly, and he didn't want it to end.

"You're not sad about any of this now, about your parents never knowing what you've become?" she asked in a deep whisper.

"No, not really," he responded at last, yielding to the closeness. "I think they'd be pleased if they knew. I'm happy with the way my life has progressed, and I enjoy what I do. The only thing bothersome about it is that it's a very lonely occupation. I really wish, Natalie, that I'd had you along to keep me company on every single adventure."

She didn't know how to take that at first. She pulled her hand away from his face as her eyes grew to round pools of uncertainty lightly traced with caution. Then her mouth broadened in a smile.

"I'd be trouble."

"But wickedly fun trouble," he teased.

"You'd grow bored with me, Jonathan."

He snickered. "I can't imagine ever growing bored with you, Natalie."

"That's a singularly odd statement coming from a gentleman known for his carousing nature," she returned in a light rebuke. "And at some point we'd get caught. I couldn't lie to my parents about where I was going every time."

"You could marry me, and then I could take you with me anywhere."

He'd suggested that in a jovial tone, and very easily, which surprised him. But it shocked her. He could feel her heartbeat steadily increase beneath his fingertips, hear the shallow, nervous breath escape her lips.

She stared at him, unsure. Then she grew markedly serious, and in the space of seconds the mood between them changed to one of sharp static.

"I will never marry someone like you, Jonathan," she asserted with a sorrowful, profound conviction. "You're a wonderful man, so charming, and I think *very* clever. But I've seen what unfaithfulness can do to a marriage. I've experienced it, and I will never put myself through that— not if I can choose. If I marry at all, it will be to someone devoted to me, and I don't think anyone who has been with many women can be devoted to just one for an entire lifetime."

For the first time ever, Jonathan felt the crushing weight of regret and a sickening wisp of something like panic slowly taking form in the pit of his stomach. Real and centered determination graced her features, and it bothered him more than he thought possible.

"But you wanted to marry the Black Knight," he insisted, sounding calmer than he felt. "He was rumored to have been with many."

Her eyes narrowed; she set a grim line to her mouth. "It was just that, Jonathan, a rumor, which, sadly to me, has turned out to be true."

That irritated him a little. "So how many is too many, Natalie? Three? Fifteen? Or did you expect to marry a virgin?"

She had no idea how to respond to that as the conflicts within her surfaced for his view, shining in her expression.

"I think most ladies are fortunate enough to marry virgins," she answered forcefully.

He slowly shook his head. "I think most ladies are naive or unknowing."

That made her mad, and for a moment he was certain she would leave the bed. But she didn't; she kept her eyes locked with his and didn't appear to notice that he still held his palm on the base of her throat.

Then her face went slack, and gradually she lowered her lashes and surrendered. "Perhaps men are, too," she whispered almost inaudibly.

That admission softened his heart. He knew what she meant, realizing at once how difficult it must be for someone who had never experienced the pleasure of the bedroom to have to understand and then deal with all that pertained to it. She had yet to enjoy the best of it but had already witnessed what was ugliest—a firsthand betrayal.

"Why did you risk your reputation—your entire future— to help your mother when she's been the one to cause such resentment in you?"

Her eyes opened to his again, her brows pinching delicately in noticeable confusion.

"I didn't come to France for her, Jonathan," she revealed in a dark, low voice. "There is very little I hold dear in my heart for a woman who nagged me for twenty-two years about being virtuous, who is so quick to denounce any lady for immoral behavior when she herself lied in the most hurtful way imaginable." She shook her head in disgust. "I wouldn't go to Rochester for my mother. But I would go anywhere on earth to save my father from the disgrace of her adulterous affair."

At last it all became clear to him. He understood her motivations.

"Does your father know?" he asked quietly.

"About the romance?"

He nodded negligibly.

She snuggled down deeper into the pillow and under the coverlet. "He knows. He loves her still, which is hard for me to imagine." Her expression clouded. "He was devastated when he learned the truth, Jonathan, when she admitted that she loved this Frenchman. In all my life I'd never seen my father like that. He was heartbroken. Tensions in our household ran high for a long time, and things are just now starting to settle down to how they were before. But their marriage will never be the same for them. She's ruined that. I just hope you're able to get these letters before society learns of her indiscretion. I don't think my father would live through the humiliation."

Jonathan ran his thumb along her neck, feeling her pulse beating strongly, enjoying the warmth and softness beneath his fingertips. Moonlight made her pale skin glow with the sheen of pearls, her hair shine silver. With his free hand he touched it, lacing it through his fingers as it spilled over her breast and onto the sheet.

"You cannot predict the ups and downs of love and marriage, Natalie." She was uncertain of that statement, and he gave her a comforting smile to explain. "What I mean is that it's impossible to know how any individual will react to life situations. You cannot judge a person by his past."

She stiffened. "My father had no past—"

"That you know of," he cut in. "And your mother likely didn't. I'd bet money that she was a virgin on her wedding night and yet it didn't stop her from becoming unfaithful."

That made her uncomfortable, and Jonathan, for what it was worth, felt a small measure of triumph.

Then she breathed in very deeply, with resolution, her eyes piercing his through the darkness. "I will never marry a man who is likely to hurt me. Sharing intimacies with different women before marriage would only make a man more prone to realize what he's missing when the honeymoon is over."

"You don't know that," he argued soberly.

"The point is not whether I know this to be true, Jonathan, but simply that I won't take the risk," she replied with conviction anew. "I won't marry a man who doesn't love me like my father loves my mother. He knows her favorite color, her favorite wine, her favorite flower. He can order dinner for her down to the specifics because he knows exactly what she likes. He knows her moods, her joys and fears, and adores her because of the good things and in spite of the bad."

Leaning toward him, she clutched her pillow with a brilliant excitement she could no longer contain. "I want love to be fun and exciting and new; something shared—a romantic . . . secret between just the two of us. I want my husband to know that I loathe embroidery and riding horses and gossip between ladies; that I adore chocolate and dark, rainy days and Shakespearean comedies, and the thrill and sparkle of the city at night; that my favorite color is rich, midnight blue; that I've always wanted to attend the opera in Milan and dream of one day traveling to China.''

In a rush, the enthusiasm fled her face as she shook her head in small movements of contempt. ''Geoffrey Blythe doesn't know these things about me. He knows I'm from a good family and that I have a decent dowry, which would likely pay off any future debts of his if he doesn't lose it first. Even worse, he'd never care to learn my interests and desires. All that matters to him, and all the other gentlemen who call on me, is that I was born of quality and will bear hearty sons. Yet my mother would marry me to any of them tomorrow. If they don't love me for who I am, what's to keep any one of them from growing bored with me and the marriage bed and moving on to another? My mother doesn't know that my father loves autumn in the country, adores long walks through the forest, and reads poetry when he's worried. She doesn't *love* him, and I won't marry for anything less.''

Her passion entranced him; her sweetness rocked him. He couldn't find his voice after such an intimate disclosure of hurts and longings, and even anger at the indignities of life. He stared into large, beautiful eyes, felt the heat of her beside him, aching anew to take her into his arms and comfort her completely. He understood the reasons behind her conclusions, and yet he wanted to shake her into believing in him, in the truths of his past, the nature of his desires, and the longings in his own heart. But right now, more than he'd ever wanted anything else, he wanted Natalie to trust him.

From instinct more than calculation, he boldly began to caress her neck in soft, wispy movements. She didn't react outwardly to the touch, just continued to stare at him through the measured stillness. He knew she was thinking about what she'd just said to him, attempting to gauge his reaction, waiting for his response.

''Do you know,'' he whispered very slowly, never taking his eyes from hers, ''just how badly I want to make love to you? Not to your body, Natalie, but to you? Do you know how hard it is to wait for something wonderful?''

Her determination faltered at those words, or perhaps just his confidence, her eyes betraying the first real flicker of doubt, of charged emotions and confusion of purpose.

And from that small hesitation on her part, which he considered to be a positive response, and from his own surge of raw need, he took the ties by his fingers and gently pulled until they gave way, opening the very top of her gown.

Her breathing became shallow, but she was captivated— by his daring, by cravings within her that she was, with each passing day, finding increasingly difficult to resist.

With cautious reverence coupled with a nervousness he'd never felt before, Jonathan placed his palm directly on her skin between her breasts, taking only seconds to savor the heated silkiness beneath his hand and fingers. Then, before she could protest or move, he slid it to the side and covered her bare breast completely.

She sucked in a clear, sharp breath from the contact, but beyond that she remained still, focused, eyes fusing with his—not from fear but with a growing sense of wonder.

His throat tightened; his body ached with an incredible urgency. Gently he stroked her flesh, back and forth and in soft circles, as he brushed her nipple to a hard, round point against his thumb and fingers.

At last she swallowed with difficulty, eyes gleaming with tears before she finally closed them, serenely, grasping his wrist and pulling his hand out from beneath her nightgown. But most perfect of all was that she didn't let it go. She clung to it, cradling his arm tightly against her chest, be- tween her breasts, as if it were a priceless thing she feared losing.

Jonathan remained still beside her, watching her for a long time as she succumbed to sleep, feeling the steady beating of her heart against his hand.

Thirteen

Jonathan stepped through the main doors of the Sorbonne and out into the bright afternoon sunshine. Slowly he descended the steps past students in their nearly uniform dress of dark-blue trousers and black jackets, toward the streets filled with low-income workers, aspiring artists and writers, and elegant gentlemen in plaid trousers and beautifully embroidered waistcoats as they sauntered along the boulevards with carefree distinction.

The political climate throughout Europe was becoming increasingly unsettled. There were grave economic problems in his own country as well as on the Continent. Paris itself was a mass of unrest—talk of revolution and reform during both private and public meetings between the Legitimists, Radicals, Republicans; between peasants and artisans; and of course among those of the middle class. Tensions continued to mount in the city, which was the sole reason Jonathan had found them lodgings outside of it, much to Natalie's irritation, a woman who adored the excitement of it at any time.

His first stop had been to the office of the French National Guard, which had turned up little information regarding Paul Simard and his family. The Guard had its own degree of problems, having been neglected by Louis Philippe for seven full years now. Louis Philippe was king of the French—the Citizen King—not king of France, and as a man he loathed conflict to the point of ignoring those who would protect his throne should unrest grow to actual rebellion. Jonathan didn't know if this was good or bad. Indeed, he really had no opinion on the matter, except to understand how such insistence on peace at any cost could undermine the man's power in a country that reveled in demonstrations and reform. Louis Philippe had allies in England, of course, as their own Queen Victoria approved of him in general, if one could ignore the scandal only last year when he insisted on the marriage of his son to the sister of the queen of Spain, and she had once welcomed him to Windsor, bestowing on him the Order of the Garter. Now there were scandals anew of a domestic nature, regarding France's electoral mismanagement and the bribery of Louis Philippe's minister of war.

Things were progressing toward a negative end. It could be felt in the air. The French people of nearly all classes were restless, and the opposition was beginning to organize, each group espousing its individual cause through angry speeches given during banquets devoted to that purpose, arranged by various political groups. Sir Guy had been correct. The current king was losing the battle, and in Jonathan's opinion it would only be a matter of time before civil unrest turned to violence and Louis Philippe stepped down to certain exile or was assassinated by those with influence like Henri Lemire.

Jonathan stood on the crowded street corner, dressed in the same business attire he wore the day he'd met with Madeleine, only mildly uncomfortable in the mid-July heat. Luck had been with them on their rather uneventful journey to the capital city, as the last week had remained overcast and unusually cool for the middle of summer, the sun making its first appearance in days just two hours ago.

He watched the movement on the city street for several minutes, only vaguely aware of the congestion of people, the shouting and traffic noise, of the smell of unwashed bodies and horse manure commingling with those from street vendor carts overflowing with roasted chicken and lamb, baked breads, and freshly picked flowers.

Jonathan had to admit he was now deeply troubled—not so much by what he'd learned during his thirty minutes in the university, which was disturbing enough, but by his conscience. Three days of investigation in Paris had brought him little word on Robert Simard. He had started at the National Guard, hoping to gain information about the man's father as a former officer, only to learn almost nothing except that his son, Robert, had once been a professor of letters at the Sorbonne. And so he had journeyed there with high hopes this afternoon, the soonest he was able to secure an appointment with the chair, but his hopes had consequently been cut to pieces when he learned Robert Simard had been living quite happily as a well-respected teacher, devoted husband, and loving father of six in Switzerland for the last five years. This, then, could only mean one of two things: Natalie was mistaken about the love letters—where or who they were coming from—or she had lied to him.

Jonathan thrust his hands in his pockets, turned, and slowly began to walk the street—south, he thought, but he wasn't really paying attention. He would need to hire transportation back to the inn where they were staying now, and that was several miles out of the city, but first he wanted to think.

The last few days with Natalie had been difficult for him. His feelings for her were confusing, and, if he considered them honestly, starting to run very deep. Yet he was unsure of the reason for this, or what exactly it would mean for his future. Their attraction to each other only seemed to intensify by the hour, and Jonathan was fairly certain this would not be quenched by a simple bedding. He'd all but concluded they would be lovers, and he also knew that deep inside of her she realized this as well, regardless of whether she chose to acknowledge it.

Yet what tore at his gut was knowing just how adamantly opposed she was to even the *thought* of being married to him. Her convictions were involved, and to Jonathan's growing concern, he was starting to think that even if he seduced her, which he was nearly convinced he could do, she would still not consent to becoming his wife. He could force the issue, but that would likely only produce an irreparable rift between them, and from that she would never learn to trust him, nor to love him as a man. She liked him, enjoyed him, desired him passionately, but that was as far as she allowed her feelings to go. He now had to admit it would please him tremendously if Natalie actually fell in love with him, and he assumed he felt that way because she was the first woman he'd ever known who was so thoroughly opposed to it. If she loved him, and admitted it to herself, she would probably give in and marry him, which was the outcome he desired. But he didn't know how to argue her stubbornness, and her firm assumption that he would ultimately hurt her. She didn't trust him with her feelings, and he had no idea what to do about that.

Jonathan groaned uncomfortably, stopping in mid-stride, which almost caused a rotund woman with a child in each hand to collide with him, though he hardly noticed this as he rubbed his eyes with his fingertips, deep in thought.

It all would have been so simple if Robert Simard still lived in Paris and had been blackmailing her mother as Natalie had concluded. The letters themselves would have been easy to steal. What bothered him most about this, however, was the idea that she might have fabricated the entire story. But for what purpose? To get him to take her to Paris? Even if she had political ties and a desire to see the fall of the current king, why would she need to be here amid the unrest to witness it directly? Why would she resort to prevarication and bribery when he would so soon discover the story of her mother's adulterous affair to be untrue? She wasn't dim-witted, and just the idea of her going to such trouble seemed far-fetched, even ridiculous to him.

No, Jonathan was certain, after careful consideration, that she had told him the truth as she believed it. And she hadn't invented the tender display of emotion that had so sharply affected him their last night in Marseilles. She was pained by the entire matter, of that he was sure, and even without her own attempt at deception and blackmail he would have helped her. The necklace she now kept hidden in the bottom of a trunk was meaningless to him. It was her innocence, her respect and admiration, her soul that he prized.

So, standing in the middle of a busy sidewalk in the center of Paris, the late sun gradually falling behind tall buildings, the sounds and smells of clopping horses and bustling pedestrians filling the air, Jonathan found himself despondent, feeling helplessly alone, and unsure what to do next. Mostly, he realized, he was consumed with the discomfiting notion that he would soon have to inform Natalie that he had failed her. That's where the weight of his conscience kicked in.

He had no idea what to tell her. Robert Simard was a married teacher living in Switzerland, making a decent living and raising a family. The chance that he was the blackmailer was remote. The man would have very little to gain and much to lose if he were discovered or arrested. That meant someone else had the letters, or said he did, and was using Robert Simard's name precisely because he knew the Frenchman was living quietly in another country. This scenario made far more sense. But who? He would likely never discover this. The only way he could possibly gain more information would be to talk to Natalie's mother himself, and he absolutely dreaded that idea. It was also possible this was all contained in England, that someone unknown to Natalie's mother had learned of the affair—and the subsequent correspondence—and was blackmailing her from the comfort of his or her quaint English parlor. But again, there were too many questions, not enough leads, and nothing he could do in Paris without more details.

Jonathan vacantly stared down the street, stalling. Natalie awaited him, hopeful that his day in the city would prove to be productive, and she would be crushed to learn he didn't have the letters in his possession. What unsettled him most, though, was the concern that when she learned he had nothing to give her, she would become angered at his incompetence, consider him a liar, or worse a fool, pack her bags, and return to England without him. He had enough of an ego to realize he wouldn't take that chance. In France he was essentially in charge of her; she was dependent upon him. In England, if she wasn't his wife, she could refuse to see him altogether, and that would be the end of everything.

His only other option, and of course the delicious, gratifying one, would be purposely to deceive her, then take her virginity as she'd offered him in Marseilles. But Jonathan, even reflecting on his sometimes unscrupulous past, had never been so devious as to take a woman's innocence with an outright lie. He now faced a huge moral decision—a test of his character as a man. Yes, he would marry her. Her reputation would remain intact. That was not the issue. But could he mislead her so blatantly that she willingly gave herself to him in exchange for a falsehood? He didn't know, but he didn't think he could. And yet the alternative was to lose her.

Jonathan turned around and started retracing his steps. A gust of wind picked up to blow old newspaper and leaves from the street against his legs. It was getting late. She would be waiting for him, and he would need to make his decision on the ride to the inn.

Fourteen

Natalie hated waiting for anything. It made her feel nervous and agitated, and when she had to wait for something as important as the love letters that would keep her father from ever having to succumb to a lifetime of shame and social pity, she could hardly sit still. Jonathan had told her flatly that he wouldn't pursue this delicate issue if she insisted on going to the city with him, and she'd relented because, when put like that, she had no choice. But now, as she sat on a cushioned wrought-iron bench in the plush rose garden behind the Auberge de la Cascade, she felt growing aggravation. It was already dusk, and he had yet to return with news. He was the most exasperating man she'd ever known, and when she didn't impulsively want to wrap her arms around his neck and kiss him desperately, she wanted to strangle him. Like right now.

Leaning back completely against the soft yellow cushion, Natalie closed her eyes, placed her hands in her lap, tapped her fingers together, and tried to think of something else.

She had no idea why the owners called this the Inn of the Waterfall. There wasn't one anywhere near it. It was, though, a perfectly enchanting place to stay, being fairly isolated in a country meadow, surrounded by lush, well-tended gardens containing mostly roses but also other seemingly exotic vegetation—flowers and plants she'd never seen before. They weren't all that far from the city, but one would never know it to wake up to the sound of birdsong and the scent of moist roses drifting in through open windows.

The two-story inn had only six sleeping rooms besides the kitchen, dining room, and a centralized salon, which was decorated in burgundy and various shades of green. Their own room, overlooking the rose garden in back, was delicately feminine in design, trimmed in plum, teal, and soft yellows, and contained only a small, comfortable bed, two reading chairs, a bedside table, and a fireplace. They'd been staying there for days now, and although she found it peaceful and lovely to look at, Natalie was becoming quite bored. Jonathan had deduced this readily enough, and had this morning mentioned that he'd attempt to confiscate the letters today if Robert Simard could be found. Then they could at last move on. But to what?

The thought of returning home depressed her. For the last few weeks she'd been living a sort of fairytale existence. She adored France, its people and relaxed culture. And being there with such an enjoyable escort made it all the more delightful. That was the sad part, really. The adventure had been thrilling, but it wouldn't have been nearly so if she'd come with anyone other than Jonathan. Returning home, mission completed, with the knowledge that she would no longer be spending her days in his presence, filled her with an unusual sense of regret and an agitation of its own kind.

She was growing to care too deeply for him. She realized this now but hadn't the vaguest notion of what to do about it—other than get away from him, which was impractical while they remained on the Continent. If she acted on her feelings, they would only cause her pain in the end. Jonathan was a social charmer, a man who flirted unconditionally and took mistresses at his leisure. He could never be faithful to one woman, and that would be the only way she'd have him. She'd tried to make that clear in Marseilles, stating her convictions reasonably and without pretense.

She refused to be his lover and had certainly said as much, but naturally, abiding by his reputation and character, he'd promptly touched her on an intimate part of her body, bringing all the hunger she felt within up front for exposure to his ego. He wanted her physically, and even now, shivering inside at the thought of unknown pleasures, she realized she wanted him, too, and that's what she had to fight. She was losing her heart to him already—which made her terribly mad at herself—and that was enough. She'd get over the romantic dreams eventually. But if she gave him her body she would lose a part of herself forever.

Natalie slipped off her shoes and pulled her bare feet up and under her gown, hugging her knees against her chest, trying to push the indecent thoughts from her mind. She'd taken a long bath that afternoon—for lack of something better to do, really. She decided that because they were still in the country, she would dress casually, donning a simple, white silk blouse and a rose-colored muslin skirt without stays. She'd also decided to forgo plaits and ribbons, instead wearing her hair down to dry in the warm, light evening breeze. Her mother would faint dead if she had even the slightest idea of where she was right now, what she wore—or didn't wear as in the case of a corset and stockings—that her unruly curls were hanging loosely down her back, in the open air where *anyone* could see. Fashionable English ladies wore binding layers to cover them nearly head to foot, even for a casual stroll through the park on the hottest of summer days. This was stupid and unnecessary, in her opinion, but then her opinions never had the least effect on her mother. She would call it loose; Natalie called it freedom.

Smiling in satisfaction, she turned her face to the last of the setting sun. She could do what she wanted here, and was utterly contented to know Jonathan didn't care as many gentlemen would. He was refined though not at all stuffy, proper yet playful, concerned for her safety yet he allowed her the relative freedom to do as she liked. He was engaging and exciting and smart, and one of the closest friends she'd ever had, accepting her exactly as she was, applying no conditions. With any hope at all, he'd want to remain her friend for years to come.

It would, of course, be sad to leave the comfort of his daily presence, and she had to concede she had unusually mixed feelings about how their relationship would continue once he married, which, oddly enough, he seemed desirous of doing suddenly. She also had a little trouble envisioning him kissing another woman with the same intensity with which he kissed her, although she tried not to think about that. She adored his kisses herself, and in truth would miss those intimate moments most of all.

Natalie sighed and gradually opened her eyes to a vivid floral array of all colors, and striking gray-blue eyes as they gazed down at her from only three feet away.

She blinked, somewhat startled to see his handsome form towering over her, hands on hips, features unreadable. Immediately she succumbed to embarrassment, as if he were intruding on her very private thoughts. Knowing he witnessed the blush in her cheeks but attempting to ignore it herself, she smiled into his eyes. "I didn't hear you."

His brows rose. "Obviously."

When he added nothing, she carefully asked, "How long have you been standing there?"

"What exactly were you thinking?"

The blunt question intimidated her a little, but she refused to let him see it. And because she didn't want him to know she thought about almost nothing but him, which was precisely what *he* was thinking, she turned it around to her advantage.

"I was thinking about you, Jonathan," she admitted, eyes large, expression shining with exaggerated innocence. "I was thinking how enjoyable our time has been together in France, how romantic you are, especially when choosing lodgings, how I shall miss the tender kisses between us once we return to England." She paused, then smiled again mischievously. "And other things."

That answer thoroughly confused him. He had no idea whether to believe her, which was naturally what she wanted. For seconds he just looked at her, considering the truth behind her words.

"Other things? What more could there be?"

She lifted her shoulders negligibly. "Trivialities."

"Ahh . . ." He strode to the bench with that evasion, turned and sat heavily beside her, blocking what remained of the sun with his large body as he leaned forward, feet spread apart, elbows on knees, hands clasped in front of him. "Were you really thinking of kissing me?"

It was a boastful question tinged with a real desire to know, and she couldn't help but brighten inside. "Of course, Jonathan," she answered pleasantly. "You're a marvelous kisser. But then one does get better at almost anything with practice, and I know you've had plenty of it."

He gazed out to the roses, shaking his head in a small measure of defeat as his lips turned up. She could see amusement etched on the side of his face, although he tried to hide it.

"I suppose you've broken the rule, then, darling Natalie. You were marvelous at it the very first time."

He had to say that and throw a spark to the brush. She'd had the upper hand with her comments, keeping him guessing as to her thoughts and intentions, and like always he knew exactly what to say to return the advantage to him.

She straightened a little and changed the subject. "Let's see . . . What did I do today? Oh, yes, I took a long bath, listened to the innkeeper loudly scolding local children for picking strawberries from the garden vine, watched bees pollinate flowers, and other equally exciting things. Did you do anything quite as thrilling while you played in the big city without me?"

He tossed her a quick glance, possibly to see if she were really annoyed, then looked down at the graveled pathway as he began tapping his fingers together in a triangle in front of his face. "I'm sure your day was far more relaxing than mine."

"I've been relaxed for a week now."

"It's also safer here—"

"What are you keeping me safe from, Jonathan? Pick-pockets?" She gasped sarcastically and clutched her throat with her palm. "Goodness gracious, what if I caught one in the act? I wouldn't know what to do with a thief if I had one in my hands."

He pressed his lips together to keep from laughing, or perhaps just to stop himself from delivering a crass rebuttal. Before he could attempt one, however, she jumped to the most important issue.

"And while we're on the subject of thieves, were you able to steal my mother's indecent love letters?"

His tensed a little, breathing deeply, hesitating just long enough for her to gather the worst.

"You didn't find Robert Simard, did you?" she asked in a tone nearly pleading for reassurance that he had.

He continued to stare at the ground. "I know where he is."

She had no idea what that meant, uncertain if she should feel relieved or worried. He wasn't acting at all like a professional thief who'd completed a successful day of work.

"But you don't have the letters," she affirmed slowly.

After several silent seconds, he started shuffling his right foot back and forth along the gravel.

"Robert Simard lives in Switzerland," he revealed quietly, "with his wife and family, and has done so for five years. It's highly unlikely he's involved."

It took a long time for his words to penetrate her mind, for her to grasp the information and compile it into coherent thought. She scrutinized the thick, shiny hair falling over his brow, the dark stubble on his chin and jaw as evening growth began to shadow his face. She could feel the heat from his shoulder and leg so close to her, and in a moment of absurdity, she wondered why she noticed these things when her life suddenly seemed to be whirling out of her control.

"He's a well-respected professor of letters, Natalie," he carried on, subdued. "With students, a wife, and six children, I don't see how he'd have the time to blackmail your mother even if he wanted to. I also learned he's held in high moral regard by his peers and makes a good living. He doesn't need the money, and I can't imagine him going to this much trouble for revenge. If he were caught and arrested he'd lose everything he values."

Natalie's mouth went dry. Her heartbeat quickened. Never had she imagined it could be anyone else. "I don't understand," she mumbled. "My mother is positive it's him."

Jonathan turned and looked at her directly, brows creasing. "What makes her think so?"

She shook her head faintly. "I-I'm not sure. I know he detested her and felt she was the one to start the affair, seducing his father who was also married."

"Was that likely?"

"Probably." She closed her eyes and wiped a palm across her brow, feeling hot color creeping into her cheeks again, finding it now difficult to look at him as she revealed private family secrets. "She's received three anonymous, threatening letters demanding money, by courier, and that's how she's been paying. By courier. She refuses to tell the authorities, obviously because of the social implication, but I also suspect because she may have been unfaithful before—with someone in England—and doesn't want that to become known."

After a second or two of silence, she opened her eyes to his once more. He regarded her attentively, thinking.

"And your father knows of the relationship she had with the Frenchman, but is ignorant of someone blackmailing her with the threat of exposing the explicit love letters she wrote to him?"

"Yes. Exactly."

He waited. "Is he aware of the letters she wrote Paul Simard?"

"Yes," she said very softly. "Their existence came out during an exchange."

"An exchange?"

That made her uncomfortable again, and she sank a little lower on the bench. "Between them. A—heated argument."

"I see. . . ." After another short pause, he asked guardedly, "Was your father ever in residence when the courier arrived?"

She frowned. "I don't know. Why?"

The breeze shifted, blowing her hair in front of her face, and without thought he reached up and brushed it from her cheek, studying her silently, his gaze taking in her features one at a time. He was piecing together a puzzle of his own, but he didn't share it with her. He was being cautious—overly so.

"What are you thinking, Jonathan?" she demanded gently.

He hesitated before answering, so clearly weighing the decision to reveal his opinion on the matter, but she refused to back down.

Finally he lowered his voice to a deep whisper. "The letters obviously exist, but I don't know who's threatening your mother, Natalie, or where this person is exactly. I'm willing to steal them for you but I need more information. And I need more time."

"Where else can you look?" she murmured bleakly. "Where would you start?"

His eyes crinkled as he attempted a comforting smile. "I don't know yet. But we may need to stay in France longer than expected."

Never in two years had she considered that the Black Knight might fail. He was the best, a legend with remarkable successes attached to his name. Only moments ago she had lived with the joy of being in France with him, and with hope. Now she struggled beneath the crushing weight of an imminent defeat.

"My parents will be returning to England soon, Jonathan."

The reassurance expressed in his features gave way to concern. "When?"

"In three weeks," she replied, running her palm up and down her leg. "That doesn't give us much time together."

He sighed and sat back fully against the cushion, knees apart, hands folded in his lap. "No," he admitted, once more turning his gaze to the roses. "But probably enough."

She wondered how he would know this, but since he added nothing more, she didn't push for detail. He was evidently considering ways he might help her and hadn't mentioned the emeralds at all in the discussion, or her promised gift of appreciation. He felt a genuine commitment to her, and that was all she could ask of him. She treasured it because she had no one else in the world now.

Suddenly, sitting alone with him in a glorious flower garden, through the soothing sound of rustling leaves and the scent of roses lingering in looming twilight, time stilled as a breath of clarity enveloped her. Jonathan had always been truthful with her, even now, as he was likely embarrassed by his lack of success and unsure of what to say. And from her own sense of compassion, with the tender filling of her heart, she recognized just how deeply her emotions ran— not with distress or anger at his apparent failure, but with a flourishing devotion only to him.

She dropped her knees to her side, resting them along his thigh, then reached for his arm, locking hers around it and pulling it against her bosom. Curling her feet up farther under her gown and snuggling into him, she leaned her head on his shoulder.

"You'll find them for me," she whispered passionately, staring out at the roses. "I believe in you, Jonathan. You're my truest friend."

Jonathan had never been more profoundly moved. His throat closed tightly from a sudden, violent invasion of his soul, and he couldn't speak, couldn't respond. He'd never expected this reaction from her, such sweet acceptance of his words, such total faith in his experience and abilities— in him. He felt an immediate rush of guilt for selfishly exaggerating the truth just to keep her by his side as long as possible, and annoyance with himself for wasting time in the city when he could have been here; for not believing in her.

A magical silence surrounded them, and he relished the moment, her head on his shoulder, her body so close to him, warm and soft. The sun had finally slipped below the hills to the west, and the windows of the inn were illuminated with lamplight, causing a golden hue to spread across the garden.

He lowered his head just enough to feel her hair on his cheek, closing his eyes to the softness of it against his face, brushing it back and forth with his lips, inhaling the scent of it, wanting nothing more than to sit there with her for hours, savoring their extraordinary closeness.

And then, very slowly, it began. She turned to him, and with a delicate, almost hesitant touch, pressed her lips to his cheek. She kept them there for seconds before moving them to his jaw, then gradually upward to his temple. They weren't kisses exactly—just a soft caress of her warm mouth against his skin.

An instantaneous fire erupted within him; outwardly he didn't move, could hardly breathe. He kept himself motionless, basking in the feel of her legs against his thigh, her full breasts against his arm, in the gentleness she gave him freely at that second in time. It would be enough, for now, if she pulled back. But she didn't. She lifted her free arm, placing her palm on his neck, running her thumb along his jaw, her fingers in the hair at his nape.

Still, he did nothing, waiting for the affection she unveiled to end, though hoping desperately that it wouldn't. She had never reached for him before, had always denied the strength of the attraction between them, so perceptible to him even the night they had met five long years ago. Then at last, as if gradually coming to terms with an internal struggle she could no longer avoid, she ceased all movement of her lips and fingers, and lifted her head to look up into his face.

His heart began to pound. The glow from the inn cast only a dim light on her features, but even in the shadow of dusk he read her thoughts, comprehended the ache she felt for an experience she had never known, witnessed the charge of emotion to escape her eyes and sear through his own.

Jonathan would always count this as one of the most powerfully touching moments of his life. She stared into his eyes conveying only a trace of apprehension, but more clearly an overwhelming marvel of something discovered, something new and wonderful.

Gingerly she raised her fingers to his lips, skimming them in slow form, her gaze never moving as she attempted to assess his response to the contact. And from that he could hold back no longer. He kissed them delicately, first one, then another, then all of them, one at a time, as he reached for her face with his own hand, placing his palm on her cheek and stroking it with his thumb.

They remained like that, caught in time, until finally, in a deep, choked voice, he whispered her name and she gave in, closing her eyes and turning her head just enough to kiss his palm, to rub her cheek in his hand.

His heart melted from wonder; his body weakened from incredulity at the change in her he had never anticipated.

Eyes shut, she leaned up to his face again, placing tiny kisses on his cheek and jaw, his chin and lips.

He responded in kind by at last pulling his arm free of her grasp, turning slightly and cupping her face in his hands, returning with kisses of his own, brushing his lips against her cheeks and forehead and lashes. She placed her palms on his shoulders, her fingers caressing him through the layers of his jacket and shirt.

Jonathan realized where she would take him in only the deepest corner of his mind, but he couldn't allow himself to believe she would take him there tonight. Not yet. Dreams became a painful thing when hoped for too much and never fulfilled. He wanted what she would give but he would only guide, never push her toward it.

Sometimes, though, the best of dreams became breathtaking reality, as this one did when at last, after only the briefest hesitation, she reached forward through a sigh of surrender and placed her mouth directly on his.

Jonathan knew this was the final yielding of her innocence to him. Perhaps she had yet to acknowledge the loss tonight of what would be her greatest gift, but he knew, and he would give her so much more in return for it. He would give her all that he was.

Taking the directive, he wrapped his arms around her, pulling her into him, molding his lips to hers, relishing in her softness, her tenderness, in the warmth of the breeze and the smell of flowers lingering in quiet nightfall. She kissed him back fully, pressing her breasts against his chest, moving her mouth in rhythm with his, opening for him should he decide to invade. And he did, tasting the sweetness, his breath quickening, hunger mounting, one hand splayed across her back, the other through her hair.

She pulled him tighter still, her own needs rising to surface as she resigned herself to the passion, a tiny whimper escaping her as he flicked his tongue across her top lip. She ran her fingers through his hair, teased his lips with urgency from hers, unconsciously rubbed her thigh against his.

But it wasn't until she turned into him and crossed her leg over his in an attempt to move closer that Jonathan knew he'd had enough of the prelude. They were still in the rose garden, behind an inn full of people, and in only moments they would lose themselves to each other and forget that.

Reluctantly he stilled, placed both palms on her cheeks, and gently lifted his mouth from hers. He pulled back just enough to gaze at her beautifully flushed face, her closed eyes and parted lips, moist from contact with his. Her breath came fast and unevenly, and within seconds she raised her lashes to look at him.

She knew. He could see it in her eyes.

Managing only a hint of a smile, Jonathan slowly traced her bottom lip with his thumb, then whispered huskily, "Come with me."

She blinked, her thoughts unsteady, and then she nodded.

He released her cheeks, took her hand in his, and stood, helping her rise and stand beside him. Quickly she reached for her shoes and slipped them onto her feet, then he turned and led her along the narrow gravel path toward the back of the inn.

Neither spoke as she followed him through opened French doors. He strode with purpose past the salon now coming to life with mingling visitors taking hors d'oeuvres as they awaited dinner, then up the central oak staircase. On the landing he turned left and headed to their room— the last on that floor. Still clinging to him with her left hand, she passed him the key she'd kept hidden in one of the pockets of her skirt and he swiftly unlocked the door, entering the darkened room without delay. Just as rapidly she stepped in behind him before he closed it and once again bolted it for the night. Silently, in near blackness, he released her hand and walked three feet to the bedside table, lighting the small lamp sitting upon it. That done, he pivoted back to her, eyeing her at last with penetrating confidence.

She stood uncertain but not fearful, and still aroused enough to want to continue where they'd left off—he could see it in her shining cheeks and full, rosy lips, her glazed eyes. Quickly he removed his jacket and waistcoat and tossed them on a nearby chair, then reached up and untied his neckcloth, dropping it on the table behind him.

"Are—are we going to kiss some more, Jonathan?"

She exuded a certain nervousness, but her voice was thick and saturated with desire, and it took everything in him not to yank her against his chest, to draw the breath from her with a bruising kiss, to pull her harshly against his aching erection, to force her to feel—to know—what she did to him. But her inexperience also gave him pause as he considered just how slowly the night was going to move for them.

Softly, eyes transfixed on hers, he started by stating the obvious to the naive woman he was about to seduce. "I'm going to make love to you, Natalie."

The muffled sound of roaring laughter filtered through the floorboards from the dining room below but did nothing to quell the sudden charge in the air between them. It was final now, he'd made his intentions clear, and after only seconds of absorbing exactly what he'd said, she faltered from the words, bringing her hand up to clutch her throat.

Faintly she replied, "I think I'd rather just kiss."

Her timid sweetness liquefied him. She fought the passion because she was so raised, but he was also quick to note that she hadn't denied what was about to take place, hadn't protested the impending occurrence. She knew it was going to happen. She'd accepted it, too, and this realization made the blood rush through his veins.

"Kissing is part of making love," he said quite seriously, moving his fingers to the buttons on his cuffs, "and I intend to do a great deal of it with you."

"Kissing?" she asked hopefully.

He smiled into her eyes. "Everything."

Hugging herself, she glanced to the bed—downy soft and covered with an embroidered quilt of pale yellow daffodils and plum roses—so inviting. "I don't think this is a good idea, Jonathan."

She was losing her nerve, or perhaps just becoming aware of the immediate complications to arise from their actions, and he refused to allow anything to invade the pleasure about to be realized by both of them. They were ready for each other, and now was the time.

Jonathan took a step toward her and reached for the hand she still held at the base of her throat. She looked up at him again as he raised it to his lips and delicately kissed her knuckles.

"I need you," he said softly, gazing into luscious green eyes spilling over with trepidation.

"You'll ruin me for my husband," she pressed with fading resolve.

His lips drew back in mild amusement. "A legitimate argument, but in your case I sincerely doubt it."

That both confused and startled her. She swallowed and attempted a general negation. "This isn't right."

"It's romantic and secluded," he whispered decisively, turning her hand over and grazing his lips back and forth along her wrist. "It's perfect."

She shivered, and for a moment she just watched him, mesmerized. Then she shook her head in tiny movements; her last attempt to save herself. Voice quavering, she insisted, "I won't be your lover, Jonathan."

That staggered him. "Oh, God, Natalie, why do you keep thinking that, saying that?" He dropped her hand and abruptly cupped her cheeks, forcefully lifting her face to within inches of his. "Can't you see what's happening between us? There's no barrier left but the physical. You already are my lover. You already *are*."

She blinked quickly, astonished by the intensity of his assertion. Then her eyes filled with tears, and she closed them to his gaze.

Jonathan hesitated. He was so certain she was willing, brimming with desire for all he could give. Leaning forward, he rested his forehead against hers. "I want you to be a part of me, Natalie. I want our feelings for each other to be real—something experienced and shared—not just vaguely sensed."

She shook her head again as tears streamed down her cheeks and onto his thumbs. "It's not supposed to be this way," she whispered.

He touched his lips to her forehead and brow, the bridge of her nose, her wet, salty lashes. And with comprehension of his own acceptance, he whispered against her temple, "It was always supposed to be this way."

She calmed from his words, so gently shattering and full of meaning. And finally, as his mouth moved down the side of her face to brush hers once again, she relented in a delicate breath of anguish. "I can't resist you anymore. . . ."

The world opened for him, and with a surge of sublime satisfaction, he kissed the tears from her cheeks tenderly, pushed his fingers through her hair to grasp her head more fully, then took her mouth with his to begin the act that would change the course of their lives.

Natalie surrendered to him as honesty conquered her at last. She could fight the power no more as she willingly gave in to the consummation of something started nearly five years ago in a flower garden. She knew then only of innocent longings and romantic dreams. Now she understood hot, raging desire between a man and woman that could never be satiated by denial or good intentions, just as she knew that same desire was soon to carry her someplace new and thrilling, to an exotic and gratifying place of discovery.

He started slowly with her, kissing her lips delicately, standing inches away, touching her only with his hands in her hair. She allowed herself to respond, to enjoy the moment for everything it was, attempting to shove the consequences of their forthcoming actions from her mind. She placed her palms on his shirt—not to keep him at a distance, but because she suddenly felt the overwhelming urge to touch him.

He sighed heavily with that, deepening the kiss as his mouth began to move in a slight, pressured rhythm with hers. She was only vaguely aware of her surroundings, of the dim lamplight shining upon them and the rich fragrance of flowers drifting through the open windows, of the people downstairs and the world outside. Her life was here in this room; their time was now. Everything faded but Jonathan.

With a dissolving anxiety she wrapped her arms around his neck and pulled herself into him, tasting him, kissing him back with a delightfully building tension. Through no intention of her own, her senses came alive, reacting as they did the day they'd kissed on the Mediterranean shore— seemingly ages ago, yet remembered like yesterday.

He responded by embracing her fully, lowering his strong arms to encircle her waist, pulling her against his chest as the kiss grew ever more demanding. He teased her lips open, gliding his tongue across them until they parted enough for him to probe her mouth deeply. She gave him access, enjoying the sensation with an ever increasing abandon, flicking her own tongue against his as he was teaching her to do.

A husky moan escaped his throat, just barely heard, and it gave her encouragement. He was experienced at this, she wasn't, and somewhere inside she feared disappointing him. She wasn't at all certain what to do next.

As if reading her thoughts, keeping his mouth on hers, he began caressing her back, up and down with the palm of one hand, while reaching forward with the other to stroke her face, to massage her neck and shoulder lightly.

She relaxed her body into his, relishing the feel of his large, muscular form against her smaller one. She loved the hardness of him, the smell of his skin and hair, the strength he possessed both inside and out.

He pursued, his mouth demanding now as his breathing grew shallow. Natalie knew with satisfaction that she affected him without even attempting to. As he did her. She had never been so forward with a man, had never come so close to giving all, but suddenly she was desperate for everything—for touching, taking, pleasing. She ran her fingers through his hair, pulling him even tighter against her, taking the initiative at last by sliding her tongue into his mouth, timidly at first, then with wonder as he groaned and came alive with fire.

Quickly he broke free of the kiss, moving back at last to look down at her face.

Time stopped as they stood together, breath raspy between them, eyes fusing with a newfound understanding of wants and needs and feelings. His expression shone vividly of longing and promise, and she knew she was giving him a view of the same. Then he dropped his hand to her breast and softly began kneading it over her blouse.

She drew a sharp breath from the initial contact but couldn't move as once again she succumbed to a burning within. He watched her closely for reaction, grazing her nipple back and forth with his thumbnail, causing it to harden to a fine point of exquisite sensation, entrancing her, weakening her. Then he brought his other hand forward for more of the same, staring into her eyes, caressing both breasts and nipples, making her gasp, forcing her to cling to his shirt.

"Jonathan. . . ."

It was an arduous pleading from deep in her throat, and he understood it. He dropped his head to her neck, running his mouth over her flesh, attempting to distract her with his tongue as he reached behind her again to unfasten the buttons of her blouse.

And he distracted her perfectly. She placed her arms around his neck once more, fingers in his hair, drawing him closer, kissing his face, feeling his lips against her ear, his chest rubbing her breasts to a marvelous tingle. Only vaguely was she aware that he'd untucked her blouse and had moved to the buttons of her skirt. She stayed absorbed in him, in his kisses, in his total awareness of her.

Then at last he leaned back just enough to pull her blouse over her head. But before comprehension of his actions had a chance to permeate her mind, he found her lips once more, capturing them with his own, searing them with charged heat he could barely contain. In seconds her skirts slid down her legs to the floor as well, and she stood before him in only a thin linen chemise.

His tongue invaded her, searching for hers, not gently this time but with a thrust of expectation, removing all final thoughts of indecency with hot, sweeping need. He placed a hand in her hair, holding her head to him, and with the other he grasped her breast, the contact becoming urgent as he rubbed her nipple back and forth and in small circles as it rose to a peak against his palm and fingers.

She wore almost nothing now, had never been so exposed to a man, and yet she no longer cared—couldn't think of her world beyond this room, this man, this feeling of being vibrantly brought to life. All that remained of uncertainty evaporated with an indescribable impatience to experience the unknown pleasures he promised with his mouth and hands. She clutched his shoulders with tight fingers, feeling the scalding heat of his body beneath his shirt, only dimly aware that he pushed her back to the edge of the bed.

Quickly he pulled his mouth from hers, and she raised her lashes to look at his face. He stared down at her, lids heavy over glazed eyes, his hair mussed and hanging loosely over his forehead, his breathing just as rapid and uneven as hers. A spellbinding fever of aching passion radiated from deep within him to envelop her almost violently—a magnificent desire she knew he possessed for her alone. And it absorbed her.

With renewed immediacy, and an instinct she didn't clearly understand, she raised trembling hands to his shirt and began to work swiftly through each button, top to bottom, staring starkly into the vivid gray-blue depths of raging physical hunger in his eyes.

He started helping her, from the bottom, until their hands met in the center of his chest. He seized her fingers, lifted them momentarily to his lips before releasing them, then pulled the shirt from his body. Eyes still locked with hers, he placed his palms on her shoulders and pushed her until she eased down on top of the quilt. Then, standing over her, watching her, he furiously began working through the buttons on his pants.

Natalie closed her eyes from a trace of renewed embarrassment when she realized what he was doing, her mind beginning to race with the details of what was so soon to transpire in this room, on this bed. In Jonathan's embrace. Seconds later she heard the rustle of clothes, then felt him lie beside her, not quite touching, although she could feel the heat of his body penetrate hers from ankle to shoulder and she knew he now wore nothing at all.

His hand raked through her hair, his lips touched her temple in wispy movements, and her heart beat relentlessly in her chest from knowing she was about to give herself immorally to a man who was not her husband, from nervousness, but more than anything from yearning and a desperation to feel and be touched.

"Look at me, Natalie," he urged in a voice marked with rich tenderness.

She shivered from the intimacy between them and raised her lashes once more, refusing to glance down but feeling the curls on his bare chest as he leaned against her shoulder.

He peered into her eyes, moving his fingertips up and down her arm in a fine trace of her skin. "Do you understand what's about to happen?"

She nodded, wanting to cringe from sudden shame. But he must have anticipated this reaction, for he drew the tips of his fingers up to her collarbone, then over her chemise once more, lowering them to her breast, her nipple, expertly building the fire again in the center of her.

"Someone's told you?" he asked more directly, concentrating.

She clutched the quilt beneath her with both palms. "Yes," she managed through a staggered breath.

That seemed to relieve him. His features softened, and then he lowered his lips to her neck, kissing her briefly before nuzzling her ear, taking the lobe in his mouth, sucking it. She closed her eyes to the feel of his lips and tongue and hands creating their magic. He ran his palm over her breasts in growing demand and she was instantly ready for more, the need in her mounting with each bold caress.

She reached for him again, her fingers in his hair, pulling him into her, now longing for a uniting of bodies and feelings and souls. He moved his head to place tiny kisses on her neck and chest, running the tip of his tongue across her shoulder, stroking the top of her arm with his mouth. And at last, as if in answer to a silent promise, he very slowly drove his hands between her legs, over the only remaining barrier to the place of his desire.

A piercing pleasure shot through her. She gasped from passion revealed, from the undercurrent of crisp, erotic tension as it erupted at the surface. He massaged her there, over thin linen, two times, three times, just as intimately as he did that beautiful day at the beach. She succumbed, her body begging for more as she pushed her hips into his hand. And at long last, taking the cue, he withdrew it, sat up a little, and pulled the chemise from her bare flesh in one quick, experienced movement.

He sucked in a jagged breath. She squeezed her eyes shut to his feverish gaze, afraid to look at him—touch him—knowing he was staring at her from above. For an endless moment he scrutinized her naked form, very slowly running the tips of his fingers along her leg from her ankle to her hip. Finally he lowered himself to her level again and began to caress her bare arms, neck, and breasts once more, his palms lightly stroking, causing gooseflesh to appear where he played with the peaks and valleys within his reach. He brushed her nipple with his fingertips, his lips on her neck and cheek and jawline, kissing her tenderly, then resting his mouth at her temple.

"You're perfect to me," he whispered against her.

She melted into the moment. He was making it perfect for her, teaching her, loving her with his body. Then he lowered his head and took her breast into his mouth.

She arched her back and nearly cried out as he began to lick and suck and kiss her nipple, teasing it with his lips, his tongue, grazing it with his teeth. He placed his hand over the other and kneaded the bare flesh, rotating his fingertips across smooth skin, lightly squeezing the nipple to a hard point, and Natalie thought she would die. She put her hands on his head, her fingers through his hair, lifting her body into it, panting and whimpering as he licked and sucked and excited her so expertly.

He groaned, coming alive from the eagerness she expressed, raising his head just enough to lay a trail of fine kisses from her breast to her neck, sliding his tongue along the crevice of her throat to her chin. He leaned closer to her, the matted curls on his muscled chest teasing her nipples, and for the first time Natalie felt the part of him he intended to put inside of her rubbing against her hip—hard and hot and shocking her to reality.

As if realizing suddenly where she placed her thoughts, he reacted by taking her mouth with his in a deep, penetrating kiss, his tongue darting past her lips in a desperate search for hers, grasping it and sucking it urgently when he found it. She moaned, rubbing her legs back and forth along the quilt, her palms on flushed skin as they moved down his neck to his shoulders, her mind emptied of everything but Jonathan caressing her body with expert fingers, Jonathan kissing her to reckless heights, Jonathan ready to make her a part of him. He was everything to her at that moment. He was her past and future and the depth of her heart.

Then she felt him move his palm from her breast to her waist in a wispy touch that sent a quiver through her body. He grazed the skin of her hip, then her belly, brushing it in slow circles, kissing her mouth with growing need and staggered breath until at last he boldly placed his hand on the soft curls between her legs.

She gasped against his mouth, but he didn't release her

lips. He continued with the kiss, positioning his free hand on her forehead, his thumb on her brow, holding her steady. Then without pause, he pushed his fingers down between her thighs.

She clutched his shoulders with rigid hands. Her throat ached; her body craved a release from the torment. He waited only seconds before he began to stroke her sensually, moving his fingers gingerly at first, then more and more intimately until she felt the slick heat mounting and a glorious tension gather strength in the center of her belly.

His touch inflamed her. The fever grew within as he pulled his lips from hers and began a trail of kisses to her breasts again, finding one waiting peak and flicking it with his tongue, sucking, rubbing it with the bristles on his cheek, piercing her with sharp fire. His fingers pursued their magnificent torture, and instinctively she began to lift her hips to his hand in tempo with his ever-intensifying rhythm, her palms on his shoulders, thumbs pressing against his collarbone as he stroked harder, faster, building the inner fire to the edge of explosion.

She turned her head to the side, moaning his name as his mouth teased her breasts and his hands worked their magic, taking her there, to that point of bursting rapture. And just as she thought she'd reached it, he abruptly slowed his actions then ceased all movement, forcing her to gasp in protest as she clawed at him with her nails in his shoulders.

"Please . . . ," she begged—a scream in her mind but just a whisper through her lips.

"Soon, my sweet love," he promised through a harsh breath. He kissed a line down her stomach, stopping to trace a pattern in her navel with the tip of his tongue. Then at last he lifted his large frame, crossed his knees over hers, and centered himself between her legs.

Somewhere deep in her mind, Natalie knew they were almost there, understood what he was doing, and she wanted him inside of her now with an intense ache she'd never felt before. Unconsciously she arched her hips up to touch him, and he reacted with a small jerk of his body and a hiss through clenched teeth. He waited above her, arms to the sides of her shoulders to support him, and at last she opened her eyes to his again.

She never expected to witness such depth of feeling from him, and yet it was so clearly forthcoming from his brilliant eyes. He tightened his jaw in an effort to control himself, perspiration gleaming on his brow, the muscles of his neck and chest and arms standing out in cords of strength and beauty as he towered over her. He reached for her wrist, pulling her hand from his shoulder, raising it to his lips to kiss her palm gently.

Through a dark whisper, he revealed his passions to her innocent heart. "I've waited years for this moment with you, Natalie."

She began to tremble from the sweetness of his words, the grave meaning behind them, from the fierceness of his gaze.

Seconds later, he moved her palm to his chest, placing it in the center, holding it there where she could feel the quick beating of his heart. Then he steadied himself, cupped her face in his hands, and slowly began to press the tip of him against her cleft.

Immediately she tensed, and he felt it, stopping the movement, giving her time. He kissed her cheeks, her lashes, the sides of her mouth.

"It's going to hurt," she managed to whisper.

He breathed deeply. "Not for long."

She nodded faintly, turning her head just enough to kiss the side of his hand, rubbing her cheek against it, detecting the faint musky scent of her—of lovemaking—on his fingers as they brushed the side of her face.

"Natalie. . . ."

His voice sounded pained, intense as he traced her lips with his thumb. She focused on his eyes so close to her own and gave in to the force between them at last, exposing her feelings to him through her soft expression, showing him exactly what she knew he'd wanted to see for so long, what he'd always hoped was there.

"I know, Jonathan," she said passionately.

That startled him; she saw it in the widening of his eyes, heard it in the quick rush of breath from his lips. Comprehension filled him, and in a choked voice, he whispered, "Wrap your legs around me."

She moved them up and down the outside of his thighs just once and then encircled him tightly, placing her free hand on the back of his neck, caressing the curls on his chest with the other.

He poised himself for a second time at the hot, slick center of her, then gazed through her eyes to touch the warmth of her soul. "I swear to you, my darling Natalie, that I will never hurt your heart for giving me everything you are."

Tears overcame her, and with that he covered her mouth with his, tensed his body, and drove himself deeply inside of her.

She felt a half second of pressure. Then sharp pain gripped her from the inside, causing her to arch against him as she dug her nails into his skin. He clung to her tightly, his hands firmly holding her face, his mouth on hers, blocking the cry from her lips. He didn't move his body at all but remained perfectly still, encased in her.

Natalie tried to breathe deeply, to concentrate on the gentleness of his mouth and the heat of his hard, masculine form covering hers. Within seconds the pain began to lessen, and she once again became conscious of her surroundings—of the soft quilt beneath her, the fragrance of roses in the air, of Jonathan's warm body joined intimately with hers, the familiar feel and scent of his skin.

A tear trickled down to her temple, and he wiped it away with his thumb. Then as he felt her gradually relax, he began to intensify the kiss again, massaging her scalp with his fingers in her hair, prying her lips apart with his tongue and a flourishing eagerness to invade.

Natalie caressed his neck and chest with her fingers, kissing him back at last as she moved her mouth in time with his. Within moments his breathing grew shallow again, and very slowly he attempted to pull out of her.

She winced, stiffening beneath him.

He stilled from her response. "Tell me if it hurts," he whispered against her mouth.

She nodded, and he waited, straining from the urge to move, his features taut. He reached for her breast, running one hand down her shoulder until he covered the waiting peak with his palm, rotating his hand over it, teasing the nipple with his fingers.

Natalie succumbed to the touch, her body coming alive again as desire sparked anew. She ran her tongue along his lips, savoring the feel of him inside of her as his hands and mouth coaxed her body toward a delicious crest of a marvelous satisfaction. Sensing her need, feeling her respond, he gently attempted to glide out of her once more. And as before she cringed from another stab of acute discomfort.

"Jonathan . . ."

He paused for her again, and Natalie recognized, perhaps only dimly, how incredibly difficult it was for him to do this. His breathing was labored, his muscles tense, his body hot. He kneaded her breast with one hand, brushed her cheek with the fingers of the other, kissed her mouth with an aching determination. He was so gentle and giving and patient, and she wanted so badly to please him.

She began stroking his neck and shoulders, raking her fingers through the curls on his chest, caressing his legs with her feet and toes. She kissed him back fully at last, flicking her tongue across his top lip and then opening for him as he searched for hers. Finally, through the strength of their passion, she felt her own instinctive urge to move.

She rotated her hips beneath him, and he moaned low in his throat, reacting with an eagerness as heavy as her own. Slowly he slid out of her and then back in once, and she stiffened again from the tightness.

Natalie felt her first real flicker of failure. He sensed this in her, too, for he released her mouth and lowered his forehead to rest against hers.

"You move," he said huskily.

She licked her lips, unsure if she'd heard him correctly, trying to grasp coherently what he was telling her. Then he rubbed her nipple between his forefinger and thumb, fanning the fire, and she instinctively lifted her hips against him again.

"Yes . . . ," he whispered. "Move any way it feels good for you."

"Will that work?" she asked through a hesitant breath.

He dropped small kisses on her eyebrows and cheeks, her temple. "It will work perfectly."

Unsureness caused her to pause, and then he started a trail of delicate kisses down her throat and chest—soft touches from warm lips to hot skin. He raised himself up slightly, brushed his lips back and forth across her nipple, then circled it slowly with his tongue, and failure was forgotten.

She gave a small sigh of raw desire, closing her eyes, tilting her head back, her hands flat on his shoulders. And without thought of perfection, she pushed against his body with her hips—first once, then again, gently enough not to provoke any movement from him. He made no sound, but his muscles flexed beneath her fingers, and she knew she affected him by even that small action.

He took her nipple into his mouth once more—to taste and suck and flick with his tongue, his free hand stroking the other, and the instinct within her finally took over. She widened her knees, pushed herself into him, and slowly started circling her hips against his.

She felt pressure at first, but he didn't move, and gradually she picked up the pace as the ache between her legs diminished.

He continued to tease her breasts with his hand and mouth—stroking, caressing, holding back his own impulse to proceed to the height of satisfaction with driving force.

She pulled her fingers up his cheek, her skin tingling from the marvelous sting of his day-old beard, moving her hips faster, pushing harder against him, keeping her eyes closed and imagining Jonathan inside of her, taking her to a wondrous peak of fulfillment.

A soft groan escaped him then, which pleased her because she knew she was doing it right. He pulled his mouth from her breast, kissing her neck and chest as he leaned up to face her once more, skimming her arm with his fingertips before raking them through her hair again to cup her head in his palms.

Her heart pounded; her pulse raced as she moved faster and harder, now rocking her body against his with a building fever.

"Natalie. . . ."

She opened eyes drugged with desire to the darkness of his. He watched her, absorbed in her actions, his breathing shallow, and yet leaving all movement to her. The moment was delicious and sensual and satisfying, and growing in brilliance. And he knew.

"I've dreamed of you for years, Natalie."

She rocked into him, whimpering. He took her hand, lifting it to his lips, brushing each finger against them.

"I've dreamed of this night," he disclosed in a voice urgent with need. "I've dreamed of making love to you, of being inside of you, of taking you to a place you've never been, of watching you discover it with me."

She whispered his name in a daze of wonder. He ran his tongue up her middle finger, taking it into his mouth, sucking it.

And that put her over the edge. She cried out for him as she ignited in a blaze of ecstasy, in a glorious climax made perfect by him, made perfect with him, like their beginning together only infinitely more beautiful because he was taking her with him this time.

He leaned over to kiss her mouth, tensing his body as her spasms inside pulled at him, as she rocked against him and tightened her grip on him with her thighs.

"Oh, God, Natalie, I've dreamed of this," he said in a rough whisper, his lips against hers, holding her head with strong hands. "I've dreamed and dreamed . . ."

He gave in to the moment and let himself go. Groaning from deep in his chest, his head shot up, and he drove his hips into hers, grinding them, rotating them against her as he matched her rhythm, his eyes squeezed shut, fingers tight in her hair.

Natalie watched him find his pleasure in her, mesmerized, feeling the power of him radiating through her, holding him firmly against her as his body shuddered violently from the strength of his release.

Finally he eased in his effort and lowered himself back onto her, his heart thundering next to her own, his breathing erratic and fast. He buried his face in her neck, inhaling fully, touching her skin with tender kisses as she gradually slowed the movement of her hips until she stilled completely.

They lay joined together for minutes as her pulse returned to normal, as she slowly drifted back to reality, to the consideration of where they were and what they'd done. She moved a little, and he felt it, shifting his body to take the weight off.

She kept quite still, placing her palms on his back. He didn't appear to want to leave her immediately, and so she allowed him to caress her, taking comfort in the closeness. At last she felt him move to his left and slowly slide out of her. He turned onto his side and sat up a little as he reached behind them to pull down the quilt.

"Jonathan—"

"Shh. . . ." He touched her lips with his fingertips. "Sleep with me, Natalie. Let me hold you."

She obeyed without argument, partly because she couldn't think of anything comfortable to say to him, but mostly because she realized he was giving her time to adjust to all that had just happened. He reached over to dim the lamp, then lifted his body and pushed the quilt under both of them so that they lay directly on the sheet. Then he encircled her waist, drew her against him, and covered them both, wrapping his arms around her body, clinging to her, his face in her hair, breath on her cheek.

"Everything's changed, Jonathan," she whispered.

He sighed and snuggled into her. "Yes, it has."

She remained silent after that, listening to the slight rumble of voices downstairs until they dissipated as guests retired for the evening. He never moved, and after a while his breathing grew slow and even, and she knew he'd fallen asleep.

Natalie gently rolled over, careful not to wake him. Sleep eluded her as she stared vacantly at the open windows, hearing the rustle of leaves outside, feeling the cool, night-time breeze on her bare arms and cheeks.

She had become exactly what she despised in her mother. She had fallen victim to her desires and had given Jonathan everything. Yet none of it was his fault. *She'd* begged him to take her to France, *she'd* slept in the same bed with him when she should have insisted against it, *she'd* worn her hair down so indecently. But more than all of that she had started the kissing in the garden that had led to the end of her innocence. This was her fault because she could not control her desires, and he was her weakness.

Choking back tears, she carefully sat up, then stood and walked across the cold floor to her trunks. She felt a slight trickle of fluid between her thighs, and it filled her with a sudden, furious shame. He was a man, and his passions guided him. But she was a properly raised lady. Her upbringing was supposed to protect her from sexual hunger, and yet it only made her feel guilty when she followed her physical instincts. She had wanted him desperately, desired him still, and yet she would never be his mistress.

Quietly Natalie lifted the lid to one of her trunks, reached in for her nightgown and pulled it over her head. Since she had nowhere else to go for the moment, she returned to his side and gazed down at his face only dimly illuminated by a trace of moonlight.

He was beautiful to her and always had been. He was the center of all of her dreams and yet he could never be hers because she would never be able to trust him with her heart. Regardless of what he'd said during the heat of passion, she knew he'd grow bored with her in time. He would move on to another, and she would be left with the pain—the jealousies and the wounds that would never heal.

Natalie eased between the sheets once more, avoiding his touch as she turned away from him to stare at the darkened wall. In the few weeks that she'd been with Jonathan in France, she'd cried more than she had in the last five years. Now she closed her eyes and allowed the tears to slide silently down her face once again, staining the pillow beneath her.

Fifteen

Natalie opened her eyes to a direct stream of sunlight striking her face. She blinked and squinted at the invasion, unsure of where she was. Then memory flooded her as she recognized the soreness between her thighs. She turned her head to the left to find Jonathan staring at her, propped up on one arm, his cheek in his palm.

"I love your hair," he said contemplatively, lacing it through his fingers as it cascaded across the pillow.

She groaned softly, pulling her gaze from the starkness of his to take a sudden interest in the tiny plum rosebuds painted on the ceiling. "I should have worn it up."

He drew his thumb lingeringly across her hairline from her forehead to her temple. "I prefer it down."

"If I had worn it up, nothing indecent would have happened last night," she clarified with a small shake of her head.

His lips curled in faint amusement. "What we did last night would have happened if you were bald, Natalie."

She squirmed a little, peeking at him through her lashes, placing her hands on her stomach and locking her fingers together. His eyes skimmed her nightgown as if he'd just come to wonder why she'd put it on, then he leaned forward to brush his lips back and forth along her cheek.

"Are you all right?" he whispered.

She nodded fractionally.

When she added nothing more, he pressed for detail. "What are you thinking?"

His voice suggested concern over what she was feeling, but she couldn't allow herself to consider his worries. Instead, she glanced back to the ceiling and said dryly, "That we missed dinner, that everyone heard us because the windows were open, and that it was much more work than I was told to expect."

He grasped her chin and turned her head so she had no choice but to look into his smiling eyes. "You were the most scrumptious dinner I've ever had. If anyone heard anything they'd simply assume we were doing what married couples do, and next time I'll do most of the work."

Her cheeks grew hot as she blushed deeply, trying to sit up.

He grabbed her around the waist to hold her against the bed. "Who told you what to expect?"

"Jonathan—"

"Who?"

With a tight throat, she answered, "Amy."

His brows pinched with his now-crooked grin. "Amy, your ever-valuable, sneaky, lying maid informed you of the intimate happenings between men and women?"

"Yes."

"I shall have to thank her for all she's done for us."

That subdued her, although she wasn't sure why exactly. "You'd be thanking her for nothing," she informed flatly. "She told me I wouldn't have to do anything but wait for my husband to finish and that it would never last more than ten minutes."

Now he was thoroughly amused. "I promise, where we are concerned, it will always take longer than ten minutes."

Natalie boldly held his gaze. He was lingering on the assumption that they would be doing this again, and if she allowed that to go on, she'd start believing it herself.

She shook her head with determination, her lips thinning

against an impending argument. "We will not be doing this again, Jonathan."

He didn't argue at all. Rather, he mildly offered, "I gather, when describing the activities of the marriage bed, Amy didn't tell you it happens more than once."

She stiffened and he held her tighter. "This is not a marriage bed."

He stared hard at her for a moment, then leaned into her and touched his lips to her cheek, gliding them across her skin in soft, sensual strokes. "I suppose in the most legal sense it's not."

"We're not married," she insisted.

"Not legally, no."

She wanted to say, "How factual you are," but his warm, broad chest pressed against her arm, his rich, male scent filled her senses, his mouth on her skin made her tingle, and this could only lead to trouble. "Jonathan, behave yourself or you'll not see the emeralds again."

She'd tried to be stern in warning, but it didn't exactly come out that way—more like a tease, although it had the desired effect.

Reluctantly he lifted his head. "Ahh . . . the emeralds." With great exaggeration he fell back flat against the bed. "I forgot about the emeralds."

Natalie huffed in feigned disgust. "That seems rather stupid for a thief of your caliber."

"You've captivated me, Natalie," he admitted through a sigh, teasing her in return as he gazed to the ceiling. "I've lost all sense of time and constraint."

She didn't know whether to laugh or hit him. Instead, she fidgeted with the quilt, pushing it down to her waist as her body grew warm beneath it. "You've apparently lost all sense of propriety as well."

His eyes shot back to her face, his countenance sobering. "I knew exactly what I was doing last night."

She softened her voice, attempting at once to return to the point. "Then I hope the memory of it is enough to placate your desire and you can at last get to the business of finding my mother's letters for me. That is, in fact, why we're here."

He gaped at her, seemingly bewildered. Then he slowly shook his head. "Natalie, I desire you so badly that I'm in pain this very second. The only reason I'm not ripping off that silly nightgown to take you again is because of the pain it would cause you. I imagine you're quite sore."

She heard birds chirping in the distance, smelled flowers and the lingering fragrance of a midnight rain, and yet suddenly everything washed from her mind but the drowning humiliation of the brazen behavior she'd shown him the previous night. Abruptly she turned to sit up, and this time he released her without question.

Stiffly she dangled her legs over the edge of the bed and stared at the wall in front of her. "Time is short, Jonathan. I need you to find my mother's letters so we can return to England."

Thick tension saturated the air, and for seconds he said nothing. Then she heard him rustle the sheets behind her as he adjusted his body to face her back.

"I've intended to do that all along."

The sincerity in his voice calmed her a little, and she looked down at her hands clasped together in her lap. "I know you have." She drew a deep breath for encouragement because she was about to expose her trust in him. "The emeralds are in one of my trunks."

"Really?" he exaggerated.

She closed her eyes, smiling to herself. Of course he would have known that. Where else would they be? He'd even likely found them by looking through her things, probably when she slept, which apparently was the way his devious mind worked. He was a thief after all, experienced with deception and discovery, and her own stupidity at forgetting that disgusted her. But what warmed her heart was the sudden consideration that he had brought her to Paris without really having to do so. He'd done it for her, and she owed him the rest of what she'd promised him.

"The comte d'Arles and several others are hosting a banquet tomorrow night, to raise money quickly for their cause,'' she revealed sedately without looking at him. ''Louis Philippe returns from holiday on Sunday, and they're planning to unseat him as he's escorted through the city.''

The bed creaked as he sat up behind her. ''What did you say?''

The tone of his voice dropped so dramatically she turned to him, trying to ignore his half-naked form as the sheet fell to his hips. ''The comte d'Arles is hosting—''

''I heard the part about the banquet.''

It wasn't his harsh interjection but his penetrating stare that unnerved her. ''Several of them are planning to unseat King Louis Philippe,'' she repeated. ''On Sunday. I thought, considering your affiliations with those in government, you'd find the information interesting—''

''Interesting?'' he cut in. ''I find it interesting that you kept this from me, Natalie.''

The anger he expressed in look and manner took her by surprise. He scrutinized her with hard calculation, and she frowned in a fast irritation of her own. ''I didn't keep anything from you. It's simple gossip I overheard at the ball in Marseilles.''

''French nobles meet in secret to discuss the assassination of their king, and you find this to be simple gossip?''

She stood and faced him, startled by the disgust now flowing from his voice. ''Why on earth would you think this is about an assassination attempt?''

Immediately he threw the covers from his body, and she spun around just as quickly to avoid looking at him.

''What did you think 'unseat' meant, Natalie, that they were going to toss him from his carriage?''

She would have laughed at the thought had he not uttered the question with such coldness. She hugged herself, her palms rubbing against her cotton sleeves, staring at the rose-print wallpaper, listening to his clothes flap as he swiftly dressed.

''We were at a party, Jonathan,'' she reasoned, exasperated. ''The wine was flowing, and people say all sorts of things under those conditions. I assumed it was boastful talk between gentlemen who'd had a little too much of it.''

"And yet you didn't overhear this in the ballroom while everyone laughed and drank and danced, did you?'' he returned abrasively. "These men were closeted in a private meeting when they discussed it.''

She frowned. "How did you know that?''

"I saw you, Natalie. Walking away from the count's private study.''

"You were *spying* on me?''

He brushed over that to add frankly, "I wonder where precisely you place your loyalties.''

She gasped at his audacity, his unfairness in assuming an involvement on her part, and she whirled around to confront him. His clothes nearly covered him now as he rapidly moved his fingers through the buttons on his shirt.

"That's a cruel thing to say, Jonathan, and quite preposterous.''

He ignored that, reaching for his neckcloth.

"I didn't know," she insisted. "I didn't really even think about it. My ancestry has nothing to do with this. The French are always considering ways to dethrone the current king, and most of it is nonsense.''

He glanced at her, pausing just long enough for her to know she'd made a perfectly logical point. Then he turned to the wardrobe, pulled out the appropriate pair of shoes to match his attire, and sat on the edge of the bed to address them. Still he offered nothing in reply, which in turn ignited her anger.

"I fully intended to tell you this, Jonathan, when you gave me my mother's letters. That should have been yesterday.''

She knew her biting comment would elicit a response. His head flipped around so quickly his entire body jerked from the movement. For a flash of an instant he gaped at her, making her feel that perhaps the blow had been too brutal. Then he shook his head in disbelief.

"This information was your promised gift in return for the letters?''

She straightened, unsure, dropping her arms to her sides.

"Of course." She hesitated as her brows furrowed lightly with conjecture. "What else would I have to give you here? My ivory-handled fan? I know you didn't want my cameos."

He stared at her so sharply, sitting so incredibly still, she thought for a moment he'd quit breathing. Then, whether it was from his continued silence or the shrewdness of his gaze, she couldn't be certain, clarity filled her in a surge of pure denial and a shock she couldn't begin to describe.

"You—you thought I would give you *me*?" she mumbled, her voice sounding small and foreign to her ears.

For seconds he did nothing, just watched her, a vivid uncertainty augmenting his expression. And that's when she knew.

Rage enveloped her. She fisted her hands at her sides, her body becoming rigid where she stood, eyes burning with tears she refused to shed. "You thought I'd give you my virginity in exchange for letters?"

Her sudden realization made him noticeably uncomfortable. He wiped a palm awkwardly over his brow, standing to face her. "Natalie—"

"How could you think that about me, Jonathan? How could you think I'd do that?"

He placed his palms on his hips, stalling. "I don't know," he answered gruffly. "It just—seemed logical."

"Logical?" Her features twisted in deep pain. "You thought I'd give myself to you in *payment?*"

"Jesus, that's not how I looked at it," he asserted through a rush of air, taking a step toward her.

Icily she whispered, "Of course you would think I had virtues like my mother."

That stopped him dead in his stride. He stiffened, his eyes shining into hers with dark brilliance. "I knew you were a virgin, Natalie," he said very quietly. "But I also knew, just as you did, that eventually we would make love. Your desire for me was no secret. It was blatant."

"You're such an arrogant man," she spat. "I wanted you to help me. I thought you were my friend."

His cheek twitched, his lids narrowed. "Friendship aside,

the sexual attraction between us couldn't be denied forever. This started the minute you walked into my town house."

She fought the urge to slap him for that—for his gall, for understanding her mind so intimately, and for using his experience against her innocence to a purely selfish end.

"It's my fault, then," she admitted sarcastically, digging her nails into her palms. "I should have prepared myself for your advances. Unfortunately I don't know anyone who knows more about sexual attraction than you, Jonathan."

His eyes widened just enough for her to know she'd stung him with that. But fury seeped from her in waves now, and she refused to stop there. His motives were becoming so very clear at last.

She swallowed as tears she could no longer control filled her eyes. "I suppose you'll next tell me that everything you said to me last night was rehearsed. Or perhaps you simply called upon phrases you've used before? I'm sure you know exactly what to say to a woman at precisely the right moment."

She realized immediately that she'd gone too far. At first he appeared only stunned by her vehemence. Then intense pain sliced through his eyes, and she knew she'd wounded him deeply. It shook her, too, and she wavered, but she refused to back down completely.

After moments of excruciating silence, staring at each other from across the corner of the bed, his features softened to an unspeakable sorrow he couldn't conceal, and he slowly lowered his gaze.

He turned away from her, walked three feet to the chair, picked up his jacket, and moved to the door. When he grasped the handle he looked back into her eyes.

"You're going to have to come to terms with this on your own, Natalie," he warned in a clear, grim voice. "I can't make you trust me and I can't change my past. If you cannot accept it for what it is, you alone will ruin everything between us, and we'll have no chance at all."

He opened the door and glanced to the plum carpeting

beneath his feet. "I'm going into the city to discover what I can about the banquet tomorrow night."

Without waiting for a reply, he stepped into the hallway and closed the door behind him.

Sixteen

Natalie sat primly on a high-backed, pink velveteen chair in the private, third-floor suite of the Hotel de Monceau. She had arrived only minutes ago after a day of frustrating investigation of her own, traipsing through Paris by herself and with all her luggage in an attempt to find Madeleine DuMais.

She'd discovered Madeleine's whereabouts by no unusual manner, but by moving from one elegant hotel to another until she did so. The Frenchwoman was in Paris because she'd accompanied M. Fecteau in some secrecy to the capital city to finish her business with the British government regarding the emeralds. This much Natalie had known before coming north herself. But it wasn't until this morning, after the fiasco with Jonathan, that she'd considered seeking her out.

Her first inclination after their horrible argument had been to leave France entirely. She had packed her trunks quickly once he'd left and had removed herself from the distress she felt within the four walls of their beautiful room at the Auberge de la Cascade. She'd traveled to the city with every intention of catching the first train to Calais, then booking passage to Dover. She could be home in three days if all went well. And yet something restrained her. At first she thought it was just the simple feeling of regret for the words she'd spoken to Jonathan that morning. But after attempting to find transportation to the city, and then spending half of her day paying an enormous sum to have her trunks carried all over town, she realized she stayed in France because of her confounding feelings for him—the man who lied to her, humiliated her, deceived her, helped her to his advantage, made love to her so perfectly, and carted her tremendous wardrobe through France because she'd asked him to.

Yes, she had to admit she'd had second thoughts about running home strictly because of the inconvenience she'd caused him for weeks without a serious complaint on his part. She'd been an imposition to him, steering him away from his work, distracting him with her presence and demands, stealing his emeralds, which she still had in her possession. And that's exactly how her relationship with Jonathan had always been—confusing, amusing, and ridiculous. Before she tossed it all away, if she hadn't lost everything already, she needed the advice of an experienced woman, and that's how she'd found herself in Madeleine's hotel suite at last, seven exhausting hours after deciding to locate her.

She'd been greeted at the door by a tall, prosaic-faced maid with dark-brown hair and eyes, wearing a starched gray gown, white apron, and cap. She took Natalie's name and after only moments, ushered her into the sitting room to await her mistress.

She sat in something more like a parlor, actually, adorned in shades of pink, tastefully done—not garish as one might expect. The decorations were sparse, as the room was somewhat small, containing only two velveteen chairs facing a settee of the same material and a mahogany tea table between them. To the west, behind her, was a wall of windows, now open to allow for any breeze that might find its way inside, offering a splendid view of the lush park across the street. Pink brocade wallpaper with tiny velveteen flowers of an unknown variety covered the other three walls, from the plush carpeting to the ceiling. Three oil paintings of Parisian sights graced the long wall, and at opposite ends were a large fireplace with a carved mahogany mantel, and the door leading to the sleeping room.

The look could certainly have been overdone, Natalie mused, sitting erect and fanning herself against the persistent heat. But of course it wasn't. The suite was sophisticated and feminine, quite Parisian, and it certainly suited Madeleine.

"Goodness, Natalie, I'm so surprised to see you."

She turned to the soft, airy voice of the Frenchwoman coming from the doorway leading to the bedroom where she'd been taking an afternoon rest. As always, Madeleine DuMais was stunning to look at, elegant in stature as she gracefully walked across the pink carpet toward her, her beautiful, smiling face brimming with questions, the full skirt of her blue silk day dress flowing gently around her legs as if a natural part of her frame.

Natalie felt small and awkward suddenly in her modest traveling gown of mint-green muslin. Her damp skin caused wayward curls to stick to her cheeks and her corset to crunch her ribs together as she tried to sit properly. Of course, she would never again leave even her bedroom without a corset, but considering that now only turned her mind to the indecent memory of not wearing one in Jonathan's presence. She didn't need the distraction right now.

"I do hope you'll forgive me this intrusion, Madeleine," she said pleasantly, lightly fanning her face. "But I was in Paris and thought perhaps I'd call. Are you well?"

Madeleine's dark brows arched faintly at the question. She moved her lithe form to the settee opposite Natalie and sat in one swift, fluid motion. "I'm quite well, thank you, except of course for the heat." She smoothed her skirt, straightening the hem to swirl around her legs, and turned her body so that she pointed just to the side as she faced forward, folding her hands in her lap. "I hope you, too, are well?"

"Oh, yes, very well, thank you," Natalie returned politely. "It's been so hot, but the showers we've had for the last several days have been a lovely diversion. I do prefer the coolness in England to the heat of southern France, although the weather in Paris has been rather mild. One cannot complain.''

''No, indeed one can't,'' Madeleine agreed easily. ''In the winter months, however, I prefer the warmth of Marseilles.''

She smiled. ''I do think it's natural for one to prefer the comforts of one's home, regardless of the weather—''

''Natalie, where is Jonathan?''

She blinked at the candid question, pinching the handle of her fan as it stopped in midair. Madeleine knew very well she wasn't here to exchange pleasantries and was now insisting on the point of her visit.

She hesitated, licking her lips. ''I'm not certain where he is. Have you seen him?'' She was deathly afraid he was here, resting with Madeleine, but she quickly shoved that thought from her mind. She truthfully didn't think it likely.

Madeleine breathed deeply, leaning back serenely against the thick cushion. ''I haven't seen him since we left Marseilles, and he didn't tell me you'd be coming to Paris.'' She lowered her voice. ''Are you looking for him or running from him?''

Natalie almost laughed. She would have had the events of the past two days not made her so unsettled. ''Actually, I-I was thinking of leaving France without his knowledge. My trunks are downstairs with the concierge, but first I wanted to visit with you.''

''I see. Is everything all right?''

Natalie felt color rise in her cheeks and compensated for it by swishing her fan again. ''We . . . had a bit of a quarrel.''

Madeleine's head tilted fractionally. ''Did you?''

Natalie could think of nothing more to add and was starting to feel restless. She turned her attention to the window, gazing blankly at green, leafy vines hanging from a white trellis.

''Have you eaten today, Natalie?''

Her gaze shot back to the Frenchwoman. ''Eaten?''

Madeleine scrutinized her for a moment, then leaned forward and rang a silver bell sitting atop the tea table. Immediately her maid appeared, and Madeleine ordered in French.

"Marie-Camille, have the hotel chef prepare a cold tray, something cold to drink, and something"—she glanced at Natalie—"something chocolate."

"Madame." Marie-Camille curtsied, turned, and walked out of the sitting room.

Natalie lowered her fan to her lap, fidgeting as she attempted to straighten her body so her corset didn't cut into her breasts quite so much. Madeleine adjusted her skirts then spread her hands wide, her palms flat against the settee cushion. "Perhaps you'd like to tell me what happened?"

She wasn't exactly prepared to be vivid in detail, but Madeleine was sincerely asking, and she did, after all, come here for advice.

Without pause, she started at the beginning. "I asked Jonathan to bring me to Paris. I needed him, as the Black Knight, to help me locate letters of a private nature, written by my mother."

"So he finally told you who he was?"

"I discovered his identity myself, the night of the ball," she countered at once, hoping to disguise her irritation. The world of deception wasn't open strictly to professional thieves and spies. Feeling proud of her deductions, she added, "He also verified my conclusions regarding your . . . affiliations with England."

"Did he," she stated without apparent surprise or concern. "Well, then, we have no secrets between us."

She seemed pleased with this, and Natalie relaxed a bit, deciding it best to divulge everything. "I also have the emeralds."

For a moment Madeleine stared at her, nonplussed. "The emeralds stolen from the comte d'Arles?"

What other emeralds were there? "Yes, of course," she answered courteously. With a small smile of triumph, she boasted, "I stole them from Jonathan."

"That's impressive. Evidently your talent and mind are on the same level as his."

Natalie nearly beamed in satisfaction. Quite a compliment, coming from a British spy.

"Was this the topic of your quarrel?"

She tried to organize her thoughts before she spoke. "No, actually. The quarrel was . . . on a more personal level."

Madeleine waited, then asked, "Of a romantic nature?"

"Yes."

"I see. . . ."

Madeleine watched her so intensely Natalie began to have second thoughts about the exchange. Her emotions were far too volatile right now, her nerves on end. She squeezed her fan in her lap to keep from screaming, because a lady did not scream. Her logical mind told her to blurt everything at once, or maybe just run. Her heart urged her to weep again, which in turn made her furious. She'd never felt so confused.

"Natalie, have you and Jonathan been intimate?"

Her eyes opened wide. Her skin flushed, and her gown felt scratchy all over. This was not something an unmarried lady discussed with anyone. Yet she could think of no other way to search for direction other than to confess such intimacies, and wasn't that why she'd wanted to talk about it with an experienced woman anyway?

"Yes, we have," she admitted through a whisper of sadness and regret, sagging into her binding stays at last.

Madeleine drew a long, steady breath, but her eyes never left hers, and she held no judgment in her expression. "Are you upset about it?"

"I think I am more angry at myself for allowing it to happen," she replied, turning to view the clock on the mantel, watching the second hand tick past the nine, then the ten. Miserably she said, "I told him in Marseilles that in exchange for getting my mother's letters, I would return the emeralds and give him something else, something priceless to his convictions. I was only speaking of information I had overheard at the ball, but he assumed I meant my innocence."

Madeleine chuckled, and Natalie glanced back at her,

noticeably bothered. "I fail to see how such an indecent notion on his part could amuse you."

"I wasn't laughing at you or your serious predicament," she soothed, smiling and shaking her head just enough that her chestnut curls bounced along her cheeks. "But that reaction is so very typical. Men always think in sexual terms, Natalie, and I don't suppose they can help themselves. It's their nature. And because of this instinctive nature, I don't imagine Jonathan thought twice about what you proposed. More likely he'd been dreaming or fantasizing of a time when you could be together, and when you offered him something priceless, he assumed you meant exactly what he wanted to hear."

Natalie's stomach tightened, aching not from lack of food but from the very troublesome thought that Madeleine might be right.

"He said he thought it was a logical assumption," she confided.

Madeleine's grin broadened again. "Of course he did. I'm sure it never occurred to him that it could be anything else."

She made it sound so simple, so normal, not despicable as her mother would think if she knew. Thank God she would never know.

"Did he seduce you?"

That cut into her thoughts, catching her by surprise, and her first consideration was to lie. But Madeleine didn't appear to be judging her. She needed the woman's guidance and she wanted her friendship, which surprised her even more than the question of seduction.

"No, he didn't exactly seduce me. I never discouraged him," she admitted, squeezing her fan now to the point of breaking. "I kissed him first, very innocently, and then he expertly took my heart in his hands and sliced it into pieces."

That was boldly exaggerated, she realized, but she could think of nothing else to explain her agitation.

"Really." Madeleine regarded her frankly from head to knees where they became hidden beneath the tea table, her fingers gently caressing the velvet settee seat, her expression only mildly curious. "So you must have handed it to him on a platter?"

"I beg your pardon?"

Madeleine's forehead creased delicately. "Your heart. Did you give it to him on a platter?"

She had absolutely no idea what that meant. The French could be so odd with their use of English words. "I'm sorry, I don't understand."

Madeleine's rose-painted lips turned up again minutely, and her thick lashes fell mischievously over her fair eyes. "Are you in love with him?"

That question made her queasy. Perspiration made her back sticky and her petticoats cling to her legs, and suddenly she wished she were standing naked on a deserted, tropical island in a rain shower—far away from home, far away from France, far away from everything.

But Madeleine waited patiently, and she supposed she needed to be honest with her about this as well. "No, of course I don't love him," she replied with a dry mouth and a suddenly speeding pulse. "What we feel for each other is an acute case of physical attraction that is now moving toward a destructive end."

She caught just a hint of disbelief on the Frenchwoman's face, which irritated her.

"Well," Madeleine concluded, "since you do not love him, you could not have handed him your heart on a platter; therefore, I fail to see how he could have sliced it into pieces."

Natalie's mouth dropped open to say something brash, or perhaps to correct the woman's reasoning, and then she abruptly closed it again. She had no idea how to respond, so it was indeed a relief when Marie-Camille knocked at the door at that moment, then entered pushing a tea cart.

Silently she rolled it toward them, stopping beside the tea table. With swift hands, she placed a tray of breads, sliced tomatoes, and cold breast of duck on the polished mahogany surface, then followed it with a cheese board, a platter of sliced chocolate cake, silverware, small china plates, lace napkins, and two tall glasses of lemonade. That done, she looked expectantly at Madeleine who dismissed her with a nod, and she discreetly took her leave.

"Please," Madeleine directed with a slight lift of her palm.

Natalie looked at the platter of sliced tomatoes, sliced chocolate cake, sliced duck, thought about sliced hearts, and nearly laughed from the constricting tension within her. Sometimes life was absurd.

Placing her fan to her side, she skipped the preliminaries, reached for a plate, and helped herself to cake. Her thoughtful hostess grinned and did the same.

"So," Madeleine began after her first small bite, "you do not love him but you seduced him. What did you do next?"

Natalie swallowed the creamy chocolate icing as if it were paper. The Frenchwoman's manner was becoming quite indelicate, and yet Natalie understood the attempt to help her sort through her frayed emotions.

She shook her head negligibly. "I don't know. And I didn't exactly seduce him," she corrected. "I only just kissed him. He took it from there."

Madeleine peeked at her from under her lashes. "Men usually have no trouble with that. And yet you let him so you were also responsible."

Natalie swallowed her third bite of cake and set her plate back on the tea table, her appetite greatly diminished. "Of course it shouldn't have happened," she acknowledged in a small, shaky voice. "It was immoral, and I am ruined."

Madeleine scoffed. "That's nonsense. You are no longer a virgin. That is all. An intimate experience doesn't ruin you for anything."

Natalie felt her bones grow rigid. "It has ruined me for marriage."

"Only if you allow your indiscretion known to your husband, who would have to be someone other than Jonathan."

Natalie tilted her head in mystification. "I could never lie to my husband, and the thought of marrying Jonathan is ludicrous."

Madeleine placed what was left of her cake on the tea table as well, then leaned on one long, graceful arm as she draped the other across her legs, allowing her tapered, manicured fingers to dangle in the air. "There are ways to hide your lack of virginity from a future husband. But before we discuss that, would you please tell me why marriage to Jonathan is ludicrous?"

The woman was so utterly direct. It unruffled her, and yet Madeleine's candidness had much to do with why she'd chosen to seek her counsel in the first place. Temperately she announced, "Jonathan is too much of a wayward spirit. He's . . . experienced."

Madeleine's features grew broad with amazement. "And this is bad?"

That stumped her. "Of course it's bad. I cannot trust him because of his promiscuous reputation." She hesitated, then said sadly, "He has a past."

Madeleine began swinging her foot gingerly beneath her gown, causing the silk to shimmer from sunlight shining on it through the windows. "Everyone has a past of some kind, Natalie, including you."

"I don't have a past."

"If you marry, and it is not to Jonathan, you will have a past."

The statement slapped her with a crude, logical truth. Disgrace burned in her anew, and she recoiled from it, raising her fan again and brushing it back and forth in front of her face with the hope of keeping her reaction unnoticeable. "The matter is irrelevant," she said weakly. "I refuse to marry a man who is likely to keep mistresses, and Jonathan could never be faithful to me."

Now Madeleine seemed genuinely dazed. "Why don't you think so?"

That exasperated her. "Because of his experience, Madeleine. Why on earth should he cease his rakish behavior, which he seems to enjoy so much, just because he speaks wedding vows to me or anyone?"

"What makes you think he wouldn't?"

She had no idea how to answer, and she was starting to

tire of the questions. Madeleine obviously noticed, for her expression grew serious once more, and she leaned forward to clarify.

"Natalie, most gentlemen of your class marry because it is expected of them. They need heirs, or property given them through a dowry, as well as the convenient sexual outlet marriage provides. Love is rarely a motivating factor for these men in choosing a wife, and they expect to keep a mistress or two while married. Wives usually know this as well, and if they, too, have no deep love for their husbands, they are many times relieved that their husbands look elsewhere for gratification, especially if they've carried several children and their bodies are tired."

"I'm aware of this, Madeleine—"

"I'm sure that you are, but let me finish." Her tone grew pensive as she carried on. "Jonathan does not need a wife—not, at least, for a dowry or an heir to inherit an estate. He has freedom now and wealth of his own, and can choose his companionship—or lack of it—at his discretion. If he would go so far as to marry you, he would be doing so because he *chose* to. I can't think of a reason why he would marry you or anyone if he wanted to continue his libertine tendencies. That would only complicate his life."

Natalie leaned back heavily, feeling the softness of the chair against her spine as her nerves prickled her skin. "Aside from one teasing moment, he's never formally suggested marriage," she mumbled, deflated.

The Frenchwoman silently eyed her in deliberate thought, her fingers rubbing absentmindedly along her seat cushion.

"Natalie, this is rather personal, of course, but consider very carefully what I am asking." She briefly pressed her lips together. "You have been intimate with Jonathan. During this intimate time did he . . . do anything that would prevent you from carrying his child?"

She felt the sharp stab of a sudden, fearful shock. Never once had the thought of carrying his child crossed her mind.

The idea was outrageous. Unthinkable. And very plausible. "I-I'm not sure of this."

Madeleine nodded negligibly as if drawing conclusions of her own, her gaze never wavering as she continued to study her with assessment. "There are a number of things a man or a woman can do during these intimate moments that can very nearly prevent pregnancy. Since this was your first time with a man, it is unlikely you thought of this. Jonathan, however, probably did. If intimate moments occur without planning, the best thing for a man to do is withdraw himself when he reaches . . . a critical point. I'm sure you now understand when this is." Very softly, and without a shade of embarrassment, she articulated, "If Jonathan did not do this, he most certainly knew he could be giving you his child. And I am also certain, if he did not intend to marry you, he would never have taken that chance."

Natalie blinked rapidly, startled and blushing fully from the blunt explanation, ashamed at the thought, and if she considered her feelings honestly, warmed somewhere very deep within. She wiped a shaky palm over her forehead, closing her eyes.

"But he knows I won't marry him. I told him so directly, before this . . . episode."

"Maybe he thinks you'll change your mind."

She dropped her arm to her lap and raised her lashes again, mouth thinned, voice flat with impatience. "He knows how I feel about this, Madeleine. I cannot trust him to be faithful and I refuse to give my heart to someone I can't trust. I *told* him this."

"Men can sometimes be very arrogant."

At last the Frenchwoman understood. Natalie rolled her eyes and spread her hands wide. "Exactly my thoughts."

"They can also be rather insistent when they want something very desperately."

"They—" She stopped short and stared. "I'm sure he didn't want me that desperately."

Madeleine smiled wryly and reached again for her plate of cake. "Are you? Why?"

The woman was maddening with her incessant questions. "He could have anyone."

"And yet he wanted you."

"I was simply there and available to him."

Madeleine shifted her gaze to her plate. "Natalie, half the world is populated by women. They are all around him, and Jonathan is a very attractive man. As you just said, he could have any number of them at any time." She meticulously cut away a bite of chocolate cake with her fork, her finely penciled brows furrowed in deep concentration. "I would suspect he's been faithful to you since you left England, and consider this: he's had no reason to be. He's not married to you now. He owes you nothing and still he's giving himself to you, and you are pushing him away."

Lifting her fork halfway to her lips, Madeleine paused, glancing up to add incisively, "I wouldn't begin to presume what his feelings are for you or how he views your relationship. I would suspect one of three things, however. He does not love you and is merely using your time together for nothing more than physical enjoyment and a summer of pleasure. He loves you but is confused by his feelings and does not yet realize this himself. Or he loves you and knows it but will not tell you because he's afraid you won't love him in return and he doesn't want to witness your rejection of him."

She placed the cake on her tongue, drew her lips across her fork, and chewed slowly, allowing her bold words to be absorbed.

Natalie watched her in silence, devoid of expression, listening in morbid fascination.

"In my experience," Madeleine continued after swallowing, "men are deathly afraid of rejection by someone they love, much more so than women, and I think this is because their pride and egos are of such great importance to them. This is also why it is more difficult for men to be honest and express their feelings." She placed her fork on her plate again and lowered her voice to a cool whisper. "Until you trust Jonathan enough to give him your heart you will likely never know what he feels for you beyond casual friendship. But let me ask you this.'' She bit the side of her lip, tilting her head. "Regardless of who you marry, do you expect to be faithful to your husband?"

Natalie could hardly breathe. "Yes,'' she managed through a clenched throat.

Madeleine smiled again satisfactorily. "So, since this is something you cannot prove, the intent on your part is all anyone can ask for. Including Jonathan. I'm sure you'd ask neither more nor less of him.'' Her pale-blue eyes sparkling, she concluded, "Life and love are full of risks, and think how very dull our world would be if nobody took them. Such risks are really what make daily experiences so enjoyable.''

Natalie sat very still, weighted to the chair, unable to suck in an ounce of air, and she wasn't sure if that was because of the heat, her constricting corset, or the difficult turn of events changing her relationship with a man she didn't logically want but couldn't passionately deny. Pulling her eyes from Madeleine's, she reached for one of the lemonade glasses with a trembling hand, raised it to her lips, and took three full swallows to moisten her dry mouth.

The circumstances were all wrong, indecent, but Madeleine's conclusions were fair, even perhaps correct. Everything the woman had said made sense. And it scared her.

Natalie set her lemonade and fan on the tea table, stood awkwardly, and walked on unsteady legs to the windows. She gazed out to the green grass and flowers in the park, the sway of oak trees, watched the scramble of pedestrians on the street below, smelled city dust and traffic drifting in with the breeze, felt late-afternoon sunshine on her face.

"How can I place my trust in someone who might grow bored with me and one day regret the past he gave up?'' she whispered. "What if I'm just a . . . diversion for him now?''

"You cannot read his mind, Natalie, nor gaze into the future,'' Madeleine returned just as quietly. "Nobody knows what will happen in twenty years. Maybe you'll be so bored with each other you'll both have separate homes and many lovers.''

Natalie turned to the woman once more, unable to disguise her expression of indecision and worry.

Madeleine softened. "But it is probably more likely you'll be content and find yourselves more deeply in love than you can imagine you could be. Frankly, I think the two of you are well suited. As for being Jonathan's diversion, I sincerely doubt this. I cannot fathom why, with a world of women to discover and seduce, he would choose a beautiful virgin for a summer of play. It's too much effort and not worth his time. It is, however, worth everything if he can romance you into becoming his willing wife, his friend, and his love. That is his risk."

Natalie groaned and placed her face in her palm. Her life was never supposed to be this complicated. It had been planned for her the moment she was born—the proper raising, the good marriage to a respectable gentleman, the life of tedious social outings, and night after night of submission to a boring, uncaring husband so she could give him sons. Nothing else was expected of her. But instead, she alone had presumptuously decided she would have something different, something more, something extraordinary with an unusual and wonderful man of her choosing. It dawned on her now, in vivid clarity, that marriage to a man who loved her, who took risks with her, who played with her and teased her as his friend, would probably be the force that would keep them happy and together through the years. Marriage to a stuffy gentleman of quality, as she was brought up to expect and endure, who cared nothing for her beyond her usefulness as a household manager and mother to his heir, would be the initial turn toward unfaithfulness—perhaps for both of them.

For the first time in her life, she felt a pang of sadness and compassion for her mother. She had married a man she didn't love because she was raised to expect nothing else. The only excitement in her life had come from her short, passionate love affair with a Frenchman she could never claim as hers. That her father had fallen in love with her mother over time Natalie now had to admit was unusual, although the path of love rarely seemed to be usual or logical. Marriage for love was a dream, not a reality, in her world. She'd known this all along. That was the hope she'd carried for the Black Knight for years.

But the Black Knight wasn't her dream; he was her fantasy—an unreal and childish expectation of a blissful happiness that had never existed and could never be. If Madeleine's words were to be taken as truth, Natalie knew her dream was a tangible, beating heart full of hope now sitting in the palm of her hand, waiting to be grasped and cherished. The only way for her to live this dream, though, would be to expose her deepest thoughts and feelings to Jonathan, and with a gut-tearing sorrow, she just didn't know if she could ever come to terms with them and do that.

Natalie raised her head and clasped her arms around herself in a protective hug. "I don't know what to do. I said some very cruel things to him this morning. He may never forgive me."

"Nonsense." Madeleine placed her now-empty plate on the tea table, stood, and fairly glided across the carpet to stand beside her at the window. "He will recover from it easily enough. Men do with the right persuasion, which is nearly always sexual in nature. I suggest you put your naked form in front of him, make love to him again, treat him as if he were the only man alive, and he'll never remember you said anything at all except what a perfect lover he is."

Natalie suppressed a giggle at the thought, both scandalous and delightful. Her mother would swoon to hear such audacious talk between ladies in a pink parlor during tea.

Madeleine stood next to her for a moment before draping an arm around her in a gentle embrace. "We will discuss what to do next," she soothed, "and the decision, of course, is yours. If your trunks are at the hotel, we will have them brought up, and you may stay here tonight. That will give you time to think."

Natalie shook her head and momentarily closed her eyes. "I didn't leave a note for him, Madeleine. He'll think I left him for England—with his emeralds."

The Frenchwoman softly laughed. "I have the grave suspicion he'll be more concerned about you and your thoughts and whereabouts than a silly necklace. And good for him. Let him worry."

Natalie wanted to argue that assumption, but Madeleine turned her toward the tea table and spoke again before she could comment.

"Now please, eat something before you wither away to nothing. Then we will dress in finery and spend an enjoyable evening on the town—without the nagging presence of any member of the male sex." She shook her head in feigned disgust. "Such disconcerting creatures they are."

Natalie hinted at a smile, then moved back to her chair without remark, strangely comforted by the sudden closeness she felt to the colorful, sophisticated Frenchwoman who had become her friend.

Seventeen

Jonathan stood alone at the end of the buffet table, thoroughly miserable. The banquet had only just begun, and few people as yet graced the hall of the comte d'Arles's private Parisian home. It was the same home, in fact, that the man was attempting to sell and in which Jonathan had pretended to take an interest. His false identity was still believed, which was probably the only reason he'd been able to work his way in to observe the festivities tonight. He had arrived early, partly because he had nothing else to do, but mostly because he wanted to get this dreary evening finished so he could at last return to his own country, his home, his dog, and Natalie—the stubborn, idiotic, calculating enchantress who held him captive and shredded his reason.

It had been only a day and a half since he'd last seen her, and yet it felt like ten years. He was furious with her, crazy for her, and worried out of his mind. Logically he realized she could get home without him, that she spoke the language and carried sufficient funds for the trip. But the people of France were restless; it wasn't entirely safe for her to be traveling alone, and he sure as hell didn't want her locking herself away from him in her bedroom in England, either. He wanted her in his, wherever that might be, even if the only way to convince her she belonged there was to pound it into that scheming little head of hers. But of course that wouldn't happen unless she saw him, spoke to him again.

God, it was just an argument. They'd said some hurtful things to each other, but he never thought she'd *leave* him. If he'd had the slightest idea of her intentions he wouldn't have left her alone; he would have dragged her with him across town. He would never forget the panic that had flared through him when he'd stepped inside their room at the inn only six hours later, ready to face her wrath, only to face instead an empty wardrobe and an unmade bed with crumpled sheets to remind him of the night before.

She had trouble accepting his past. He knew that, understood why, and was willing to give her time. But what frightened him now was that she'd decided to give up on them without trying, without accepting how much she cared for him, and that's why she had left. She was giving up on them, and it was ripping him apart inside. What made him want to laugh, though, instead of tear the room to shreds was the simple acknowledgment that he'd never once, in all of his nearly thirty years, thought a woman could do this to him.

Jonathan looked down at the full glass of whisky in his hand. He'd been holding it for ten minutes and had yet to take a drink. It was probably outstanding, smooth, and would no doubt go straight to his head to make him at first carefree then later more despondent than he felt already. He didn't need that. He needed to keep his mind clear for the events to ensue this night.

Placing the glass on the table to his left, he leaned his head back against the tapestry-covered wall behind him, watching those around him with only mild interest. This home was smaller than the count's home in Marseilles, but just as extravagantly decorated in dark oaks and plush auburn, teal, and gold. Rich food lined three buffet tables, the drink flowed, the smoke of expensive tobacco filled the air, and yet this wasn't a party—not, at least, like the ball two weeks before. Few women were in this hall tonight, and although everyone dressed in finery, it was silently under-

stood that the reason for this commingling was to raise
money to pay Louis Philippe's assassin. And that would
have to be a great deal of money. Only a professional would
risk such a calculated attempt to murder the king of France.

Jonathan had wanted to go to the authorities, but he had
no proof of anything, and what would he tell them? That
several nobles wanted to change the course of history? Natalie had been right about that being boastful talk, which
was why he couldn't fault her for not immediately confiding this to him. Deposing the king was a common thought
among the French and no doubt wouldn't surprise or concern anyone of authority. But if the assassination attempt
was planned for tomorrow, and tonight's banquet was the
front for Legitimists to strengthen their political ties, boost
their egos, and collect their needed funds, he might learn
something he could forward. He had to take the chance.
Tomorrow he would leave the country.

Jonathan scanned the crowd. The count had yet to appear
for the evening, but the room was quickly filling with people, mostly men, starting some rather boisterous exchanges
at tables and in corners. Eventually it would get crass, and
the women would leave. At least now he had something
appealing to look at, although he was actually starting to
bore of doing even that.

Jonathan closed his eyes with a light groan and folded
his arms across his clean, pressed frock coat, uncaring
whether he wrinkled it.

The world was filled with beautiful women, and he
would admire them until he died. But he couldn't have
them all. Of course he'd been with many before Natalie,
and apparently everyone alive today was aware of this fact.
Curiously, though, he now found himself unable to recall
the specifics of even one episode with any of those women.
They were all enjoyable romps that extinguished his desire
and gave him a short time of companionship at his will. It
wasn't that these women meant nothing to him, but that
they only meant something sexual, and they, for their part,
were perfectly aware of this. Nobody, including him, had
ever been truly disappointed or hurt, and physical pleasure

had generally been the only reason for coupling in the first place.

His sexual experience with Natalie two nights ago, however, was in many ways different. It certainly wasn't the most relaxing of his life, and to be fair he'd probably have to say it wasn't the most erotic. But if he had to choose one word to describe their first time together, that word would be "beautiful." Their lovemaking had been beautiful to him, which made him smile inside because he didn't think beautiful was a word the average, rational man would ever use to describe a bedding. And of course it was something he'd keep to himself. Maybe someday he'd tell Natalie.

He'd lain with her afterward, satiated and overwhelmed, and so stirred emotionally he couldn't think productively, or talk. He'd never experienced that before with anyone. She'd been at one time innocent and soft, yet magnificent in her desire to please him. That's how he knew it had meant something deeply to her, too. It was her first time; she had nothing to which she could compare it. But he knew because he'd observed many women in bed with him, and not one of them had ever expressed such intense feelings for him as Natalie had during that one hour. It was obvious to them both, and she was scared of it. She had run, and now he'd have to coax her into trusting him, which he was fairly certain he could do over time. Of course, he'd probably have to kidnap her first, as she likely wouldn't see him if he called on her formally. Then again, maybe she'd be pregnant. Another first for him, he conceded with a grin. His greatest fear in life had always been getting a woman with child, and now it occurred to him that under the circumstances that would be the best thing that could ever happen to him.

Jonathan rubbed his eyes with his fingertips and opened them again. The group assembling in the hall had grown, and it was becoming stuffy and warm. A quartet played a Bach minuet in the distance, but no one danced. Everyone mingled, which he supposed he was going to have to do to keep up appearances. He gazed indifferently at men in bright, embroidered waistcoats and black top hats, women wearing swirling skirts of red, purple, and yellow silk; lime-green, white, and midnight-blue taffeta. The latter made him think of Natalie because it was her favorite color, and he knew she'd look smashing in it with her hazel-green eyes, creamy skin, and reddish-blond hair curling down over her breasts.

Then he realized it *was* Natalie wearing the midnight-blue gown, walking slowly toward him, a half smile on her lips, her eyes absorbed in his, and the emeralds gracing her neck.

Jonathan stared. The vision of her seemed so illusory, and yet it was her, in a gown fitting snugly to her long, narrow waist, sleeves puffed off the shoulder, the bodice cut far too low over her full breasts. Revealing so much of her splendid figure in ball gowns was something he was going to have to discuss with her, and he wondered for an absurd moment why he suddenly thought of such a thing.

His first impulse was to grab her wrist and yank her against him, but that would only cause others to stare and likely serve no purpose but to irritate her. She had nearly reached him before he stood erect again and masked his astonishment, which irritated him because she'd probably already noticed it. His heart began to pound, his hands started shaking, and he put one behind his back and reached down with the other to clutch the glass containing his untouched whisky so she wouldn't notice that.

She sauntered up to him, her features unreadable, and he raised his glass to his lips and took a full swallow, to calm his nerves, to hide them. But his eyes never strayed from her face.

He'd never seen her so breathtaking. She was beautifully clothed and adorned, the emeralds adding an elegant touch, drawing attention to her pale, tapered throat. She'd piled her hair high on her head, allowing stray curls to fall loosely around her forehead and cheeks, down her back. And she'd very definitely painted her face, which pricked him with amusement. That was Madeleine's touch.

"Hello," she said softly, standing in front of him at last.

"Hello," he replied, just as quietly.

She hesitated after that, watching him closely.

"You're wearing my emeralds," he offered to break the strain.

She smiled awkwardly and glanced quickly at the buffet table. "I thought it might help tonight."

That admission was the final touch. She'd made a decision on her part, and being here now was the proof of all that she felt inside for him. She might never put her feelings into words he could hear, but her actions, the fact that she was at the banquet instead of bound for England, cast the last fraction of doubt aside.

But he would bask in his joy internally. For now.

He took another sip of his whisky. "It will certainly cause an uproar when the comte d'Arles appears and sees you wearing his necklace."

She twisted gloved fingers tightly together in front of her. "My thoughts exactly. I-I thought it might draw them out."

"How clever you are, Natalie."

"I've always thought so," she agreed, pulling her painted mouth up coyly.

She was just so incredibly sweet. His heart ached, and he longed to touch her, to hold her against him and rub his cheek against hers and breathe in the scent of her hair—

"I thought you'd like some champagne." Madeleine interrupted his thoughts, standing beside them, exquisite as always in shining rubies and a gown of deep burgundy.

She held a glass out to Natalie who mumbled a quick thank you and took it in one of her hands.

Madeleine sparkled as she raised calculating eyes to his. "I see several acquaintances of mine, Jonathan, so forgive me for leaving the two of you alone. Have a lovely chat." Without waiting for a reply, she lifted her skirts with dainty fingers and whisked away.

Very tactful, he mused, and he'd have to thank her for that sometime.

He focused again on Natalie. "You stayed with her since yesterday, I presume?"

"Yes," she returned without prevarication. "I found her

in her hotel suite, and we've had a delightful time together.''

"It seems she's had quite an effect on you."

She paused. "Do you mean the face color?"

"Mmm."

"You don't like it, Jonathan?"

He cocked his head and inspected it. It was subtly applied, with only a shimmer of pink to her lips and cheeks, and a brownish tint to outline her eyes. He shrugged negligibly. "I don't suppose I dislike it."

She seemed satisfied with that. "Not that your approval matters—"

"Of course not."

"—but tonight will be the only time in my life I'll wear it, I'm sure. My mother would disown me if she knew, but I am in France, doing what French ladies do, and Madeleine said it would accent my best features."

"Did she?" He reached forward and lifted a curl of her hair as it hung over her right breast, rubbing it between his fingers. "She must not realize your best features never see the light of day."

She narrowed her eyes, shaking her head in disgust. "Jonathan—"

"I was angry that you left me," he cut in quietly. "And hurt."

She stiffened as the conversation turned serious, breathing deeply and dropping her lashes so that all she could see was his waistcoat. "I'm so sorry for what I said," she admitted shakily. "I was ... overwhelmed by everything that happened. Confused."

The urge to pull her against him was so powerful now he squeezed his glass until his fingers whitened. "I was overwhelmed, too, Natalie," he confessed instead. "It was a night of firsts for both of us."

She looked up, disbelieving. For seconds she didn't know how to respond, or what exactly he meant by that, but her eyes bore into his, searching, and he refused to move his gaze.

In a voice both husky and tender, he whispered, "Tell

me how you feel in your heart, and I'll forgive you."

A shrill burst of laughter sliced through the air, followed by a shout or two from one end of the hall to the other. Horrible timing, and it broke the spell between them.

She jerked her head to the sound, skimming the room uncomfortably. "This isn't a typical party, is it, Jonathan?"

"No," he answered through a sigh. "You probably shouldn't be here, either. It's likely to get . . . lively later."

That annoyed her a little. Her mouth tightened, and she tapped her fingers rapidly against the rim of her champagne glass. "You cannot spend your life protecting me from likelihoods."

He didn't know how to take that. Part of him was startled to hear such an implication from her. But she still looked across the hall, surveying party guests, which he supposed caused the uncertainty in him because he couldn't see her eyes.

"Maybe that's something I'd enjoy," he countered.

For a moment she did nothing. Then, with another deep inhale, she raised her gaze to lock with his again. "Madeleine said you, being a typical man, would forgive my words of yesterday morning if I told you what a magnificent lover you are."

He sipped his whisky to hide his choked expression. "Really? I'm almost afraid to know what she's been teaching you."

"And you probably never will," she intimated in a tone of triumph. She raised her champagne to her lips, briefly tilted the glass to her mouth, then slowly lowered it again. Resolutely she admitted, "I do, however, think you are a magnificent lover."

He reeled from that, melting inside. "You're forgiven." Grinning devilishly, he added, "But you have nothing to compare it to, my darling Natalie."

She ignored that, took another long swallow of champagne, licked her painted lips, and pressed on. "I've made some decisions about us."

The muscles in his shoulders flexed from the immediate buildup of anxiety and he shifted from one foot to the other, his skin growing warm under his formal attire. "I'm engrossed, so please enlighten me."

She closed her lids serenely and whispered, "I've decided to become your mistress—"

"What?"

She reached out with one hand and lightly placed her palm on his chest. "I want to wake up every morning in your town house and put on a silk wrap and have coffee with you in your kitchen."

With her eyes shut and her expression flat, Jonathan had no idea if she was serious about something so outrageous, or teasing him. He was very nearly speechless.

Then she raised her lashes, peeking up through them, and her face beamed with mischief. "But I refuse to wear the one worn by your former mistress. You remember her, don't you? The tall, perfectly formed creature with the long, dark hair. What was her name?"

He squeezed his lips together to suppress a laugh. Right now, in this crowded, stuffy hall, where conversation was political and growing louder by the second, everything dimmed but her.

"I don't now recall," he mumbled thickly.

She dropped her chin fractionally, one corner of her mouth turning up faintly. "How very clever you are, Jonathan."

"I've always thought so."

She grinned. Someone brushed against her, and he grasped her elbow, drawing her so close to him her taffeta skirt blanketed his legs from his thighs down.

"But do you know what I do recall about that morning in vivid detail?" he carried on contemplatively, feeling the warmth of her body penetrating him.

She arched her brows in innocence. "Probably how nothing has ever fanned your pompous ego so much as to have two women discussing you at your kitchen table over coffee."

"No, that happens to me weekly," he corrected with an exaggerated sigh.

"I've no doubt."

He caressed her elbow with his thumb in long, smooth strokes. "What I recall about that particular morning is your peach gown clinging to your marvelous breasts. I recall you stupidly cutting your hand on a sword. I recall your sweetness, your conniving little mind, and your stunning, pleading eyes all working together to persuade me to do something irrational like cart you off to France with me. But most of all, I recall how startled I was to find my dog's nose between your perfectly formed thighs and how, at that very moment, I would have done anything on earth to switch places with him."

Her skin flushed, and her lips thinned. "You're despicable."

"You're beautiful," he whispered huskily.

That twist surprised her, but she caught herself, rubbing a palm along her forehead and shaking her head stiffly in negation. "Madeleine is beautiful. I have a face that freckles from too much sun and thick hair so wavy I cannot, for the life of me, control it."

Jonathan refrained from a delicious, offhand reply, because it occurred to him suddenly that he'd been given the opening he needed. And he would use it. It was time to make her understand.

He took another drink or two of whisky in an attempt to calm the unexpected anxiety rippling through him. Then almost methodically he set his glass on the buffet table and looked back into her eyes, stalling only for a moment to collect his thoughts.

"Natalie, I think Madeleine DuMais is probably the most physically beautiful woman I have ever seen in my life."

She blinked, flustered by that admission and noticeably dismayed, which he had to admit thrilled him in an odd way.

He continued before she could comment, concentrating on every word. "And you're right, she is nothing like you. She is exotic and untouchable. You, on the other hand, are approachable and enjoyable. She's the kind of woman who will live on through the ages because men will write songs about her. You are the kind of woman men want to cuddle next to and wrap themselves in. She is regal and polished. You are amusing and vibrant. You're the kind of woman I want in my bed, to hold and make love to and satisfy. She's the kind of woman I'd like to . . . stuff, and hang over the mantel in my study to admire when I work."

She giggled from that, and Jonathan smiled contentedly into her eyes.

"You are the kind of woman who sweats—"

She gasped through a laugh, appalled. "I don't sweat. Horses sweat."

He ran his hand from her elbow down her arm to clasp her fingers lightly. She didn't appear to care as she locked them around his.

"What I mean is that you are real," he explained with a mounting nervousness he refused to let her detect. "Madeleine is a doll. When she looks at me, I see a remarkable beauty—like a priceless painting with fine lines and brilliant color to stare at and appreciate. When you look at me, I see smoldering passion and giving loveliness and a desire to please."

His tone grew reflective, his gaze intense, and he lowered his voice. "When you look at me with your stunning eyes and expressions of longing, my heartbeat quickens, and all I can think of is taking you in my arms and kissing you breathless, of holding you against me and comforting your hurts and laughing in your joys."

A wave of uneasiness descended upon her. Her fingers moved, and she tried to pull them from his grasp.

He wouldn't let them go. The noise grew to a thunder around them, the room smoky and hot, the people unruly as they heavily imbibed fine liquor. A most unusual place to assert himself, but considering how unusual their relationship had always been, it seemed appropriate. No. It was perfect. She sensed what was about to occur. He knew it and marveled in it.

Leaning very close to her, he pulled her champagne glass easily from her grasp and placed it next to his on the table. Then he reached up and lightly cupped her chin, forcing her to remain face-to-face with him, staring starkly into her eyes.

"Madeleine is a lovely woman, Natalie," he revealed in a whisper. "But you are the strength of my soul, do you understand this?"

She started trembling, and it jarred him with a surge of tender emotion.

"You are everything I need. You are the beauty that belongs to me. I feel nothing special for her, but you nourish every sense I possess. I don't care anything for Madeleine, or any woman in the world who is as beautiful as she is. But I do, very much, love you."

She stood entranced by his words, shivering uncontrollably, barely able to breathe, eyes huge and unblinking.

Jonathan calmed inside, knowing at last that she understood. She said nothing in reply but she radiated a mixture of complex feelings that seeped through his skin and warmed his heart. And above them all, through the pleasure of absolute confidence, he knew she believed him.

He smiled gently, caressing her jaw with his thumb. "I knew I loved you two nights ago, when we sat together in the garden. And I also think you knew how I felt then or you wouldn't have let me love you in bed. I've never had anything so wonderful fall into my lap and surprise me so much."

She blinked finally, with a wavering gaze, but he continued to hold her face a breath away from his.

His mouth widened to a playful grin. "Perhaps it's more accurate to say I've never had anything so wonderful climb into my lap."

A trace of a smile tugged at her quivering mouth, but her eyes filled with tears, and he realized she was close to breaking down.

He swallowed hard to keep his own feelings contained, so powerful and indescribable. Then he leaned over and touched his forehead to hers. "If you cry now, my sweet Natalie, you'll smear all the color you painstakingly applied to your face, and it will run down your cheeks."

She laughed softly at that, holding his fingers tightly and

placing her free palm on his chest, shivering despite the heat in the hall and the raucous activity surrounding them.

He wiped a sliding tear away with his thumb, wishing he could embrace her completely, wishing they were far away from here, back at the inn together, that he could have told her these things in the rose garden where he had discovered them.

He softly kissed her brow, then moved his mouth to her cheek, grazing it with his lips, smelling flowers on her skin, aware of her fingers coiled around his, of the sentiment flowing from her to bathe him in contentment.

"I know you love me, too, Natalie," he said in a breath against her ear. "You started loving me years ago."

She shook her head vehemently.

"Shh . . ." Her reaction was one of confusion, he knew, not contradiction, and he cupped her cheek, holding her steadily against him, his lips brushing her temple. "I know you do. Trust me with it, Natalie."

"Jonathan . . ."

Her voice sounded so pained, so small, and he ached inside for her. Then he caught a glimpse of Madeleine walking toward them, followed by the comte d'Arles and four or five others, dressed impeccably and ready for battle if the hard lines of their features were any indication.

"We're about to be rudely interrupted," he whispered, sighing with aggravation. He kissed her cheek and pulled himself upright. "The timing in this romance of ours has always been laughable." He braced her face in his hand and looked into her eyes. "Regardless of what's about to happen, believe what I've just told you, sweetheart. Play the game brilliantly now and don't, in any way, stay mad at me."

Natalie couldn't respond to his last remark. Her mind had gone numb; her body shook from bewilderment and shock at the impassioned intimacies he'd shared with her that she never expected to hear from his lips, but that yes, she believed because she wanted so desperately to. He frayed her sensibilities to the edge with his smile, his light caress, his deep, velvety voice that resonated longing and desire and his own devotion to something new and marvelous.

And then Jonathan moved to the left of her a little, leaving her in plain view of those approaching. She had imagined the evening to be taut with an excitement of its own, and she'd been looking forward to it with rational thought, hoping to surprise Jonathan with her appearance in his priceless jewels, and she knew she'd accomplished at least that. He'd been most definitely surprised to see her, had looked even astounded if one could describe his facial features exactly, and that alone had filled her with self-assurance and pleasure.

Then he'd stripped it all away in minutes with his gentle tongue and caressing words, to leave her feeling dreadfully exposed in the presence of the comte d'Arles and others who sought to alter history with the sale of the emeralds clasped around her neck. Her only protection now was Jonathan because her mind had crumbled to nothing with his oddly timed confession of love. She wanted to hit him. She wanted to cry. She wanted to wrap herself in his embrace and never leave. Instead, she poised herself for the impending confrontation and wiped her cheeks with her white gloved fingers, glad to note her eye color hadn't rubbed off as feared.

Suddenly the two of them were surrounded by several angered Frenchmen, and Madeleine, who had carefully moved in to place her body protectively on Natalie's right. The count's side whiskers flared from clenched teeth, and his black eyes bore into hers for a long, static moment before he lifted them to Jonathan.

"Monsieur Drake," Henri began in a controlled but frigid voice, "how coincidental that we should see you here at my Parisian home tonight. And with your wife who is wearing my jewels. You found them, I assume, and are returning them to me?"

Someone coughed within the small, hovering crowd at the offensive implication that the Englishman had more correctly stolen them. Abruptly Natalie realized how stupid it had been for her to wear them here. She and Jonathan stood against a wall, encircled by Legitimists who wanted their king dead and would use the emeralds to fund his murder, and who would also go to extremes for their cause. Only two things could come of this: the deceitful men in front of her would physically rip the necklace from her throat, or she would have to hand it over to them. Either way Jonathan would lose, and for the first time, as the fog in her head began to clear, she wondered why he hadn't been cross with her for her lack of judgment.

Someone in a far corner of the room yelled, "Death to Louis Philippe!" while others cheered in response. A low rumble filled the hall, and Madeleine, standing between Natalie and Henri, was the first to react civilly to the count's question, gingerly touching his arm with a hand encased in black satin. "I'm sure you didn't mean to be so abrasive, Comte—"

"Please stay out of this, Madame DuMais!" the man bellowed in French. "I did not ask for your opinion."

Madeleine pulled her hand back, having the good graces to appear startled, although Natalie knew she probably expected such a reaction to her comment.

Jonathan cleared his throat to speak at last, and, still clasping her fingers, squeezed them in reassurance. "I believe there has been a grave misunderstanding on your part, Monsieur Comte."

Natalie stiffened at his boldness. His tone was firm and forthright, though not unkind, as he subtly returned the insult without any obvious awareness that he did so.

The count blinked, temporarily stumped by the reply as spots of red appeared on his puffy cheeks. His body, clothed in dove-gray superfine, stood out like a shield, and his expression was murderous. If she were alone with him like this she'd be frightened.

The tall man with the droopy eyes who had been so forward and enraged in Marseilles reached in between the count and Madeleine and clasped the emeralds around her throat with long, bony fingers.

Natalie gasped and pulled back a little. Jonathan reacted just as quickly by grabbing the man's wrist.

"I wouldn't do something unwise," he warned through clear eyes and a dangerously dark voice.

Madeleine took the cue. "Indeed, Monsieur Faille, that is quite enough. We should at least allow the Englishman to explain himself."

"Explain himself?" he seethed, looking from Jonathan to Madeleine and then to Natalie. He reddened, and the muscles in his neck stood out against his black cravat, but he jerked his wrist free of Jonathan's grasp and dropped it awkwardly to his side again. "How can he explain his stupidity in allowing his wife to be seen here tonight in these?"

A logical point, Natalie considered, and it left Jonathan in a difficult position. She felt his warmth beside her, his fingers wrapped firmly around hers, sensed his annoyance at the situation they now faced. But surprisingly he conveyed no concern or even nervousness in his stance. He was smooth in voice and confident in bearing.

Ignoring Faille, Jonathan looked squarely at Henri to divulge his secrets at last. "These emeralds weren't stolen from you—"

A thunderous cheer erupted in the hall, followed by several angered shouts, causing his words to be cut off. Two or three in their vicinity turned spontaneously at the noise, but both Natalie and Jonathan kept their eyes on the count who glowered at them in bright fury, his thick body stiff, forehead perspiring, eyes bloodshot from drink and the heavy tobacco smoke saturating the air.

Jonathan stood relaxed, waiting for his moment to strike. Natalie knew this as she knew him. He was poised, prepared, and knew exactly what he was doing. She trusted him.

"Indeed, Comte," he continued as the ruckus died a little. "These are not emeralds at all. This is a paste necklace I had made for my wife in Paris only several days ago. She admired the one worn by your daughter at the ball in Marseilles, and I consequently saw fit to indulge her."

Natalie stilled and slowly turned her head to stare at him. His mouth twisted into a caustic smile for Henri alone.

"Stealing precious emeralds is risky, Comte. Likewise, only a fool would risk letting his beloved wear priceless, stolen jewels in public. What my wife wears now is green glass worth only a trifle less than the pearl-studded pin in your lapel."

Natalie bristled beside him, her feet rigidly set, body like cold stone. The revelation registered like a blow to the gut, clarifying everything—the lies, the deception, the humiliation and hurt. For two weeks he'd allowed her to think she'd bested him, only to play her for the fool in the end. He didn't look at her but he felt her reaction because he curled his fingers around hers even tighter, refusing to release them.

Commotion ensued between those in their general vicinity. Someone in the hall stood on a table and, raising a glass that sloshed with amber liquid, began a lengthy, drunken exchange regarding the politics of the current government and those of a better time. Many yelled back in agreement, others stood atop chairs and countered. Natalie had never seen anything like it, and anywhere else she would have been fascinated to observe gentlemen, and even some ladies, behaving so shamelessly. But at this moment her attention stayed riveted on those directly in front of her—on the comte d'Arles and his fellow Legitimists. On Madeleine, and Jonathan—the world's most crafty liar.

"I don't believe you," the count spat in deadly calm. "Both your credibility and my imagination and tolerance cannot be stretched that far, Monsieur Drake."

Faille moved closer, blocking light from the large chandelier with his head.

"He is lying, Henri," said another stout Frenchman. "Nobody could produce paste so perfectly in less than a fortnight."

Quite possibly true. Still, Jonathan disregarded them all, glaring subtly at Henri. "And yet I assure you this necklace is a well-crafted forgery."

Natalie shuddered, enraged at his arrogance, the devious use of his cleverness. But through it all she believed him. The jewels around her neck were glass. This was the Black

Knight at his best—shocking everyone with daring and unforeseen disclosures. And yes, she'd play her part brilliantly because he'd asked her to. He wouldn't have done so unless he trusted her not to spoil his life's work in a loud, crowded banquet hall in Paris. She would never do that to him, and he knew it.

Natalie angled her body so that she moved a step forward, in front of the artful thief of her insane desire. She rubbed her thumb across his knuckles to assure him, and with that wordless gesture, he finally let her go.

"Goodness, gentlemen, such a misunderstanding where there is no cause," she reasoned as a woman intolerant of foolish men. With a forced smile she placed her palm on Henri's arm. He flinched, but she pretended not to notice. "Please, monsieur, I insist you have these."

"Natalie, darling," Jonathan pleaded, aghast.

She sent him an icy grin. "It's quite all right, my darling. Proof is needed now, and under the circumstances, we can't expect to leave here tonight with them." Her eyes melded with his in feigned sweetness. "You'll buy me lots and lots of others, I'm sure." For a second she thought he would break his character and laugh.

She sighed and turned her attention back to the count, who now seemed genuinely taken aback by her suggestion, that she could be so easily swayed. Actually they all appeared uncomfortable as it occurred to them that by her offering to hand over the faux jewels without argument, the Frenchmen had been wrong in their assumptions and had insulted an influential Englishman and his innocent wife in the count's Parisian home. Natalie concluded this at once and played upon it by patting Henri's arm in a small measure of condescension, expressing a silent understanding toward the absurd complexities of the male ego.

Then without further response, she raised her fingers to her neck and unclasped the necklace, pulling it forward and holding it out to the count.

Dazzling emerald green and gold glittered under candlelight—a magnificent forgery she loathed losing.

Henri took it from her with thick fingers, clutching it, his heavy brows knit together as he turned it over to study its structure. "For a woman, you are indeed"—he cleared his throat—"astute, Madame Drake. And you are also honest."

"So is her husband," Madeleine interjected with a tactful drop of her chin.

That was the final offense. The count and other distinguished noblemen had acted disgracefully toward her and Jonathan, and that acknowledgment had come from a Frenchwoman. A splendid touch. Natalie felt the air grow thick with embarrassment and triumph.

Someone shouted obscenities, and they all turned.

And then she heard the pops, two of them, followed by screaming and a sudden mass of confusion.

Jonathan grabbed her wrist and yanked her to the ground, her feet tangling in petticoats and yards of blue taffeta as she tried to steady herself. She heard yelling in the distance, wailing. Madeleine shouted something in French from behind her, but she couldn't understand it. The count pivoted unsteadily, knocked in the back by several people pushing through the crowd. Faille snatched the necklace from Henri's hands and sprinted along the edge of the buffet table toward a side entrance, tripping twice over his gangly legs before he reached it.

The yelling continued, disarray grew, then another pop exploded above the noise, which Natalie now registered to be a pistol shot. Jonathan pushed her to the edge of the buffet table so that she couldn't see much of anything but him and scattering feet. He said something to Madeleine in French, then turned back to her, grabbing her face with firm fingers.

"Madeleine's getting you out of France—"

"I'm not leaving!" she blurted angrily without clear thought, attempting to steady her unbalanced figure so she wouldn't topple over and crash into the table.

He gritted his teeth. "The authorities will be here soon, maybe even the National Guard if things get uglier." He tightened his hold on her cheeks. "You can't get arrested, understand?"

She grimaced at his hardened features, fuming from his determination. Someone fell against the table knocking over their discarded glasses of champagne and whisky, causing the contents to splash over the side and down the front of her gown.

The noise grew. A chair, heaved across the floor, crashed through a window twenty steps away from her, and Natalie started to tense in fear. "I'll leave, but you're coming with me—"

"I can't," he argued, looking directly into her eyes. "I have to tell somebody in authority about tomorrow."

"Madeleine can do that."

He shook his head. "No one will believe her. She's French and a woman, and they'll either suspect her involvement or disregard her. I will probably be taken seriously but that means I can't leave until tomorrow at the earliest. She can get you out tonight."

"We must go while people are still disoriented!" Madeleine interrupted in a shout above the roar, kneeling behind Jonathan.

Natalie refused to look at the woman or give in so easily. "I'll stay at the hotel with her until you come for me—"

"Dammit, Natalie, no! You—" He stopped, releasing her cheeks, then raking the fingers of one hand harshly through his hair to calm himself. "If these people attempt to assassinate the king, the streets will ring with unrest, and you might not get out at all. Things are already dangerous enough. You did a marvelous job for me, sweetheart, but it's over. Go home *now*."

She glared at him and hit a fist against his chest. "I *hate* you, Jonathan."

He have her a sheepish grin. "I know. Now go."

He turned toward Madeleine, and Natalie grabbed his coat sleeve. "Do *not* die."

The shouting grew louder, the whimpering shrill.

He rolled his eyes in exasperation. "I would never deprive you of the pleasure of killing me yourself."

She opened her mouth to say something clever, then shut it again. With that he kissed her hard on the lips. "Get out of France, Natalie, before you're detained or arrested. Your mother would *not* approve.''

"She wouldn't approve of you, either," she nearly screamed.

He glanced at her face for a final time. "Yes, she will."

Then he disappeared into the scrambling crowd as Madeleine dragged on her arm until she found herself outside and standing on the dark and dangerous street.

Eighteen

Moonlight sifted through gauze curtains to illuminate the entry hall as Jonathan stepped into his town house. He paid his hired driver after the man set his trunk on the floor, then dismissed him, locking the door to the outside world. It was nearly midnight, and he was exhausted, relieved to be home.

Loosening his neckcloth, he moved quietly through the first floor toward the center staircase, deciding against lighting. There was no need. His intent was to do nothing but fall into bed and sleep off the weariness of the last few days. Tomorrow, well rested and prepared to face his future, he would make his first formal call on Miss Natalie Haislett.

She'd arrived home safely, that much he'd learned, but whether she'd speak to him again soon was anybody's guess. It had been nearly a week since the disastrous party in Paris, and all had not gone well for the Legitimists. But he was tired of concerning himself with their cause. His life was in London, or more precisely Natalie was in London, and his life was with her.

He missed her, and he'd never missed a woman before. She had wrapped herself around his heart, and he had succumbed. She would forgive him for the last little lie about the emeralds and marry him, not only because his egotistical mind would accept nothing less, but because she loved him, too, and he knew this.

Jonathan climbed the stairs to the second-floor landing, unbuttoning his cuffs, then working through those at the bottom of his shirt as he walked into his darkened bedroom. Immediately he saw her and stopped short.

Her body lay under his covers, a silver shimmer outlining the curve of her figure as moonglow streamed through the tall window behind her. She stirred and turned in his direction, noticing him as he stood staring at her. Silently she sat up and stepped onto the carpet to walk toward him, completely unclothed.

"Jonathan?"

His body reacted from joyous wonder at finding her between his sheets, from the husky, intimate way she said his name, from the naked vision of her coming to his side.

"Were you expecting someone else?" he softly teased.

"Yes, I was expecting my lover," she answered with a casual air and a toss of her curls. "He hasn't arrived yet, though, so I suppose I'll have to settle for you."

One side of his mouth curved upward. "I think I can make you forget him."

Her brows rose. "Really? How arrogant." With light-hearted irritation she added, "But then, since you're the one who's here and available to me, I suppose I, too, shall take it upon myself to make you forget all the other lovers you've had in this bed."

His smile widened. "You did that in Paris, Natalie. I can't now recall having a lover before you."

She sighed and inched her body up so close to his he felt the heat of it. "That's the correct response, Jonathan, and naturally what I'd thought you'd say."

He touched her cheek with his palm, and she quickly covered it with her hand, turning her face into it, kissing him. She stood before him like a goddess from his deepest fantasy—skin gleaming like pearls, body sensual and soft, hair curling thickly over her breasts, eyes dark in shadows.

"I missed you," she whispered.

And he was lost.

Jonathan seized her elbow and pulled her against him, wrapping his arms around her waist, drawing her into him so she could feel the evidence of his desire, dropping his lips to brush hers.

"Madeleine told me—"

"I don't want to talk about Madeleine," he murmured against her mouth. "I want you to tell me what's in your heart, Natalie."

She reached up and placed her palms on his cheeks. "I'm furious with you."

"I know that already."

She touched his lips with delicate kisses. "I need you."

"I know that, too."

She shivered as he glided his fingertips up her waist until his hand found her breast. He cupped it, stroked it, feeling hot skin beneath rising gooseflesh, making her gasp when he gently squeezed her nipple to a peak.

"Tell me what I need to hear," he begged in a whisper.

In a silky, passion-filled voice, she pleaded, "Love me, Jonathan. . . ."

From that small demand, urgency overpowered him. He took her mouth completely with his in blatant hunger, drawing the breath from her with a harsh kiss of strength against softness, passion and longing against sweetness and forgiveness and acceptance. She parted her lips without insistence, eagerly welcomed his tongue with a sweep of hers, and his blood began to boil.

Gently he pushed her toward the bed with one hand while working through the remaining buttons on his shirt with the other. She grasped his shoulders as he led her, tasting him with a growing impatience to feel.

The back of her knees touched his quilt, and with that she pulled away from the kiss. He stared down at her face hidden in darkness, features unreadable, and yet he sensed every feeling for him she possessed. They emanated from her, shrouding him in warmth and comfort like summer sunshine on skin.

She lowered her body onto the bed as he swiftly discarded his clothes, and then he was beside her, touching her, kissing her mouth and neck, cheeks and brows and eyelashes. She moaned softly as his hand found her breast again, running his fingers along the base of it, cupping it, kneading it tenderly.

His shaft, hard and hot and ready, grazed her hip. But instead of shying away from it as she had their first time, she pushed herself into it, closing her leg over his to mold him to her tightly. He groaned from the contact, encircling her waist with his arm as they now lay nearly side by side, kissing deeply, breathing rapidly, wanting.

She put her hands flat on his chest, massaging his muscles with vigor, then lowering them between their bodies until she found the coarse curls below his navel.

He drew back, releasing her mouth and sucking in a sharp inhale at a boldness in her he hadn't expected. Then she touched the hot, smooth length of him, her expression of uncertainty only vaguely discernible through filtered moonlight.

"Yes," he assured her in a gravelly whisper, caressing the softness of her breast.

Cautiously she explored him with her fingers, moving them up and down his demanding erection, teasing the curls at the base, grazing her nails along the outside. Then she took him fully in her hand, her thumb finding an emerging satiny drop on the surface that she smoothed across the top in one slow circle.

Jonathan had trouble breathing, holding back. He ached to join with her, to embed himself in her heated softness, but wanted more desperately at that moment for her to discover the hard angles and strength of his body, the physical differences between them. He reached down with his hand and covered hers, staring gravely into her eyes, showing her how to stroke him, moving her hand slowly up and down the length of him until she grew confident in the movement herself.

He placed his hand back on her breast, rubbing the rosy, hardened tip with his fingers. The other he laid flat across her forehead, smoothing her hair back from her beautiful face, taking in every feature with only a faint stream of light.

"Tell me how you feel," he urged again quietly, his voice thick with longing.

Her body trembled as her breathing became a pant from his steady caresses. "Don't ever leave me, Jonathan."

Those barely audible words came from deep within, through an ache of something she couldn't yet define for him. He forced himself to stay calm, to hold back his release as she continued to stroke him with her hand, swallowing harshly at the wonder of having her beside him, desiring him, wanting him always. "I love you, Natalie. . . ."

She drew a shaky breath from the power of her own feelings, and he could wait no longer.

He covered her mouth with his, kissing her delicately at first, then spreading her lips with his tongue, invading the warmth of her with thriving need. He reached down with his own hand and touched hers again as she stroked him intimately, grazing her fingers with the tips of his. Finally necessity invaded, and his heart pounded and he knew he was close to losing himself. He closed his palm over her knuckles to stop the movement, and she responded. He kissed her deeply, brushing her brow with his thumb as he pulled her hand from him and placed it to her side.

He released her mouth and began a line of gentle kisses down her neck and chest, circling the tip of her breast with his tongue, then taking the nipple in his mouth, kissing and sucking until she whimpered. He lowered his hand to the curls between her legs, skimming his fingertips along the soft flesh of her inner thighs before finding the slick, wet folds and parting them to stroke her slowly, deliberately.

She gasped and curved into his hand, moving her fingers to his hair as the anticipation in her grew. He quickened the pace, sucking her nipples, one after the other, increasing the pressure of his fingers, then finally pushing one inside of her as he found the hidden nub of her pleasure and began circling it with his thumb.

She pressed into him, lifting her hips in rhythm, setting

her own pace, closing her eyes once more to the feel of his rousing invasion.

He drew his lips down her belly, pausing to rub his cheek in the curls between her legs, inhaling the scent of her, marveling in the beauty of her as he brought her closer to her glorious crest. He touched his lips to her thigh, and she stiffened a little, confused through the haze of desire, unsure of his intentions.

"Just feel me," he whispered before pulling his hand away and quickly replacing it with his mouth, tasting her, penetrating her with his tongue.

"Jonathan—"

He ignored her momentary shock, sliding his palms beneath her to hold her still, licking her within until she accepted the intrusion and began to burn once more in a craving fever.

She clutched him to her, her fingers through his hair, breath quick and uneven as she started pushing her hips against his mouth. Expertly he flicked the center of her in steady measure, taking her to the edge of satisfaction and then withdrawing the pressure, again, and then again.

Finally she moaned his name in delicious torment, and he stopped the teasing and carried her there. Her thighs tightened. She pressed into him. Then the pleasure shattered within her, and she cried out, rotating her hips while he flicked and stroked and licked her with his tongue.

He felt the quivers within her subside, and quickly he moved up to cover her with his body, lowering himself between her legs, adjusting her hips beneath his. He hesitated for a few seconds, hearing her fast breathing, feeling the dampness of it on his skin, and at last she opened her eyes to his.

He watched her face in near darkness, tracing her lips with his fingertips as he entered her, deeply, resisting further motion while she adjusted to the pressure and fullness of him.

She welcomed him, encasing him in hot, tight softness, expressing no pain this time, only desire of completion and the hope of pleasing him. She wrapped her legs around his thighs, her arms around his neck, pulling him as close as she could.

Everything about her bewitched him, as it always had—her glossy hair spreading out in a silvery sheen across his pillows, her magnificent eyes now circles of black satin, caressing him, hypnotizing him, the soft feel of her, the tempting scent of her, and now the sweet feminine taste of her as her honeyed moisture lingered on his lips.

"I will never leave you," he whispered with an intensity that staggered even him.

She inhaled a deep, shaky breath, feeling the radiant power between them, comprehending it. "I know."

He placed his forehead on hers, wove his fingers through her hair, and steadily began to glide out and then back into her, keeping the action slow and small until he felt her relax from the tightness and grow accustomed to the sensation.

She started her own little movements against him, running her inner thighs along the outside of his, and he gradually quickened the pace, driving deeper with each penetration. She arched her body enough for him to realize she wanted more, and he gave, changing the rhythm until she adjusted, circling his hips to help her find fulfillment again.

She matched the force of each thrust as passion grew, resting her palms on his neck, her breathing shallow once more. He lowered his hand to her breast and clung to it possessively, sliding his fingers across her nipple, then circling it, squeezing it.

She turned her face into the pillow, and he increased the tempo, rotating his hips against her, kissing her temple and cheek and the curve of her throat.

He held back for her, concentrating, kissing her face, sucking her earlobe, grazing it with his teeth, kneading her breast with expert fingers. The heat she radiated scorched his skin, her breath caressed his cheek, and his body strained with a fire of its own as he neared his own climax.

She writhed beneath him frantically, whimpering, and finally he could stand no more. He reached the edge of sanity, raised himself up to see the beauty of her face, and just as quickly she grabbed his hips with tight hands, forcing him to remain inside of her.

His body tensed. Then he let himself go and exploded within. She continued to move her hips, circling them against him, pushing into him, digging her nails into his skin, until at last she whispered his name and captured the exquisite pleasure for a second time. Her legs jerked wildly, her deep muscles contracted around him, and he watched her, felt everything, savored it all, loved it all.

Loved her.

Nineteen

Jonathan stirred, squeezing his eyes shut to the brightness of early morning. His body felt stiff beneath the sheets, his mind sluggish, and then the memory of the night before returned, and he knew his face glowed with a smile that would embarrass him in front of anyone.

He raised one eyelid, squinting, reaching for her with his palm, but she wasn't beside him. Then he heard her downstairs, in the kitchen below, and the soft hum of her voice was enough to drag him from between the covers.

Jonathan dressed to his waist, splashed cold water on his face from the full pitcher on the washstand, ran his still-damp fingers through his hair, and left the bedroom.

He descended the stairs quickly, strode through the hallway, and stopped in the doorway to his kitchen, because the sudden sight of her dazzled him.

She stood by the stove, facing him, hands behind her back, wearing only a silk wrap in deep red, tied by a sash at the waist, which left it open from the thighs down and in a low plunge between her breasts. She'd pinned her hair loosely atop her head, although strands of it curled wildly down her temples, neck, and back.

She smiled hesitantly, cheeks flushing a gentle pink when she became aware of his presence, eyeing him through half-raised lashes, and Jonathan was certain he'd never seen anything more alluring in his life.

God, she was so beautiful, so sweet and soft and feminine, affecting him in ways he'd never imagined. His body tightened, his breath caught, and he wondered what she'd think if he pulled slowly on the sash, ran his tongue across her collarbone until she moaned, and just took her—

"I've made you coffee," she said timidly.

"You've made me happy and satisfied as I've never been before, Natalie," he corrected in a thick drawl.

A smile tugged at her lips again, and she glanced to her bare feet to escape his heated gaze. "You're delusional."

He chuckled and sauntered toward her. "I think it's more accurate to say I'm blessed and I know it."

She shook her head and whispered, "Jonathan, last night—"

"Was perfect," he finished for her.

She almost laughed, restraining herself with difficulty. "That wasn't what I was going to say."

He took her chin with his fingers and lifted her face so she couldn't help but look at him. "You were going to say it was less than perfect?" His eyes grew round with innocent hurt. "I'm devastated."

The collar of her robe threatened to fall down her arm, and she yanked it up, trying to remain stern even as her eyes crinkled with amusement. "We need to discuss serious issues before we get into anything . . . intimate."

"Ahh . . . Of course." He released her chin and looked over her shoulder. "It's boiling."

She turned awkwardly in the tight space between his bare chest and the stove. "Finally. Go sit at the table."

He considered moving away from the distracting warmth of her body and the smell of lilacs in her hair, but doing so was difficult. And was it lilacs? He couldn't remember what lilacs smelled like exactly, but lilacs were supposed to smell heavenly, and of course her hair smelled clean and flowery and felt heavenly against his—

"Jonathan, sit," she ordered, cringing and lifting her shoulder against his intrusive face. "You're breathing down my neck."

He sighed loudly and mumbled, "If you insist."

"I do."

He glided his tongue along the smooth rim of her ear. She shuddered but ignored him, and at last he withdrew from the sensuous feel of her silk robe rubbing his chest and stepped toward the oak table where they'd had their first coffee together more than two months ago.

This morning, however, she'd already set two places with saucers, spoons, and a bowl of sugar and a pitcher of cream between them. In the center of the table were chocolates, laid out on a plate in the shape of a heart.

He stared at them nonplussed, head cocked to one side, a crooked grin on his mouth. "Chocolates for breakfast?"

She said nothing, and after a second or two he turned to her. She carried their cups in her hands as she walked in his direction, careful not to look at him.

"What is it?" he asked suspiciously, pulling a chair out for her.

She glanced at him mischievously, then placed the full cups of coffee on the saucers. "It's symbolic, but I'll get to that in a moment."

Withholding comment on the symbolism of chocolate at half past seven in the morning, he sat after she did, beside her, studying her and the pearly cleavage exposed between crimson silk, her long, lowered lashes, the way her forehead creased into two fine lines of concentration as she added half a cup of cream and at least three teaspoons of sugar.

Entranced, he lifted his cup to his lips and suddenly wished he'd added the same. The coffee was bitterly strong, nearly undrinkable, but she had made it, and he pretended not to notice.

"You're staring at me again, Jonathan," she scolded in a low voice.

He smirked. "A naughty habit that I imagine will haunt me for the next fifty years."

She smiled, gaze lowered as she sat back in her chair. "I hope so."

It was her first verbal concession to her own acceptance of a lifetime spent with him, and the thought, the idea, made his heart start to beat hard and fast. He took another drink of the incredibly awful coffee to hide his elated expression should she decide to look up.

"How did you get in here, Natalie?"

She stared at the chocolates. "I found a key under a flowerpot sitting on the stone steps that lead to the servants' entrance."

"My housekeeper, Gerty, is rather forgetful," he explained without surprise.

"I assumed so."

"Did you?"

She disregarded the implication in his simple question, apparently deciding he didn't need to say aloud that he wouldn't leave a key for a mistress to enter through the servants' door. That was far-fetched, and she knew it.

Finally she took a sip of coffee, then made a face of disgust. "It's not very good—"

"It's fine," he countered, bringing his cup to his lips without expression. "How long have you been here?"

That made her uncomfortable, and she twisted her body just enough in the chair that the silk opened a little more, exposing her right breast nearly all the way to her nipple. She didn't notice, though, and he wasn't about to tell her.

She glanced out the window. "I've been here since Tuesday."

That jolted him. "You haven't been home?"

"No. I've been waiting for you."

He knew he beamed from that remark. Probably too much.

She touched a loose strand of her hair and coiled it around her finger absentmindedly. "Your servants will be back soon, won't they?"

"I'll probably request that they return Monday," he replied. "There are only the two of them, and they're paid regardless."

"So I can stay the weekend."

It wasn't a casual question but a pointed statement full of hope, and suddenly he wanted her sitting in his lap, her mouth lingering on his, her bare bottom rubbing against him.

"I need to know some things, Jonathan."

He raised his cup to his lips. "Hmm?"

Seconds later she moved inquisitive eyes back to his. "First," she began thoughtfully, "beyond the fact that I know Louis Philippe is alive and well and still in power, I have no idea what happened in Paris after I left."

He lifted his brows and relaxed in his chair. "Well, not much did happen, really. The comte d'Arles and six or seven other Legitimists were arrested early Sunday morning. The assassination attempt was carried off as planned, and there was a scuffle among the crowd. But the king was never very close to danger."

"Thanks to you, I suppose," she put in with a prideful tilt of her head.

He grinned again. "No, actually, he was fairly well guarded anyway."

"How humble you are today, Jonathan."

Shrugging fractionally, he conceded, "I do take credit when it's mine."

She almost laughed. "Yes, indeed you do. You're very good at that."

Jonathan turned his attention to his cup, tracing the rim with the pad of a finger. "Several were injured along the parade route, though. Two or three critically. The little information I revealed couldn't prevent unrest." His expression became guarded, his voice taking on a more serious air. "Louis Philippe won't last a year, Natalie. His reign, if one could call it that, is nearly over already. The people are restless and ready for change."

"And our good friend the comte d'Arles?"

Jonathan shook his head, frowning. "He's probably home in Marseilles, the entire episode behind him. He and other nobles of his generation are far too prominent to be kept in custody during such a time of civil unrest. There's more at stake for the French government than attempting to prosecute influential, wealthy men for an assassination plot that cannot be traced to them directly.'' He looked back into her eyes. ''The Legitimists want Henri on the throne, and maybe they'll get their wish eventually.''

She considered that for a moment, sipping her coffee, staring at the table.

''Are you going to tell me about the chocolates?'' he pushed at last.

''Are you going to tell me about the emeralds?'' she returned matter-of-factly.

He sighed and rubbed his forehead with his fingertips. ''I forgot about the emeralds.''

''Again?'' she charged sarcastically. Stirring yet another teaspoon of sugar into her coffee, she scrutinized him as she would a naughty child. ''That's a nasty habit of yours as well, Jonathan. A decent thief shouldn't forget the objects of his endeavors so frequently.''

''That's why I need you, Natalie,'' he admitted. ''I'm getting too old to do this work on my own. I'm becoming forgetful.''

She stared hard at him. ''You're not even thirty. And don't change the subject.''

Resisting a smile, Jonathan leaned forward, resting his forearms on the hard oak surface of his table as he turned his cup around in his hands. ''I gave the real emeralds to Madeleine in Marseilles the day after I stole them. She got them out of France—before the ball. We couldn't chance having them found once the count realized he had glass jewels in his possession.''

Natalie placed her elbows on the table and covered her face with her palms. ''So you carried two identical forgeries to France.''

''Two forgeries and the onyx necklace,'' he replied. ''I didn't know what I'd need, or what I'd leave behind in the safe the night of the ball. In the end I chose the onyx.''

''So I stole a glass necklace from your trunk. How ridiculous I must have looked to you.''

''Don't be embarrassed,'' he said softly, watching traces of pink flowing into her cheeks that she attempted to hide. ''Your shrewdness took me quite by surprise.''

"This also explains why you weren't angry with me."

"I wouldn't have been angry at you for stealing real emeralds, Natalie," he maintained in a tone filled with deep meaning. "I was fascinated by everything about you on our little adventure."

She thought about that for a minute, then shook her head in her hands. "I'm disgusted. Madeleine knew this all along, and still she let me believe I had the real jewels, encouraged me to attend that dreadful party in Paris."

He waited, then reached for her wrist, which she tried to keep from his grasp to no avail. He pulled it from her, wrapping his large hand around her soft, smaller one. "Madeleine's smart, Natalie."

She groaned and briefly closed her eyes, one palm clasped with his across the edge of the table, the other resting on her forehead. "No, she's astounding. The two of you make a magnificent team."

He wasn't sure if she was being serious or sarcastic, but he rubbed her fingers with his thumb and lowered his voice to a soothing caress. "Madeleine works on her own. She always has and probably always will. But she sensed very early that I was devoted to you—that I wanted to work with you, to be with you. That I was falling in love with you."

Her warm fingers stiffened in his hand, but he held fast to them. "You and I are the team, Natalie. You're aware of this or you wouldn't be here now, wearing red silk over bare skin, smelling like flowers and warm sheets and a night of lovemaking, tempting me with your smile and eyes." Gravely he whispered, "I think it's time for you to tell me."

Static charged the air, and Natalie knew, with a sudden tightening in her belly, that confession time had come. It had, in fact, been coming for weeks. He realized it as well, sitting smugly next to her at the table, rubbing her fingers with his, waiting arrogantly for her buried secrets to be revealed.

She straightened a little and covered her coffee cup with her right hand, clutching it as her pulse sped up with anticipation and a creeping fear of the unknown. He felt her reluctance to begin but said nothing in response, just watched her intently with his beautiful eyes as they gazed through hers to touch her deepest feelings.

"Madeleine *is* smart, Jonathan," she started huskily.

That wasn't what he wanted to hear. He hadn't expected to talk more of the Frenchwoman, and he couldn't hide the dismay in his expression, which she had to admit pleased her.

She attempted a smile. "The chocolates were her idea."

Now his brows furrowed in confused interest.

"Well, not exactly," she clarified with a small shake of her head. She paused to collect her thoughts, and he held even tighter to her fingers. "I told Madeleine that I thought you had cut my heart to pieces the night I gave myself to you. She defended you by saying that couldn't have happened unless I had given you my heart as well." She glanced quickly at the chocolates then back at his face, her stomach now in knots, pulse racing, mouth dry. "I never really did that, did I, Jonathan?"

His body stilled, and he barely breathed. "No."

Natalie locked her gaze with his. "That's what the chocolates are for," she disclosed in a raspy, nervous breath. "They symbolize my heart. I'm giving it to you now."

For an endless moment he stared into her eyes, clinging to her fingers. Then he whispered, "Why?"

She succumbed to tears she could no longer fight. "Because I love you."

It was as if the mysteries of the universe were unveiled for him in that instant. Air hissed through his teeth as he inhaled, and his eyes, his features, every part of him beamed in a vivid pleasure she felt as an ache in her own chest.

"I'm afraid of it, Jonathan."

He caressed her with his gaze, her fingers with his thumb. "I know you are."

She dropped her lashes at last, staring at her coffee cup through blurring vision and memories of so long ago. "You were right, too. In Paris. You said I started loving you years ago, and I did. But I couldn't talk about that night because I was mortified after it happened—about the way I kissed you and the things I said to you. I'm embarrassed about it to this day.'' She shook her head. ''I was so very foolish then.''

''I didn't think you were foolish. I thought you were enchanting and beautiful, so innocent.''

Those softly murmured words were meant to calm, and they liquefied her. ''I thought you were beautiful, too, Jonathan, and dashing and sophisticated. I dreamed about you for months after that night. I dreamed of your lips on mine and hearing you tell me that you loved me, too.''

''You were so young, Natalie.''

She raised her eyes to his again, and the look he gave her—one filled with such utter gentleness and keen comprehension of her feelings—nearly took her breath away. Her throat constricted, and she swallowed hard, wiping away a single tear as it slid down her cheek.

''Yes, I was young,'' she explained in a rough, faraway voice. ''And naive. I didn't know you then, didn't really know anything except that I felt a small, innocent love for you in my heart like . . . like the beauty of a single rose, or a violin or harp playing a soft melody.'' Her gaze became intense. ''But the love I feel for you now is different. I know your weaknesses and strengths, your moods. I know how much you adore women—''

''Natalie—''

''Shh . . . Let me finish, my darling Jonathan, before I lose my nerve.''

He lifted her hand to his lips, tenderly kissing her fingers, her knuckles, and wrist until she felt a tingling within. Still, he never took his eyes from her face.

''I love you so much more as you are today,'' she continued passionately. ''And you wouldn't be who you are without the experiences of your past, and this includes the women you've known. I love your intelligent humor and the way your mind works so cleverly to expose the ultimate good. I love the way you argue with me over silly things like the appropriate dinner wine and stealing the covers. I

love the way you flatter me with a small, suggestive glance
and tease me with your voice and make love to me as if
you're sharing the secrets and longings of your soul. I know
how much you adore your ridiculous weapon collection,
and the theater and fine brandy and expensively tailored
clothes. I know your favorite color is lustrous, ruby red and
that your greatest worry, your greatest fear, is losing me.''

He'd gradually stopped kissing her with her intimate disclosure, his breath becoming uneven and raspy as she felt
it on her wrist. For a second or two, Natalie was certain he
was close to losing his composure in front of her.

She smiled with trembling lips and squeezed his hand,
her voice once again dropping to a whisper of profound
intent and fervent conviction. ''I said I loved you then like
a rose or a harp—something innocent and delightfully
sweet—and I did. But I love you now, Jonathan, like a—
a conservatory filled with the dazzling color and fragrance
of hundreds of exotic flowers, like a symphony of music—
from flutes to French horns to cellos—playing rich concer-
tos and beautiful waltzes.''

She leaned toward him, running her thumb along his
knuckles. ''I don't need to promise to love you, Jonathan.
I love you enough to last a lifetime, and you know this
already.'' Eyes once more brimming with tears, she confessed in warmth, ''But I swear to you, right now, that if
you promise to cherish my heart with all the love and goodness in yours, I will give myself to you completely, faith-
fully, and trust you always with everything I am.''

For a long time he just stared into her eyes. She'd given
more than he'd expected to hear, much more. She could
see the wonder in his gaze, feel it flow from him in currents,
and suddenly emotion surfaced and the love he felt for her
was a discernible force, radiating from him in joy, suffusing
her to wash the past away. Forever.

''Natalie . . .''

It was a whispered plea for her to come to him, and she
responded, raising herself on unsteady legs and walking
two feet around the corner of the table to his side. He
brought her knuckles to his lips, not kissing them this time,

but just placing them against him, gliding the fingers of his free hand down her silk wrap as she stood before him— from the side of her breast, over her hip to her thigh. Then at last he pulled her onto his lap.

She curled into him, erasing the world outside with his powerful embrace, fitting her bottom snugly against his hips as she wrapped her arms around him and nestled her face in his neck.

"I will never break your heart," he assured her in a violent, whispered vow, his cheek to her temple, his lips to her ear.

The strength of his conviction unraveled her, and she started to cry softly, silently, against him.

He held her quietly for several minutes, pulling the pin from her hair so the mass of it flowed in waves over her shoulders and down her back, tunneling his fingers through it, kissing her forehead and brow, cradling her in his arms. "Did you know, Natalie sweet, that since that night in the garden five years ago, I've never been able to get you out of my mind?"

She sniffled but didn't move her face from the curve of his throat. "With such variety at your fingertips? I don't believe you."

He chuckled in a velvety tremor that shook her to the spine.

"I lied to you in Marseilles," he admitted, choosing his words carefully. "The truth is, after that night, I didn't ask about you occasionally—I thought about you constantly for months, and later asked about you often."

She stilled in his arms, but he carried on without notice.

"I knew who courted you from time to time, and I was more than irritated when I learned Geoffrey Blythe had serious intentions, because it was so obvious to me that the two of you didn't suit." Very slowly he added with a thread of discomfiture, "No less than seven times during the last five years, Natalie, I dressed for you to notice me and left this town house to call on you formally."

Amazement pulsed through her, and she raised her head to lock her startled eyes with his.

He smiled wryly. "I wasn't sure how you'd receive me, knowing my reputation, and especially after sharing that first incredible kiss and your innocent confession of love for me. And because of this uncertainty I never got past a drive down your street, except once. About a year ago I actually rang the bell and spoke to a parlor maid, but you were out, and I was too nervous to leave a card."

His eyes grazed her features as his palm slid across the wetness on her cheek. "I swear it was by fate that you walked into my home when you did. You were embarrassed to be here, but in some small regard I expected it. I was surprised to discover you in my study that morning, but not at all surprised that you'd come back into my life." He grasped her jaw with tight fingers as his tone grew passionate. "You're so vibrantly alive, and your presence and friendship enrich my life in so many ways, giving me something I've never experienced with anyone else. I dreamed of loving you like this, Natalie, and yes, I cherish it. I always will."

She didn't think she'd ever been more shaken by a disclosure in her life. His beautiful gray-blue eyes pierced hers with stark memories, with honesty and abounding hope. She placed a palm on his cheek and drew it over a day's growth of stubble, the tingle of it on her sensitive fingers making her toes curl and desire for him burn anew. Then she touched his lips with hers, kissing him, tasting the lingering traces of coffee and inhaling the warm, masculine scent of his skin.

He reacted in kind, pulling her closer, untying the sash at her waist, demanding more as his hand reached in to caress her back and hip in sensuous strokes.

"Marry me, Jonathan?" she begged against his mouth.

"I was beginning to fear you'd never ask," he whispered in fast reply.

She smiled inside, squirming against the marvelous feel of his growing erection now stiffly nestled in the curve of her bottom. "Our courtship has been so unconventional."

He moved his hand to her breast, sliding his palm across

her nipple in slow circles until it hardened, and she sighed from the welcomed invasion.

"To avoid gossip," he said against her mouth, "we'll tell everybody I courted you in Newburn while you were there visiting your great-aunt for the Season. I, of course, was there on a scouting expedition for ancient English swords."

She laughed softly against him, and he pulled back a little.

"We'll say we met at . . . ." He tilted his head in thought. "At Mrs. Peabody's soiree."

She frowned. "Who's Mrs. Peabody?"

"I've no idea, but I'm certain there's more than one in Newburn."

"As ingenious as that is, my mother won't believe it," she warned in a teasing voice, brushing her fingers through his hair.

His eyes rounded in challenge. "I'll charm her into believing it. I can be very convincing."

"Indeed," she said dryly. "I imagine you'll spend years using your convincing charm on her."

He pursed his lips. "I think . . . perfecting it on her would be more accurate." Another small laugh escaped her, and he leaned in again to nuzzle her neck. "What about your father?"

She inclined her head to give him better access. "At this point my father would approve of my marrying almost anyone."

He chuckled. "Then you're stuck with me, I'm afraid."

"I think I can manage to be happy," she purred.

His lips moved provocatively over her flesh again. "With the courtship issue respectably explained, we can be married within the month."

"That's not enough time to plan a wedding, Jonathan."

"We have to, Natalie, to avoid scandal," he clarified, nibbling her lobe with his teeth. "In case you're carrying my baby."

Color crept into her cheeks. "Oh."

She felt rather than saw his broad smile of satisfaction,

annoying her that he should enjoy flustering her with such considerations.

"And speaking of your parents," he whispered, his mouth to her skin, "I fixed your mother's little problem." He pushed the silk over her shoulder and trailed her throat with his tongue until he sucked her collarbone.

"Wh-what?"

"The problem with the letters," he explained seconds later, his breath so cool against her suddenly burning flesh.

His hand found her nipple again, teasing it, brushing it lightly with his thumbnail. Then he leaned over and licked it, sucked it, and she reached for him in response, raking her fingers through his hair and delighting in the sharp, tingling pleasure she felt between her legs.

"Mmm . . ."

"Did you hear me, Natalie?"

He stopped tormenting her with his hands and mouth until she raised closed lashes to look at him.

"What about the letters?" she asked in a rush.

"Do you remember a footman employed in your household called John Russell?"

She tried to force her head to clear, to concentrate on what he said exactly. "I think so."

But Jonathan made it so extraordinarily difficult for her to focus. He pushed his hand through the silk until it fell open completely and draped down the sides of her body. Then he slid his palm lower and lower on her belly until he cupped her between her thighs.

"Jonathan—"

"Russell was dismissed about three years ago by your mother for stealing silver," he continued, watching her, his voice now labored with his own need.

Deliberately he began to stroke her as she tried so very hard to pay attention to what he was saying.

"He overheard the arguments between your parents, and when he was forced to leave without reference he began blackmailing your mother with rumors of the love affair. There were never any letters—at least not in England."

Through the fog and his ever more intimate coaxing of

her body, Natalie was beginning to understand his words. She grabbed his wrist to still his hand.

"What are you saying, Jonathan?"

He grinned almost bashfully. "In about an hour, Sir Guy Phillips and one or two others are going to call on Russell at his home to discover the duke of Newark's priceless emeralds in a flour tin. They will then inform the man that in exchange for his silence about your mother, he will not be arrested and prosecuted for stealing a necklace he, of course, didn't steal at all. The emeralds will then be returned to their rightful owners, and your mother should finally be free of her scandalous secret."

Natalie's heart thundered from pure emotion—from physical passion he built in her so tenderly, from exhilaration at the Black Knight's conquest in her honor, but mostly from joy in discovering a love in Jonathan Drake.

"You did this for me," she said in awe she couldn't mask.

His expression melted, and he resumed the sensuous stroking of his fingers. "Last night, before I came home." He put his lips to hers once more to whisper, "I'd do anything for you, Natalie."

And she believed him. "Love me. . . ."

"I do."

"Take me to bed," she pleaded.

He grasped the back of her head and planted his mouth firmly on hers to kiss her deeply, his tongue invading her, sweeping across her lips in slow form, making her body turn to liquid fire, making her wait, making her insane with want as he glided his fingers in steady rhythm over the slick heat between her legs.

With effort she pulled her face away from his. "Jonathan, *now*."

He stood, lifting her easily in his arms. "I'm going to Amsterdam in five weeks," he mentioned as an afterthought, brushing her cheek with his as he carried her to the stairs. "To steal an already stolen Rembrandt at auction."

"Wonderful. . . ."

"Join me?"

"That's a ridiculous question, Jonathan," she replied breathlessly, tightening her hold about his neck and pushing her breasts into his chest. She traced a line along his ear with her lips, then admitted in a whisper, "I'm already mentally planning my wardrobe."

He tripped, nearly dropping her before they reached the bedroom.

Author's Note

While I was writing this story, I knew having Natalie hide an emerald necklace in the heel of her boot might seem far-fetched to some readers. This plot device was not merely a product of my imagination.

According to family legend, ancestors of mine—two brothers—left Germany bound for America in the late 1790s. Before they sailed for New York, they were warned that there was a good chance their ship might be stopped by pirates, who were roaming the seas quite frequently at the time, and that their possessions would likely be stolen. Shoemakers by trade, they heeded this warning, and before leaving to begin their new lives in America, they sewed all their money into the soles of their shoes. Who would look there?

In the end, their ship was indeed raided by pirates, and while others lost family fortunes, these brothers made it safely to New York with their hidden money intact.

Adele Ashworth
My Darling Caroline

A Lifelong Dream

Lady Caroline Grayson had always wanted to study botany—and had already bred a rare lavender rose—but as a woman in nineteenth-century England, her intelligence and talents were ignored. Caroline was determined to see her dream become a reality—even if it meant masquerading as a man to be accepted at a university. But when her father arranged for her to marry, she agreed—knowing she could not become a conventional wife...

A Flourishing Love

Yet marriage wasn't what she thought it would be. Her attractive new husband gave her the freedom she never expected—and the respect she had always deserved. At first she tried to resist his admiration, his love...and especially his touch. But soon she was surprised and overcome by her husband's—and her own—passion. Now Caroline might have to make the most difficult choice of all—between her lifelong dream and the depth of her love for an extraordinary man...

❏ 0-515-12369-2/$5.99

TIME PASSAGES

- ❏ CRYSTAL MEMORIES   *Ginny Aiken*   0-515-12159-2
- ❏ ECHOES OF TOMORROW   *Jenny Lykins*   0-515-12079-0
- ❏ LOST YESTERDAY   *Jenny Lykins*   0-515-12013-8
- ❏ MY LADY IN TIME   *Angie Ray*   0-515-12227-0
- ❏ NICK OF TIME   *Casey Claybourne*   0-515-12189-4
- ❏ REMEMBER LOVE   *Susan Plunkett*   0-515-11980-6
- ❏ SILVER TOMORROWS   *Susan Plunkett*   0-515-12047-2
- ❏ THIS TIME TOGETHER   *Susan Leslie Liepitz*
                                             0-515-11981-4
- ❏ WAITING FOR YESTERDAY   *Jenny Lykins*
                                             0-515-12129-0
- ❏ HEAVEN'S TIME   *Susan Plunkett*   0-515-12287-4
- ❏ THE LAST HIGHLANDER   *Claire Cross*   0-515-12337-4
- ❏ A TIME FOR US   *Christine Holden*   0-515-12375-7

All books $5.99

FRIENDS ROMANCE

Can a man come between friends?

❏ A TASTE OF HONEY
by DeWanna Pace   0-515-12387-0

❏ WHERE THE HEART IS
by Sheridon Smythe   0-515-12412-5

❏ LONG WAY HOME
by Wendy Corsi Staub   0-515-12440-0

All books $5.99